DEFIANCE

A Novel

By

Titia Bozuwa

Published by Piscataqua Press
An imprint of RiverRun Bookstore, Inc.
142 Fleet Street | Portsmouth, NH | 03801
www.riverrunbookstore.com
www.piscataquapress.com

ISBN: 978-1-944393-64-9

Printed in the United States of America.

Also by Titia Bozuwa

Joan, A Mother's Memoir (2000)

In the Shadow of the Cathedral (2004)

Wings of Change (2007)

The Emperor's Guest (2009)

I dedicate this book to the memory of

Gijs Bozuwa,
For his loving and unstinting support from beginning to end
***

And to:

Mary Avery, Maggie Kennedy, and Rob Nelson
For their listening and encouragement
***

Three amazing women in my past inspired the character of the baroness.
They have my eternal admiration and gratitude:

Johanna Wetselaar-Ament (my mother),
Louise Hugenholtz-van Wassenaer, and
Jane Wilde Howe
***

Netherlands, 1944 (U)

North Sea

AMSTERDAM ★

Emst

● UTRECHT

● EDE

The Hague

Arnhem

Delft

Lek   Neder Rijn

Rotterdam   Waal

Nijmegen
Groesbeek
Grave

Kleve
(Cleve)

Germany

Veghel

● BREDA

Helmond

Eindhoven

Roermond

Belgium

★ BRUSSELS

Fr.

50 Kilometers

30 Miles

Unclassified

743256 (001524) 7-97

Acknowledgements

There are no words to express the immense gratitude I feel toward my husband, Gijs Bozuwa, for his support during the seven years it took to write this novel. He made it his priority to create time to write, and coached me through three major surgeries that interfered with reaching my goal. A month before he passed away, I finished the novel. He was a big part of it —beginning to end.

Unforgettable moments were spent at the end of many a workday with Gijs and Rob Nelson as I shared my progress and listened to their input. We debated war, religion and human nature. These discussions have now become precious memories.

Sue Wheeler gave unselfishly of her time and expertise. Her encouragement and enthusiasm were infectious. I am greatly indebted to her for the many hours she spent on my book despite declining health and eyesight.

Bett Barrett took over the editing where Sue had to leave off. She has an unerring eye for structure, language and spelling. It was great to work with her.

I'm also grateful to Arnold Leuftink, who helped me out when I got hopelessly lost trying to figure out how the great rivers throughout my native country connected. He is a researcher par excellence.

Rev. Mary James was very helpful with religious aspects. Mary Avery read parts and kept after me to finish the book, as did Beryl Donovan, my favorite librarian. Maggie Kennedy and Johanna Bozuwa read the entire manuscript and pushed me to get it into the world. I thank them all for their time and input.

Colleen Bozuwa took the picture for the cover while she was in Holland, and Norman Royle helped fashion it into a beautiful cover. They are both accomplished artists and I thank them for their time and expertise. I also want to thank Tom and Kellsey of the Piscataqua Press for their artistic eye, speed and diligence.

The book you hold in your hand required teamwork by a diverse group of people. It took more than just my imagination.

I thank "my team" from the bottom of my heart.

PROLOGUE

At a time when draught horses and river barges were still the primary means for moving goods, and the narrow roads were paved with bricks and cobblestones; when the queen still looked like a queen in a floor-length satin gown, a brilliant tiara gracing her head; when the faithful went to church in black coats and black stockings; at that time Adolf Hitler pounced on Holland, waking her up to a new reality after a deep, self-satisfied slumber. The colonies in the East and West Indies had made her wealthy. During WWI, she had managed to stay neutral while all about her empires, soldiers, and citizens were crushed or slaughtered. Surely Hitler would honor his promise to Queen Wilhelmina that he would never invade her country. At the eleventh hour, a military draft was instituted and the army beefed up, but it was too late.

On the tenth of May in 1940, as dawn gave way to a bright sun, the promise of summer hung over Holland's flat landscape after a bitter winter. To most, there was no hint that this would become an infamous day in the country's history, but during the night and early morning hours, the Germans had executed a three-prong assault on Holland. Around Rotterdam and Den Haag, eight thousand Germans fell out of the sky, a good portion of them disguised as priests, farmers, and civilians. Everybody, including the prime minister, was aghast and stunned. Once they gathered their wits, the Dutch put up a good fight. They shot down four hundred German planes. Hitler—surprised by stronger resistance than he'd expected—ordered the heart of Rotterdam to be bombed and destroyed. Nine hundred citizens died within an hour. He threatened to do the same to Utrecht and Amsterdam.

Holland capitulated on May 15. Queen Wilhelmina had left for England with her entire family, taking her cabinet of ministers with her as well as Holland's gold reserves. Her subjects were shocked. The country was overpowered and parts of it were in tatters. Daily life was brought to a standstill.

But not for long.

Ordinary daily routines were picked up again. People who'd fled to Belgium and France returned, dusted themselves off, and adapted, best they could, to the occupied status. It seemed the only sensible thing to do.

Not everyone could live by new rules and new laws, though. Not every Dutchman could swallow national pride and dance to the tunes of the Nazis. Dirk van Enthoven, a first-year medical student, had witnessed the bombing of Rotterdam. He was not in a forgiving mood. The young *Dominee* Walter Vlaskamp wondered what would happen to his church as long as Hitler believed that Christianity and Nazism were incompatible.

But for a sixteen-year-old girl like Anna Smits, life hadn't drastically changed. Her home in Arnhem was still standing. She could go back to school. Her father still left for work every morning, and there was no shortage of bread on the table. Not yet.

And in Oldenburg, Germany, Oberst von Schloss donned his army uniform, kissed his wife good-bye, and left for his post in the Netherlands.

·

CHAPTER ONE

Anna - September 1941

On a sunny September day, one and a half years into the war, Anna Smits boarded the train to Utrecht. She sank into the luxurious, velvety feel of the upholstery in a first-class compartment and blew her mother a kiss through the closed window. She willed herself not to dwell on the run-ins she and her mother had had before she could embark on this journey. There'd been no slam-of–the-door scenes. The struggle had been icily controlled. No, the importance of this moment, Anna reminded herself, was that Moeder had stopped fighting the idea of her daughter becoming a doctor.

Moeder's fashionable wide-brimmed hat threw a shadow over her face, but failed to hide the anxiety in her eyes. Or was it sadness? For a fleeting moment, Anna felt the silence that would envelop her parents when they returned home—a home without children.

"Good luck, Anna," Vader said, and put her suitcase in the luggage rack. "Make the most of it. These are your golden years."

He reached into his pocket and produced a small business card.

"You will only be a few hours away. Even so, there's a war going on, and if you should ever need immediate help, contact this man. We were classmates at Leiden University. You can trust him as you can trust me. I called him and he's aware of you."

A high-pitched whistle blew a minute after her father left her compartment. The locomotive's engine hissed and slowly pulled the train away from where her parents stood. They formed a striking couple. Her mother slender and beautiful, her father a bit taller and ruggedly handsome with blond hair that was graying at the temples. As she waved good-bye, they filled her with pride and emotion. And relief.

At the next stop, a German officer stepped into her compartment and seated himself across from her. He wore the insignia of the feared SS on the collar of his uniform. They eyed each other suspiciously.

"*Wie geht's?*" he asked.

She shrugged. The idea of carrying on a conversation with an SS man while the train progressed through an area where the vastly outnumbered Dutch Army had taken its last stand revolted her. On the day the war broke out, she had watched bleeding soldiers being unloaded on the sidewalk of Arnhem's hospital, where she'd been laid up with a broken leg. It had been all mayhem below her window. The memory was alive in her mind. She couldn't bring herself to utter even one word to this man.

The officer opened his leather briefcase and started reading a letter. A vista of luscious green pastures, lined by straight rows of poplar trees, flew by. It reassured her to see the familiar landscape in the presence of the stranger. What would the landscape of his hometown look like? Hills, forests, dark woods, rushing brooks? Hitler had arrogantly declared that the Dutch and the Germans were blood relatives within the same Germanic race. That remark hadn't sat well with Vader.

"We are totally different," he'd fumed. "The Germans are militaristic and we are individualistic."

As Anna studied the glossy shine on the officer's black riding boots, she pondered how Holland's lowlands and wide rivers had shaped her country's character. The fight against the constant threat of rising water defined its gritty nature. That made sense. But she couldn't find a plausible connection between forests and the German militaristic attitude. What could have fed this officer's decision to join the *Schutzstaffel,* the Nazis' special police force? Horrible stories of their crude violence, hauling people into concentration camps, executing them without due justice, were whispered about. She threw a sideways glance at the German, trying to read from his face if he had blood on his hands, if he was really as bad as the Dutch made him out to be. His uniform was impressive and a little scary in its twill rigidity, but his face was just the face of a man. She couldn't read any more into it than his probable age — quite young, she thought. If she were honest with herself, she would have to admit he was handsome and amiable.

The train got closer to the city of Utrecht, and Anna started to worry how she would get her heavy suitcase out of the luggage rack. Even for her strong father, it hadn't been easy to hoist it up there. Where would the officer get off? God forbid she would emerge from the train with an SS officer carrying her suitcase! She would be instantly marked a collaborator, or in a woman's case, a whore. What could she do?

The officer put his reading material back in his briefcase as the train slowed. The engine's squealing brakes echoed against the huge roof of the station, which covered the many parallel platforms.

"*Fraulein?*" the officer said. "Can I help you with your suitcase?"

"*Nein,*" Anna answered abruptly, although she was struck by his courtesy. She broke out in an uncomfortable sweat, but at that very moment the conductor appeared at the door of their compartment and stepped inside. He reached overhead and without saying a word grabbed her suitcase. Anna followed him out into the narrow corridor. He placed the suitcase on the platform and extended his hand to let her down the steps.

"Your father told me to look out for you," he whispered, and quickly hailed a porter for her.

The address she gave the taxi driver was where she would live. The university didn't provide housing. Moeder had made the living arrangement through a friend, because the business of renting a room had been complicated by the war. How could you determine if someone responding to your ad wasn't a sympathizer with the Nazis? Members of the Dutch Nationaal Socialistise Beweging (NSB) looked like any other Dutch citizen. Or if you unknowingly rented a room in the home of one, you might be identified with them.

A middle-aged woman in a cheerful cotton dress opened the door of a modest home in a row of lookalike houses. The wind played with strands of her graying hair, and her eyes, full of wit, looked directly into her own.

"You must be Anna Smits," she said with a firm handshake. "I am Betty Schoonhoven."

The taxi driver placed the suitcase on the sidewalk and discreetly waited to be paid. She should have looked at the meter before getting out. This was a ritual Vader usually took care of. She found her wallet, made a wild guess, handed the driver a ten-guilder bill, and told him to keep the change. The man looked at the bill in his hand and hesitated, then he thanked her profusely. She'd given him quite a tip, obviously. Oh, well, the man had had a good day. Betty had followed the transaction with interest, but did not comment.

A cuckoo clock struck the hour as they entered the small living room. It was neat and unassuming with comfortable chairs facing a coal stove and pink begonias on the wide windowsill, reaching for the filtered light that came through white net curtains. Several photos in silver frames stood on the mantel. Anna studied them. Children looked back at her, some with their parents. The settings reminded her of her grandmother's place: sprawling lawns, elaborate flower borders, old trees with wide trunks. Who were these people?

"Those were the children I took care of," Betty said. "I was a governess for many children."

It made perfect sense. Of course! This woman had a proven record. She could be trusted. Besides, she lived in a neighborhood the Germans would skip over when looking for rooms for their officers. They preferred patrician homes.

"I stopped working a year ago," Betty went on. "But Jan still works at a printing company. They don't want to let him go yet. He is the fastest letter setter they have."

Jan came home just before dinner, a tall, skinny man with a receding hairline. He politely asked about her train trip. When Anna told him she'd found herself alone in the train compartment with an SS officer, Jan asked if he'd tried to start a converstation.

"Yes, he did, but I pretended I didn't understand German."

"Good," Jan said.

Her room was sunny and looked out over red-tiled roofs that made a straight line against the evening sky. Below was a large rectangle of small backyards divided by solid wooden fences. Anna had never lived on a city block. Her parents' home stood on the outskirts of Arnhem, where the yards in front and back were larger than the footprint of the house. Here on this block of houses lived people who worked for other people. For people like her parents, or for a boss in a store. Anna hadn't paid much attention to the housing arrangement Moeder had made for her. She'd been too busy getting good grades as she finished school and then saying good-bye to friends. Moeder, apparently, had let standing be overruled by a wish for security. The war had already changed some of her long-held perceptions of class and propriety.

Anna pasted a framed photograph of her family on the wall next to her bed. It had been taken before her brother Maarten left for the Dutch East Indies. She smiled at the thought of him, far away, out in the boonies on a tea plantation, free as a lark, while she was embarking on a strict discipline of study. In ten years, how would they look at the choices they'd made?

Having unpacked, she sat on the edge of the bed and took stock of her first day of true independence. It could hardly be called that. Her father had foreseen that a girl alone in a train compartment might get into trouble. The conductor had saved her from extreme embarrassment. She'd made a fool of herself when she paid the taxi driver without knowing the charge. Her mother had arranged a safe haven by finding a room with Betty Schoonhoven, and her father's protection extended to calling a friend if she needed help. She wondered what situation would make her call that stranger. Tomorrow, she would have to do better. She wouldn't ask for anyone's help or make a fool of herself when she registered at the University of Utrecht.

She put on her nightgown and threw back the covers. Betty Schoonhoven knew how to make a bed. The sheets were tightly drawn, the soft pillow puffed up. She drew the cotton sheet—not heavy linen with a monogram like at home—up to her chin and felt as if she'd slipped into a warm tea cozy. As she dozed off, her mind drifted to the immediate past.

"You? A doctor?"

"Yes, me. And why not?"

"Girls become nurses, not doctors," her mother said.

Anna had weighed her options. Secretary? Nurse? Teacher? She didn't like any of those. Her reasoning always circled back to studying medicine. It sat like a magnet at the center of her thoughts.

"Not any of the women in my or your father's family has gone to university," Moeder continued.

"Then I will be the first, won't I?"

"There are better ways to prepare for womanhood, Anna. Becoming a nurse will be more helpful when you have children."

"Wouldn't being a doctor be just as helpful?"

"You would invest many years in a study that will be of no use when you get married. Carrying on a medical practice and being a wife and mother is incompatible."

"So what you are saying, Moeder, is that being married is the most important goal for a woman?"

"Well, my dear, it has been the hope and expectation of every woman for all the ages."

"Finding a husband is not my first expectation, Moeder. I want to make something of myself, be independent. I know there's nothing wrong with being a nurse, but why not become a doctor? When I broke my leg and had to stay in the hospital, I saw both. Watching the doctor intrigued me. I don't want to change bandages. I want to do the surgery!"

"You can't be serious, Anna. Wouldn't you want to marry and raise a family?"

"Maybe, but I want to become a doctor first."

Her father asked if she was ready to deal with dying patients.

"That's like asking you if you were ready to face a war. The war happened, whether you were ready or not. I think most people deal with whatever comes across their paths. Right now, I think I can handle it."

But she knew she had created turmoil in her mother. Not to follow in her mother's footsteps, to give marriage short shrift, was an affront to her personally and to her generation, but Anna had taken a stand and didn't give an inch. It was about her future, whether that fit her mother's ideas or not.

Vader, after initially raising his eyebrows, began to back her up, and eventually Moeder gave up fighting her.

The early spring of 1941 had not been a happy time for anyone. The Nazis made life miserable for the Jewish population. Hitler advanced his troops over an ever-widening territory, and the atmosphere inside her home lurched from hot to ice cold between mother and daughter. Anna's main concern was not with what happened outside. She didn't have Jewish friends. That didn't affect her daily life. Her single focus was on convincing her mother there was nothing scandalous about having a daughter enter university. Her mother, from her side, predicted Anna would never last seven years with her nose in textbooks. But Anna stuck to her plan.

Vader took it for granted that she would go to Leiden University. He had studied there, following family tradition. But by the time she obtained her high school diploma, Leiden University was no longer an option. The German authorities had decreed that all people with Jewish blood who served the government in one way or another be fired. That included professors. Professor Cleveringa, who was not Jewish, made an impassioned speech, firing up his students to go on strike. They did. The Germans closed Leiden University in retaliation. In Utrecht, the doors to its university were almost shut too, but at the fervent urging of the university's president, the students decided against an all-out strike. What kind of future would there be for the country if academic life got shut down? Anna decided to go to the University of Utrecht.

She turned over in her bed in Jan and Betty Schoonhoven's home and felt content. A deep sleep awaited her.

CHAPTER TWO

Anna – December 1941

In Utrecht, the winter made its entrance on a stinging December wind. Laundry blew horizontally from the lines strung between poles in the backyards of the Schoonhovens' neighborhood. Anna pulled on her high-collared sweater. On her way out to classes, she watched Betty fry onions and chunks of beef, adding a few cloves, mace, stock, and a bay leaf. When she returned in the late afternoon, her stomach rumbled as she lifted the lid to take a peek. The distinct ingredients had melded into a gently bubbling dark brown mass.

"Want to have supper with us?" Betty asked.

"How can I refuse?"

"By the way, your mother called. She would like you to call her back."

Anna's pulse thrummed as she dialed her parents' phone number. Moeder answered with an agitated voice. "The Japanese have bombed Pearl Harbor," she said.

"Where's Pearl Harbor?" Anna asked.

"On Hawaii."

"Hawaii! What an exotic name! It sounds very far away. Why are you calling about it?" This was annoying. She had to study for an exam on anatomy.

She was told that Pearl Harbor was the base of America's Pacific fleet and that the Japanese had practically wiped it out. America had declared war on Japan, and the Dutch government in London had done the same thing.

Another war to cope with, Anna thought. But America and Japan seemed very far away.

"It means," Moeder said, "that Japan may invade our East Indies."

The Dutch East Indies? That's where Maarten was.

"Are you sure?" Anna asked. "Why would they want to do that?"

"Anna, for goodness sake, where have you been? The Japanese are on a rampage in Southeast Asia. They want to throw all the Europeans out. They invade one country after another."

It was true. She hadn't followed the news. Her mind had been on organic chemistry, biology, and physics. The war wasn't a topic she cared much about.

"I haven't heard from Maarten in a long time," her mother said with a quiver in her voice. "I'm so worried about him."

"That's probably got more to do with the Germans than the Japanese, Moeder. The mail travels over sea, but they torpedo every ship that isn't one of their own." In her mind, Anna followed canvas bags filled with personal and intimate letters on their way down to the ocean floor. A dark feeling crept into the pit of her stomach.

"What does Vader think?"

"He's as worried as I am. He says that if the Dutch Army is as well prepared in our Indies as they were here, then you know what will happen!"

"Moeder, don't worry about what hasn't happened yet. Maarten is probably just fine."

"That's easier said than done."

After they disconnected, Anna stood with the black bakelite horn in her hand, wondering if it had been helpful to tell Moeder not to worry. She had every reason to be worried, for heaven's sake. What if her parents were right and a war broke out in the Pacific? The situation could explode. She scolded herself, ashamed of her self-centeredness. She hadn't taken the time to read any newspapers lately, as if a world in flames was of no consequence. The insistent sound of the busy signal made her replace the horn in its cradle. She pulled her fingers through her straight blond hair, as she was wont to do when nervous.

Anna had always been in awe of her older brother's daring. There had never been a dull moment in their growing-up years. Maarten would gleefully place a mouse or a frog in the maid's bed; and while Moeder received the minister of their local church on the terrace, Maarten shot spitballs from the balcony above. One landed in the man's tea. Moeder ran out of ideas for punishment. Anna had been keenly aware of Maarten's many exploits and his irrepressible urge to test boundaries. She figured that life would put enough challenges and adventures in her path without her seeking them. Through it all, she learned not to rock the family boat—except when she decided to study medicine.

Betty came into the living room to draw the curtains. Every day at sunset she made rounds through the whole house to close all shades and curtains. The Germans demanded total blackout. Since it was December, twilight arrived shortly after three in the afternoon.

"Everything all right?" she asked.

What Anna liked about Betty was her discretion. It wouldn't occur to her to ask for details. She must have been the perfect governess. With her slightly overweight body, she exuded warmth and comfort. Anna could imagine herself cuddling up to her as a child. Betty invited trust. Her own governess hadn't been the cuddly type, and neither was her mother.

"Mother says America has declared war on Japan. My brother lives on Java, and Mother is afraid the Japanese will invade. She says it's just a matter of time."

"That's worrisome, but who knows. Even if they do invade, maybe the Japanese are easier to live with than the Germans."

"That's the trouble. They've done horrible things to the Chinese. They're brutal."

"Well," Betty said, "the soup is always hottest to the tongue when it's just served."

It was pitch dark outside when Jan opened the kitchen door. The moon, no more than a sliver, hung over the tiled roofs behind him. Cold outside air, mixed with the vague smell of lead, clung to his work clothes.

At dinner, he told them the same news.

"The whole world is at war," he said, helping himself to a heap of steaming potatoes. While he mashed them with his fork and poured the rich brown sauce over them, he said, "Show me a place on earth where there is peace. The Germans and the Italians are on the African continent. Europe is under Hitler's thumb. Japan is all over the map in the Far East. Now America is involved. What a mess!"

Jan always seemed well informed. You named a place, and he could point out exactly where it was on the atlas he kept by his chair. He didn't just set letters. He absorbed their meanings. Details of history, current events, they mattered to him.

Anna woke up to a silent house the next morning. With one eye on the clock, she decided to stay in bed a bit longer. Her biology class was scheduled for nine o'clock, but the university was not a school where attendance was taken. Some students never even showed up at all for early classes. Maybe showing up late just once wasn't a cardinal sin. Her mind was not on biology anyway. Worry about Maarten had overtaken her thoughts. She cared for her brother, and the thought that harm might come to him absorbed her. The surprise of a war in the Far East—at least, to her it had been a surprise—provided a different perspective. She realized she had been blindsided by her own ambitions.

It was eerily quiet in and around the house, as if all of humanity had decided to stay in bed this December day. The familiar clippity-clop of hooves and the shouts of men egging their horses on were missing. The absence of sounds, Anna thought, could be more alarming than the rumble of artillery fire in the distance. Imagine if birds wouldn't return in the spring, frogs would not croak, bees wouldn't hum.

When she finally got out of bed and pulled the window shade up, the color of the rooftops had changed from red to white. Flakes fluttered down from a barely visible sky. Watching the snow took the mystery out of the silence. She put on warm street clothes and boots and ventured downstairs, where Betty was already putting the evening meal together in the kitchen.

"Did Jan take his bike to work?" Anna asked.

"Yes, but I don't expect he'll get back on it. They predict a lot of snow."

"I'd better start walking then. My first class starts in fifteen minutes."

"Here, Anna, take this piece of bread. You can't trudge through snow on an empty stomach."

On a bike it only took ten minutes, but stepping through the thickening snow took close to an hour. Few students made it to class. Further classes were suspended. As Anna walked through the empty halls, wondering what to do, she ran into a girl with a pile of notebooks under her arm.

"We could have stayed in bed. No classes today," the girl said. "Listen. I live not far from here. Would you like to warm your feet at my place? Your boots look soaked!"

The girl's name was Carla Vlaskamp.

The snow was piling up fast; sidewalks seemed to have disappeared. Carla laughed. "I guess we'll have to goose-step like those German soldiers in a parade." She lifted her booted foot up high before taking the next step. Her dark curly hair peeked out from under a woolen cap, and her brown eyes sparkled with

15

merriment.

"Look at that poor woman over there," Anna said, pointing out a figure who struggled with a heavy bag. Carla jumped ahead and touched the woman's shoulder.

"Let me carry that," she said, and took the bag from her hand. "This is no weather to be out in, lady. Do you have far to go?"

"Just around the corner. They say there's more snow coming, and I had little food left."

They took the woman in between them, hooked into her arms, and delivered her to her front door.

"You're good at picking up strays," Anna said as they turned the street corner.

Carla gave her carefree laugh and pulled at Anna's sleeve. "Come on. Let's hurry and warm our feet by the stove."

She unlocked an impressive front door and motioned Anna to step inside, onto the white marble tiles of a long hall with an elaborately carved staircase at the end. To avoid having to give quarters to German officers, the owner, a widow, had rented out every available room to students. They climbed up the spiral staircase, boots in hand. Anna admired the Delft blue tiles that skirted the lower part of the white walls. The fine details in the ceiling decorations reflected the pride of the original owners and the devoted craftsmanship of its builders. Houses in this part of Utrecht were over three hundred years old. Carla's room was at least three times the size of her own in Betty's house.

Carla gave her some newspaper to stuff her boots with. "It will dry them out quicker," she said. "My mother tells me not to put leather shoes too close to the fire. It cracks them." She held a match to the white asbestos columns of the gas-fired stove. With a soft puff, they filled with blue flames tinged with pink. It seemed as natural as breathing to allow Carla to take the lead. The woman in the street hadn't hesitated to hand over her precious load of groceries, and here she was herself, doing what she was told, crumpling up old newspapers.

"What do you study, Carla?"

"Medicine. I'm in my third year. And you?"

"Medicine also. This is my first year."

"There aren't too many of us. Most women at the university seem to prefer the humanities."

"I wouldn't know," Anna said. "I've hardly met anyone outside of my own classes."

"That's because meeting other students has become so hard since the Germans closed all student clubs. We used to go there after classes. That's where you met people who studied different disciplines. It's where you ate and made new friends."

"What harm could student clubs do?"

"The Germans think that when more than five people congregate, they can band together. It could be debating clubs, not just student clubs. Members of any club might get it into their heads to start an uprising." Carla rubbed her nose with a quick gesture. "The Germans are quite paranoid, don't you think?"

There was a knock on the door.

"Come in," Carla called.

The door opened, revealing a tall figure in the doorway.

"Hello, Dirk," she said. "We're having a newspaper-stuffing party."

With his hand outstretched, Dirk walked over to where Anna stood.

"Hello, I am Dirk van Enthoven."

Hazel-colored eyes looked into her light blue ones, probing, curious, steady. His handshake was firm, his wide forehead crowned by dark blond hair. Everything about him seemed solid and definite.

"My feet feel like clumps of ice," he said. "Can I take off my shoes? I may have holes in my socks, you know."

"Go right ahead," Carla said. "We'll help you stuff your shoes, but we won't mend your socks. Those days are over."

"I'm well aware." Dirk laughed. "God forbid you'd be accused of being domestic."

She stuck her tongue out at him and threw some newspapers in his direction.

Anna, not knowing what else to do with herself, offered to stuff Dirk's shoes while Carla rummaged in a closet to get cups and saucers. She felt him watching her. A palpable field of energy surrounded this man, and it made her at once shy and curious.

"I take it you're a student?" he said.

When she told him she studied medicine, he said, "That makes three of us in this room."

Anna opened one of the papers before crumpling it and studied the headline. "Look at this," she said. "'Cafés and cinemas are ordered to display a sign that Jews are not welcome.' When I first saw this, I thought the café owners and cinemas would ignore that stupid order."

"Did they have a choice?" Carla asked.

"There's always a choice," Dirk said.

Anna realized belatedly that calling a Nazi order *stupid* was a dead giveaway that she wasn't a Nazi sympathizer. Should she have been more cautious? With Jan and Betty, she had no doubts. The three of them were beyond pussyfooting around with their remarks about the Nazis. It would have been wiser to throw out a fishing line first to get a feeling for where Dirk's sympathies lay.

"What do you think is stupid about that order?" he asked.

"Stupid may not be the right word," she answered, "but I don't think it's fair to brand a group of people. They are legitimate Dutch citizens. They should have the same rights as any of us."

Dirk watched her as she pushed the paper down hard into the front of his wet right shoe. There was something very compelling about this Dirk. Even as he casually leaned his elbows on the back of a poorly upholstered chair, he exuded authority, and she felt challenged by it.

"None of us have all the rights we used to have," Carla said. "We wouldn't be here in my room if we did. We would be drinking beer at the Club."

It was quiet, as if the silencing snow had fallen inside, even as they watched it come down on the other side of the large window, each flake illuminated by the low light of a streetlamp. Anna put Dirk's shoes next to her boots.

"What headline will you read us next?" Carla asked.

"Let's see." Anna picked up another paper and took her chances. "Our beloved, fearless police leader, General Rauter, announces that all political prisoners held in the Scheveningen prison will be freed tomorrow as a gesture of goodwill toward the Dutch population."

Carla laughed. "Isn't that lovely!"

A smile played around Dirk's lips. He raised his eyebrows and looked at Anna. She handed him the newspaper. "Here, you can see it for yourself."

He took it from her hand and laughed.

After they savored their hot coffee and ate all the bread and jam they could find in Carla's closet, they became more serious, mutually aware that their earlier lighthearted mood was trumped by the dark cloud that hung over their future, one that threatened their shared goal of becoming physicians. Carla sat on her bed, leaning against the wall. Dirk made himself comfortable in a fauteuil and rested his long legs on the coffee table. Anna sat cross-legged on the floor facing both of them. To her surprise, she felt relaxed in their company.

"That beloved General Rauter you just quoted has no conscience," Dirk said. "They picked the right man for the job. He's ruthless."

"How do you know?" Carla asked.

"My parents have an elderly Jewish couple living next door, and these days, when you know a Jew, you also know about Herr Rauter. Our neighbors fled Germany after the Kristallnacht."

"I have to be honest," Carla said. "I never understood what crystal had to do with that night."

"Neither do I," Anna said. "I really don't know much about what's behind the Nazi anti-Semitism."

On the night of November 9, in 1938, Dirk told them, the Nazis demolished synagogues all over Germany and Austria. They smashed windows of Jewish homes and businesses. Everything was fair game. Any brownshirt could walk into a Jewish home and pull the tablecloth from the table with everything on it, even while the family was having dinner. There was so much broken glass everywhere that, from then on, the night was referred to as Kristallnacht. The splinters and broken pieces had looked like crystals in the sun the next morning.

"How awful! How stupid!" Anna said.

"You seem to like the word *stupid*," Dirk said with a faint smile. Anna wished she hadn't said it.

"Jews were threatened at every turn after that," he went on. "People couldn't believe this madness would last. Hitler's dictatorship would be overthrown. But some feared it could only get worse and the best thing to do was to pack up and leave to wherever they would be welcome. That's how my parents got Jewish neighbors from Germany. They had hoped to get to England. They had their papers ready, the boat trip paid for, and then the Germans invaded Holland."

"How are they doing now?" Carla asked.

"Fair. Life isn't pleasant. Money isn't the problem. To have money makes no difference. It seems like every day there's another restriction put on them. Anna just read one of them. General Rauter pulls a nasty rabbit out of his hat every other day."

"My God! How could it have come to this? It is insane," Anna said. Again, she regretted her choice of words. *Insane* was not that much different from *stupid*.

"That's a hard question. So much goes into it," Dirk said. "There's always been anti-Semitism in the world. Ever since Jesus died at the hands of the Jews, even though he was a Jew himself and the Roman soldiers were the ones who nailed him to the cross,

Christians won't let them forget that."

They got into a discussion about the why of it all. Dirk said his father's take on it was that Hitler used slumbering sentiments to promote his own rise to power. He needed a villain, and a Jew was an easy target to get people behind him.

It was quiet again in Carla's room. Anna felt as though she'd never heard about this war before. She had no stake in it, no role in it, but Dirk seemed totally absorbed by what was going on. Practically everything he'd said so far had to do with the war. It came across as his personal concern. Moeder was right: Where had she been?

Dirk got up and walked over to the window. "It stopped snowing."

"Then I should be going," Anna said. "My boots must be dry, or at least warm."

"It's still messy outside," Carla said, joining them at the window.

"Where do you live?" Dirk asked.

"Ten minutes from here on a bike, if it doesn't snow."

"I will bring you home," he said. "I have a shovel we can take with us."

His offer took her by surprise. Color rose to her cheeks. She pulled her fingers back through her hair in a quick gesture. As he opened the front door into the darkness of a white December night, cold wind blew snow into her face and covered her eyelashes. She looked up at Dirk, who laughed and pulled her woolen cap down to cover her ears. This Dirk was amazing. Good-looking, a gentleman, a sense of humor, yet more serious than any boy she'd ever met. *Stop right there*, she told herself. *This was what any well-brought-up young man would do. Nothing special. Don't flatter yourself or get any ideas.*

CHAPTER THREE

Anna – April 1942

After a bitter winter, the calendar could finally be turned to April. Anna biked past blooming daffodils in a park filled with them, and they helped her forget the things that were wrong with the world. The sun crept inside the yellow trumpets waving in the breeze on their sturdy flat stems. A smattering of a smaller variety with white petals and orange hearts poked up their heads in between their taller yellow sisters. The superintendent of public parks may not have been sure if the German bosses allowed orange-colored flowers in the borders, Anna thought, since they forbade any show of loyalty to the royal family and the House of Orange. Their aversion only encouraged Dutch citizens to sneak in the color orange wherever they could. Anna used an orange pencil to underline sections in her various textbooks. It wouldn't win the war, but it made her feel better.

Unfortunately, the sunlit daffodils also brought to mind an ugly shade of yellow that had popped up simultaneously with the hyacinths and the daffodils. Every Jew was ordered to pin a yellow piece of cloth in the shape of the Star of David on their outerwear. In its center, in thick black letters, was the word JOOD. Its purpose was to show the world who among them was Jewish.

And all the cheerful daffodils in the world couldn't chase away morbid thoughts about what might be happening to Maarten. Early in March, the Japanese had invaded Java. First they sank most of the Dutch Navy's fleet; and as they reached the shores, the sadly underequipped Dutch Army could not keep them off the island. Just as her father had predicted. After the capitulation, there was a news blackout from the Dutch East Indies.

In view of the German Occupation, she'd often thought Maarten had made the right choice go to the Indies, but that was questionable now. It had angered their father when he left in 1938. Vader had wanted him to study at Leiden University in the family tradition. But Maarten felt there was no future for him in Holland, and he had no patience to wait out the Depression. He worked himself into the management of a tea plantation on Java. Anna thought of the framed picture of Maarten on Moeder's desk, where he stood surrounded by natives, a dead tiger at his feet. What would happen to him now? A feeling of dread filled her. The worst part was not knowing.

These thoughts continued to run through Anna's mind as she made her way to anatomy class. Dirk was waiting for her in front of the university building. A flutter of excitement shivered through her when she spotted him, his arms leaning on the handlebars of his bike and one foot on the sidewalk for balance. No matter what pose Dirk was in, his slender body had a natural ease and elegance to it.

"Shall we go for a bike ride along the Amsterdam-Rijn Kanaal?" he asked.

"What a great idea. It's a good day for it," she said. "Can you wait till three o'clock?"

At three, Anna raced out of class to the bicycle rack outside. Dirk was already there, sitting on his bike and holding hers alongside. She jumped on it, and they biked fast to get out of the city. Beyond the outer limits were lush green pastures filled with cattle. They got off their bikes to watch the frolicking cows that were freed from their stanches in smelly barns after long winter months.

"I never thought of a cow as a sexy animal," Dirk said, "but there's lust in the way they go for that early spring grass, don't you think? Look at how they wrap their tongues around a tuft, grab it, and put it away, ready for the next bite. Amazing. They're veritable mowing machines."

"They are free and happy. I am jealous," Anna said.

"Jealous?"

"Yes, jealous. They spent a long winter cooped up, confined to no more than six square feet of space, standing in their own manure, having to produce milk. It's the perfect simile for the German Occupation: we have to produce milk and cheese for the *Heimat,* but what do we get in return? We long to be set free, just like these cows."

"You have a point, but I don't think your metaphor is very elegant. How about chickens?"

"Are they any better off? They live in chicken coops, summer and winter."

"How did you learn about cows and chickens? You didn't live on a farm, did you?"

"No, but my grandmother has many farms around her house."

Flirtations and banter came easily between them. Over the harsh winter months, a circle of friends had formed around Carla. She had the largest room, and there were few other places to meet. Wine, beer, and *jenever*—Dutch gin—were scarce, but some students raided their fathers' wine cellars on weekends. When they were feeling cooped up, they would visit a café, but they usually recoiled from the sign at the entrance that said, *"Joden zijn niet welkom."* They didn't blame the café owner. He had little choice. They wouldn't stay long if German soldiers entered the café. In no time, the soldiers' loud singing and their *hoempa* music got on their nerves.

Dirk and Anna followed the path on top of the dike along the canal. Greening meadows reached to a distant horizon, where a few small towns broke up the flat line.

"I've wanted to ask you what made you decide to study medicine," Dirk said as they settled on the grassy slope of a dike. "But we're always in a group of people, and it didn't seem right to ask such a personal question."

"One of the reasons was that I broke my leg the day before the war started. I'd fallen off my bike. So, I was in the hospital when wounded soldiers were brought from the Grebbenberg. I watched them being unloaded on the sidewalk from my hospital room."

"What did that do to you?" Dirk was fully concentrated on her answer.

Should she tell him? She had never told anyone how deeply that sight had stirred her. She took a deep breath.

"I had two reactions. Horror and an impulse to help." She stopped and looked directly at Dirk. "Silly, I know, but I was just a kid."

It came out as an apolgy, but Dirk said, "Go on. Tell me more."

"The doctor who set my leg fascinated me. I looked at everything he did as if I were watching a movie. The nurses were helpful, but it was the doctor who made me think: I want to do this. And when I saw those wounded soldiers lying on stretchers the next day, I thought the same thing. An urge to do something. Of course, I kept those thoughts to myself."

"Why?" He shifted his tall body so he could lean on his elbow and look up into her face.

"Because nobody would understand. When it came time to think about the future, my mother suggested becoming a nurse if I wanted to help people so badly. I had always been busy playing doctor to my dolls and teddy bears. My room was a veritable sickbay. But being a doctor was not in a woman's future, my mother said. In her upbringing, becoming a wife and a mother was the goal. The funny thing is, my grandmother encouraged me, not my mother. By the time I had to defend my choice, I had thought long and hard about it. I had talked to our doctor. He was a family

25

friend. I often stopped by his office on my way home from school, just to smell that peculiar doctor's office smell. He always gave me the time of day, no matter if people sat in the waiting room. He encouraged me. My grades were good. I knew I could handle the study. What I had to overcome was prejudice against women in academia."

"You're helping to break the mold. How did you get your parents to agree and let you go to Utrecht?"

"Oh, I'm stubborn!" Anna laughed.

Dirk took her hand and stroked it. "And what else?" he asked, looking up at her.

He took her off guard. She tamped down a rush of excitement and finally said, "I don't know."

"I know," he said. "You're courageous." He took both her hands in his. Looking into his eyes, she had no doubt that when Dirk van Enthoven spoke, he meant what he said.

"Now you have to tell me what *your* first day of the war was like," she said.

He scooted closer to her on the grassy knoll. His eyes focused on the wide canal below. A barge came by, its hull deep in the water, headed in the direction of Germany, probably loaded with copper. All citizens had been ordered to hand over whatever they owned in the way of copper. It wasn't a long shot to conclude cartridges for bullets would be made from them. Some people complied, but many copper lanterns, bowls, candlesticks, and other family heirlooms found their way into holes, dug surreptitiously in backyard gardens.

A serious expression spread over Dirk's face.

"My father saw the war coming. Still, we were surprised when it actually started. He'd made plans to escape with the whole family. I have an older sister and a younger brother. I live in Den Haag. Airplanes woke us up that morning. Many got shot out of the sky and came down burning. The noise was unbelievable, with all those planes roaring overhead and being shot at, and you didn't know where they would come down."

"All I heard were cannon booms in the distance," Anna said.

"My father told us to pack a rucksack," Dirk went on, "only important things, he said. We got on our bikes and hit the road. Not the main road. Some were no more than wagon tracks in clay."

'Where were you headed?'

"To Hellevoetsluis. That day it seemed at the end of the earth."

Anna created a map of the coastline in her mind and searched for Hellevoetsluis. Dirk sensed her struggle.

"It's on Voorne, one of those islands south of the Maas River. Vader knew a skipper there with a seaworthy fishing vessel. All we had to do was get there and we could escape to England."

"If it had worked, you would now be serving in the British Army, and we would never have met!" Anna said.

He smiled and put his arm around her. Male sweat, mixed with the smell of coffee and Palmolive soap, permeated his Harris tweed jacket. It sent Anna's heart floating. His fingers were close enough to her face that she could smell the herring he'd held up by its tail and popped into his mouth when they'd passed a stand with *nieuwe haring* before they left the city.

They'd been stopped many times, Dirk told her. "'Where are you going?' German soldiers would ask. My father always gave the same answer. 'To my mother's farm in the next village over.'

"The Germans dropped pamphlets from the air. *Deutschland* was not fighting against *die Niederlande*, but against England, the pamphlets proclaimed. The German Army would protect the lives and property of every peace-loving civilian, but any opposition would be punished by death."

"Peace-loving! And that after *they* attacked. What nerve."

"We found that pamphlet while we saw smoke rise over Rotterdam. The roads were chock-full with people coming toward us, fleeing the city. The look in their eyes was awful. We finally got to that small harbor. The ship was waiting for us. It would be the last one to make it out to the North Sea and on to England."

"What happened?"

"After we got on board, a family just like ours stood on the quay, pleading with the skipper to let them on board. My father went back down the gangplank and got in on the conversation. A moment later, he came back on board and ordered us off the boat. The dangers for this Jewish family are greater than for ours, he said. We put our rucksacks back on and got on our bikes."

It sounded biblical to Anna. Sacrifice one family for another.

"Your father is high-minded," she said. "What did *you* think? And the rest of your family?"

"His decision didn't come out of the blue, really. The conversations around our dining table had been about Hitler and the Nazis for several years. We all saw it coming, not just my father."

"Saw what coming?" Anna asked.

"That Hitler has plans for the Jews that go beyond our imagination. We've only seen the tip of the iceberg, Anna."

In a sudden impulse, she threw her arms around him. A vague fear gripped her.

"What's going to happen?" she asked. "What will Hitler do to these poor people?" But she was really thinking about Maarten. The reputation the Japanese had earned during their war with China, which had been filled with atrocities according to leaked stories, boded ill for the people on Java. If the Germans had plans for the Jews, what plans did the Japanese have for the Dutch colonialists?

"He wants to get rid of them," Dirk said. "Slowly but surely, he'll create a hell for them."

He made the statement with authority, and over the few months that Anna had gotten to know him, she'd learned he was not given to exaggeration. In Carla's hub of friends, Dirk was not the loudest. He hung back amid heated arguments, hearing all sides. More often than not, his was the last word.

"Let's not think about that now, Anna. It's spring. It's a happy day and we're alive. Let's enjoy it." With that, he rolled her onto her side and fitted her body to his.

"You know?" he said. "I love you."

Anna's heart quickened as she looked up to him, surprised at his change of mood. Holding her face in his hands, he kissed her tenderly.

Another barge came by and tooted its horn. The skipper waved, and his wife smiled broadly as she hung her laundry out to dry on the deck. They waved back.

CHAPTER FOUR

Anna – May 1942

"That was a very good-looking young man who brought you home the other day," Betty said. Anna felt a blush creep from her neck into her face. "Is he a student?"

"Yes, he studies medicine."

She could tell Betty had more questions, but trained by years of discreet service, she refrained from posing them. With a spoonful of thick barley soup close to his mouth, Jan asked, "What's his name?"

"Dirk van Enthoven," Anna said.

Jan looked at her directly. "Can you say his name again?"

"Dirk van Enthoven."

"Interesting name," Jan said, and continued eating.

She was annoyed at their questions and at her own blushing, but it was true. She was in love. Every time she bent over her textbooks, she reminded herself she'd come to Utrecht to study medicine, but it didn't take long for the words on the page to flow together and reconstitute into a picture of Dirk's face. He was everywhere in her mind. He sucked up all other thought. What was it about him? Was it because he was older than any boy she'd ever gone out with? Had she fallen for his good looks? How could she have drifted into love when she hadn't really wanted to? What she *did* want was become a doctor. There was a lot at stake. Not the least to prove to Moeder she was capable of achieving what she'd set out to accomplish. Dirk van Enthoven was a disturbance, a distraction, a fork in the road.

Again, she couldn't shake Dirk off the page of her physics textbook. But then, what was wrong with being in love? It should be possible to study while being in love. Except for the Duke of Windsor and a few notable others, men hadn't let women thwart their ambitions, and women shouldn't give up their dreams because of men either. Still, she berated herself for being so distracted.

Could she blame it on the Occupation? The war hadn't been front and center in her thoughts in her last year at high school. The German presence had been no more than a nuisance then, like their decree of a curfew after eight at night. Of all the restrictions that were put on the population, that was the only one that had touched her daily life. But the Germans had become more than a nuisance since then. They were a threat, and the one who pointed that out to her was Dirk. He told her of things going on she hadn't been aware of because the Nazis controlled the news. Over distribution radio, they had gleefully informed the Dutch people that the Japanese Army had conquered the island of Java, where Maarten lived. They emphasized that it had taken no more than a few days to force the Dutch-Indonesian Army to capitulate.

News you could trust came over the BBC from London. *Radio Oranje* was beamed directly at Occupied Holland. Every evening at eight, the newscast started with a Morse code signal—the V for victory, which were the first four bars of Beethoven's Fifth Symphony, *ta-ta-ta-taaa*—and it ended with Vera Lynn singing "We'll Meet Again." The Germans had forbidden listening to it, but since few people complied, the Germans then ordered everyone to hand in their radios. Severe punishment was promised if the *Ordnung* wasn't adhered to. Like obedient children, most people handed in their only trustworthy source of news. Better to comply than to be taken to a police station.

Anna suspected Dirk had access to a hidden radio somewhere. He talked about news that didn't come over the distribution radio and wasn't printed in the papers. She respected his privacy, never asked him about it, and he didn't volunteer. They'd established a level of unspoken trust. Her parents' good friend, Dr. Blom, had told her over Christmas vacation that one of the most prized qualities in a physician was the ability to observe and keep quiet about it. As a joke, he'd added that doctors would probably make good spies.

Early one beautiful Sunday morning, Anna met Dirk in a park close to the university. After their happy time on the Amsterdam-Rijn Canal, they'd sought quiet places. There was so much to find out about each other. But on this day, Dirk's mood didn't match the weather. He was angry at the Germans. Very angry. An Ordnung had been posted demanding all Jews hand in their bicycles. What was worse, Jews could no longer use public transportation. They had only their feet to get them from here to there. This last order came on top of many others. Jews couldn't touch their own money in the bank; they were not allowed to swim in public swimming pools, or go to the beach, or take in a movie. The Nazis' intended message was clear to Dirk. Jews were trash and they deserved to be treated as such.

When he related the latest news, Anna asked, "Aren't there any people left in Germany who will stand up for them?"

"Hitler brainwashed them," Dirk said. He kicked a pebble down the gravel path. All around them, tulips were in full bloom and flowerbeds formed a tapestry of squares—yellow, purple, white, pink.

"Brainwash an entire population?"

"He promised them glory. He fired them up with fiery speeches. He also created a police force to enforce his ideas."

When she had still lived at home, Anna's father had pointed out pictures in the newspapers of huge crowds of young people with their right arms lifted to greet *der Führer*, who stood high on a podium in a general's uniform against a bank of red flags with the black swastika starkly displayed in its inner circle. The minister of propaganda, Joseph Goebbels, was a master at organizing rallies that outdid any spectacle anyone had ever seen, giving Hitler the imposing backdrop he needed to fire up his Hitler Jugend, which stood before him at attention in their uniforms, as if they formed an army. Instead of guns, they held flags.

"I saw one of Goebbel's propaganda movies when it was screened in 1940," Dirk said. "Goebbels forced every SS officer and soldier to sit down and watch it." He kicked another pebble. It landed among a stand of bright red tulips. "The movie was filled with ridiculous stereotypes."

Der Ewige Jude (*The Wandering Jew*) was a so-called documentary, filmed in Poland, where Jews made up 10 percent of the population, most living in ghettos. It was meant to contrast Jews with the Nazi ideal of Aryan men who lived healthy lives. Jews were parasites who took pleasure in money and favored a hedonist lifestyle. In one scene, rats came out of a sewer, Dirk told her. Its obvious message was that just as rats are the vermin of the animal kingdom, so Jews are the vermin of the human race. By the time the audience left the theater, it had been convinced Jews were the cause of everything that had gone wrong in their nation. They would be better off without them.

Anna drew her fingers through her hair, leaving it in strands over her forehead. A feeling of total misery overtook her.

"I can't stand it," she said. "What must we do?"

"I like the way you put that. *Must*," Dirk said, and hooked his arm through hers. She looked up at him and realized once again that Dirk had thought about these things so much harder and so much longer than she had.

"It's not only the Jews, Anna. Once you and I have our medical licenses, we will be confronted with another injustice. Hitler has no patience with the mentally retarded or children with birth defects. He makes them quietly disappear. If you don't fit the mold of the Aryan super race, you're on your way out. And he will make doctors do it for him."

They sat on a bench at the edge of a pond. Two swans glided by, their necks curved gracefully toward the water's surface in stark contrast to the ugly cruelty Dirk was revealing to her. She felt limp, like a balloon with the air pressed out of it. She remembered how she'd been wary of the young SS officer in the train when she came to Utrecht, but not afraid. She just hadn't wanted to be seen with him. Now, knowing how ruthlessly his ilk treated the Jews, Anna felt sapped. She leaned against Dirk's shoulder, looking for protection. He wrapped his arm around her, and they sat like that for a long while.

Before they got up to leave, he turned her face toward his and kissed her, his lips pressing against hers with passion and urgency. The park was quiet, inhabited by nesting birds, swans, ducks, and large goldfish, whose furtive movements were visible under the pond's surface. The trees were budding, and spring had turned the well-tended lawns into a deep green. They strolled over the gravel paths that curved this way and that in a graceful design, and the world seemed to belong just to them. With Dirk's arm linked into hers, Anna felt intrinsically connected and reassured. She hadn't come close to plumbing the depths of the current and looming dangers. What had been most important to her since the German Occupation began was getting her own way and studying medicine. That realization filled her with guilt. She loved Dirk even more for not pointing that out.

"Carla announced last night that her brother is preaching in a small village not far from here this morning," Dirk said. "I've never met him, but he sounds like an interesting man. We could bike over. What do you think?"

"What kind of church?" Anna asked. Her parents were not

churchgoers. Outside of Christmas and Easter, they didn't do much about their professed Protestant religion.

"The Remonstrant Brotherhood."

"Well, okay. Let's go."

They rounded up their bikes and peddled through the city. Only the sound of ringing church bells, high ones and low ones, broke the silence. Once out of the city, they followed a dirt road that was lined on both sides by rows of poplar trees, whose slender trunks had given in to the prevailing wind. Their crowns uniformly leaned to the right, like reeds in a breeze. As they approached the small village, the steeple of the church rose like a beacon on the horizon.

CHAPTER FIVE

Anna – Same Day – May 1942

They were early. Only a few congregants stood in the yard. Anna and Dirk put their bicycles in a rack under the roof of a plain woodshed. Women greeted each other with a nod. Men lifted their fedoras in a practiced gesture of acknowledgement. Anna felt out of place. For one thing, she didn't wear a hat, even though it was customary for women to wear hats to church. She didn't own one. Her long blond hair would have to do. Her cotton dress was unpretentious, put on earlier without a thought of going to church. Dirk, who wore his customary jacket and tie, resolutely stepped into the church's vestibule where the sexton, a short man wearing black leather gloves, was pulling on a heavy rope. Down and up, down and up. On the up motion, he seemed to levitate, his feet coming off the ground at least two inches. Beads of sweat glistened on his forehead. It was hard work to make the bell peal, but if its loud, deep tones could wake a sleepy village to say it was Sunday, the day of the Lord, then the sexton would have done his duty.

Dirk fetched a booklet from a rack and took Anna by her elbow as they entered the church, into suffused light that streamed through tall windows and settled on whitewashed walls. A huge brass chandelier hung over the middle of the aisle. At first glance, it was the only decoration. The simplicity of this small church's interior, with its gray slate tiles and dark oak box pews, charmed Anna. It seemed to send the message: don't distract me.

Dirk opened the door to a pew near the back, underneath the organ loft. After they sat, he pulled out the booklet he'd picked up in the vestibule and pointed to the large letters on the first page.

The Remonstrant Brotherhood is a community of faith, which rooted in the Gospel of Jesus Christ and true to its principle of freedom and tolerance seeks to worship and serve God.

All around them was a respectful silence as congregants slowly filtered in. "Have you been in this church before?" Anna whispered.

"Not here. There is a large Remonstrantse Kerk in Den Haag that I go to."

A line farther on in the booklet caught her eye. *Remonstrants are by no means always in agreement with one another on questions of faith and social issues. What binds them is the statement of principle.*

Dirk stood up to let Carla and a friend into their pew. The church was filling up. Just a few more minutes and the service would start. In front of her sat mostly middle-aged couples. To the left and right were people her own age. They might all be Carla's friends who'd come to listen to her brother, who was the guest minister that day. Carla was the kind who gathered people around her. Anna often thought of Carla as a vase, with her many friends forming the bouquet.

Hearing a stir behind her, Anna turned her head and blanched at the sight of a man in a black uniform entering the sanctuary with a proprietary air. His shiny black riding boots clacked loudly on the slate floor as he walked right up to the front, where he set himself down in the first pew. His entrance was well timed, just moments before Dominee Vlaskamp entered the chancel from a side door, followed by four deacons, all men in solid black suits and black ties, who took their seats in the box pew next to the chancel.

Dominee Vlaskamp looked to be in his late twenties. A tall blond blue-eyed man, he would do well on a Nazi propaganda poster. Yet in his simple black robe with a small white jabot under his chin, he cut a striking contrast to the man in his flashy black uniform.

Dominee Vlaskamp looked around the church, and his gaze rested momentarily on the surprising presence of a uniformed member of the NSB. Possibly, there were other members of the NSB in the church, but not in uniform, and that made all the difference. With remarkable calm, the minister took his place while the organ finished its prelude. The service had begun. After the usual psalm readings and hymn singing, Dominee Vlaskamp climbed the spiral staircase of the pulpit, which rose above the chancel. For purposes of acoustics, an equisitely carved roof hung above it, fastened to the brick wall behind it with two cast-iron rods.

The Bible reading was from the Gospel of Luke, chapter 10, verses 25–37, the Parable of the Good Samaritan. With a clear and purposeful voice, Dominee Vlaskamp read the story of the lawyer who'd asked Jesus, "Who is my neighbor?", after he'd acknowledged that one of God's commandments was that he should love his neighbor like himself. Jesus answered him with the story of a man who walked down a steep hill from Jerusalem to Jericho and fell into the hands of robbers. The robbers stripped him, beat him, and went away, leaving him half dead. First, a priest and then a Levite came by, but when they saw him, they passed him on the other side of the road and continued on their journey. When a Samaritan came by and saw him, he took pity. He bandaged the man's wounds and put him on his own animal, brought him to an inn, and took care of him. The next day, he gave two denarii to the innkeeper and told him to take care of the man till he came back. Jesus asked the lawyer, "Which of these three, do you think, was a neighbor to the man who fell into the hands of the robbers?" The lawyer answered, "The one who showed him mercy." Jesus said to him, "Go and do likewise."

All around Anna, people sat in rapt attention. She wondered

where Dominee Vlaskamp was going to take them with this scripture reading. One of Rembrandt's paintings depicted the Good Samaritan. She had seen it in the Rijks Museum in Amsterdam—the Samaritan in rich clothing and the victim of the robbers, half naked, being lifted from a white horse. The innkeeper had a white beard, and Rembrandt had effectively used his famous ability to render light to make the victim's body on the white horse stand out. Even though she had admired the technique, it hadn't touched her as much as a painting by the Frenchman Aime-Morot, who had depicted the Samaritan as a simple merchant, stooped under the weight of the victim, whom he hoisted as best he could onto his small donkey. The way the totally naked victim leaned on the Samaritan had filled her with empathy. The profound meaning of suffering and caring came through powerfully.

In Anna's limited experience, ministers seldom took a direct route to the message they really wanted to deliver. Dominee Vlaskamp was no exception. He led the congregation into his interpretation of the parable by describing the road that led from Jerusalem to Jericho. It was steep, because Jerusalem was 640 meters above sea level and Jericho was 258 below it. A winding, meandering road, conducive to ambushing.

"Jesus," Dominee Vlaskamp said, "knew that his audience—the lawyer among them—was well aware that it was called the Way of Blood because so many had met deadly fates there. Jesus also knew the Jews he was talking to hated the Samaritans. Samaritans were considered half-Jews. Inferior, in other words. The Samaritans hated the Jews in return. So, Jesus deliberately shocked his audience."

The energy in the church shot up. The word *Jew* spoken out loud these days was provocative, especially when mentioned in the same sentence with *hate*. Anna put her hand on Dirk's thigh. His muscles felt tight under her fingers.

"Jesus's words are for all the ages," Dominee Vlaskamp went on. "The reason his parables are so masterful is because he knew how to touch on complex issues with a vivid image and a simple story that went straight to the core. The issues and the ethics of this parable are still with us today. And we have to ask ourselves: Do we love our neighbor as ourselves?"

Anna shifted in her seat. From here the minister had only one way to go, and that was all the way. In the Nederlands Hervormde Kerk she and her parents attended in Arnhem, nothing spoken from the pulpit had made her nervous. But Dirk had told her that in the Remonstrantse Kerk, people didn't sit on their hands. They wanted to *live* their faith.

"If we set this parable in today's world," the reverend said, "who would be the poor man by the side of the road? Who would be the priest who wouldn't dirty his hands on him? And who would be the Levite who crossed the street and walked away?" He paused. "Who would be the Samaritan?"

Anna's mind was on fire. The images of the first days of the war that she had spent in the hospital rushed back. The wounded soldiers, the blood on the pavement, the doctors and nurses scurrying around. But that was not the complete answer to the question posed. What about the priest and the Levite?

Dominee Vlaskamp dared the congregation. "Haven't we seen people suffering in the street in our day? Haven't we seen helpless people being robbed? Of their possessions and especially of their freedom? And what have we, people of faith whose stated principles call for freedom and tolerance, what have we done to help them?"

A woman with a wide-brimmed hat in the next pew turned to her husband and gave him a meaningful look. He nodded back at her.

"Several things are going on in this passage of Luke's Gospel. It isn't just about the victim and the healer. It isn't just about the two men who looked the other way. It is about one group of people hating another. About one group that doesn't accept the other as full members of society."

Untermenschen. Under-man. Inferior. That's what he meant. Just that morning Anna had heard the word for the first time.

"Think about this deeply," the reverend continued. "Whom do you identify with in this story? Do you feel like the victim? Are you the healer, the caretaker? Are you a hypocrite like the priest and the Levite? Or are you one of the robbers, who brutally takes away what rightfully belongs to another? What do you think it teaches us today? When you reach a conclusion, remember Jesus's words: Go and do likewise. Amen."

Silence.

Anna was unable to breathe. Around her, people shifted. There was coughing and shuffling of feet. Dirk reached for the hymnal as the organ started up. The deep tones vibrated in Anna's tight chest.

After the benediction, the people headed toward the exit. All except the NSB officer in front. He followed Dominee Vlaskamp, who had disappeared through the side door with the deacons while the organ was still playing. Anna watched him. The blood drained from her face.

"What's going on, Dirk?" she asked.

"I wonder," he said slowly.

They went outside where clusters of people stood wrapped up in troubled conversation. The sun shone brightly in the sky. A flock of swallows swooped over them. It was a glorious spring day. The side door opened, and out stepped the minister with the NSB officer, who took him to a car parked in the yard.

Anna gasped. Dirk abruptly went over to the car and demanded to know where Dominee Vlaskamp was being taken.

"To the police station," Dominee Vlaskamp answered before the NSB officer could. "Please tell my sister not to worry."

A German soldier in a green uniform slammed the door of the staff car before another word could be said. He got into the driver's seat and sprayed pebbles as he charged ahead down the street.

The courtyard went quiet. People were speechless.

CHAPTER SIX

Anna – Same Day – May 1942

After the car left the churchyard, the congregants stared at one another, thunderstruck. What would happen to that nice young man who'd been their guest minister today? Had the higher-ups in the NSB been ordered to check what was being preached from the pulpit of their church? Anna eavesdropped on a small group next to her. The owner of the wide-brimmed hat, who'd sat in the pew in front of her, stood at its center.

"You know what happened last Sunday, don't you?" she asked in general. "Every Roman Catholic priest read an open letter from the pulpit condemning the German authorities for making Jews wear the Star of David. Priests were arrested afterward."

"They're talking about closing clubs that don't have a Nazi on their board of directors," a young man said. "They're pushing their way into our society."

The other members in the group shook their heads in sad agreement. Just like Utrecht's Student Club, Anna thought.

"The Catholic bishops are furious," another man said. "They're urging their faithful to leave infiltrated clubs. The lines are drawn."

Dirk took Carla, who looked pale and shaken, by the arm and steered her to the shed where their bikes were stored. Anna and their other friends followed.

"Let's leave together," he said, "all of us. I know a small café between here and Utrecht."

There were eight of them, all students—though not all medical students—and all Carla's friends. They biked in single file over narrow paths that led to a farm that was part café. You had to know about it to find it. They placed their bikes in a rack and found woven reed chairs and tables in the garden. There were no other guests. Five cows stood behind a barbed wire fence. They briefly raised their heads with their outsized eyes and sloppy wet noses. Curiosity satisfied, they returned to rhythmically grabbing the succulent grass. Dirk pushed three tables together, and the rest dragged eight chairs over. The heavy smell of cow manure, mixed with the sweet smell of a flowering lilac tree, filled the air. The farmer's wife came out on wooden shoes. Over her black dress she wore a colorful apron that fell from her waist to just above her ankles, exposing her black wool socks. They ordered coffee and an *uitsmijter*, a traditional Dutch sandwich.

"Dirk, how can we find out where they've taken my brother?" Carla asked. She still looked awfully pale, but some color had returned to her cheeks.

"I bet they took him to a police station in Utrecht," he said. "They wouldn't bother with the police in a small village. I know somebody there. I'll check with him. Maybe he can find out where he is, but you'll have to be patient."

"What can they charge him with?" Herman asked. He was the one who'd sat next to Carla in the church pew and he sat close to her now.

"Most likely it will be something like stoking unrest from the pulpit."

"Your brother was very subtle in the way he brought his message," the student on Carla's right said. "I mean, his choice of scripture was such an effective way to characterize the Nazis, the NSB, the Resistance, and the Jews. There was no escaping what he was driving at."

"I know," Carla said. She fidgeted with her silk scarf, adjusting it around her shoulders, taking it off, twisting the tip around her index finger.

Piet, a heavyset geology student with gentle eyes set in a bit of a baby face, sat across from Anna. She had met him several times over the winter at Carla's place.

"As we were biking over," he said, "I kept asking myself: 'So, whom do you identify with, Piet?' I know whom I would like to identify with, but I don't think I qualify."

"That's the important question, isn't it?" Dirk said as he moved aside to let the farmer's wife put down steaming cups of coffee and a pot with more.

After she had gone back into the café, another student said softly, "I know who I am. I am the victim."

"You?" Dirk said. "You feel like a victim, Daan?"

Daan reached into his pocket and pulled something out. In a swift movement of his head, he looked at the door to the café. When he was sure it was closed, he flashed the yellow Star of David at them. Dead quiet followed his revelation. So quiet, they could hear the chewing of the cows. White petals from the flowering apple tree fluttered through the silence and landed on the table.

Otto, a veterinary student, was the first to speak. "This doesn't make sense. You don't look Jewish at all."

"I know. That's why I have it in my pocket and not on my jacket. I am half-Jewish."

"Sweet Jesus," Piet said.

"How do you handle this?" Herman asked. "What if they stop you? Do you have an identity card? The one with the J on it?"

"Yes, I do. So far, I haven't needed to show it. Of course, I am careful where I go. My dad is as blond and blue-eyed as I am, so we go places together, even if it's where Jews aren't allowed, like on the tram or the train. So far, so good."

Anna shivered. Daan could be in a lot of trouble. As usual, everyone looked at Dirk for guidance. The muscles in his face tightened. Finally, he said, "Obviously, you trust us. That is an enormous compliment. I for one pledge that I will never pass this information to anyone. No matter what."

"Likewise," Otto said, and before the farmer's wife came back carrying a large tray with their lunch, everyone in the circle had pledged to keep Daan's stunning news to themselves.

The *uitsmijters* tempted them to dig in. Anna's mouth watered at the sight of fried egg, sunny-side up, on a thick slice of ham. She fancied that the chicken strutting through the yard had laid the eggs. The ham had probably been smoked in the farm's chimney over the winter. Maybe the bread had been baked that morning by the farmer's wife, and the butter churned from the milk those cows across the fence had produced. It gave her a warm, cozy feeling, as though things were still as they used to be and no war had interfered. It was quiet for a while but for the clicking of forks and knives.

"We're at crossroads," Carla said. "What's expected of us? Jesus did not preach rebellion. There are many Christians, Walter told me, who feel you can't sabotage the Germans if you follow the Bible. When biblical Jews complained about paying taxes to the Romans, Jesus told them, 'Give to the emperor what is the emperor's and to God the things that are God's.' But what if you feel in your gut that you can't look away when innocent people are brutalized? What values do we live by?"

"Your brother seems to have made his choice," Piet said.

"Yes. Walter feels we shouldn't let ourselves be led like meek sheep. Who can live with a Fascist regime?"

Emmy, a student in French, took a last bite of her *uitsmijter* and poured herself more coffee from the blue enameled coffee pot. "The Samaritan," she said. "He's the one we would all like to identify with. The trouble is that, suppose we see a German soldier beat a

Jew into submission. There's little we can do. He has the gun. We have bare hands."

Again, they fell silent. The world around them was alive with sounds. The chickens talked to each other as they picked at blossoms in the flower border. Birds sang in the apple orchard. A dog farther down the road barked. Everyday sounds.

Dirk broke the silence among them. "We have more than just our bare hands. We have brains."

"And a passion for freedom," Daan added.

"How can we use that passion to make a difference?" Anna asked.

Dirk looked at her and gave her a thumbs-up. "That's a question each of us will have to answer."

The farmer's wife came out to present the bill, which was modest for the feast she'd treated them to. They all chipped in and left her a generous tip.

It was time to head back to the city and face the reality of Walter's arrest. Carla suggested they meet again at six at her place. First, Dirk had to find out where Walter was being held. He got on his bike, turned around once to smile at Anna, and took off.

Everything she'd heard and seen swirled through Anna's mind, as if she'd been thrown off a bridge and landed in an eddy that was sucking her down. The German Occupation presented a moral dilemma. After listening to Walter's sermon, she could see that now. There were choices to be made. The war had not impacted her own life yet. She'd come to Utrecht to study medicine, and nothing the Germans had done had stood in her way, except to put a clamp on the social aspects of student life. Even that wasn't much of a hindrance since she didn't know what she was missing. What had really thrown her off was Daan's admission that he was half-Jewish. He and people like him needed protection. The horrible facts Dirk had been telling her were no longer information she could store separate from her own reality. The urge to help was rising up in her, yet she felt as powerless as when the bleeding soldiers had been rushed to the hospital when the war started. She still had been a child then, not equipped to help. To feel powerless was disabling. Dominee Vlaskamp had found the strength to give a provoking sermon. Had faith empowered him?

She had time to kill before meeting again at Carla's, so she got on her bike without a destination in mind. She was just peddling and thinking. Hardly any cars were on the road. Gas was rationed. Only doctors and a few others had permits to fill up their tanks. As she passed the railroad station, she stopped to look at the posters that plastered its walls. Germans loved posters. Blatant propaganda. A Nazi specialty. An entire wall was devoted to promoting their push to get Dutch men to work in Germany. The men depicted on the posters were physically strong, with bulging biceps and fiercely determined looks. The Aryan ideal. The slogan underneath said *"Wie in Duitsland werkt dient het Nederlandse Volk."* (Working in Germany serves the Dutch people.) The raw truth was they desperately needed workers to replace their own who'd been drafted. The more territory Hitler conquered, the more troops he needed to occupy it. South from Norway to Yugoslavia and east from Holland to Russia. What good that did for Holland was a mystery, because the workers were paid a pittance and lived in forced labor camps. Those who returned vowed not to go back.

Anna headed for Carla's place. She was too restless to bike to her own room and get a bite to eat. Carla was alone, staring out the window. Anna asked if there was any news. Carla said no. She asked if Carla was all right. Carla shrugged. They sat together in tense silence for an hour until they heard footsteps outside. It took Dirk just seconds to make it up the stairs with his long legs, three treads at a time. A blush crept into Anna's face when he strode through the door. His presence was reassuring. Even if he brought bad news, he would put it in perspective.

"Walter is being held at the police headquarters in Utrecht. He's being interrogated, and I don't think they will let him go yet."

"Who is leading the interrogation?" Carla asked with a quiver in her voice. "The police or the Gestapo?"

"There is little the Dutch police can do without the Gestapo looking in on them."

"How long do you think they will hold Walter?"

"I don't know. It depends. If he's involved in the Underground, he will have to be very careful about what he says. The Gestapo always tries to force detainees to give up the names of coworkers."

Carla shook her head. "I have no idea if Walter is involved in the Underground."

"Of course not. What you don't know, you can't give away. He wouldn't want to put you at risk. The less you know, the better."

Carla paced the floor as the news sank in. Otto and Emmy arrived, and gradually the room filled with their entire group.

"What's the news?" Emmy asked.

"Walter is being held at the police station here in Utrecht," Dirk said.

"Is Walter married?" Herman asked.

"No," Carla said.

"How about your parents? Should you let them know?"

"They live in Breda. It's just Walter and me."

"Let's wait and see," Dirk said. "That would be my suggestion. There's no sense in alarming your parents. I will keep tabs on the situation. They might release him tomorrow."

A pall fell over the room. They'd started the day as a boisterous group of students, but events had given them a shared secret, and Walter's sermon had kindled a chilling awareness of the world outside the walls of academia.

"I've been thinking about our conversation at the farm café," Anna said. "I don't know if I can call myself a Christian. I can't approach the fix we're in with the kind of faith your brother has, Carla. But his call to action spoke to me."

"That makes two of us," Piet said.

"You have the compassion, Anna," Dirk said. He sat across from her on the floor, his long legs folded under him like a Buddha.

"Compassion drove me into medicine," she said. "Not any particular faith."

"Then compassion might drive you to oppose the Nazis," he said. "Being a member of a church is not a requirement, you know. Besides, having compassion is a big part of being a Christian."

His eyes locked onto hers, and she felt his love in the way he looked at her. When they'd sat by the side of the canal only a week ago, he'd called her courageous. What did he expect of her?

They'd all had plenty of time between leaving the café and gathering at Carla's to think about how they could answer Dominee Vlaskamp's challenge. They talked about it until it was time to make it home before curfew. Nothing was decided. The question they wrestled with was how to go about opposing such a brutal enemy. To some, it seemed a pipe dream. But Dirk said, "Resistance doesn't happen overnight. An opportunity has to present itself."

Anna wondered again if Dirk was already connected to an organized resistance. She didn't want to ask him. As he had said to Carla, "What you don't know, you can't give away."

Over the next days, between exams, they kept meeting at Carla's to find out if her brother had been set free yet, but there was no news.

"One more week and we'll be on summer recess," Otto said.

"Three months of doing nothing!" Piet said. "Frankly, I'm not looking forward to it." He'd plunked himself down on the floor, leaning against the frayed couch, nursing a beer. "My parents live in Drenthe. Not the most fascinating place in the world. Besides, I'm an only child. I dread all the attention focused on me."

Piet hit a nerve in Anna with his "only child" statement. She was like an only child. Her parents hadn't heard from Maarten since the Japanese had conquered Java.

"Daan," she asked, "where do your parents live?"

"In Den Haag. Why do you ask?"

"I just wondered. Will you be safe? Here you're one in a crowd of students."

"Don't spend the summer worrying about me, Anna." Daan took a bite from a warm chicken croquette he'd plucked from an automatic dispenser down the street. It was one of those modern wonders. You could feed yourself from a hole in the wall, where an invisible hand kept things like croquettes and fish sticks warm for you in exchange for a few quarters. "I am very good at amusing myself. One of my passions is drawing and painting. The Gestapo can't stop me. Once I get into drawing, the summer will be over in a whiff."

Anna admired his attitude, but she worried. She shifted in her chair and ran her fingers through her hair, leaving it an unorderly mess.

"I also live in Den Haag," Dirk said. "I'll get in touch with you. Be sure to give me your address before we leave on break."

It reminded Anna that she needed to give Dirk her own address in Arnhem. Already, the prospect of not seeing him for several months was unbearable.

The news of Walter's whereabouts reached them the last time the Group of Eight, as they now called themselves, met before the academic year ended. It was a bright early-summer day. They chose a quiet spot in the park where they created a circle with their bikes and sat in its center on the neatly clipped grass. They felt safer this way. Ever since their Sunday in the country, they'd been careful not to gather in places where they could be overheard.

Anna could tell something was troubling Dirk as soon as he stepped off his bike. He sought out Carla to sit next to. He stretched out his long legs, but quickly drew them up and put his arms around his knees.

"I don't have good news," he said. "Walter has been transferred to Scheveningen."

Carla stiffened. She pressed her hands to her face.

Dirk put his hand on her arm. "Somebody I know back home called me. He says the Germans use the prison in Scheveningen to store people until they figure out what to do with them."

Anna's suspicion that Dirk had contacts with the Resistance grew. He knew a whole lot more than any of them. As usual, nobody challenged him if this was really true. Did the others share her suspicions?

"What are they after?" Otto asked. His frown paralleled the anger in his voice. The dark hair of his furrowed eyebrows made him look severe.

"I think they suspect he works in the Underground. If he is not part of the Underground, they can't get any information out of him. My hope is that after a while, the Gestapo will give up. I think he was moved to Scheveningen because it's next to Den Haag. That's where the Gestapo has its headquarters, and that's where their seasoned interrogators are."

Carla dropped her hands into her lap and stared at Dirk. "Is there anything we can do for him? Anything?"

"I wish I knew the answer, Carla. But I just don't know. I've thought of going there and asking some questions, but my contact tells me there's no use in doing that. The Germans would slam the door in my face. The only reasonable thing we can do that might be effective is to find some influential person who could exert pressure on the Gestapo."

"Are there such people?" Emmy said. "Is there anybody we might know who can change a Nazi's mind?"

"It would have to be either a German officer or a member of the NSB," Herman said. "And not of low rank either."

"My father is a judge," Emmy said. "I doubt he keeps company with the kind of people you're looking for."

"It's a long shot, I know," Dirk said. "I hate to send us off with this news just before break. Who would have thought we would ever wince at the mention of Scheveningen? I used to go to the beach there every sunny summer day."

"Me too," Daan said. "As a kid I built sand castles, and as a teenager I flirted with the girls."

Dirk got up and walked over to his bike. He reached inside the woven basket strapped to its handlebars and produced a white paper bag.

"When I need a fix, I eat chocolate. So, I brought us some truffles. I hope they didn't melt on the way over. Here, let's pass them around."

"You mean to say that you used your distribution coupons to buy us chocolate?" Daan asked. "That must have taken your entire allotment for the month of May."

Anna looked over to Dirk. He shrugged and smiled at her. She just loved that man.

Before the curfew went into effect, they said good-bye. Carla would go back to Breda the next day, Otto to Rotterdam, Piet to a small place in Drenthe, Emmy to her home in Haarlem, Herman to his parents' summer cottage in Loosdrecht, and Anna to Arnhem. Only Daan and Dirk went to the same city. None of them had any solid plans for how to spend the summer months. The borders were closed. Traveling to foreign countries was out. Working in a summer job was not an option. It wasn't part of student life. The possibility didn't even enter their minds. Their fathers paid for their education. If your father couldn't pay the tuition, you didn't study.

Anna said she would visit Carla in Breda. Herman invited everyone to come to his house on the lake. Dirk would visit Daan in Den Haag. They vowed to stay in touch, and begged Carla to let them know any news about her brother.

CHAPTER SEVEN

Anna – Late Spring 1942

Anna sat at the desk of her youth where she'd studied hard to get into medical school, and had daydreamed about living an independent life, away from provincial Arnhem, away from being an only child in a strict household. It hadn't even been a week since she'd come home, and already she was thoroughly bored. With her head propped up on her hands, she stared out the window at the massive chestnut tree that dropped white petals from its blossoms, which looked like candles, the way they sprouted straight up from wide branches, as erect as the ones in the heavy silver candelabrum on her grandmother's dining table.

Nothing much had changed in the backyard, except the seasons. That morning, she'd watched the gardener deadhead the petunias and pansies that lined the wide flower border. He'd tied the pink peonies to sticks so their heavy blossoms wouldn't tip over. The edges got trimmed and the grass cut with a push mower. Neat, organized, nothing left to chance.

It hadn't been easy to slide back into the groove. Like the garden, the house was kept neat, and the various routines were mapped out like a train schedule. Breakfast at eight, coffee at eleven, lunch at noon, tea at four, dinner at six. Mondays were for laundry, Tuesdays for ironing, Wednesdays for cleaning, Thursdays for sewing. On Fridays, the shopping was done for whatever the milkman, the baker, or the vegetable vendor didn't deliver to the door. Her mother had patterned the schedule after the way life had been when she grew up. The major differences were that Anna's father was not a wealthy landowner and that Maarten and Anna attended public schools. Mother had brought Sarah, a trusted housekeeper, from the estate with her when she started married life, and Anna could not remember a day that Sarah hadn't been part of the household.

Here at home, she missed her brother even more. It was like an ache in her side. With his independent spirit, he'd pushed the limits of anything and anyone, and he'd shown a special talent for putting his parents on edge. Yet when she thought about him now, it was his sense of humor and lovable nature she remembered best. They'd been written on his face, centered in his intense blue eyes, with the wavy blond hair falling over his high forehead, so much like Vader's.

She'd fallen off her bike once, when she was six, because Maarten had challenged her to bike along the very edge of the canal downtown. He'd been behind her, egging her on. She had been petrified she'd fall into the water. Instead, she fell on the streetside, on the uneven, hard cobblestones, and badly twisted her ankle. When she screamed, he jumped off his bike and made a quick decision. The only other form of transportation immediately available was a bike with a loading platform in front, ordinarily used for deliveries. Maarten hijacked it from the surprised owner, who took over Maarten's bike, and Maarten pedaled her straight to Dr. Blom's office. The thought of calling his parents from some nearby house hadn't occurred to him. Why wait for instructions when it was clear what needed to be done? Moeder had been incensed when Anna hobbled into the house with a big bandage wrapped around her ankle, but Vader had pointed out that

Maarten had acted responsibly. Anna never told either one that Maarten had caused the sprained ankle in the first place. Loyalty had been the basis of their sibling relationship.

Anna sighed. She ran her fingers through her hair, wondering why Maarten had gotten all the curls while she was stuck with unruly strands. Good looks had not been equally distributed between them. Maarten had inherited his father's strong facial features. In the female line, her mother's natural elegance had not been passed along to her.

Outside, the gardener put the lawnmower back in the shed. She should probably go downstairs for the daily midmorning coffee ritual. When she first came home, a richly decorated hazelnut cake had awaited her. Sarah had brought in hot coffee on a silver tray, and Moeder had sliced the cake, arranging the pieces on precious china plates that were only used at special occasions. Vader had even come home from work early. It was obvious her parents were happy to have her back. They wanted to hear her stories, but what could she tell them? That she had fallen in love with Dirk van Enthoven? That she had become acutely aware of the havoc the Germans created in the lives of the Jews and many others? That she was worried sick about a minister called Walter Vlaskamp? That she believed she would somehow have to take some kind of moral stand against the Nazi's sick agenda?

She told them none of it. She'd passed her exams, she said, and they hadn't been as hard as she'd feared. The formality of the living room, with its dark leather wallpaper, heavy cretonne curtains, and elegant Empire furniture, stifled her into silence. The setting seemed far removed from the life she'd led at the modest home of Betty and Jan, and from the lurking dangers Dirk had opened her eyes to. Her mind was still with her friends in Utrecht, and with Walter Vlaskamp, who had spent almost a week at the police headquarters there and now had been sent on to Scheveningen. The name of that town had always had a pleasant ring to it. It was where wide sandy beaches bordered the North Sea. In everyone's memory, it smelled of suntan lotion and rang with the sound of screeching seagulls following the herring fleet as it returned to harbor, or the sound of a jazz band playing at the hugely popular pier. Scheveningen was synonymous with lighthearted pleasure.

Not anymore. The Germans had closed the beaches while they built fortifications, the so-called Atlantic Wall, to defend against a feared English invasion. The dunes were filled with land mines, barbed wire, and guard posts. In the middle of this bleak territory stood the prison, where people that had any suspicion pinned on them got dumped. Black-market racketeers, Jews who'd transgressed ordinances, people with false identifications, Resistance workers, they all were crowded into the prison of Scheveningen, which soon was referred to as Het Oranje Hotel. The thought that Walter was one of the prisoners was agonizing.

Anna took up the Parker fountain pen—her grandmother's graduation gift—and started a letter to Carla.

Arnhem, June 1, 1942

Dear Carla,

I hardly dare ask, but have you heard anything yet about Walter? This is a stupid question, because you promised me to call if there was news. It's just that I am furiously hoping and praying that the Gestapo will let him go. The sooner the better. How are your parents? They must know by now that Walter is being held. And how are you doing? Too bad we don't live a bit closer, but I'm planning on coming to Breda one of these days. I've never been there before. It's a beautiful city, I hear.

I don't know about you, but I'm having a hard time adjusting to domestic life. Breakfast at eight, lunch at noon, dinner at six... I feel I've been taken over by a clock. I'd forgotten how regimented life could be. My situation at home is a lot like yours: the only child while our brothers are away.

I've joined a small tennis club for something to do. Some of the girls I went to high school with talked me into it. I like the game and the exercise, but it's interesting to see how little I have in common with them now. I was the only one to go to university. The others either went into nursing or secretarial work. Straight out of school they fall into the regimented life! We probably will have to make up for it later in our lives, but when I listen to their stories, I like the student life better, for now.

I'm catching up on my reading. My father has a great collection of mysteries. I'm working my way through a row of Agatha Christie's books. Can you concentrate on anything while you wait to hear from Walter? Let me know when a visit would suit you. I would love to see you and cheer you up a bit!
Love, Anna

She sealed the envelope and stuck a stamp on it—one without an image of Queen Wilhelmina—and reflected on the fact that it was easier to cheer someone up face to face than sending encouragement through the mail. Blue ink turned every word into a cold statement of fact. A gesture, a hug would accomplish more. Worrying about Maarten made her realize that Carla must be living in daily agony, knowing that her brother was in the infamous Oranje Hotel. The rumors that came out of there about people being tortured were scary. She could only hope they were exaggerated.

She got on her bike and rode over to the railroad station to mail her letter. While there, she looked up the times of departure for trains to Breda. It would be a complicated trip. At least two stopovers. Her gaze wandered to the schedule for Den Haag. That would be easier. No stopovers. She was tempted to throw caution to the wind and get herself on a train that would take her to Dirk. No. She would rather be invited.

She took her time biking back home, her soul aching as she pined for Dirk.

CHAPTER EIGHT

Walter – June 1942

The low-ranking Gestapo officer pushed Walter Vlaskamp out of the *overvalswagen* as if he were an unwilling child. It had been a long, rough truck ride from Utrecht. On a hard wooden bench in the covered cargo area without windows, he'd had no clue where the road led. It took him a moment to adjust to the bright sunshine after his feet hit the ground. Slowly, he made out a massive brick building. It looked familiar. He'd seen it before, but only from a distance. Its front looked like a fortified medieval castle, with two towers, each three stories high, and an elaborate, heavy oak door in between.

Scheveningen! Dear God, they're taking me into a prison for criminals. The heavy boys.

With nine other men, he'd been taken from the police station in Utrecht. There hadn't been much talk on the way. Deaf and dumb, like lead soldiers in a child's toy box, they'd sat next to one another, each with a secret he wasn't going to divulge in front of the Gestapo. Walter assumed the others were trying to guess his secret, as much as he wondered about theirs. Don't waste your time, he felt like saying. I have no secret to hide. I am just a naive clergyman.

Once inside, they had to undress and were searched, straight up and down and bent over. Most of what they had on them was taken. The guards divided their group among three one-person cells, each three meters long and two meters wide. It had one bunk with a thin mattress against the wall across from the door, a slop jar in the left corner, and a water jug in the other. A peephole for the guards sat like an evil eye in the upper part of the thick door; and a serving hatch had been cut into the middle. Light came from a weak electric bulb hanging from the ceiling. Some natural light fell through high windows.

"So, this is Het Oranje Hotel," a man with a grizzled beard, one of Walter's two roommates, said. "I had expected better accommodations, like a nice hospitality suite with a private bath."

"It will take some imagination to pretend you're in a royal suite," Walter said.

"Wherever she is in her exile, I hope Queen Wilhelmina doesn't have to use a slop jar. That would be a real come-down."

Walter studied his two roommates and wondered what they might have in common. It would be crucial to passing the time. He'd never been in a situation where there was absolutely nothing to do. He'd hoped he would be spared this. The interrogating authorities in Utrecht thought he was a member of the Underground. They just didn't believe him when he insisted he was not in any way connected to the Resistance. They could prove nothing against him, so they had threatened him, pressing for information he didn't have. How could he convince a police officer he was just a minister doing his work by reminding the faithful that the great stories of the Bible related to present times? Compassion, justice, faith, the discernment of others' sufferings were the Christian values a minister should remind his flock of. And that's what he'd done when he'd taken over the pulpit from a vacationing minister in a small village church. Who would have thought that a high-up in the NSB party would walk in and take offense at his sermon? Although he had to admit, the timing had been asking for trouble, only one week after the Roman Catholic Church had read an open letter from every pulpit in the land, condemning the order that Jews wear the Star of David. But that had been the whole point. He agreed with the Catholic clergy. He would give the same sermon if he had to do it over again.

The brick walls around them rose to a high ceiling. Just below the ceiling were three windows. The middle one could be pulled open to a narrow slant with a thin rope to let in fresh air. Walter wasn't tempted to try to escape through it. Even if they stood on each other's shoulders to reach the windows, how would the last man get out? Besides, having seen the fortifications of the place, he didn't harbor any illusions about what would happen once they got to the ground on the other side. No, the three of them were caught in what looked and felt like a brick oven.

"It's not a good idea to call each other by our true names," the third man said. "What you don't know, you can't tell. Call me Scar." He pointed to the long scar that ran over his right eyebrow.

"That sounds reasonable," Walter said. "You can call me Blue for my blue eyes, and I'll call this guy Grizzly." He gestured to the man who looked to be the oldest.

Giving themselves nicknames didn't provoke laughter. Not even a snicker. Silence. Each evaluated his surroundings and his fellow prisoners. Walter looked at two bricks with scratches on them. He got closer and noticed the scratchings represented words. They were hard to read, and it took him a while to make them fall into one sentence.

Do not fear those who kill the body, but cannot kill the soul.

Someone had sat in this cell expecting to die. And now, he read those letters painstakingly scratched into the hard brick with what? A safety pin? It was so different from reading them in his well-worn Bible. In his rented apartment in Leiden, a pipe with curling smoke in his left hand, an azalea plant in the windowsill catching the setting sun, maybe a steaming cup of coffee next to him, this sentence would have struck him differently. He probably would not have concentrated on the killing of the body, though if he remembered correctly, this sentence was part of Jesus's warnings to his apostles that they might be killed in his name. "But the one who endures till the end will be saved" was in that same passage. Emphasizing the soul might have been his preference for the pitch of a sermon. The prisoner who had vacated this cell had looked death in the eye. Whoever he was, he had been defiant, that was clear. He hadn't let the Nazis break his spirit or take away his faith.

"Look at this," Walter said to Grizzly and Scar. He read it out loud to them.

"Sounds like something from the Bible," Grizzly said.

"It's from the Gospel of Matthew. I know that much, but I can't remember which chapter."

"Are you religious?" Scar asked.

"I'm a minister."

"What's a minister doing in a prison, for heaven's sake?" Grizzly said.

"I preached a sermon the Nazis didn't like."

"And they put you in prison for that? That's the limit," Scar said.

"They think I work for the Underground, but I honestly don't. They pushed and pushed for information that I didn't have. Apparently, I'm better at convincing my parishioners of the love of God than the Gestapo of my innocence."

"I hope they didn't give you the fingernail treatment," Grizzly said. "Did you hear the screaming that one night in Utrecht? They'd caught a young man ransacking the archives at the City Hall. Later they threw him in the cell I was in, and he showed me where they'd yanked the nails from his fingers. Brutal. But the kid didn't squeal. They didn't get one name out of him, and they tried hard."

The sound of heavy footsteps came from the hallway. The serving hatch opened.

"Pick up your mugs, you lazy bastards," a guard shouted, pointing to the tins they'd been handed when they were locked up. Something looking like soup was poured into them, a mishmash of things boiled in water. Without spoons, they slurped the soup from the sharp edges of the tin. Was this a meal? Even so, they licked their tins to the last drop for the lack of tools to clean them with.

"Like pigs lapping up the slop in their trough," Walter said.

He dreaded the hours before the next meal. Starting a conversation with two men who weren't comfortable sharing either their identies or their life stories would require time. They had no reason to trust him.

"I don't think we'll get overweight in this place," he added, "but our muscles will be as thin as spaghetti when we get out."

"*If* we get out," Grizzly said.

"Of course we will get out," Scar said. "Even if it is only as far as the execution place over there in the dunes." He pointed to the window.

"OK. Ever heard of calisthenics?" Walter asked.

"Something religious?" Scar asked.

"Nothing to do with religion, just with fitness. Since we don't have room for exercises, we can contract our muscles. It doesn't require room or motion, yet you work your muscles."

"Show us," Grizzly said.

Walter took off his shirt and balled his biceps and counted out loud.

"See? It's that simple. You can contract every muscle in your body, and you can increase the time you do it."

Scar and Grizzly looked at each other doubtfully, but they did take off their shirts and flexed their biceps.

"Next we'll be singing hymns," Scar said. "This reminds me of training for boxing. That's how I got my scar."

"You might become more frightening than the guards," Grizzly said.

They did the exercising for a while, then Grizzly noticed Walter glancing at the slop jar.

"Go ahead. You need to take a piss. Think of it as the public urinal downtown. Really not much different."

Walter felt self-conscious. It wasn't as if he'd never used a public place to relieve himself. As a student in Leiden, drinking all that beer, he had known very well what the insides of the city's urinals looked like. But this was different. The thought of spending days, maybe weeks, in this cell without any privacy revolted him.

The minutes turned into hours, and, incredibly, afternoon passed into evening. The monotony was finally broken by noises in the hallway. Moments later, the serving hatch opened again and three slices of bread with a nick of butter were shoved onto the tray. Later the door opened and two straw mattresses were thrown in.

"These are for sleeping, not for sitting on, you understand?" the guard barked. "Tomorrow morning you roll them up and put them against the wall. "

"How thoughtful of him," Grizzly said. "We don't have to share that cot between the three of us! I'll take out three straws and we can draw who gets to sleep on the cot."

Grizzly poked the mattress and he found three straws of different lengths.

"The longest one gets the cot. First you, Scar. Blue next."

Walter got the cot. "We'll take turns," he said. "You're both older."

The cell turned dark after sunset, and they spread the straw mattresses over the floor. There were no blankets. They didn't have pajamas. Nobody had toothpaste or soap.

Walter sank down on the cot. He felt broken. It was the first time since he'd been taken to the police station in Utrecht that he could lie down. A bone-deep weariness set in. He was on the brink of despair, but he kept it at bay by mumbling the Lord's Prayer. *Your will be done on earth as it is in heaven.* How much of his own will would be required to get him out of the fix he was in? *Trust in the Lord,* popped into his mind. Walter thought about the ease with which those words had so often come from his lips. Saying them now was very different from when he consoled people in distress, even dying. In this cell and in this moment, he felt the words deeply in his gut. They issued a challenge. He would be measured by them. That he was sure of. The thought weighed him down.

The straw in their mattresses rustled as Grizzly and Scar tried to get comfortable. Walter wondered what their ages were. With a grizzled beard, you would have to be at least in your forties. Scar looked to be younger than Grizzly. What had they done to deserve to be locked up like this?

Faint light filtered through the high window. Maybe the moon was out. He couldn't remember if it was a half moon or full moon on the evening before the Sunday he was arrested. It seemed ages ago. The only manifestation of Mother Nature he could pick up on was the distant sound of waves rolling onto the wide beach where he used to frolic with his friends.

Throughout the night, doors banged and guards yelled. Among those brutal sounds, Walter heard the cries of children. Oh, dear God, what were children doing in a place like this? If he guessed right that they were Jewish, his own suffering was negligible in comparison. By what law of nature, by what standard of humanity, could Nazis justify their goal of casting out the Jews, especially innocent children? Walter was perplexed. Race-hate crimes were incomprehensible to him. The Jewish persecution had not brushed up to him as closely as hearing those bewildered cries in this dark cell. They broke his heart.

Finally, morning came. Light crept into their cell. Walter guessed it was about six o'clock when the door opened just a crack, and each of them was handed a small bucket of water for washing up.

"It was more fun playing in the sand with a little bucket like this," Grizzly said. "Come to think of it, this cell is about the size of my sandbox of fifty years ago."

"Be careful not to spill a drop," Scar said. "I have a hunch this is all we'll get for the day."

After they'd dunked their hands in the cold water and splashed it over their cheeks, they heard loud yells. "Coffee! Coffee!" The hatch opened, and as they held out their cups, hot coffee poured down. The guard was none too careful. Some poured on the floor, and Scar jumped when a stream flowed onto his hand. An unbuttered slice of bread followed.

Another day with nothing to do. They weren't allowed to sit down. Scar took out a small comb he'd miraculously hidden from the guards. It was made of steel. His girlfriend was a hairdresser, he told them, and they used steel combs instead of the ones made of horn. It had a pointed handle, and he started to scratch on a brick.

"There! This is for the two days in this cell. We might lose count, you know."

Walter and Grizzly looked on in silence. Two days! How many more? But Scar wanted to talk. He switched his tone from the ironic to the factual.

"I'm a bricklayer," he said as his index finger followed the mortar lines between the bricks. "I laid miles of streets on my knees."

Walter and Grizzly listened. They didn't want to ask where those streets were, but Scar told them.

"Remember the strike in Amsterdam last year? We ripped up those bricks we'd laid. And it felt darn good. We were so mad with what these bastards were doing to the Jews, we sabotaged the trams, ripped up the streets. We were really getting somewhere. Enough hands on deck to do the job. People were out of work. Might as well throw bricks if you can't lay them. Better than working for the Germans in their factories making bullets for them."

"It didn't end very well, did it?" Grizzly said quietly.

"True. The Germans sent their Totenkopf infantry in. I tell you, those soldiers with the skull and bones insignia on their caps? No scruples."

"Is that why you're here?" Walter said. "Because you threw bricks?"

"Not directly," Scar said, but he said no more.

The third evening they were there, the door opened and an old man was practically flung into the cell by a guard, the way you throw a dirty towel into a laundry bin. The poor man fell to the floor and stayed there, dazed. Walter helped him up.

"You can take the cot," he said.

"Thank you," the man said. "I am most grateful."

Walter eased him onto the cot. Grizzly and Scar stood back against the wall. They were silently evaluating the newcomer, who would make their crowded quarters even more so. The old man seemed to know what they were thinking.

"I have been treated like a criminal, but all I am is a Jew."

"It doesn't seem to make much difference these days, whether you're of the Jewish or the Aryan race," Grizzly said. "You land in the same cell. By the way, we've given each other nicknames. I go by the name of Grizzly."

"They call me Scar, and the fellow over there we call Blue. How about calling you Abraham?"

The old man nodded, a wan smile on his wrinkled face. He rolled over on his side, pulling his knees up almost to his chin. To see him in that fetal position, Walter felt a deep compassion. He knelt beside him, took the man's two hands, and gently folded them in prayer. The psalms, he thought quickly. That was what Christians and Jews share from the Bible.

"'The Lord is my shepherd; I shall not want. He makes me lie down in green pastures: he leads me beside still waters. He restores my soul.'"

The Jew looked up at him and whispered, "The twenty-third Psalm." He closed his eyes as Walter kept reciting.

"'Even though I walk through the darkest valley, I fear no evil; for you are with me; your rod and staff—they comfort me."

Tears fell off the old man's cheeks. Walter raised himself up to leave the man to his own thoughts. When he turned around, he noticed Scar's and Grizzly's hands folded in prayer. They looked self-conscious, almost apologetic.

"Let's roll out the mattresses," Walter suggested. "We can share."

Incredibly, the minutes ticked away and the days passed until they added up to a whole week. What was the purpose of being here? they wondered. If the enemy wanted to get some useful information out of them, then why didn't they interrogate them? At least it would be a change of scenery. Four men in a cell that, as Grizzly had pointed out, wasn't much bigger than his old sandbox could turn a visit to the Gestapo office into a welcome break from the deadening monotony their lives had turned into. But, of course, they only kidded themselves. The day would come when they would have to face their tormenters. Both Scar and Grizzly were working on inventing an alibi that was as tight as a drum. They allowed glimpses into the reasons they'd been picked up and thrown in jail, and Walter now understood their initial reaction of "What's a minister doing in a prison, for heaven's sake?" Giving a tendentious sermon was a mild offense in their eyes. These men had taken extraordinary risks. Scar said he'd met Resisters in Amsterdam during the strike there. They formed a group with the goal of breaking into city halls. Every citizen—married or single, adult or child—had a card in the archives of the city where they lived. It registered their birth date, address, job, religion, and race, and included information about grandparents. If your grandmother was Jewish, you were considered a Jew. And if you moved, your card went with you. There was no getting away from that card. The Dutch were diligent administrators, almost as thorough as the Germans, who recorded everything to the finest details. Since the German Occupation had taken over all government offices, all they had to do was go through the files at the municipal archives to know who was Jewish.

Scar did not elaborate on what role he'd played in the organization. If he'd been caught red-handed, he might have been shot right there and then. But he must have been close enough to a break-in for the Germans to want to interrogate him.

When they talked about these things, Abraham said vehemently, "Of course, we stated our religion! The Jewish people are proud of their heritage. We never dreamed it would be held against us."

"You thought you lived in a free country. And you did till two years ago," Walter said.

Abraham turned to Scar. "It pains me to think you and people like you have to risk your lives to save ours. It is a noble deed. I thank you."

It took a few more days for Grizzly to come around and give some insight into why he had been picked up. It weighed heavily on him, Walter could tell. For long periods he would lean against the wall and look up at the high window, as if the solution for his dilemma would come at him through the sky.

On the twelfth day of their forced togetherness, Grizzly said out of the blue, "I uncoupled a string of wagons. Freight wagons."

Walter, Scar, and the old man looked up in surprise but didn't ask for more information.

"I work for the Netherlands Railways on night duty. In Utrecht."

"That's a busy junction," Scar said.

"It is."

Through the partially opened windows, they heard seagulls screeching. It must be a windy day, Walter thought. Sounds of seagulls and pounding waves traveled toward them on the wind.

"Eight wagons were filled with brass and copper. *Our* brass and copper. The pots and pans and the candlesticks everyone was ordered to hand in. Those wagons were part of a big transport to Germany. These eight were at the very end. My men and I left them standing on the rails when the train with the rest of the wagons left."

"Was it noticed?" Scar asked.

"It was midnight. The Moffen don't want people to see what they're taking out of our country. But, of course, they were bound to find out. I am probably not the only one in this prison. They couldn't point their finger at just one individual. There were no witnesses. So, they arrested the whole crew on duty that night."

"Were you the foreman?" Scar asked.

Grizzly sighed. "Yes."

It fell silent inside the small cell.

Twelve days earlier, Scar had wanted to make sure they only knew each other by nicknames. Walter hadn't expected them to divulge their secrets. What moved these two men to make these confessions? He couldn't relate to their motives, since he didn't have a deed to hide. Neither Scar nor Grizzly had asked him for strict secrecy. Walter regarded their trust as a gift from God.

"My wife and I," Abraham said, "we were taking a stroll with our dog. When we turned the corner of our street, there was a checkpoint. We had the right identification, but we'd forgotten to wear the yellow star. They shot our dog on the spot. Then they took us over here. Oh, my God, what have we come to?" His voice trembled.

They listened to the crashing waves and the strong wind that turned the crack in the window into a whistle. A haunting sound. Except for the old man, they stood leaning their backs against the brick wall. How appropriate, Walter thought.

The following day, their cell door opened wide and a Gestapo sergeant, accompanied by a prison guard, stood on the threshold. They hadn't seen anybody but each other for almost two weeks. The door had been opened only once to throw in the old man. The sight of the guard with the Gestapo unnerved them.

"Albert Kok," the guard called out, as if they were housed in a large hall.

Grizzly stepped forward and was handcuffed.

"God be with you," Walter said to him.

"And also with you," Grizzly answered.

Then he was led away, leaving Abraham, Scar, and Walter stunned by the rude interruption.

Grizzly didn't return. Not that day and not the next.

CHAPTER NINE

Anna – July 1942

T he locomotive huffed and puffed through the friendly landscape of Noord-Brabant, a southern province Anna had never visited before. It offered a distinct change from the low-sky country up north she was used to. There the wide rivers had created fertile pastures on their banks. As she looked out the train's window, the early-morning sun fell over unpretentious farms—focal points among small fields of strawberries, cabbages, and pole beans. The barnyards looked intimate, and neighbors lived close by.

There was no need to worry about an SS officer stepping into her compartment. Several of the cars that made up the whole train carried signs: *"Nur fur Wehrmacht."* Forbidden for civilians. The cars reserved for the German Army were practically empty, while the rest of the cars were chock-full with civilians. To keep her mind off the close quarters she'd been pressed into, Anna pretended she was entering a foreign country, crossing closed and forbidden borders.

Finally, the train stopped in Breda. Carla stood on the platform. Anna leaped out of the train compartment like a dog let out of the house after a rainy day. Arm in arm, they walked through the blissful shade of a park, Het Valkenberg, part of the castle next to it. Trees that looked hundreds of years old, and probably were, hulked over later park plantings, and although she was only paying peripheral attention, Anna felt herself in the presence of history.

"I have loads of questions," she said to Carla. "First, have you heard anything about Walter?"

Carla answered with a short yes. She didn't elaborate, and Anna's mood sank. The past weeks had been devoid of news about Walter. She'd been following the daily papers to see what was going on outside Arnhem, especially in Den Haag, but the newspapers were in the hands of German editors, and there wasn't much to learn from them beyond Ordnungs and shameless propaganda. On many days, she'd wanted to jump on a train to Den Haag, but knowing that it was not proper to barge in on Dirk unless she was invited, she'd held herself back. Then an urgent telephone call came last night from Carla to please come to Breda right away. She gave no reason for the haste. With Carla's curt reply to her question about Walter, Anna feared the worst.

They walked by the castle. Years earlier it had been turned into the Royal Military Academy, but the Germans had taken it over for their army headquarters. Soldiers and officers darted in and out over the quaint drawbridge. Anna hadn't seen that many military in one place since the start of the war. The elegant castle sat unperturbed in its wide moat, but the "Heil Hitler" shouts between the officers and soldiers coming and going destroyed its beauty.

They turned the corner and stood in full view of a Gothic cathedral. Its elegant spire rose high above the houses and above the staging around its foundation. Carla said the staging had been up for as long as she could remember, and she wondered if she would ever see the day it came off. From the belfry, joyful notes floated downward over the busy market, where farmers sold vegetables and women in native costume shouted praise for their fresh fish. At a flower stand, Anna bought a large bouquet of orange zinnias for the hostess she was soon to meet.

A penetrating antiseptic smell greeted them when Carla opened the door of her parents' home on the Veemarktsstraat. Her father was a dentist, and his practice was on the ground floor. They quickly walked through a hallway and up a staircase, where several doors lined the landing. Carla opened one for her, and Anna let out a cry as she stepped over the threshold. There, on a couch right in front of her, sat Walter Vlaskamp. Dirk, sitting next to him, jumped up to greet her, and in his tight embrace the bouquet of bright zinnias fell on the parquet floor. Walter got up as well. She didn't know how to address him. He couldn't know her. She had just happened to be in the congregation on that infamous Sunday in May.

"Dominee," she began, but he cut her short.

"Anna! I have heard much about you. Please call me Walter."

"This is too funny. We've never been introduced, and yet I worried more about you than I ever worried about anybody."

"It must have helped, because here I am, a free man, thanks to your good friend here."

"Dirk?"

"Yes, Dirk. He pressed the Gestapo hard to let me go."

Anna's eyes widened. Dirk changing the iron will of the Gestapo?

"That's too flattering, Walter," Dirk said quickly.

There was another person in the room. Mrs. Vlaskamp emerged from the shadows, a striking woman with intelligent brown eyes and curly hair cut in a style remarkably different from the fashion of the day, which favored a hair roll. Her short, free-flowing hairdo came across as a statement of prized individuality.

"Please sit down," Mrs. Vlaskamp said warmly. "A cup of coffee?"

The living room was many shades brighter than the one at Anna's home. Tall, wide windows let in a stream of sunrays that bounced off the whitewashed walls and highlighted several eye-catching paintings. They reminded her of French Impressionists.

Maybe they were. She preferred them to the stilted portraits of deceased forebears, whose admonishing looks had followed her around her entire childhood.

"When did you get here, Walter?" she asked.

"Last night, just before curfew. I walked out of Het Oranje Hotel around noon yesterday with nowhere to go. The Gestapo doesn't provide taxi service when they decide you're no longer of use to them."

"What did you do?"

"I remembered Carla had talked about a friend who lived in Den Haag. So, I walked to a café and looked up van Enthoven in the telephone book, praying I had the right one. Thank goodness there aren't too many by that name. Dirk came on his bike ten minutes later."

Walter looked thin and exhausted. Having seen him only once, and then in a wide black robe, she was unable to compare his physique from then to now, but he had no doubt lost many pounds. Bags under his eyes told of sleepless nights.

Mrs. Vlaskamp carried in a tray with cups of steaming coffee. It smelled like the real thing. Right behind her was Carla with a cake in one hand and small plates in the other.

"Mom saved all her sugar coupons for the day you would return, Walter. So, now we can dig into a genuine hazelnut cake!"

Carla cut the cake into equal pieces, except for one slice that was twice as large as the others. Hazelnut cakes must be what mothers think of when their children come home, Anna thought. It was the one thing her mother had in common with Mrs. Vlaskamp.

"Do you mind if I ask Walter to tell once more how he got released, Mrs. Vlaskamp?" she asked.

"Of course not. It's music to my ears."

"Actually, my tale is short," Walter said. "I was finally called to appear before the Gestapo."

Anna had never set foot inside a courtroom. She made some wild guesses, and what she pictured, true or not, was a large room with dark oak paneling and tall windows. Seated at a long table covered with green felt and on a raised platform, the Nazi flag behind their backs, sat five Gestapo officers. Two soldiers stood at attention at either side. That's how she imagined the scene. Walter filled in the proceedings.

"This is how it went," he said. "Name?"

"Walter Vlaskamp."

"Profession?"

"Minister."

"What's your religion?"

"Protestant."

"Which denomination?'

"I am an ordained minister in De Remonstrantse Broederschap, officer."

"Where is your parish?"

"I am waiting to be called to one."

"So, what did you do while you were waiting?"

"I was filling in for ministers in churches around the country who were sick or on vacation, officer."

"You're sure? How much of your time did that take?"

"All of it."

"Are that many ministers sick or on vacation in your denomination that it fully occupied all your time?"

"Yes, officer."

"Do you swear that you were not involved in illegal activities?"

"I swear that I have not engaged in any illegal activity, officer."

"Then there was a break," Walter said. "They whispered to each other in German. They seemed to agree. The interrogating officer turned around and said, 'Then you may go, Mr. Vlaskamp. Sergeant, lead the man away.' And so I was walked out of the room and was set free. I was dumbfounded. I'd answered all of those questions before at the police station in Utrecht. Over and over again."

"Do you have any idea what changed their minds?" Anna asked.

"It's not *what* changed their minds. It was *who* changed their minds. Dirk can tell you better than I can."

"You're overstating my role, Walter," Dirk said, but he went on to explain his part.

When he had returned home for vacation, he'd immediately set out to find a way to get Walter out of prison. He found out that the Catholic priests, who had been arrested in droves after they read the bishops' condemning letter from their pulpits, had been allowed to return to their parishes with few exceptions.

"The Roman Catholic Church has power," Dirk said. "My father reminded me of the political dance Hitler was in with the Vatican."

In 1930, to secure dictatorial powers for himself, Hitler had needed to eliminate the only other political party left besides the Nazi party. The German Center Party, which was predominantly Catholic, vehemently rejected National Socialism. The Reich Concordat, an agreement between Hitler and the pope, was the instrument Hitler devised to reach his goal. The German Center Party was disbanded. Hitler became dictator, and the church was granted help with new schools and other favorable measures. Quid pro quo. It left German Catholics politically leaderless. Millions joined the Nazi Party out of fear. They were practically forced to do so.

"Hitler," Dirk said, "is acutely aware of the many people who are still devoted to the Roman Catholic Church. When my father told me about these political maneuverings, I realized that, unlike the Catholic Church, we had no bargaining chips. To start with, I didn't even know if De Remonstrantse Broederschap had a hierarchy."

Anna forgot about her coffee. She didn't want to miss a word.

"Our denomination has existed for many centuries," Walter said, "but it never succumbed to creating a hierarchy. We're too individualistic."

Dirk smiled. "I noticed."

Lacking a pope or a cardinal to vouch for Walter's innocence, Dirk looked for a member of the church who had a societal role important to the Germans, but who was not a Nazi sympathizer. He brainstormed with the pastor of his church in Den Haag, and they came up with Mr. L., who was the Director General of the Bureau of Food Supply. The distribution of food was important to the Dutch and the Germans alike. Mr. L. held the key. He needed to be sure that enough food remained for the Dutch population, in equal and fair distribution, while the Germans tried to cart off the cream of the crops. His position between the Occupiers and his own people was precarious and often misunderstood. Dirk and his minister went to visit Mr. L. at his home one evening to explain what they were after. Would he be willing to vouch for a young minister of his own denomination, who had preached a daring sermon but was not connected to the Underground?

"What made you so sure Walter wasn't connected to the Underground?" Anna asked.

"I was 99 percent sure," Dirk said. "How I came to that conclusion, I cannot tell you."

It was the first direct hint Dirk had given that he had more than superficial connections to that secret world. Knowing now how Walter had been treated just on the suspicion of having worked in the Underground made her shiver with fear for Dirk.

"Anyway, Mr. L. said he would think about it and let us know. It was hard to ask him to vouch for someone he didn't know and who wasn't important in the great scheme of things, but he was impressed with Walter's courage to give that sermon. It took him a week to line up a plan. He didn't give us details, but you can see the result for yourself."

Anna was in awe. Her intuition had not betrayed her. From the moment she met Dirk, she'd recognized his audacity, his innate sense of justice, his compassion. In the way he'd come toward her on that snowy day when they first met with an outstretched hand, the way he'd calmly looked into her eyes, the ease of his banter with Carla, his preoccupation with the fate of the Jews, all of it had registered with her in a flash.

"What was it like in Het Oranje Hotel, Walter?" Carla asked.

"It's a good place to stay away from." He left it at that.

Mrs. Vlaskamp invited them to the dining room for lunch. She had arranged the zinnias into a spectacular centerpiece, mixing in some silver foliage from her small city garden. Carla's father remarked on what an appropriate choice orange flowers were for the celebration of Walter's return from Het Oranje Hotel. Anna was seated next to him, and over his shoulder, she noticed movement in the street. A policeman shoved a young man through the wide door of a big house across the street. The dentist intercepted her gaze.

"We live across from the police station, Anna," he said. "It keeps us on our toes. We know who the bad actors are in Breda."

"Who knows?" Carla said. "They could be innocent men like Walter."

"You're right. Stealing jewelry is a minor offense these days compared to cutting telephone wires to SS headquarters," Dirk said.

"I used to wonder what went on across the street," Walter said. "Now I know."

It was quiet around the table for a moment. The urge to ask Walter what exactly had happened in Utrecht was palpable, yet the tempting moment went by. It would be selfish curiosity to fish for the details of what must have been a harrowing experience.

"What time does your train leave, Anna?" Dirk asked.

"Four o'clock."

"Mine leaves at four-thirty. I'll see you off."

The bells of the church's carillon were quiet as they walked through the market on their way to the station. Merchants had mostly packed up and left. Men from the city's cleaning crew, wearing high rubber boots, swung their brooms, pushing garbage and horse droppings into piles. From the other end of the market, a big truck approached spraying water over the cobblestones. They glistened in the sun. Market day was over.

Anna realized that Dirk had coaxed her out of the Vlaskamp home with an excuse so he could walk her to the railroad station. They looked for a secluded spot off the main path in Het

Valkenberg. Under the wide canopy of a beech tree, on the quiet side of a pond, an empty bench awaited them. A weathered brick wall, separating the park from the castle, protected them from behind. Dirk pulled Anna down on the wooden seat. She didn't have time to look into his eyes before she felt his lips on hers. Weeks of anxiety and unanswered questions melted away in a passionate kiss. How she had hoped for this moment, for this confirmation of his love. She'd felt so far away, as if their friendship in Utrecht had been nothing more than a fool's dream.

He came up for air and looked into her eyes. "God, I love you!"

He lifted her up and set her on his lap. Two pigeons flew over from the other side of the pond and cooed around their feet, picking at leftover crumbs spilled by a previous visitor.

"I'm sorry you didn't hear from me, Anna, but things were hectic."

"Don't apologize. I understand."

"That's another thing I love about you. You understand and you don't ask any questions. Do you trust me?"

"I do. Completely."

She got up to straighten her cotton summer dress, but Dirk gently pulled her back onto the bench. He had something on his mind, she could tell. His gaze went inward, as it had last winter when he told Carla and her about his Jewish neighbors in Den Haag. She waited.

"The Germans are tightening the noose, Anna. Every week there is another restriction for the Jews. The last one is that Jews cannot have contact with Gentiles and vice versa."

"Daan?" she said.

"Yes. It makes it harder to go and see him. What they're trying to do is create a ghetto in Den Haag, the way they tried to make a ghetto out of the Jordaan in Amsterdam, by forcing all Jews to move into designated areas."

"Do you think they will succeed? It didn't work in Amsterdam."

"Who knows," Dirk said. "My father told me that in German newspapers, there is mention of Jews from all occupied countries being transported to a place in Poland or eastern Germany. There they can live together and only harm themselves, it said. Out of sight. Hitler had personally given the order. That means he wants them quarantined from his exalted Aryan race."

"What a sickening thought. I hope it's rumor. It's got to be! It's too outrageous to be true."

"You have to wonder what their next step will be," Dirk said. He looked at his watch. "Time to go."

She got up and put her hands on his shoulders. "Do what you have to do, Dirk. I won't ask any questions."

He lifted her hands from his shoulders and held onto them as he stood. "Thank you, Anna," he said softly.

Anna returned Dirk's blown kiss from her window seat in the crowded train compartment. The locomotive belched steam, and the shrill whistle of the conductor sounded as the steel monster lurched into motion. Gradually, Dirk turned into a thin stripe on the platform. She waved until he became no more than a speck in the universe.

Her reflection in the window stared at her. Automatically, she brushed a stray strand of her thin, unmanageable hair back from her forehead.

Why me? she wondered. Dirk van Enthoven could get any girl he desired, for he was the kind of man who drew a lingering eye wherever he went. Her mirrored image didn't provide a clue to the mystery of how she could be so lucky. She lacked a peachy complexion, and her nose ended in a bit of a bulb. Her looks couldn't match Carla's, of that she was sure. Carla, with her wavy, thick hair and twinkling brown eyes, with her infectious laughter and vivacity, turned heads. When she first met them, Anna had thought Carla and Dirk were intimate friends. If her assumptions had been correct, then Dirk must have put a quick end to it. But Carla didn't seem to begrudge her their budding love. Maybe things would have gone differently if it hadn't been for the war, which seemed to have swallowed them up.

The train was picking up speed, and the landscape glided by like scenes in a movie without a plot. One moment, she watched a heavy-set woman hang out bed sheets on a line; the next, a boy ran a hoop over a brick road with a stick. Down the same road, a farmer giddy-upped his horse pulling a full wagon with shiny milk cans. Moving images that were not connected; taken together they represented daily life.

Anna's mind drifted off to what a meeting between Dirk and her parents would be like. Dirk's good looks and manners would impress Moeder, but it wouldn't stop her from probing his background, as she'd done with a girl Maarten once brought home. The poor thing hadn't passed Moeder's criteria, and Anna wondered if it had influenced Maarten's decision to seek his fortunes on the island of Java. He'd left shortly after. They still had heard nothing from him since the Japanese had invaded Java.

Before Anna reached Arnhem, she'd made up her mind to leave the war out of the introduction, if and when it came to pass. She would present Dirk as just a fellow medical student.

CHAPTER TEN

Anna – August 1942

It was hard to tell who was more shocked—the German Army or the Dutch population—after a daring bomb attack in the center of Rotterdam blew up a train carrying German soldiers on furlough to their Heimat. Everyone understood the Underground had planned it. Actually, it was only partially successful. An innocent rail inspector on a bicycle had unwittingly touched a wire, so not all of the explosives had gone off, but enough of them to incense the Germans. When they failed to find the perpetrators, they took five hostages and promised to execute them if no one stepped forward within a week. The country held its collective breath. The list of hostages was eye-popping: Willem Ruys, internationally known president of the Rotterdam Lloyd Steamship Company; Count E. O. G. van Limburg Stirum and Baron Alexander Schimmelpenninck van der Oye, both highly regarded members of Dutch nobility; Robert Baelde, attorney in Rotterdam; and Christoffel Bennekers, past police chief of Rotterdam.

This news fell into the Smits household like a bombshell. One of the hostages, Baron van der Oye, was Moeder's cousin. Anna had met him only once, at her grandfather's funeral, and she could hardly remember him. Moeder was indignant at the thought that people of their standing could be put to death without due process and, what's more, without being guilty. She refused to believe the Germans would go to this extreme. Vader said the Germans would think twice before making good on their threat.

Amid this gloom and anxiety, Dirk wrote that he would like to get away from the city and take a bike ride to Arnhem. Would he be welcome? "Of course," she wrote back, and set out to sell the idea to her parents. It would be a surprise to them. Dirk's existence was her well-kept secret. Not for any particular reason. It was just that she had learned to let Maarten do the rocking of the family boat, while she kept things to herself. She didn't lie. She kept secrets. After observing the give and take in the Vlaskamp family, she realized her relations with her parents could be described as distant. Good manners were ingrained and practiced. A life lived on solid Christian values—mixed with an emphasis on noblesse oblige —was expected as a matter of course, not in need of debate. At Dirk's house, he'd told Anna, sparks would fly around their dining room table. His family debated the daily news, history of the far past and the recent past, any subject worth having an opinion about.

"Moeder," Anna said two days before Dirk was due to arrive, "a third-year medical student I got to know in Utrecht is making a bike trip and asks if he could stop by. He's starting from Den Haag."

"Would you like him to? What's his name?"

Anna had anticipated the question. His name would be a way to place Dirk on the social ladder. Anna swore her mother could spot a baron a mile away.

"Dirk van Enthoven."

Moeder repeated the name. "There is a professor by that last name. Could that be his father?"

"I have no idea. I never asked."

Moeder found this implausible, but it was true. She had no idea what Dirk's father did for a living, and neither did she care.

"Well," Moeder said, "if you like him, then ask him to stop by. Quite an honor to have caught the attention of a third-year student. Invite him for lunch."

Anna was uncharacteristically nervous anticipating Dirk's visit. She worked off energy by rearranging her room. Sarah kept it spotless, but it begged to be more than dusted. Really, her room was just a tired holdover from childhood. It didn't look like the room of a serious medical student, with teddy bears and other sentimental reminders of childhood. Those old standbys got stuffed into a closet.

Of course, Dirk might not get to see her room at all. She'd never been alone in a room, especially her own room, with a boy. Classmates had occasionally come over, both boys and girls, always in small groups. Moeder was of the chaperone era. Contact with boys was restricted to dancing lessons and formal balls. Meetings between the sexes were supervised, organized, and conspicuously surrounded.

Anna set out to cut the healthiest and prettiest flowers she could find in the August garden below—shasta daisies, blue lavender, and tall ruby-red phlox. She made a mess wielding the gardener's scissors, letting cut stems drop to the kitchen floor. She was aware of the exchange of glances between Moeder and Sarah as she carefully carried the bouquet upstairs.

Dirk met the Smits family on August 15, 1942, a day of infamy. At dawn, the five hostages were executed. Vader had come home early from the bank with a special edition of the local newspaper and had just read the shocking news to his wife and daughter. Shortly after, Dirk was ushered into the living room by Sarah, who'd been the only one to hear the doorbell ring. Although Anna stood with her back to him, she sensed his presence and turned around. She wanted to rush over to him, but he put his finger to his lips as he took in the scene before him. Anna's father stood with his arms wrapped around his wife's shoulders, trying to console her, and Anna understood Dirk didn't want to intrude. Neither did she want him to go away. It was an awkward moment. Did Dirk know what her mother's tears might be about? She picked up the newspaper from the coffee table and wordlessly handed him the first page. As he looked at the bold headline, a dark shadow fell over his face. "Oh, God, no!" he whispered.

Vader reached into his pocket, handed his wife a handkerchief to wipe her tears, and walked over to Dirk, who still stood on the threshold, ready to turn around and leave.

"Welcome, Dirk. I'm sorry our meeting has to coincide with tragic news."

"I apologize for bursting in," Dirk said. "I didn't know the execution had gone through. I was on my bike since early this morning."

"You don't have to apologize, young man. One of the hostages was my wife's cousin, so it hit hard in our home."

Moeder wiped her tears and turned around to face Dirk. With inbred grace and the self-discipline that had been drummed into her by a strict governess, she gathered herself and took on the role of hostess.

"How do you do, Dirk? So nice to have a chance to meet you," she said, and offered her hand.

"I didn't pick the best moment, I'm afraid," he said. "I offer you my condolences, Mevrouw Smits."

Moeder abruptly switched the subject. "How long did it take you to bike over from Den Haag?"

"Actually, I did it in two parts. I spent the night with a friend halfway. So, it was only a three-hour ride this morning."

"Let's have Sarah bring in some coffee. I think we all could stand some caffeine. Tell her to brew real coffee, Anna."

The late-morning ritual of Moeder seated in a fauteuil behind a low table pouring coffee from a silver pot was a familiar sight, but there was one difference. Her hand was shaking. Dirk got up to take his cup. His tall body bent at the waist, he hovered over her mother, and she looked up at his open, confident smile. Her gaze lingered there for a moment with a hint of approval. Anna saw it all.

Sarah had set the table for lunch and, at a signal from her mistress, brought in a dish of fried calf's brains in a caper sauce over a bed of cooked rice. Moeder was testing Dirk, Anna thought. She wanted to see how he handled something that wasn't everyday fare.

"I read about the Atlantic Defense Wall," Vader threw out as an opening to conversation. "Since you live in Den Haag, Dirk, have you seen it? What does it look like?"

"Not pretty," Dirk said. "Nobody is allowed into Scheveningen without a pass. The hotels have been taken over by workers from Germany. They build bunkers in the dunes. The beaches are full of barbed wire that you can see and land mines you can't see."

"I wonder who pays the bills," Moeder said.

"They take the money from our National Bank and call it the cost of occupation," Dirk said.

"Thank God our queen took the country's gold reserves with her to England," Vader said. "At the time people were indignant, but as a banker, I think it was a wise decision. Not that it makes things easier for us right now. "

"What gives Hitler the right to turn our beautiful beaches into a fortress? It makes me so angry," Moeder said.

"Hitler takes the law into his own hands, Mevrouw Smits. He has a proven record."

"The law certainly wasn't applied this morning when they executed my cousin." There was indignation and anger in her voice. "Of course," she added, "the perpetrators could have stepped forward. *They* were the guilty ones. How could they let five important men die? I think of them as cowards."

"Moeder, how can you call them cowards?" Anna said. "They are patriots! Just as much as the hostages were."

She had challenged her mother only once in her life, and that was when she wanted to go to medical school. Maybe it was time to stake out positions. She was tired of the icy silence around real issues.

"Patriots? Are people who blow up factories and trains patriots? We used to call them criminals!" Moeder straightened her spine against the back of the formal dining chair.

"They are patriots because they stand up for our freedom," Anna said. "They risk their lives to prevent the Nazis from winning the war. Anything we can do to slow the plundering gets us closer to an end to the war."

"If you take action, you have to bear the consequences," Moeder said. "These men you call patriots, Anna, didn't. They let others die instead."

Anna sat at the edge of her chair, ready to retort, but Dirk got ahead of her. "It must have been an agonizing decision for the Underground to make. It takes my breath away. I realize how bitter this is for you personally, Mevrouw Smits, but I'm afraid they really had no choice."

Moeder looked surprised by his piping in, but she took a friendlier tone when she asked, "How so, Dirk?"

"The Gestapo would have tortured the perpetrators until they had beaten every name of connected resisters out of them. If the Underground had given in to this kind of blackmail, then that would be the end of the resistance. And, of course, that's exactly what the Nazis are after."

"If we don't resist, this war will drag on," Vader said. "Dirk is right. The sacrifices are sad and horrible, but no war was ever won without sacrifice."

Sarah appeared in the kitchen doorway, as if she sensed it was time for a distraction. She busied herself by taking the dishes away. Anna noticed Dirk's plate had no leftovers.

"What's your next stop, Dirk?" Moeder asked.

"I have a friend in Lunteren."

"That's not far from where I grew up."

Anna brightened. "I'll go with you as far as Ede, Dirk. My grandmother will need some cheering up, I think, after what happened this morning."

An hour later, with her parents looking on, Dirk helped Anna fasten an overnight bag to the baggage carrier of her bike.

"Thank you for lunch, Mevrouw Smits. It was delicious. May I ask what I was eating?"

"Calf brains in caper sauce. I am glad you liked it."

"Ah, brains. Good idea. We'll need them to get through this war."

They waved and took off. It was a nice day. The bright sun lifted some of the hovering gloom that had dominated Dirk's visit. As soon as they got out of sight, Dirk put his arm around Anna's shoulders and kept it there as they biked along paths that took them past farms and fields, over cobblestone roads and — the closer they got to Ede — along narrow dirt roads. At a small café with a terrace, they stopped to have a soda. Dirk spread out a map of the area.

"What street does your grandmother live on in Ede?"

"Actually, she doesn't live in Ede. Her place is outside of it."

"Can you find it on this map? It's a very detailed one."

"I'm not very good at reading maps, but I will get you there. It's only a ten-minute bike ride from here."

They skirted the small city of Ede and biked in a westerly direction alongside wheat fields, where blue cornflowers poked out their heads at the edges. No grain had been imported since the war started. Bread was rationed, and the farmers were ordered to plant their fields with wheat. Now, in the month of August, the farmers took advantage of the sunny weather to harvest their crops.

Anna knew she was close to her grandmother's place. She stopped and got off her bike, dropping it to the ground on a harvested field where cut wheat stalks had been bundled. Three sheafs leaned into each other, tied together at the top. The result looked like a tent, and the whole field was dotted with these golden tent-like contraptions. The stalks were drying, ready to give up their precious seeds.

"Let's take a break before we have to be polite and conversant," she said. She smiled as she walked to the middle of the field and nestled herself into a three-sheaf tent. Dirk looked down at her.

"Do you want me to sit down on those prickly stubbles?"

"Yes. I know you're really too tall for this tent. But this is a test."

"A test of what?"

"A test of love."

"Do I have a choice?"

"Not if you love me."

She'd never been so bold in her life, but she suddenly felt the urgency of time. Not many hours were left in this day. More than that, an ominous threat hung in the air that gripped her heart. Where was this war taking them? What could happen to Dirk?

He backed himself into nature's little tent. His long legs had to remain outside and, sitting up, his head touched the straw top.

"Now that you lured me into your trap, young lady, what exactly do you want of me?"

"To get out of this uncomfortable position, you have to give me a kiss. That's the price I demand."

He laughed and gave her a peck on her cheek.

"You're a tease, Dirk."

"And you?"

He took her in his arms, and they stayed in the tent for a long while.

With bits of straw clinging to their clothes, they got back on their bikes. Passing by several farms, Anna waved at the folks working in their yards.

"Do you know these people?" Dirk asked.

"Yes. I spent many summers at Oma's place."

"We must be close then."

They followed a bend in the road, and there in front of them stood a castle. A coat of arms and the name *Kasteel Koppelburg* appeared on the wrought-iron gate.

"OK. You're in a funny mood today, Anna. Don't tell me this is where your Oma lives."

"I couldn't be more serious."

Dirk stared at the wide three-story building. The massive front was divided into three sections. The red brick middle section was taller than the white-painted wings. Four graceful pillars sustained an elaborate balcony over the entrance, and a gravel driveway circled around the clipped front lawn, accentuated by graceful lanterns at regular intervals.

"You have told me precious little about your background, Anna."

"Yes, I know. Come, let's go in and say hello to Oma. She's a neat lady. You'll like her."

"What's her name?"

"Baroness van Haersolte."

It was quiet between them for a moment. The look on Dirk's face turned inward as he adjusted to the blinding light Anna had thrown into a corner of her life.

"Well," he said, "let's see if she will accept the company of two bikers with straw sticking out all over."

"Oh, she will. If it makes you feel better, I'll clean you up."

As she pulled bits and pieces off his slacks and shirt, Dirk asked if she'd ever plucked a chicken. "Yes," she said, "but that was easier. The chicken lay still."

"Don't monkeys clean each other up?" he said, laughing as he picked some stubborn straw from her dress.

They leaned their bicycles against the carefully pruned branches of a miniature apple tree that was tied onto the castle's wall with a wooden frame. A side door led straight into the kitchen, and that was how Anna entered the castle.

"Miss Anna! What a surprise," the cook said. She wiped her wet hands on her large apron and came over to hug Anna.

"Hello, Mien, how are you? What are you cooking? We may be staying for supper, you know."

"Oh, not the kind of things I used to make, Miss Anna, when we had plenty of meat," Mien said. She threw a curious glance at Dirk.

"As long as it isn't calf's brains, Mien. We had enough of those today. By the way, this is my friend Dirk van Enthoven."

"Glad to know you, I'm sure, Mr. Enthoven," Mien said.

"How is Oma, Mien?"

"Holding up well after that bad news about her nephew. You know how she is."

"You think it's too much of a surprise if we just go upstairs, or should we have Janus announce us?"

"She'll be glad to see you, Miss Anna. Just what she needs."

They climbed the few steps leading to a large hall where paintings of Anna's forebears decorated the walls. It was dark in spite of the white marble floor. Anna walked over to a tall mahogany door and turned the brass handle. Inside the salon, by the window, sat her grandmother. A book lay in her lap, unopened.

"Oma!" Anna called out.

The baroness stirred, seemingly waking from deep thought, but her eyes immediately focused on her granddaughter.

"Anna, my dear! How lovely to see you," the baroness said.

Anna embraced her grandmother. Rays of the late afternoon sun highlighted her silvery gray hair and were reflected in the diamond ring on her left hand. In the large room, filled with precious furniture and Oriental rugs, her grandmother was its luminous center, its focal point.

Anna kneeled at her feet and took her hands into her own.

"We bicycled from Arnhem to come and see you, Oma. The news this morning was so awful. Moeder was quite distraught. I'm sure it is hard on you also."

"Indeed it is, my dear. Poor Alexander. He was such a good man. He will be missed by his dear wife and three children. I can't begin to imagine what this day is like for them."

Anna hadn't thought of the execution in terms of personal loss. She'd felt anger first and foremost. It was different for Oma and Moeder.

"Oma, I brought a friend. He came to see me in Arnhem, and since he is on a bicycle tour and his next stop is Lunteren, I thought

I would join him for part of the way."

"Lovely. Introduce him to me," the baroness said, and got up from her chair. She was quite tall, or maybe her ankle-length black silk dress made it seem so. Her hair was done up in a bun, fastened in the back with a comb carved from horn and shaped like a quarter moon. A velvet ribbon lightly bound loose skin folds in her regal neck.

Anna watched Dirk cross the room with his inimitable confident stride. These two people, about to shake hands, were her two most favorite souls in the whole world.

"This is Dirk van Enthoven, Oma."

The baronness evaluated Dirk with a practiced eye, and then invited them to sit with her near the window. She pressed a button and Janus, the butler, appeared. She asked him to bring tea and something to go with it.

"I assume you are also a student in Utrecht, Dirk?"

"Yes, I am. I am a third-year medical student, madam."

"Did you bicycle from Utrecht to Arnhem and then to here?"

"I started out from Den Haag, where I live, but I stayed overnight with a friend halfway. I don't have a set route."

"Ah, the freedom of youth. No demanding itineraries. Enjoy it while you can. Your chosen profession will give you plenty of restrictions."

Janus reappeared, pushing a cart with teacups, cookies, and a pot of tea under an embroidered cozy. The baroness took command of it.

"Oma, where did Alexander Schimmelpenninck live? I know very little about him."

"He lived in the same city as you do. I'm surprised you haven't met his family. He was a judge there. If Hitler thought he was creating a love affair with the Dutch population, then he ruined his chances for reciprocation this morning."

"The number of citizens in love with the Nazis is dwindling fast," Dirk said. "There will be a reaction to this brutal act."

"Moeder was angry that the Underground didn't come forward

with the perpetrators. That would have saved Alexander's life. What do you think, Oma?"

She didn't answer right away. Instead, she took the teapot out from under the cozy and poured the tea. Her movements were deliberate and thoughtful.

"I think," she said finally, "the Underground had no choice. Regardless of Alex being my relative, it is the principle that counts. We cannot give in to a regime we fundamentally disagree with. If we want to shake off the yoke of oppression, then we'd better stand our ground."

"How will this war end? How long can it last?" Anna didn't direct her question to anyone in particular.

"It won't last forever," the baroness said with authority, "because Hitler is greedy, and greed is seldom rewarded in the long run. Think of Napoleon. Hitler is a terrible leader. It is all about himself. Quite different from our queen, who was born to the task of ruling."

"I agree that Queen Wilhelmina is a far better example of a ruler than Adolf Hitler," Dirk said, "but history is filled with rulers born to the task who left less than an impeccable record."

The baroness looked up in surprise. Anna could tell her grandmother appreciated Dirk's audacity. She had always admired a mind capable of astute observations, and Dirk hid his gift under a relaxed demeanor. The way this visit was developing boded well for the remainder of the evening.

"Well, it seems we have a lot to talk about," the baroness said. "Surely you don't want to bike to Lunteren on an empty stomach."

Without waiting for comment, she again pressed the button next to her chair. When Janus reappeared, he was ordered to set the table for three. Anna winked at Dirk. There could be no better illustration of what kind of a woman her grandmother was.

While waiting for Janus to announce that dinner was ready to be served, she complimented Oma on the flower arrangement on the coffee table, knowing that the baroness had done it herself. The tall blue delphiniums, surrounded by white phlox, brightened the otherwise dark room with its heavy velvet curtains.

Dirk offered his arm to the baroness and led her into the dining room. As she seated herself, he stood gallantly behind her chair. It amused Anna to watch Dirk perform these acts of chivalry. He seemed quite at home with them.

Over cold vichyssoise soup, sprinkled with freshly cut chives, they continued their conversation. Oma wanted to know what was going on in Den Haag. Dirk told her the face of Scheveningen and Den Haag were drastically changing. The Atlantic Wall meant the Germans had taken a wrecking ball to a part of the city to build a fifteen-meter wide antitank moat. Beautiful homes and offices, even a hospital, had been sacrificed to make room for an enormous trench with barbed wire barricades on either side. Their beautiful city had been turned into a future battleground, Dirk said. The baroness sighed. She was born there, she told them.

"It's ugly, but what goes on under the surface is even uglier," Dirk said.

"Explain," the baroness commanded.

He told her the Nazis were persecuting the Jews mercilessly, coming up with rules that made their lives miserable.

"In these parts, you may not notice so much of what is going on," he said, "but in the city, it's become a suffocating atmosphere. It is worrisome. Without help, they can't survive."

"What kind of help?" the baroness asked.

"The Nazis have already started to deport some of them to concentration camps. It is rumored they are sent to eastern Germany and Poland."

"For what purpose?"

"Nobody really knows. My assumption is labor camps, but nobody has come back from there to tell us what exactly is going on."

"They have no use for them," the baroness said. "Hitler has made that abundantly clear. To think this is going on in our country! For centuries, we have sheltered minorities, religious or otherwise. Not everyone is fond of Jews, I know, but that's beside the point. We are freedom-loving people. The very birth of our country had to do with self-determination and liberty. This is unacceptable!"

"I agree, Oma. But what can we do?" Anna said. "The Germans are good at doling out punishment. Last year, when workers in Amsterdam stood up for the Jews and went on strike, they brought in their Totenkopf Brigade and randomly killed people. They were ruthless."

Anna looked around to see if Janus had left the room. She was relieved to see he had disappeared with the empty soup plates. It suddenly struck her that they'd better be careful. It wouldn't be the first time a servant turned out to be a Nazi sympathizer. God forbid! Oma was used to speaking her mind. Maybe she should warn her grandmother to be careful.

The dining room door opened, and the main meal was brought in. Each of them was served a filet of sweet water fish, surrounded by mashed potatoes and caramelized carrots. After Janus left the room, Oma picked up the thread of conversation.

"Anna, my dear, don't let the Nazis intimidate you to the point of resignation. Alexander died this morning because he had no choice. Yet his death stands as a symbol of our country's refusal to put up with a doctrine that violates our own principles. I think it will gradually become clear in what ways we can strike back. We have to examine our conscience, and then take the risks we're best equipped for."

Anna was dumbfounded. "Oma, are you suggesting we join the Underground?"

The baroness put down her knife and fork and wiped her mouth with her linen napkin. She didn't answer Anna's question right away. Her eyes, as light blue as her daughter's and granddaughter's, focused on some spot on the ceiling while she formulated her thoughts.

"Decisions like that are not made by impulse, Anna. Sound decisions you can live with the rest of your life require a history of work you do beforehand."

"How do you mean that?"

"Examine your soul, your conscience, your mind, and when the opportunity offers itself, you will know what to do."

Anna looked at Dirk. He was leaning forward, his body taut with attention, taking in every word.

"God bless you for those words," he said.

The baroness smiled at him. "Would you like to stay overnight, so Anna can show you around tomorrow? It's getting too dark to bike over to Lunteren. Even here in the country, we have to mind the curfew."

"Thank you. I would love to take you up on that," Dirk said.

The next morning, they followed Baroness van Haersolte's suggestion to explore the castle's neighborhood. Anna knew every farmer's family for miles around. Wherever they stopped, they were made to sit down in the parlor for a cup of coffee and a piece of homemade cake. While Dirk was observed with shy curiosity, the farmers swapped stories with Anna about her days of picking strawberries and helping to put up the hay. They remembered her climbing to the top of cherry trees. She meant more to these hardworking people than just being the landowner's granddaughter. She was "our Miss Anna."

They pedaled along rutted sandy roads between fields of wheat still standing and wheat already cut. In a shaded bare spot under a large beech tree, they leaned their bikes against its wide trunk and lay down in the soft grass. Rustling sounds of a bird flying to and fro between the branches quieted their minds.

They just lay there, holding hands. Far in the distance, they heard the clippity-clop of horses' hooves and the crunching of wagon wheels over a gravel road. Nature exuded peace. Amidst this God-given beauty, how could men come up with such evil and deadly schemes? Anna thought. The question was hardly a new one. Every generation since man came into being had wrestled with its own brutality. And now, it was their generation's turn. Without Dirk, she probably would not have fully understood the awful things happening around her. Without him, she might have concentrated solely on her own goal in life and kept the war at arm's length.

He turned on his side and tickled her nose with a grass blade. "You look so serious, Miss Anna. What are you brooding about?"

"That's true. I am brooding ... about what Oma said last night."

"And what's that?"

"She seemed to say I should articulate my stand in this war."

"Yes, I remember."

"It's one thing to lament what the Nazis are doing, quite another to know how to counter them." She turned her face toward Dirk and looked into his eyes. He pulled her close and held her. Their embrace contained none of the frolicking of the day before. Something vital had crept into their friendship. They both felt it.

"Your grandmother is remarkable, Anna. I've never met anyone quite like her. Meeting your parents and your grandmother adds a new dimension to the girl I met this winter."

"You'll have to take me to *your* oma some day. Does she exist?"

He laughed. "Yes, but she doesn't live in a castle."

"Please, Dirk, don't be too impressed with the castle part. As castles go, hers is not even that big."

"All right, let's talk about Oma's message then." He rolled onto his stomach, leaning on his elbows. "What irks you most about the German Occupation? What wrenches your gut?"

She stared into the large leaves of the beech tree. Together, they wove an airy blanket with patterns of light spots and smooth branches. Another two months, and they would turn to bronze.

"I despise the Nazis and their beliefs," she said.

"That's a broad statement. What gets your goat? What are you ready to defend if you had to?"

"It all comes down to freedom, I suppose. If I knew how, that's what I would defend. They are anti-individualists. Their worst crime is taking away the right to self-determination."

"Are you ready to protect that right? How important is that to you?"

"Very."

"Your oma wanted you to discover how committed you are to your own principles. To know what's on top of your list. Once you figure that out, you will know what to do."

Anna was going to speak, but Dirk reached over and kissed her on her mouth, effectively silencing her. She reveled at the way he transmitted his courage and his passion. "Don't do anything foolish, Miss Anna. I know you have a bold streak. Promise. You are too precious to me."

CHAPTER ELEVEN

Walter – Late August 1942

Walter Vlaskamp sat behind his desk. His study looked exactly as he had pictured it in prison. The azalea was bathing in sunlight on the windowsill. Smoke curled up from his pipe. A cup of coffee stood close to his right hand. Nothing had changed from the image he'd tortured himself with after he'd discovered words from the Bible etched into the brick wall of his cell in Scheveningen. Life offered different realities. Had God spoken louder in the cell than in his study? What did God expect from him? While he believed in free will, he also felt a message was hidden in the events of the past month, and it annoyed him not to be able to pinpoint it.

It seemed like all he'd done in the two weeks since he'd been released was sleep and eat. His mother had lavished her food stamps on him, and he'd regained the ten pounds he'd lost to the abominable prison diet. But he'd been anxious to get back to his apartment in Leiden. The Germans knew everything about him now. He was no longer anonymous. They knew where he lived, that he was a Protestant minister, that his parents lived in Breda — across from the police station, of all places — and he was sure they were keeping an eye on him. Best to go back to daily life and prove he was only a substitute minister. But first, some minister in the land had to go on vacation or become ill. He was anxiously awaiting a call.

A letter from his sister lay open on his inkpad, urging him to come to a vacation cottage in Loosdrecht and meet her student friends. She called them the Group of Eight. They'd heard him preach that infamous Sunday. The shock of seeing him taken away had glued them together, Carla had told him.

Walter leaned back and relit his pipe. He'd found a tin of before-the-war tobacco in his old room at his parents' home. The pleasant, aromatic smoke rose to the ceiling, and his eyes followed its path, but his mind was elsewhere. It circled back to that moment, a few weeks ago, when Anna Smits had walked into his parents' living room. The way Dirk had jumped off the couch to embrace her, forgetting they were in front of strangers, was enough proof that those two were in love. Though it had given him vicarious enjoyment, a feeling of envy and regret lingered. It was hard to ignore the aroused feelings. If only he could have left them behind in Breda.

His best friend there was Peter Turnhout. In their early teen years, they'd paddled their canoes over canals and rivers, and adventured throughout the ancient city. His true love was Peter's sister, who was a few years older than Carla. The four of them—Peter, Bertha, Carla, and himself—had been steady companions in those carefree prewar days, when life was plentiful and comprehensible. They'd been like lambs darting around spring pastures, unaware of boundaries. Bertha blossomed into a beautiful woman, her deep-set eyes as blue as a cornflower, her straw-blond hair reaching to her shoulders, her movements fluid and graceful. As they both matured into young adulthood, they fell in love, pure and simple. Walter found he shared many interests with Bertha. But one aspect of life they did not share was that Bertha's parents were devout Catholics, while Walter's family belonged to a small

Remonstrant congregation. As kids, they'd given this difference short shrift. Sharing the same ideals was more important. Their pure interpretation of Jesus's command "love your neighbor as yourself" was the basis for their desire to be of service to others.

Walter tapped his burned-out pipe on a ceramic ashtray and fished in his vest pocket for his silver scraper. The mindless exercise of scraping the bowl relieved the tension his memories had built up. He'd hardly seen Bertha during the years he studied in Leiden. Parents on both sides hadn't encouraged contact, but his friendship with Peter stayed. While he recuperated from his prison experience, Peter and Bertha had come to visit. The dormant flame of love had flared up. Bertha told him of her work as a nurse at a hospital in Utrecht. She was as beautiful as he'd remembered her, with the added glow of a soul who gives to others with a full heart.

Walter sighed and filled his pipe again. Bertha would make the perfect preacher's wife, but unless the Catholic Church was stood on its head, there was no way a wedding could ever come to pass. And for him to convert to Catholicism was equally unthinkable. He'd been very aware of this as they shared the cake she'd brought and carried on a conversation over a cup of tea. He'd tried to avoid her eyes. Life would be more bearable if he didn't know if she still harbored the love they'd once shared.

Walter reached for the phone and dialed his parents' home number. Carla answered.

"Are you coming to Loosdrecht?" she asked. "My friends are dying to meet you."

It had always been hard to refuse Carla. Her cheerful voice tingled in his ear.

"Tell me where to go and I will be there," he said.

"Bring your bathing suit and leave your clerical collar at home."

Loosdrecht was more or less in the middle of the country. Its sprawling lake was its attraction. He got instructions on how to get to a cottage that belonged to one of her friends' parents. By coincidence, he received a request in the next day's mail to substitute for a minister in Ede. Walter decided he could do both in one trip, and do it on his bicycle. He rolled up his black robe so it would fit in a canvas bag he could strap onto his bike. He chuckled as he placed his bathing suit next to it. Off he went. Thank God he'd done calisthenic exercises with Scar and Grizzly. Without them, his muscles might be screaming. Peddling alongside ripe pastures spotted with Friesian cows, he prayed for his cellmates, even as he feared all three might have been executed or taken to concentration camps. He would probably never find out.

Those bitter thoughts faded the minute he knocked on the door of a cottage at the edge of the lake. Topped by a thatched roof, it looked as inviting as a teapot under a cozy. Cheerful voices and sounds of splashing water rose from the other side of the house, so he walked to the back. As he watched his sister jump off a sailboat, the stuffiness of his study, the oppressive confinement of the prison cell, the consuming agony of a lost love, all of these burdens fell away. He surveyed the sunlit lake in front of him, and his ears filled with the carefree reveling of young voices. For just a precious instant, there was no war, no hate, no death.

Carla's head emerged from the water. "You made it!" she cried out.

Three young men and two young women turned around. They tied the sailboat to the dock and walked over the gangway to meet him. Carla, dripping wet, threw her arms around him. People he'd never met before gave him something of a hero's welcome. They introduced themselves as Otto, Herman, Piet, and Emmy. Anna he'd already met.

"I thought this was the Group of Eight, but I see only see six. Where is Dirk?"

"He's on his way," Anna said.

Herman, who was the host in his parents' absence, arranged chairs on the deck and offered cool drinks and cookies. The day was still young.

"Did you get stopped anywhere?" Anna asked. She fidgeted

with a buckle on the shoulder strap of her bathing suit, less self-assured than when he'd met her in Breda.

"No, luckily not. I've had my fill of men in uniform asking me questions."

"We worried a lot about you," Emmy said.

"Dominee Vlaskamp, did you ever find out why they held you so long?" Otto asked.

"Please call me Walter. No, not really. Maybe they were just too busy gathering facts on me. They were convinced I worked for the Underground, but they couldn't produce proof. The Gestapo may seem like a lawless bunch, but at least they still work with evidence."

He could tell they wanted to hear what it had been like in Het Oranje Hotel, yet didn't dare ask the question. Neither did he want to play the role of hero. Throughout, he'd never once felt like a hero.

"Carla may have told you we heard you preach on the day you were arrested," Emmy said. "I was impressed with your sermon. If you had to do it over again, knowing what you know now, would you give the same sermon?"

"Yes, I would."

A cheerful whistle flew over the house, and everybody looked up. Anna ran around the house to the street and let out a holler. Moments later, Dirk appeared, followed by a young man with tousled blond hair and an engaging smile.

"Daan!" everyone shouted.

Carla filled Walter in. He might not look like one, she said, but Daan was a Jew because his mother was one. He lived in Den Haag. Dirk must have a special purpose, Walter thought, to risk bringing Daan on such a long bike ride. The threat of being stopped was not imaginary. People got stopped for the most unpredictable reasons. Sometimes it was the bikes the Germans were after. In that case, one had to walk the rest of the way. But always, identification papers were required. Walter found it hard to believe Dirk and Daan had risked so much for a party on the lake. Did these happy people realize the danger they were in? Being in one another's company potentially compromised them all. Jews and Gentiles were not to gather together.

Carla brought out a large platter with sandwiches. The noon sun stood directly overhead, ready to burn Walter's skin to a crisp. The group was luxuriously tanned after weeks of summer vacation, except for Daan and Walter, who'd spent more time indoors than out.

The platter with sandwiches was soon empty, and everyone was spread out over the deck, stretched out on lounge chairs or balanced on the railings. When Dirk raised his voice, it had immediate impact. Everyone fell silent. When he was sure he'd caught everyone's attention, he continued in a hushed voice.

"I probably don't have to remind you all of our promise to never pass on the confidential information Daan gave us." He stopped for a moment and looked around. "I don't know how up-to-date you are on Hitler's plans for Jews," he went on, lowering his voice even more. "Living in Den Haag, you can't escape being informed, but this is Hitler's latest plan—force all Jewish citizens from their homes and put them on a train to Germany or Poland."

In the distance, they heard the faint splashing of oars hitting the water. Any other day, the sound would have been a gift, a sign of summer, of relaxation and peace, but on this day and in this moment, the air was still and filled with tension, the way it turns heavy when a thunderstorm is brewing.

The reason people didn't realize what was happening, Dirk told them, was because the Germans made it happen in the dark of night, after curfew. "Daan is in acute danger."

Every face turned to Daan.

"It's true," he said. "My mother, my younger brother, and I received a notice that we have to present ourselves at a nearby school in four days. We're told we can bring only one suitcase, small enough to carry."

"That's insane!" Emmy shouted. "I can't believe this!"

"Shhh. I know how you feel, Emmy," Dirk said. "But you'd better believe the unbelievable, because it's going to happen all around you, whether you see it with your own eyes or not."

The comfortable lounge chairs were vacated. The Group of Eight huddled around the low coffee table.

"There are tens of thousands of Jews living in Holland alone," Piet said. "There must be millions more spread out over Europe. What's Hitler's plan? You'd think he'd have his hands full fighting on a whole continent. Doesn't he have enough to do? This is crazy!"

Daan's expression turned somber and pained. "The Nazis think they're doing everyone a favor by driving us all to one place."

"*Ewige Jude*. Oh my God, it's too terrible for words," Anna said under her breath, and Walter recalled the old man who'd been thrown into his cell. There had been no mercy in the way the guards had treated him. The indoctrination by Hitler's propaganda apparatus had been successful. Guards bought into the idea that Jews were not human and could be treated like the lowest animal.

"Future historians have their work cut out for them trying to explain what motivates this madman," Herman said.

Daan looked around the table. "If you were me, would you go?"

The question went to the core. They could no longer just rail against the insanity of Hitler. It was decision-making time.

Anna was the first to speak. "I would not go."

"Then what would you do?" Daan asked.

"I think Walter gave us a clear answer in his sermon. There can only be one answer."

"And what is that?" Daan asked.

"We will bring you to a safe inn, Daan, like the Good Samaritan did."

Daan, who sat next to her, took her hand. He was too overcome to speak. Dirk looked over at Anna, and as they gazed at each other, Walter could read the love they had for each other. God bless them, he thought. They made a powerful team. Anyone hiding a Jew from the Nazis risked being sent to a concentration camp, or worse.

Piet walked to the edge of the water and threw the crust of his sandwich into the reeds next to the gangplank. Two ducks flew up and competed for the bread with loud quacks. When he turned around, beads of sweat dripped from his round face.

"I am all for it, Anna," he said, "but I know I am a coward. Please don't tell me what your plans are, if you have any, because I would rather not know. If there's something I can do to help down the road, I will do it, of course, but right now I don't feel enough of a hero."

"That's OK, Piet," Anna said.

"You bring up an important point, Piet," Dirk said. "From now on, we have to trust each other without asking for details and never telling what we know."

"When I was staying at Het Oranje Hotel," Walter said, "I had two roommates. We gave each other nicknames. They called me Blue. I called them Scar and Grizzly. And when an older Jewish man was literally thrown into our cell, we nicknamed him Abraham. I have no idea what their real names were, and I had only a vague notion of why they'd been arrested. It was better that way."

"That makes sense," Otto said. "But we will need a leader, a coordinator, a central command—whatever you want to call it—to be effective."

"I think it's obvious who that will be," Herman said, and looked at Dirk.

"Not *will* be," Carla said. "Dirk already is. He is our unspoken, fearless leader."

"Only if you want me to be," Dirk said.

"We're committed," Otto said. "Let's put our right hands on the table to indicate we're in this together."

Slowly and deliberately, they offered their right hands. Eight hands formed a stack at the center of the round coffee table. The stillness around them emphasized the gravity of their undertaking. Walter got up from his seat outside the circle and held his own right hand over theirs. "God bless you and keep you. Amen."

They took their hands back and looked up at him.

"Thank you, Walter," Dirk said.

CHAPTER TWELVE

Anna – Same Day

Dirk and Anna were alone on the dock with their legs dangling in the cool water. Otto, Emmy, and Piet had left. The rest of them would stay overnight. Herman and Carla had just gone off on the sailboat. Walter was washing dishes with Daan in the kitchen.

"That inn where you will hide Daan, where is it?" Dirk asked.

"I thought of Oma's place," Anna said.

"The castle? Anna, that's asking a lot of an old lady."

Walter and Daan walked down to the waterfront in their bathing shorts, looking nakedly white after their sunless summer. Anna flipped up some water with her feet, lightly splashing Daan. He smiled and took the hint. After a graceful dive, he swam away.

"I need a more gradual approach," Walter said. He dipped his toe in and slowly climbed down the rope ladder.

Anna turned to Dirk. "I can't explain it, but when Daan asked that crucial question, a great calm came over me. Oma said I had to think things through. I did. Then, when the time came, she said I would know what to do. This was the moment. I heard Oma's voice. We can't let Daan walk into that Nazi trap, Dirk. I could never live with myself."

He drew her close. "Neither could I, Anna. We have to make a good plan, though. Time is running out fast." The sound of splashing below them almost drowned out his voice. "There's no turning back to Den Haag for Daan. We're lucky we made it this far."

"He's already more than halfway to Ede," Anna said.

"That's true. If we can make it work, it will be a brilliant solution."

That evening, they all sat around the small dining room table with the doors and windows tightly closed, keeping their voices low.

"This is the plan," Dirk said. "We will bike to Ede tomorrow."

"That's an amazing coincidence," Walter said. "I have to preach in Ede on Sunday. I had planned to bike on from here."

"Great," Dirk said. "If we go in a group of four, we just look like vacationers."

"What if you get stopped?" Carla asked.

"I gave myself a new ID," Daan said. He pulled out a *Kennkarte* from his wallet. "From now on, I am Klaas Voorne. It's better than an ID with a big J across it. The card was pickpocketed for me from a stranger."

The card went from hand to hand around the table.

"I won't ask you how you got this card," Walter said, "but how does this work? The real Klaas Voorne lost his identity."

"No, he just lost his ID card," Daan said. "He can go to city hall and ask for a new one. My contact made sure he doesn't live close to Den Haag. As a matter of fact, I think he lives somewhere in Zeeland."

"That's a good distance from Ede," Anna said.

At dawn the next morning, Carla and Herman cooked a hearty portion of oatmeal and prepared sandwiches for on the way. The lake was smooth. The creaking of oars, splashing in the water, carried over the lake. The early fisherman could be heard but not seen. They kept their voices low.

"No wind," Carla whispered to Anna. "That'll make your trip easier, at least." She had tears in her eyes. "Anna, take care. I couldn't sleep last night. We may not see Daan for a very long time. I pray this war will be over soon."

"Pray hard," Anna said, and embraced her tightly. When she let go, she whispered, "This will be a scary trip."

With water bottles, sandwiches, and overnight bags tied to their bikes, they started on their journey. Carla and Herman waved them out. They looked forlorn as they stood with their arms around each other at the end of the driveway.

No wind. No rain. A ball of fire appeared on the horizon, climbing inch by inch. They passed fields where farmers milked their cows and women in long skirts and aprons hoed between rows of potatoes. Taking few breaks, they peddled through Holland's lively countryside for hours. Only Dirk and Anna knew where they were headed.

Just as the sky was clouding over, they reached the outskirts of Ede. Anna had visited her grandmother many times, but she barely knew her way around the small city, because the direct route to the castle from Arnhem bypassed it. She gambled that if she kept the church steeple in her vision, it would lead them to the center of town. It did, but not before passing the Prins Maurits Kazerne, a complex of dreary army barracks. German soldiers were everywhere. Since when was Ede a military base? she wondered, and threw a worried look at Dirk. He shrugged in response and kept his eyes on the road.

Adrenaline pumped through her veins, and she pushed harder on her pedals. Scary thoughts clouded her mind. There were plenty of soldiers here to stop them and demand to see Kennkarte. And what then? She threw a sidelong glance at the complex. It was somewhat reassuring that the soldiers marched behind high wire fences. Only two guards stood outside, one on either side of the entrance. Their job was to check out people who wanted to gain entrance. Dirk kept his gaze on the road. So should she, but her heart beat wildly. The enormity of what she was planning to do—asking her grandmother to hide a Jew and assuming that she would agree to it—was illustrated by these soldiers in their drab uniforms. She hadn't questioned herself if this was a safe adventure for everyone involved. It had just seemed the only thing to do.

They reached the center square without incident and placed their bikes in a rack on the church grounds. It wasn't the one where Walter would preach, he said, but he would check if it was open so they could rest inside, rather than collapsing on a café terrace, even though they were dying for a cold beer. It had been a long ride, and the rush of adrenaline had parched Anna's tongue.

The church's interior was cool and quiet. Dirk chose a pew in front. For a while they just sat there, letting the stillness settle their minds. Anna fought her sagging spirits after passing the barracks. Was she leading Daan into a lion's den? How many more dicey surprises were ahead of them?

Dirk took the lead. "We are about twenty minutes from our destination," he whispered. "I propose that Walter stays here. Anna, Daan, and I will bike on. Do you have an address, Walter, where we can reach you?"

Walter told them he would be staying at the parsonage of the Remonstrantse Kerk.

"Good. We will be in touch as soon as things are settled."

Walter got up and walked over to the pulpit. With his hand on the unopened Bible, he turned around to face his companions. "'Blessed is the one who comes in the name of the Lord.' That's a quote from the Gospel of Luke. Go on your mission. The love of God will guide you."

Dirk bowed his head. Then they got up and left.

In single file, with Anna in front, they biked out of the city. She got off at the gates of Kasteel Koppelburg.

"This is where we go first, Daan. My grandmother lives here."

Daan didn't react. He seldom asked unnecessary questions.

Looking closely at the miniature shield with the coat of arms artfully worked into the stiles of the gate, he said, "Nice piece of work. I like the design. It doesn't have the usual swords and daggers."

Anna smiled, but her smile faded quickly when they rounded the curve of the circular driveway. A large, shiny Mercedes was parked in front of the castle. Nazi standards were attached to the fenders on each side. The rooftop had been let down. A chauffeur in uniform sat behind the wheel, as rigid as a lead soldier. Anna's mind raced, and she stopped pedaling. Her entire body prickled with the onset of sweat. Should they turn around? The chauffeur had already seen them. The limousine was facing their way. If they turned around now, it would look suspicious. With one foot on the bike's pedal, the other on the ground, she balanced herself while her mind raced over the consequences of going inside with two young men, one a half Jew, the other undoubtedly involved with the Resistance. Oh, God! She took a deep breath. *No. I am a granddaughter. I have a right to come here with my friends.* She had made a promise to Daan. What if she recoiled from that commitment at the first sign of danger? It would have been better if she'd never started on this dangerous activity. Something like a steel rod slipped into her spine. She lifted her foot up on the pedal and kicked off, heading for the front door.

It didn't take Janus long to answer the bell and open the door. "Miss Anna! You're back. Your grandmother has a visitor," he said, and threw a glance at the Mercedes in front. "Shall I announce you?"

"No, thank you, Janus. We'll bring our bags in first. It looks like it might rain."

"Yes, you'd better, Miss Anna." Janus looked up at the threatening sky, black as ink. "If the visitor doesn't hurry up, he'll have to sit in a puddle of water."

A door opened at the far end of the hall. Her grandmother stepped out, followed by a German officer. The decorations and insignia on his uniform hinted at a high rank. As he strode along the wide marble floor in shiny black riding boots, his footsteps sounded hollow. With his officer's cap clenched under his arm, he clicked his heels, bowed, and placed a kiss on Oma's extended hand.

"*Gnädige Frau*, I thank you for your kind reception."

Oma drew back her head and returned her hand to her side in a graceful, slow motion. She looked every inch the baroness.

"*Auf Wiedersehen, Herr von Schloss*," she said. Then she spotted Anna at the front door. "What a nice surprise! Herr von Schloss, this is my granddaughter Anna, and I see she has brought some friends."

The officer gallantly bowed to Anna, took up her hand in his gloved one, and kissed it. As he straightened, she looked into his face. His eyes were fastened on hers for a penetrating, unnerving moment. It threw her off balance. This handsome man was not the monster she'd imagined when she'd first spotted the parked car. His eyes had warmth and wit in them.

"I have to leave now. It may rain any moment," Herr von Schloss said, and let go of her hand.

Dirk, who'd watched the scene from the doorstep, turned around and said in German, "It's raining already."

The black sky had opened up. Big drops pounded on the hood of the car. The chauffeur was frantically trying to raise the roof, but he struggled with stubborn buttons. Soon, the rain came down in sheets. Daan walked over to the Mercedes and with a quick turn of his hand, got the buttons into place.

"*Danke schön*," Herr von Schloss said to Daan as he slid into the passenger seat. He rolled up the window. His tunic was covered with raindrops, and the chauffeur's uniform had changed from dark to black. Anna couldn't help wonder—in spite of the tension of the moment—what kind of conversation would be going on between the officer and the hapless soldier on their way home.

'Well," Oma said cheerfully, "let's get inside and you can

introduce me to your other friend."

Dirk offered his arm to the baroness. She smiled up at him. "Dirk, I see you are still on your bike ride."

"Yes, madam. There's a lot of lovely countryside in these parts."

Daan's hair and shirt had got soaked while helping the foolish chauffeur. He smiled at Anna and offered his arm. They walked behind Dirk and the baroness into the salon. Once there, Anna said, "Oma, this is Klaas Voorne. He studies law in Utrecht."

Baroness van Haersolte seemed to like what she saw. At least, a smile spread over her face as she took in his face under the wet mop of blond curly hair. Not as tall as Dirk but equally confident, Daan had a way of engaging people right away. His manner was quiet and undemanding.

"How nice to meet you, Klaas," she said. "Are you from the island of Voorne?"

"My ancestors came from there, madam," Daan lied, "but I live in Den Haag."

Dirk, who understood that Anna needed to speak to her grandmother alone, suggested he help Daan get their bags inside. Oma pushed the button on her silver bell and instructed Janus to lead Klaas to a bedroom with a bath. As soon as they left the room, Anna peppered the baroness with questions.

"For heaven's sake, Oma, what was that German officer doing here?"

"Come and sit down with me, Anna, and I will tell you." She led her to a couch by the window. "Do you want some tea, my dear? You look ready for a pick-up. It must have been uncomfortable weather for a bike ride."

"No, thank you, Oma. I am more interested to know what the German wanted of you. I assume he didn't come to offer something."

Oma smiled. "That's correct. He is the commander of Ede's new army base, and he wants to use my home for his headquarters. He has good taste, don't you think?"

Anna was dumbfounded. Her grandmother's reactions were totally incongruous.

"I don't think that's particularly good news, Oma. Why are you smiling?"

"Because he didn't get his way."

"What? In my entire life I've never doubted you, but this sounds unbelievable. I haven't yet heard of a German officer who didn't get his way."

"He was actually a pleasant man, Anna. I didn't like his request, of course, but he was gracious and very well-mannered."

Anna began to wonder if her grandmother was imagining things, but the baroness took Anna's hand and told her exactly what happened. The commandant had been gracious enough not to spring the visit on her and had called in advance. She'd offered him tea. It gave her time to observe him, because she was sure he was after something she most likely wasn't willing to give. Anna had no difficulty picturing her grandmother initiating a conversation over a cup of tea that would lead the commandant to tell his entire life's story. Then came his order. He was terribly sorry to do this to her, he'd said, but he needed her castle.

"I still don't see how you got away with refusing him," Anna said.

"It wasn't easy, my dear. During the course of our conversation, I determined he came from Lower Saxony. That area is home to breeders of the Oldenburg horse. Your grandfather was steeped in the history of that breed. Over the years, I listened to his stories. Not always with full attention, mind you, but I was quite sure I could treat this German officer to the names of famous stallions."

Anna began to relax, though she was still shocked that Oma's place could be taken over by the German Army.

"So, when the commandant made his wish known, I didn't respond. Instead, I told him that my husband had traveled extensively in his area. The man was too polite to hammer his own point, and I could see I had piqued his interest. I abhor name dropping, but I broke my own rule and showered him with the names of breeders I remembered."

Anna had to laugh. "Did he take the bait?"

"He recognized every name I gave him. He was a breeder himself. Your grandfather bought many Oldenburg horses over the years. It is a very desirable breed."

"So, what does this all mean?"

"Most German breeds are raised on state-owned farms. Oldenburg horses are the only ones that are not. It is a private business. Men like the commandant make a lot of money breeding."

"But that couldn't be enough to thwart him, could it?"

"Correct. Maybe you weren't aware, Anna, but a year ago, the Germans confiscated my horses. I had advance notice, because it was happening all over. Your grandfather had a very valuable Oldenburg mare, his favorite horse. I just couldn't bear that beautiful animal to be used by our enemy. I had one of the farmers take her. It's not easy to hide a horse, especially one that is branded."

"Now I am intrigued, Oma!"

Oma leaned back in her chair. She was as calm as a lake on a windless day. If ever Anna needed proof of her grandmother's sangfroid, today provided it.

"Now I had a bargaining chip," Oma said. "I told Herr von Schloss that if he didn't force me out of my home, I would let him have the Oldenburg mare. And he took it."

There was a soft knock on the door. Anna got up to open it. Dirk was on the other side.

"Come in, Dirk," the baroness said.

Anna realized she had missed her chance to talk about the real purpose of their visit. The Nazi's presence had thwarted their plans. Dirk took a hesitant step into the room. How could she clue him in? But there was no time. The baroness gestured Dirk to sit next to her on the couch.

"Were you able to help your friend?" she asked. "Did he have dry clothes with him? I think he's about as tall as my husband was, but with a different waistline. Maybe we can find something that fits him."

"That's very kind of you, but he had extra clothes in his bag."

"Where is he?" Anna asked.

"Resting," Dirk said. "He's not used to such long bike rides."

Anna saw this as an opportunity to broach the subject.

"Oma, quite frankly, we are here on a mission. Klaas Voorne is in great danger. The German authorities have notified him that he has to present himself within a few days. He will be deported because he is a Jew."

"Deported?" the baroness said. She looked horrified and sat up straight, twisting the diamond ring on her left hand.

"Yes, deported," Dirk said. "Probably to a work camp God only knows where."

"But this young man doesn't look Jewish at all."

The Nazis had so relentlessly hammered home Jewish physical traits with their use of cartoons and propaganda movies, Anna thought, it had become hard to recognize a Jew who lacked them.

"His mother is Jewish," she said. "That makes him a Jew. Even if only his grandmother were Jewish, the Nazis would still consider him a Jew."

"So what is your mission?" the baroness demanded.

Anna told her about the Group of Eight, how they had met in Loosdrecht and agreed that something had to be done to keep Klaas out of the Nazis' reach.

"And you brought him here. Did you tell your friends what you had in mind?"

"No, we didn't. Just that we would find a place, somehow, somewhere," Anna said, admiring her grandmother's astute observation.

It was quiet in the room. Baroness van Haersolte turned within herself. The tall grandfather's clock ticked the minutes away with unbearable regularity, emphasizing the tense silence and the enormity of their unspoken request. Anna didn't want to look at either Dirk or her grandmother. It was a time to be inward looking. What would they do if Oma thought Klaas wasn't worth the risk? Was there an alternative?

Finally, the baroness asked if his mother was alive and if she'd also received a summons.

"Yes, she did," Dirk said, "and so did his younger brother. They were told they had to report with only one suitcase each, one they could carry themselves."

It was silent again. Anna had no idea what direction the conversation would take. Oma had asked a logical question. But hiding three people? A mother with two sons? Outside, the rain came down hard and thunder rumbled nearby. The large room was plunged in eerie darkness.

"Did you say Klaas Voorne is a law student?" the baroness asked. "How far along is he in his studies?"

"He's going into his fourth year, madam," Dirk said.

It was quiet again, except for the thunder outside. The light flickered in the lamp beside the couch.

"I am glad you came to me," the baroness said finally. "Our conversation the last time you visited, I remember it well. We can't let Hitler rule people's lives in such a beastly manner. I agree. We must find a way to protect these people. Dirk, wake up Klaas. I want to talk to him."

Daan appeared, looking slightly disoriented. Dirk had told them he had woken up with a start and wondered where he was.

"You are in a better place than if you'd stayed home, Klaas," the baroness said as she invited him to sit down.

Daan looked at Anna and Dirk, his expression revealing that he understood this formidable woman in front of him had been informed of who he was.

"Please excuse my appearance, madam," he said.

"They fit your circumstances, Klaas. Relax and let's have a talk."

Anna realized that from now on she had to think of Daan as Klaas, and she willed herself to do it.

"Tell me a little bit about yourself," the baroness said.

It was a kind invitation. Daan's bewilderment of having woken up in a castle faded as he gathered his wits and realized this might be the most important interview of his life. He settled into the elegant fauteuil—a direct contrast in style to his crumpled clothes.

"My name is actually not Klaas, madam, but it's better that I do not give you my real name. I took on a different identity."

"I see. Go on."

"I want to apologize to you. I told you a lie. My forefathers do not come from Voorne. My family is solidly rooted in Den Haag."

The baroness smiled but didn't speak.

His father was a life insurance agent, he said, his mother an accomplished painter and illustrator, his brother still a high school student.

"Do your parents know where you are?" the baroness asked.

"All they know is that Dirk would take me to a safe place. At first, I didn't want to leave them, but they insisted I should. It was hard," Klaas said, wringing his hands and fighting his emotions.

It was quiet again. The room had filled up with sorrow.

"It's time to have dinner," the baroness declared, breaking the silence. "You all must be starved. Anna, run out to Mien and tell her to make some sandwiches. We don't need to be served. It's after hours for the help. We have a lot to talk about, and we might as well do it at the dinner table."

Anna did as she was told.

Chapter Thirteen

Anna – Next Day

The previous night's rainfall had woven itself into a blanket that lay draped over the farms and fields surrounding Kasteel Koppelburg. Dirk and Anna dried the seats of their bikes and started on their way to Ede to take a train to Den Haag. They located the Remonstrantse Kerk where they hoped to find Walter. They were too early. The church was open but empty. Dirk tore a page from his pocket notebook and scribbled: *"Sorry, we can't make it to the service. We found a wonderful vacation spot. Will see you later. Dirk."* On the wallboard, the numbers of the hymns to be sung that morning were already posted, and he climbed up the stairs of the chancel to slip his note between hymns 22 and 23 in the hymnal.

Hardly any passengers were on the train on this Sunday morning.

"Just a few weeks and we'll be back in Utrecht," Anna said.

"It will be quite different from last year. I'll be seeing patients."

"Hands on?" she asked.

"No. Patients are presented in an auditorium. The professor stands on a stage. The patients are brought in for us to look at, so we can learn to recognize symptoms."

"Do the patients have a choice in the matter?"

"Of course. It's not a zoo."

"I can't wait till I get to the hands-on part of studying medicine," Anna said. "So far, it's been pretty dry. Anatomy, chemistry, biology. I wanted to become a doctor to *do* things with *people*. My mother doubted I would keep my nose in textbooks for very long. She had a point."

At the next stop after Ede, the only other person in their compartment got off and nobody else took her place. Anna leaned into Dirk and watched the landscape fly by. The fog had lifted enough to reveal the outlines of trees, their leaves pregnant with raindrops, waiting for a breeze to deliver them to the ground.

"Do you think our plan will work?" she whispered. "What if they refuse to leave? Or maybe they aren't home."

"In moments like this, it pays to have faith," Dirk said, and pulled her toward him. His certainty was a comfort. Dirk had already been initiated into this underworld of secrets and risks.

They jumped from the train onto a tram that took them straight to Daan's home. Dirk rang the bell. Daan's father opened the door just an inch, peeking outside. When he saw it was Dirk, he pulled him inside and pumped his hand. Apparently, Dirk had become a familiar face over the summer months. Upstairs, Daan's mother fell onto his neck, tears welling up in her eyes. But when she spotted Anna on the staircase behind him, a shadow fell over her face. Dirk hastened to introduce Anna as one of Daan's friends.

"I apologize for coming unannounced, but we have no time to lose," he said.

They sat around the dining room table. Dirk sprang the plan of bringing Mrs. Timmermans and her son to the country where they would be safe. His words were received in stunned silence. Anna looked around and noticed subtle signs of upheaval. Glaring gaps in a row of portraits on the fireplace mantel told of frantic picking and choosing. A bulging suitcase stood in the corner, ready to be carried to the grammar school where they'd been told to present themselves for a journey without a known destination. Twenty-four hours from now.

Daan's mother sat with her head in her hands and stared down at the white damask tablecloth. Her body was taut with tension. Anna could hardly breathe for the stifling atmosphere that hung in the air. She tried to put herself in the woman's shoes. The choices were stark and equally unpredictable. Both could end very badly. How did one choose?

"There's no time," Dirk said, "to get you and your son false identities. That's for later. Mrs. Timmermans, are you willing to get on the train today and travel to the place where Daan is? We will travel together: your husband, your son, Anna, and myself. We have a safe place for you to hide at the other end of the trip. Daan is already there. Will you trust us?"

A gangly teenager hung in the background. He resembled his father more than his mother, his hair a shade darker and not as curly as Daan's.

"Come and join us, David," Dirk called to him. "We have something important to tell you. By the way, this is Anna Smits. She is one of your brother's friends."

An hour later, Mr. Timmermans locked the front door of the house, and the five of them hurried to the tram stop across the busy street. The packed suitcases were left behind, the hateful yellow patches with the black *J* removed from their coats. At the train station, Daan's father bought three tickets, for his wife, his son, and himself. They looked like vacationers, each carrying a handbag.

A German soldier on patrol paced back and forth in the hall, a gun slung over his shoulder. Anna, Dirk, and Mr. Timmermans put Daan's mother and brother in the center of an invisible circle on their way to the platform. They didn't look different from any other group of passengers. The train was preparing to leave, white clouds rising into the air as the locomotive let out steam with a fierce hissing sound. They filled one compartment. Dirk had grabbed a tourist brochure and a map at the station in Ede that morning. Since they had told Mr. Timmermans to buy tickets to Ede, the family knew their destination. Dirk spread the map out over several laps. When the conductor knocked on the door to see their tickets, their heads were inclined over the large map with Anna pointing out places of interest, but letting her fingers skip over her grandmother's castle.

Moments later, a German sergeant walked by. The buttons on his uniform brushed against the window of the sliding door. He peeked inside, stopped, and studied the five people sitting on worn leather seats across from one another, poring over a map. Four had variations of blond hair. The woman's hair was dark. They didn't look up at him, except for Dirk, who unabashedly stared him in the eye before reaching into his pocket and producing a bar of chocolate. He unwrapped it, divided it, and started dealing the pieces around. The sergeant moved on. The encounter lasted only a few seconds. They seemed like hours. Daan's mother slowly raised her head with an expression in her eyes that Anna likened to a deer that had just narrowly escaped its hunter. Raw fright and confusion. *She* was the one the Germans were after. *She* was the one who'd passed her Jewish blood on to her sons. Hitler despised her race. Anna wanted to convey what she couldn't say: you will be safe. We will take care of you. She put her hand on the woman's arm. Of course, none of them were safe. They'd blatantly disobeyed an order that forbade contact between Jews and Gentiles.

Before leaving Den Haag, Anna had called the castle and talked to Janus, asking if he could bring the pony wagon to the station to transport some more guests. She and Dirk could use their bikes, but with the shortage of gas, there wouldn't be any taxis for Daan's family. As they stepped off the train, the pony wagon approached the empty taxi stand. The driver pulled on the reins so the two Welsh ponies stood perfectly still and waited.

"Oh, my God," Anna whispered to Dirk, pulling on his sleeve. "That's Oma."

Dirk herded the trio to the open carriage. Without acknowledging Anna's grandmother on the coach seat, he helped

Mrs. Timmermans negotiate the steep climb into the rear. The baroness, wearing a beige jacket and a wide-brimmed straw hat, a plaid blanket over her lap, didn't look back and ignored her passengers. After everyone was seated, their bags in their laps, Dirk wished them a fun trip. The baroness lowered the whip over the ponies' shiny rumps, and they obediently trotted away. Anna thought she knew her grandmother well, but this side she'd never seen before. Oma was a born actress.

She and Dirk found their bikes. Taking paths inaccessible to four-footers, they got to the castle first, where they found Daan pacing the hall. He jumped when Anna and Dirk came up from behind him, having entered the castle through the kitchen door. It was after dinnertime, and the sun was setting. Without a word between them, they went back out through the deserted kitchen and quickly walked to the stables. A man appeared out of nowhere. It was Anna's favorite farmer, the one she'd hayed with when she was a little girl, and the one who'd hid her grandfather's Oldenburg mare.

In the distance, they heard the pounding of hoofs on gravel. The rubber tires of the pony cart made hardly a noise. Even though they expected her, they were still surprised to see the baroness drive into the courtyard and halt in front of the impressive building that had once housed horses and carriages, and was now a spacious palace for the two Welsh ponies the Nazis had no use for.

The farmer held on to the ponies while Dirk offered his hand to help the baroness down from the driver's seat. Daan ran over to his parents and passionately embraced them. Back in Den Haag, Dirk had warned them not to call their son by his given name. He was now Klaas Voorne.

The baroness took off her leather gloves, which smelled heavily of pony sweat, and handed them to Dirk. She laughed. "How I love that smell," she said. "It's been a while since I held four reins."

She walked over to Daan's family. "I am Anna's grandmother," she said simply. "I am so glad to have a chance to meet Klaas's parents. I enjoy his company." She shook hands with all three. Sensing their discomfort, she added, "If only these were better times for us all, I would invite you inside. But under the circumstances, it is best that you get back into the wagon. Hendrik here will take you to a safe place. He is your guardian angel. Your tough, indomitable angel."

Hendrik was feeding the ponies lumps of sugar, and white foam slobbered on his jacket. Steam rose from the ponies' chests as the cool evening air seized them, giving rise to the small clouds. Daan's parents looked like they'd landed on a stage. It was so obviously not what they had expected. A castle? A grandmother who directed the show? They didn't know how to take it. Mr. Timmermans was the first to speak.

"Thank you," he said. "I cannot adequately express how grateful we are."

"No need to," the baroness said. "God's speed." With that, she waved and walked to the kitchen door.

"I have to stay here," Klaas said to his father. "Anna will visit you tomorrow and explain things."

The next day was Queen Wilhelmina's birthday, and Mien served up some remarkable items for breakfast: orange marmalade and tea, both from "before the war." She proudly slipped in the fact she'd been named after the queen.

"Were you also born on August 31, Mien?" the baroness asked.

"Yes, ma'am."

"You don't have to tell us in what year, but I wish you a happy birthday."

Mien blushed.

The marmalade looked exotic on their buttered slices of bread. "From before the war" had become a new adjective in daily parlance. It stood for genuine, original, superior quality, made from ingredients that could not be imported any longer and were only to be found in the back of pantry cabinets, hidden behind the hated surrogates. It wasn't illegal to have real tea or coffee, but making them hard to reach cut down on moments of weakness or wandering hands.

After Mien left the room, Anna asked Oma what arrangements she'd made with the farmer Hendrik and what to tell Mr. and Mrs. Timmermans.

"I asked Hendrik to come over after church, and I introduced Klaas as my new secretary to help out old Mr. van Dijk. He's been the property manager since long before your grandfather died. I told Hendrik that Klaas is one of your friends, Anna. He seemed to like that idea. Of course, he probably wondered why he had to come and see me on the day of the Lord to hear this. He's a devout Christian, as you know."

"I remember," Anna said. "He and his wife would dress in black from top to toe every Sunday morning."

"I asked him if he was aware the Nazis were taking Jews from their homes and sending them to concentration camps. He said he was not. That kind of news didn't appear in the papers here."

"No wonder," Dirk said. "They're transported at night to keep it out of the news."

"Klaas told Hendrik he came from Den Haag," the baroness went on, "and that his Jewish neighbors had received a summons from the Gestapo, and that tomorrow was the day they were supposed to present themselves for relocation. I could see Hendrik recoil. He asked if they *had* to go just because they were Jews, and Klaas told him the choice they had was to obey or to hide somewhere. I made it clear that I'd offered to hide the two Jews—mother and son—because I saw it as my moral obligation and Christian duty, but since Herr von Schloss's visit, I was worried my home might not be safe. He might come again, even make it his headquarters after all. The mention of Christian duty sank in. Hendrik said he would talk it over with his wife."

"And she said yes," Anna guessed.

Her grandmother nodded.

Hendrik's farm was a short walking distance from the castle. Early sunrays cast long shadows over the land. A rabbit darted in front of her from a bush, and a flock of ducks flew overhead in formation, quacking loudly. Red apples in the castle's orchard shone as brightly as freshly polished shoes. Anna sniffed the air that rose from the meadow and recognized the distinct aromas of animal life. How would Mrs. Timmermans and David fare in an environment so essentially different from living on the first floor of a house on a busy street in a big city? And how would a farmer's wife adjust to having a woman around who was an accomplished artist? Her impulsive decision to hide Daan had set events in motion at a dizzying speed. It had seemed the right and moral thing to do, but she hadn't foreseen that hiding Daan would implicate more people than just her grandmother. Hendrik and his wife had accepted people into their home they didn't even know. Walter would probably say that that's what true Christians do.

A *hooiberg* loomed up in her line of sight. It towered over Hendrik's farm and held together a mountain of hay with four poles at its four corners, topped by a mobile roof that could be moved up or down on the poles. Next spring, that roof would be close to the ground after the cattle had devoured all the hay underneath it over the winter months, and the manure pile would be stacked high next to it.

Her leather shoes crunched the gravel on the short path from the road to Hendrik's house. Solid shutters flanked the four front windows with their neat eight-over-twelve panes of glass. The combination of colors on the shutters—green, white, and red—indicated the farm belonged to the castle. All farms on land belonging to the castle had the same colored shutters. They added a cheerful note to the landscape.

Hendrik waved from the vegetable garden. She waved back, and he smiled in return. A good sign, she thought, and continued on to the kitchen door, where a pair of wooden shoes had been kicked off by whoever was inside. Hendrik's wife Bertien sat at the kitchen table with Daan's parents and brother. Pulling at her long apron was a little girl whose curious eyes were fixed on the strangers. They merely sat there taking stock of each other. What a blessing, Anna thought, that Dirk had knocked on her door that morning before the sun came up, and that breakfast had been served earlier than usual. She wasn't a minute too early, as apparently this was the first contact between the Timmermans and Hendrik's wife.

"Good morning, everyone," she said. "Are you celebrating the queen's birthday?"

"Oh, my God," Bertien said. "I totally forgot, Miss Anna. Thank you for reminding me. Used to be that I hung out our red-white-and-blue first thing in the morning. But not nowadays."

"I assume your guests haven't given you their true names?"

"That's right," Mr. Timmermans said. "We are Mr. No-Name and Mrs. No-Name and Junior. That's the only decision we've made so far, right, Bertien?"

Bertien smiled. What a good-natured woman, Anna thought, and so totally natural in her simple small-print cotton blouse and black skirt.

"We'll fix that as soon as we can get you new IDs," Anna said. "Bertien, Mr. No-Name will pay you a monthly amount that you and he agree on, and I will see to it that you get the *distributie bonnen* that you will need to feed two extra people. As for the living arrangements, you will have to work those out with each other, but remember. It is absolutely imperative that Mrs. No-Name remains invisible. You should work out a place she can slip into when there is a threat. Hopefully, there won't be one, but it's better to be prepared. Junior could help Hendrik around the farm, since he's the right age to be a farmhand, and let's be realistic. He has blond hair and blue eyes. There's nothing wrong with dark hair and brown eyes, but that doesn't seem to be the opinion of the Nazis."

For the first time, Anna saw a smile on Mrs. Timmermans's face.

"Miss Anna, I haven't even offered you a cup of coffee," Bertien said. She looked genuinely upset.

"Don't worry about it, Bertien. This is not that kind of visit. It doesn't mean I wouldn't like one, because I know you brew the best coffee for miles around."

Before Anna left, she took Mr. Timmermans aside and told him to remind his wife and son never to reveal that the man who now worked as secretary for the baroness was her son or David's brother.

"You can count on it," Mr. Timmermans said.

"It is none of my business," Anna asked, "but may I ask what *you* are planning to do?"

"I won't go back home. My office is on the ground floor. I will get in touch with my secretary and instruct her to refer calls to the main office of the company I work for. The police may want to have access to our living quarters. Who knows, they may even take it for themselves, like they've done with other houses. These are things I have to work out. But at some point, I will have to get some clothes for my wife and son. The way I see it, the most important thing right now is to stay out of the way of the Gestapo. I can stay with a cousin who lives in Amersfoort. I will let you know where you can reach me."

"I think that's wise. You would be peppered with questions if the Germans started to look for your family."

"Thank you, Anna," he said. "That sounds so lame in view of what you and your grandmother are taking on. I will do whatever I can to protect and help you."

Anna looked up at him. Daan was his spitting image.

Back at the castle, she found Walter Vlaskamp drinking coffee in the salon with her grandmother, Dirk, and Klaas. When he shook her hand, she read in his face how surprised he was that his path had led to this place.

"Walter! You found us. I hope the Gestapo isn't as clever as you are," she said.

He laughed. "Not unless Dirk calls them on the phone, they won't be."

"I was afraid Walter would be on his way to Leiden before we got in touch," Dirk said.

Her grandmother sat in her chair by the window, surrounded by Anna's three friends, each dressed in shorts and rumpled shirts. It was almost comical. Two generations removed, different lifestyles, it seemed to make no difference. That, at least, was one good outcome of the Nazi Occupation. People not likely to meet otherwise came together.

Walter had apparently just arrived. As she had done with Klaas, the baroness asked him to tell a bit about himself. Anna could tell Walter felt put on the spot. He was used to sitting down with older women and getting a conversation going. It was part of his profession. But helped by the overwhelming environment and by the baroness's force of personality, the tables were turned on him. He modestly described how he'd graduated from Leiden, studied theology, and that this Sunday he'd substituted for the minister of the Remonstrantse Kerk in Ede. The baroness wondered how he got to know her granddaughter and her friends if they studied in Utrecht and he was a Leiden man. Dirk stepped in, explaining that the sermon Walter had given in a town close to Utrecht had changed their lives.

"How so?" Oma asked.

"He had the audacity to give a sermon about the parable of the Good Samaritan and compare it to our own time. His bad luck was that a high-up of the NSB sat in the front row. Walter was taken to the police station and spent several weeks in Het Oranje Hotel in Scheveningen."

"I never heard of Het Oranje Hotel. Is it new?" the baroness asked.

"That's what the big prison there is nicknamed, Oma," Anna said.

"When did this all happen?"

"In May," Anna said. "Thanks to Dirk, Walter got out of prison at the end of June."

"Well, well, well." The baroness put down her cup of coffee and leaned back in her armchair. "I am beginning to put some things together. Could it be that Klaas is here because you appealed to these young people's sense of Christian duty, Dominee Vlaskamp?"

Walter looked like he didn't know how to take this comment, but after a brief hesitation, he said, "As a minister, it is my duty to interpret the gospel. What people do with it is up to them. The NSB officer took it one way. My sister and her friends took it a different way."

His answer was at once modest and resolute. It seemed to satisfy the baroness.

Their coffee cups were empty, and the day was getting on. Dirk said it was time for him to go home and tackle a few tasks, like getting IDs for Daan's mother and brother. Would Walter like to join him, he asked, but Walter said he couldn't. The minister he was substituting for was seriously ill. He would have to stay in Ede longer, at least until the doctors determined what ailed the pastor.

"Dirk, will you bring Anna home on your way?" Oma asked.

He smiled. "It will be my honor and my pleasure."

CHAPTER FOURTEEN

Dirk – Early September 1942

Escorting Anna to Arnhem led Dirk in the opposite direction from where he needed to go. He declined her mother's invitation to stay overnight, well aware of his rumpled, smelly summer clothes. He didn't consider himself vain, but Anna's relatives had never seen him dressed otherwise, and he preferred not to let that impression linger for too long.

It would be a strenuous ride back to Den Haag. He might not make it before curfew, but biking was his favorite sport. He had got his first bike on his third birthday, and he'd taken to biking the way a goat takes to mountain climbing. As a teenager, he'd been the proud owner of a racing bike, and had covered untold miles at great speed. He remembered those rides well, that feeling of physical strength and independence and the wind whooshing through his hair. Unfortunately, his treasured bike hadn't survived German greed. It had gone the way of so many things these days: requisitioned by the Germans. Now he used his grandfather's sturdy, old upright.

His mind whirled with the happenings of the last few months. It was all a wonder to him. He'd been attracted to Anna from the moment he saw her on that snowy day, back in January, at Carla's place. He'd seen her as pretty, unpretentious, and easy to be around, and he'd trusted her right away. Suspicions that had crept into first-time meetings with others, ever since the war started, hadn't entered into his mind. Now that he looked back on that day, he was amazed he'd told her about Kristallnacht, that he'd dropped his caution. Walter's sermon, arrest, and jailing had displayed her compassion. Everything since then had deepened his feelings for her. Physical attraction came first, as it always does. Her light blue eyes immediately stood out to him, and there was a naturally confident elegance in the way she moved that was a pleasure to watch. But there was so much more to her than good looks and blue blood. She was real. He'd seen it in the way she'd reached out to Daan and his parents. It was in her genes. Her grandmother was amazing. But he continually questioned if he'd done right by opening Anna's eyes to the plight of the Jews. He would forever be responsible for exposing her to dangers, and the baroness as well.

A German patrol stopped him as he entered the small town of Doorn. Three soldiers surrounded him and, at first, they seemed most interested in his bike. In German, they commented to each other that it must be a relic from the First World War.

"Kennkarte!" one demanded.

Dirk produced his ID card. The highest in rank took the card and quickly looked at the birthdate, turned it over, glanced at his passport picture on the back, and compared it with the face in front of him. This all happened in a flash.

"General Rauter ordered you to present at the Labor Department for work in Germany. So, why are you here riding this stupid bike?"

Dirk decided not to tell him his comrades had stolen his own bike.

"I am a student and the university is closed in August."

The soldier turned the ID over and saw that he'd overlooked the line where Dirk had entered his profession. The seal at the bottom assured he'd written it in the presence of an official. He turned the card over and looked at the picture again.

"What do you study?"

"Medicine."

Dirk knew he was on the right side of the law. What they were looking for were young men they could put to work, but students were exempted.

"You can go," the soldier said. He didn't seem happy about it. Maybe catching young men and Jews was a way to get promoted.

Adrenaline pumped through his veins as he remounted his grandfather's bike. The Kennkarte for Mrs. Timmermans and David would have to be foolproof. It wasn't as if he didn't already know that, but this five-minute encounter brought out the importance of the picture on the ID. The left and right index finger imprints didn't get looked at. They were hard for a soldier in the street to interpret. The picture was what caught their eye. And that was the hardest part to falsify. The designer of the ID cards had been very clever. It was nearly impossible to take the photograph's top layer off an existing ID and replace it with another. That had been his experience with Daan's stolen ID. It had taken the artistic hand of Daan's mother to accomplish it. She'd spent many hours on it.

Over the summer months, as he often visited the Timmermans family, he discovered that Daan was a daredevil at heart. How else could he have managed to stay in Utrecht with that ugly black *J* on his Kennkarte while Jews were forbidden to attend university? He'd simply sailed on his blond hair and blue eyes, and got away with it. Dirk had known through his father that Daan would be called up for transport sometime soon. He'd tried to prepare him, a subtle task, because he didn't want to drive him to despair. He'd gotten his hands on Klaas Voorne's ID, and had talked Daan into using it in case he might need it, which he did a scant week later. When the summons came, Daan had finally realized he'd exhausted the good works of his guardian angel.

There had to be a better way than stealing IDs from others, Dirk thought. He would talk to his father about it. Karel van Enthoven was a prominent lawyer in Den Haag, and had taken an early lead in the Underground. He had involved his son in some small tasks at first, like being a courier. It was the reason Dirk had avoided inviting Anna to his home. It was better she didn't know Vader, and therefore would never be able to identify him. Not only for his father's safety, but her own as well, now that she'd landed in the dangerous business of hiding Jews.

Soon after he arrived home from his arduous bike trip, he asked his father about the IDs.

"Yes, there's a better way," Vader told him. "Soon, we will need more than just one or two IDs. So, we're busy printing our own, never mind tinkering with existing ones. That's too time-consuming. But printing our own in great numbers is hazardous. The watermark has to be in the paper, and the paper itself is a special kind. It's made in Austria, and has to be stolen. And then the stamps and seals. It takes draftsmen, printers, and engravers. The whole enterprise is fraught with danger."

Dirk nodded. "How can I get a hold of some?"

"There's a contact in Amsterdam. How many do you need?"

"Two to begin with. There will be more, I'm sure. Right now, there isn't a general awareness of what's going on."

"That will change soon," Vader said.

His father called him a few days later to the stately house that was his office, a stone's throw from Het Binnenhof, the seat of government now occupied by Arthur Seyss-Inquart, the Reichskommissar. It had galled the residents when Seyss-Inquart chose the Ridderzaal—the Hall of Knights—as the place for his installation ceremony, the very place where Queen Wilhelmina used to address parliament on every third Tuesday in September.

Vader's secretary of many years was happy to see Dirk.

"Miep, do you still keep Haagse Hopjes in that drawer?" Dirk asked, pointing to the right side of her desk.

She laughed and produced a tin with the coveted sweets. "I'll check if Mijnheer van Enthoven can see you. He's been on the phone all morning."

Moments later, Dirk stood in front of his father's desk. The large room's furnishings were in contrast to the style of the house itself, built sometime in the seventeen hundreds. After walking through the Delft-tiled hall, Dirk was again surprised to see shiny steel chairs and a light-blond oak desk, all in the modern Gispen style. The room's furnishings reflected the man who occupied it. Karel van Enthoven's outlook on life more often than not departed from conventional thinking.

Vader took out a pen and wrote the name Leo in Greek letters on a small piece of paper. Underneath it he wrote Café Kempinsky, also in Greek letters.

"Here, take this. You will meet Leo at that place. It's located in the Leidse Straat in Amsterdam. Be there at 11 a.m. on Monday. Wear my gray fedora. He will recognize you by that hat. Leo will help you get the IDs."

"Thank you, Vader," Dirk said, and got up. "Can you tell me what this Leo looks like?"

"No. Find a table for two in a corner and order two beers. He will recognize you by your hat and the two beers."

"How can I be sure it's Leo?"

"He will offer you a cigarette and light it for you."

As Dirk reached for the doorknob, Vader rose from his chair. He was a tall man, youthful in appearance. It would be easy to mistake him for Dirk's older brother, but for graying hairs at his temples.

"I am proud of you, Dirk. Be intuitive and careful."

Once outside the office, Dirk noticed in one glance that at least five German officers walked in the street. Seyss-Inquart's minions populated this part of town. Enemies encircled his father's office. Dirk chuckled. His father was like a mole in their midst, digging secret tunnels under the seat of Nazi power.

Early in the morning of the designated Monday, Dirk took a train to Amsterdam. The country's wide landscape flew by the window. It might not be as imposing as the Alps, but it was endless. The horizon never hemmed you in. It was clear that it was laundry day. The train's path ran through a densely populated part of the city. Underwear, stockings, shirts, sanitary napkins, and bras flapped in the breeze on lines strung from one end of tiny balconies to another. Dirk felt as if he'd inadvertently stepped into a woman's dressing room. Not of just one woman, but of many.

He entered the Leidse Straat ten minutes before eleven. Café Kempinsky was a typical *bruin café*. Over time, cigarette and cigar smoke had painted the walls dark brown. A brass rod held up a once-white curtain that blocked the lower half of the front window. From the street, it was hard to see who or what was inside. Once inside, he spotted an empty table in a far corner, away from the bar. That was a relief. He wasn't used to wearing a hat, certainly not a nice fedora and never inside, but he had no choice except to keep it on as he seated himself. There were no customers his age. A few men seated at the long bar were well into their forties or older. They looked like artistic types, if he were to judge them by their nonchalant clothing, some wearing a black Alpine cap, so characteristic of painters. His fedora was somewhat out of place in this company. Hopefully, this wouldn't attract unnecessary attention. He seated himself in the corner and ordered two beers. This was what undercover agents did, he supposed. Or had he read too many mysteries? It felt a bit strange to be acting out this new role. Yet, he felt daring rise within himself. It surprised him.

The next man to enter the restaurant was casually recognized by the others, and the bartender waved at him with a jovial gesture. With abundant self-confidence, the man walked over to Dirk, seated himself across from him, took out a pack of cigarettes, offered him one, and then reached over with a lighter. Okay, this was his man.

"Nice hat," the man said.

"I borrowed it," Dirk said.

"I would keep it, if I were you. You may need it again."

Dirk concluded from this remark that Leo expected to see him back. He wouldn't have to plead with him to make the IDs in the first place. Apparently, Vader had taken care of that. This was the first step. Mr. Timmermans had given Dirk passport pictures of his wife and son before they left their home. Without them, Leo could not make IDs.

Dirk studied the man in front of him. His hands, folded around the glass of beer, were refined, his fingers long and slender. Dirk estimated his age at early forties. There was a lot to like in his face. His eyes held benign purpose, or so Dirk liked to think. His presence was commanding, yet it felt comfortable to share a beer with him.

After some small talk about medical school and the good summer they'd had, Leo lowered his voice.

"A few things to remember. I don't know and I don't want to know your last name. And you don't know mine. If you ever get caught, be sure your contact, the one that got you here to meet me, notifies me as quickly as possible. Harsh questioning can be withstood for twenty-four hours in most cases. Even if you cave in after that—and nobody would blame you—it would give me enough time to get myself underground."

"I understand," Dirk said. He wondered if Leo knew it was his own father who'd gotten him here. But really, what difference did that make?

"Furthermore, if you have a woman in your life, have her sew a secret pocket inside your raincoat. I assume you understand why."

"I do," Dirk said. "My sister is pretty handy with a needle."

"Will you have demand for more IDs?"

"I may need more later. As of now, two will do."

Dirk reached inside his jacket and pulled out the envelope with the pictures. Leo put his hand on it and left it there while he downed the rest of his beer. Only then did he put it in his pocket and then got up.

"You'll hear from me," he said.

Seconds later, he was gone. Dirk decided not to leave right away and ordered another beer.

CHAPTER FIFTEEN

Anna – September 1942

August melded into September, that peculiar time of year when gardens are filled with colorful phlox while the leaves on the trees look tired and dusty. Summer was coming to an end, and vacation would soon be over. Anna wasn't sorry about that. She'd had enough of being back under parental guidance. It was a split existence. Her mind was never where her body was. She longed for her cozy room at Jan and Betty's, for seeing Dirk and reconnecting with the Group of Eight.

When she arrived at the Schoonhovens', Jan brought her suitcase upstairs. On the way, she noticed the bedroom opposite hers had changed dimensions. She peeked inside and asked Jan why it seemed smaller than before.

"It's not a bedroom anymore, it's a hobby room for when I retire."

"Are you retiring?" she asked.

He shrugged. "Someday, I'll have to."

As she entered her room, her family picture from before the war—when Maarten was still in Holland—greeted her. It hung in the same spot as where she'd put it a year ago. Nothing had been heard from Maarten or about him. The Japanese had conquered

Java six months earlier, back in March. He'd vanished from their lives. Anna was convinced her brother would have joined the Underground, had he stayed in Holland. His sense of adventure made that a sure bet. He could well have joined a resistance group on Java. Thinking about him doing heroic things kept the demons away. She willed him to be alive, somewhere, somehow.

To distract herself from dark thoughts, she started to unpack her suitcase. The only additions to her wardrobe this fall were a silk blouse Moeder had passed on to her and a pair of stockings she'd bought with her textile coupons. The rest was identical to what she'd brought last September.

A framed picture lay wrapped inside two woolen sweaters. It was of Oma in her early twenties when she lived in Den Haag, around the time Queen Wilhelmina ascended the throne at the end of the previous century. She'd found it at the castle, in a heavy leather album in her grandfather's library. Sepia pictures of ladies clothed in reams of silk and wearing hats the size of boxes large enough to hold a cake; men with top hats and pointed, upturned mustaches; and horses with plumes on their bridles pulling shiny carriages filled the pages. Oma rode sidesaddle in the picture. Her booted left foot rested in a stirrup, the other was drawn up on the same side under a wide flowing skirt. Her head was held high, and the reins lay securely in her hands. The horse seemed to enjoy the ride, judging from the pricked-up ears and the black tail flowing in the breeze.

To think that Oma could enjoy the company of young men in rumpled shorts, as she had over the course of the past summer, and make them feel completely at ease was all the more remarkable considering her past. She had remained erect as well as supple in body and mind, in spite of drastically changed times.

Anna placed the framed picture on her desk.

A week later, the members of the Group of Eight, minus Daan, were sprawled over Carla's large room, nursing a bottle of red wine Herman had brought from his father's wine cellar. They talked about textbooks and where to buy them for bargain prices.

"Is Daan safe?" Emmy asked suddenly.

"As safe as any Jew can be these days," Anna said. She expected the follow-up question to be "Where?", but it didn't come. Even Emmy had learned to handle information gingerly.

Her question shifted the conversation to the roundup of Jews in the last weeks of August. Carla said she lived on a street that led to Breda's railroad station, and groups of Jews had marched below her window, flanked by German soldiers with guns. Enough soldiers so no escape was possible, she said.

Anna winced. Daan, his mother, and his younger brother could have been marched through the streets like criminals. She felt restless, and shifted on the old couch to release tension. The sagging springs underneath her shifted as well. Except for Otto, who leaned against the doorframe smoking a cigarette, the men sat cross-legged on the carpet.

Piet seemed agitated, combative even, the reverse of his mood in Loosdrecht, when he'd broken out in a sweat at the thought of hiding a Jew. He told them he'd discovered the Germans had set up a transit camp in Westerbork not far from where his parents lived, close to the German border. Jews were taken from there to places east. Piet had biked over to check it out. It had been too heavily guarded to get close, but he watched trains being unloaded at the station. One locomotive had pulled fifteen boxcars with human cargo. The Gestapo soldiers pushed people around on the platform with the butts of their rifles, he said. The shouts and loud commands were deafening.... He fell silent, remembering, but his eyes burned in his round face, and Anna sensed he wasn't done yet. She took a sip of wine and waited.

He continued, "A policeman came to the house next door to my parents. Fifteen minutes later, our neighbor, his wife, and their three teenage children stood on the sidewalk. The officer took the key from the owner, locked the door, and put the key in his own pocket. Then he marched them off to the station. The next day, all their belongings were carted off, and a new family moved in a week later. It was the policeman's."

Herman reached for the wine bottle on the coffee table and divided what was left.

"Did you know that for every Jew a policeman delivers to the Gestapo, he pockets seven guilders and fifty cents?" Otto asked.

"I hope you're joking," Herman said.

"I'm not. Think of it. More than ten Jews per square mile live in our country. Even if the police rounded up only a fraction, they could end up rich."

"And every square mile in Holland is as flat as a pancake," Herman said. "Where do you hide?"

Anna took the last sip of her wine and walked over to the window. The street below was deserted. It gave a nice overview of Old Utrecht with its brick houses and wide granite stoops. A gust of wind chased the first dead leaves of the season over the cobblestones. She put her hand in her jacket and felt around for a piece of notepaper. It was Daan's list. Twenty-one relatives and friends needed a place to hide. He'd begged her to help them the last time she'd visited her grandmother. It would take more positive thinking than Otto and Herman were showing right now to find places for them, although Herman had a point. It was tough to hide people in a flat landscape. A Jew in France stood a better chance. She'd counted on the Group of Eight to help her find people ready to take in a Jew. She was not encouraged.

"I have a list of people here," she said, turning to face them, "who are urgently in need of a place to hide. Who is willing to find places for them?"

Dirk raised himself from the floor and walked over to the window, sitting on the wide sill next to her. The sky looked restless behind him with clouds chasing one another over a horizon of tiled rooftops. Feeling his body leaning into her lifted Anna's mood.

"Nobody should feel forced into this," he said. "It's dangerous work."

Otto was still leaning against the doorframe. He ticked ash from his cigarette into the cup of his left hand. A strand of sleek dark hair fell over his forehead. He might be taken for Hitler if he sported a square moustache under his nose. His eyes were an unusual light color, like Hitler's. "We stacked our hands in Loosdrecht," he said.

Piet was the first to sign up. "Tell me what to do," he said.

"Who else?" Dirk asked.

All of them raised their hands. Anna took the list out of her pocket and put it on the carpet. They studied it, each looking for names and places closest to their hometowns. Daan's family and friends were spread out over the country.

"This is urgent," Dirk said. "Classes don't start till next Monday. Let's go and find places for them. We'll check again after the weekend."

Anna decided not to go home. None of Daan's relatives lived in the Arnhem area. Besides, she was wary of involving her parents. Vader might be helpful, but she didn't see Moeder getting involved with hiding Jews. From whomever Maarten had got his audacity, it was not from his mother. Although Moeder could put up a good front, like the time Dirk walked in on the family scene after her cousin was executed, Anna didn't perceive her as the best candidate for dealing with risky situations. Moeder hadn't inherited Oma's unflappable nature. Right or wrong, that was how she felt. So, Anna told Betty she would visit her grandmother in Ede for the weekend. She called Walter Vlaskamp at the parsonage to see if he would meet her at the station; she had something important to discuss. He gallantly offered to take her out for lunch.

"On Saturdays, ministers write their sermons, you know," he teased her on their way to a small restaurant at the edge of town.

"I can give you enough fodder to write a scathing sermon, if that would help."

"That sounds ominous, Anna."

A waiter came up to their table. They ordered coffee and pea soup with a slice of buttered pumpernickel bread on the side. There were few other customers. One older couple sat outside on the terrace, sipping coffee, their faces turned to the sun, soaking in the last rays of summer. At that moment, it seemed blissful to Anna to soak in the sun and not be burdened with worries about how to outfox the Gestapo.

"How are things with you, Walter? How long do you think you will stay here?"

"I don't know. Dominee Bosma is very sick. He has some respiratory problem. Poor man. He has a wife and three children. The deacons want me to stay on. It puts me in a delicate position, since I stay at the parsonage. I'm looking around for a room to rent, but the Germans of the military base here have taken all that are available."

"I know," Anna said. "The local commandant wanted to take over my grandmother's place."

"Really? How did she get out from under that?"

"That's a long story. But, you know, Walter, I think she'd rather have you in her home than German officers."

Walter looked up in surprise. "I never thought of that. I have to admit, Anna, I was surprised to find out the lady in the castle was your grandmother!"

"Oh?"

"Well, uh, you know," he stammered. "You are so ... down-to-earth. Not a hair on my head had associated you with such grandeur."

She laughed. "Oma is more down-to-earth than I am. You will see."

After the waiter put down their bowls of soup, she told Walter about Daan's list of names, and how the Group of Eight was spending the weekend looking for places to hide those Jews in their hometowns. It was urgent.

"I have to be honest, Walter. It's the reason I wanted to meet you. It's too crowded with Germans in the Western provinces. You trip over them. I think it is safer in this area, even though the army has taken over the base. But the army is not as zealous as the Gestapo. That's how I thought of hiding Daan and his family on a farm near my grandmother's place."

Walter gave her a pensive look. He took a piece of pumpernickel bread and dipped it into the pea soup. Anna knew she was asking a lot. Walter knew better than anyone how suspicious the Gestapo could get. He might still be under surveillance. Besides, he was a stranger here. Most farmers in this area belonged to the Gereformeerde Kerk, not the more liberal Remonstrantse Kerk, so he didn't have an easy way in to ask strangers for a huge sacrifice. But she couldn't think of another plan.

"Let's see how things turn out, Anna. I will do what I can. It's a good cause. But don't get your hopes up too much."

Walter walked her back to the station. Without a bike, there was no easy way to get to De Koppelburg, and he still had to write his sermon. It wasn't fair to ask him to bring her there. She took the train back to Utrecht, where she had stabled her bike at the station.

Betty was scrubbing the sink when she came in through the kitchen door. She seemed startled to see her. "I didn't expect you back today," she said.

"Hello, Betty. It's been a long day. I thought for once I would try to be ahead and get ready for Monday's classes."

"Jan hasn't come home yet," Betty said. It wasn't a casual remark.

"But it's Saturday. He doesn't work on Saturdays, does he? Maybe he went to that soccer game everyone was talking about."

"No. I don't know. Maybe he did."

Even as she spoke, Jan maneuvered his bike through the gate in the fence that enclosed their small backyard. On the carrier over the back wheel sat a large canvas bag. Jan had all he could do to carry it in as Betty opened the kitchen door for him. Anna caught a look between the two of them that made her feel unwanted. She reached out to help get the package in, but Jan refused her help. He passed her by and started up the stairs.

Anna talked to Betty for a few minutes. She told her how beautiful the fall colors were in the woods surrounding Ede, but Betty didn't react, so Anna decided to go upstairs and get organized. Jan stood in the middle of the remodeled room. He closed the door as she walked by. The sequence of events unsettled her. What was in that large package? Why were Jan and Betty so secretive? They'd never acted this way before. Were they hiding something?

As she sat at her desk that evening, she heard voices in the hallway and footsteps coming up the stairs. The door to the new room opened and closed. She heard muffled voices. Moments later, the same door opened again, and somebody went downstairs step by step, scraping something over the railing. Anna was curious and peeked into the hall. A man with a black cap was halfway down the staircase with a wide box in his hands. Jan was still upstairs and was stuffing money into a large purse. He did not look pleased that she was a witness.

"I thought I heard something," she said.

"That's just a friend of mine visiting," Jan said. "Sorry to disturb you."

"That's all right. It just didn't sound like you." She laughed. "You always *run* up and down the stairs!"

Jan shrugged. He looked self-conscious. Back at her desk, Anna pondered what could be in that large package they obviously didn't want her to know about. Could it be that Jan dabbled in the black market? It wasn't illogical in a time of war that ordinary citizens would try to get food outside of the strict system of rationing that had been imposed on them. That kind of trading was called bargaining. But Dirk had told her about a black market that went beyond bargaining, where people made good money off their fellow citizens. It had become a cynical way to make a living. She thought of Hendrik, who, in contrast, risked his life to save Jews from deportation. She hated to think of Jan in a negative way. He had always seemed too patriotic to take an illegal profit. But if not the black market, what else? Why the secrecy with large packages and money going from hand to hand?

God, let it not be true, was Anna's last thought before she dropped off into sleep.

Only Piet and Carla reported success. Carla's parents offered to take in the couple that lived in Breda. They knew them vaguely, it turned out. The husband and wife owned a camera shop two streets over. Anna was pleased, but also surprised Carla's parents would take the risk, considering the police station was directly across from their house.

"My mother says that sometimes you're better off doing clandestine things right under the nose of the police," Carla said. Patients went in and out all the time. The police wouldn't be able to keep track of everyone who came and left.

Piet returned triumphantly as well. He'd visited with an uncle, who'd recently retired from government service and had bought a stand-alone house at the edge of the city. He raised and trained German shepherds for a hobby. He and his wife would take the risk and house a couple. "My German shepherds will protect them," he'd said with a laugh. His uncle had even seemed excited about the prospect.

Herman was disappointed in his parents. They had wondered if he was in his right mind when he suggested their cottage in Loosdrecht might make a good hiding place. A house that stood empty except for the summer months would attract attention if it were suddenly occupied year round.

Emmy ran into a different kind of trouble. She'd visited an elderly couple on the list, close to her parents. They didn't want to leave their home. They hadn't received a notice from the Gestapo, so as far as they were concerned, there was no threat. The idea that they would be forced to leave their home seemed preposterous to them. Emmy had told them of the trains that left at night for

Westerbork, the transit camp Piet had discovered. They hadn't read about it in the papers, they said. Small wonder with the Germans controlling the news, Emmy said.

"They live in a nice house in a nice neighborhood," she went on. "I can't blame them for not wanting to move out. But how do you make people do something they really do not want to do? I said I would check back. I didn't leave my address."

Otto's hometown was Rotterdam. He discovered that his city was in a severe housing crisis. Everywhere he visited, homeowners had taken in people who no longer had a roof over their heads. After the bombardment, every house still standing was crowded with victims. Nobody was looking for more refugees, Jewish or otherwise.

"I was fishing behind the net," Otto said. "It was pretty depressing."

Of the twenty-one names, they could only strike off four: two couples.

"What do we do now?" Emmy asked.

"Don't be discouraged," Dirk said. "We have various possibilities in the pipeline. And don't forget. All people involved have to make some life-or-death decisions. They need a bit more time than we were willing to give them."

Neither Dirk nor Anna divulged any information about how they'd spent the weekend. It was assumed they'd done their bit for finding places.

Carla passed around mugs of surrogate tea, and Anna carried hers over to the window. Before she sat down on the windowsill, she noticed a sleek car parked across the street. The heavy oak front door of the house across the street opened, and a German officer stepped out, looking smart in an ankle-length leather overcoat. A soldier-chauffeur jumped out of the car, saluted with his arm raised in the Heil Hitler salute, and held the passenger door open. The officer saluted back and nestled himself inside. Anna chilled at the sight and stowed what she had witnessed away in her mind without sharing it with the others.

The get-together broke up shortly afterward. Anna left with a heavy heart.

CHAPTER SIXTEEN

Walter – Fall 1942

Walter sat behind a desk that didn't belong to him, writing a sermon for a congregation he hardly knew. It felt like violating someone else's space, although he had been invited to fill that space and take over from a pastor who seemed much loved by his congregants. The outpouring of compassion for the pastor's wife, when it became known Dominee Bosma had fallen victim to tuberculosis and been admitted to a sanatorium, testified to the man's popularity. Walter faced the task of filling the shoes of a man who wore a size larger than his own. What kind of a man was the owner of the comfortable desk chair he was sitting in? A picture of what he assumed were Dominee Bosma's parents stood in front of him. From a silver frame, they looked into the world with trust and confidence. Salt-of-the-earth kind of people.

Walter looked around the room. How better to judge a man than by the books he owned? One shelf was filled with classics, like Shakespeare's plays and Tolstoy's *War and Peace*. More space was given to modern literature and avant-garde theology. Colorful begonias brightened the wide windowsill, and a reproduction of Rembrandt's *The Good Samaritan* hung on the wall. He'd been struck by it the minute he walked into this room. Was it God's way of signaling that giving one sermon wasn't enough to motivate people to protect Jews?

There was a shy knock on the door. Walter rose to open it. In the hallway stood the eldest of the Bosmas' three young children. This one was Bram, and he was five years old. Walter looked down and Bram looked up.

"Can I come in?" he asked.

"Of course," Walter said.

"This is my father's room, you know."

"That's right, and it will always be your father's room."

"But you're not my father and you are here," Bram said, leaning against the desk.

"When your father returns, he will be sitting in this chair. And I won't."

The boy thought this over.

"When is Father coming back?" he asked, a frown forming on his pristine forehead.

"When he's better," Walter said.

"Will that be soon?"

"Come and sit in my lap, and we will pray together," Walter said, and lifted him up. They settled into the comfort of the desk chair. Walter pressed the boy's slight body against his own and folded Bram's hands into prayer.

"Dear Lord, we pray that you will make Bram's father better soon. As soon as possible, because we miss him so very much. Amen."

They sat quietly. There was another knock on the door, this one more resolute.

"There you are!" Mrs. Bosma said to Bram. "I looked all through the house for you."

"We prayed together, Mama," Bram said, and jumped down from Walter's lap. "God will bring Father back soon."

Mrs. Bosma, who looked to be in her early thirties, settled her one-year-old daughter on her left hip. The little girl grabbed a strand of her mother's dark blond hair, which fell in curls to her shoulders. Walter admired her grace and quiet courage. The last few weeks would have been enough to break anyone's spirit.

"Bram," Mrs. Bosma said, "go downstairs. Riet is waiting for you with hot chocolate." Bram was out the door in a wink.

"I'm sorry he disturbed you, Dominee Vlaskamp, but he knew that if he knocked on the door, he would be let in. That was the rule with his father."

"That's quite all right," Walter said. "Maybe this might be a good time to talk about how to arrange things. It seems to me you should keep living here and wait for your husband to get better. This parsonage is home to your children. Staying here would be less disruptive for you."

Mrs. Bosma walked over to the window and looked out on the street. "We've lived here for almost six years," she said. "You are very considerate, Dominee Vlaskamp, to offer this possibility. My parents are in the Dutch East Indies. The way I left it with my husband was to ask my in-laws if I could move in with them."

"Where do they live?"

"In Amsterdam."

"That would be quite a switch for the children. Besides, I wouldn't advise anyone to move in with in-laws. You stay here, Mrs. Bosma. I can find a place to stay close by. I am single and my needs aren't great."

"You are very generous, Dominee Vlaskamp."

"Please, call me Walter."

"I will, only if you call me Ruth. I appreciate your offer, but I don't know how the deacons will react." She shifted the weight of her daughter onto her other hip. "Living in the parsonage is part of a minister's salary, and with the army base here, rental places are scarce. You may not be able to find one."

"A friend's grandmother lives in the area, and I will visit her soon. She may have an extra room. And as to the deacons, I will talk with them."

Ruth moved toward the door, and Walter got up to open it for her. He couldn't help noticing how pretty she was as she turned around. Looking into her face was like stepping into a patch of wildflowers. The bright, healthy color on her cheeks and the resolute look in her eyes bespoke a free and loving spirit. One more reason to find another place to rest his head, he told himself.

It took fifteen minutes to reach the front gate of Kasteel Koppelburg. The sprawling building looked imposing. Standing there with his bicycle in his hand, the idea of asking for a room seemed outrageous. If Anna hadn't brought it up, he would never have entertained it.

A butler opened the door. The baroness was expecting him. He was told to wait in the hall. As he watched the man stride away through the white marble hall, he took in the environment with a more careful eye than when he'd come unexpectedly to see Dirk and Anna. The portraits on the wall told of the castle's successive owners. There were no paintings of women in the row, yet he had a hunch that the most powerful in the succession of owners was awaiting him in the salon.

Baroness van Haersolte sat in an empire-style chair next to a tea table. Walter bowed slightly and took her outstretched hand.

"Dominee Vlaskamp, how nice to see you again. Anna wrote me you might be paying me a visit. Please sit down. How do you take your tea? I'm afraid I don't have a slice of lemon to put in. Lemons are off the market these days."

Walter sat down on a small couch across from his hostess. "Sugar will do, madam."

"Anna wrote that the minister you were filling in for has become ill. This must have consequences for you."

"Indeed it does. Dominee Bosma contracted tuberculosis and was moved to a sanatorium."

"Oh, dear. How unfortunate. I heard he was liked by his congregation."

"Yes, that is my impression as well. There was a great outpouring of sympathy."

"How old a man is he?" the baroness asked.

"I haven't met him, but I judge his wife to be in her early thirties."

Baroness van Haersolte picked up her cup and stirred the hot tea with a small silver spoon. She was clearly thinking over what Walter had just said. He took a sip of tea and waited.

"I am not familiar with the Remonstrantse Kerk. I belong to the Nederlands Hervormde Kerk," she said.

"Both churches go back to the time when Martin Luther wrote his challenging ninety-five theses in 1517," Walter said. "But churches never stand still. They evolve. They grow and split and grow again. A mirror of our fickle human nature, you might say."

The baroness looked up at him. "Do you consider that a good thing, Dominee Vlaskamp?"

"Actually, I do. If we think of God as our rock, we continuously move around that rock to find new facets, new ways to apply God's truth to the way we live, or vice versa."

"Hmm … That's an interesting thought. But whatever the differences between our churches, they both have deacons. And those deacons may have a lot to do with your immediate future." The baroness looked intently at him. Either Anna had already asked for the favor of a room in her house, or she was remarkably astute in correctly guessing the reason for his visit.

"The deacons have asked me to stay on till Dominee Bosma returns," he said.

"That's a logical decision on their part. Are you inclined to accept the position? Curing tuberculosis is a lengthy process, as you must be aware. And a cure is by no means assured."

Walter liked the way his hostess went straight to the heart of an issue. In a few well-placed questions, she had framed the situation he was in.

"I have told the deacons I will stay on as long as I'm needed."

"Do the Bosmas have children?"

"Yes, they do. Three. All under five years old." He wouldn't be surprised if the next question was where he would live. He was right.

"Does Mrs. Bosma have a place to stay while you live in the parsonage?"

"I have offered her to stay in the parsonage. I think she should not have to uproot the children. I am a bachelor. My needs are not great." He began to feel uncomfortable, because the moment of asking her for a favor had arrived. But the baroness spared him.

"Would you consider giving Klaas Voorne some company? It must be quite dull for him to live with an old lady." Walter saw the twinkle in her eye.

"That's extremely generous of you. Mrs. Bosma tells me it is hard to find a place to rent here. Of course, I would want to pay you."

"Turning over your food stamps is all I ask of you, Dominee Vlaskamp, and the pleasure of your company. I am sure the three of us will have interesting conversations. Living in a place like this may seem glamorous, but it can also be lonely."

On his way out, Walter ran into Klaas, who stood in the hall with an impressive stack of papers under his arm.

"Walter, how are you? Great to see you. How are things in the outside world?"

"Not as tranquil as in Kasteel Koppelburg. How are you adjusting, Klaas?"

"Amazingly well. Let me show you my office."

They entered a room with a wide desk in the center and bookcases lining three walls. The fourth wall was devoted to mounted deer antlers. The stuffed head that once belonged to a buck protruded into the room from its place of honor above the door. Walter walked over to examine a charcoal drawing in the making. It sat on a painter's easel off in a corner. "Who is the artist?" he asked.

"Oh, I am working on it in the evenings to pass the time."

"Are the evenings long?"

"Yes. After dinner, time seems interminable."

"Maybe I can help you get through them," Walter said. "I will be moving in shortly."

Klaas was ecstatic.

"Anna brought up the idea of me staying with her grandmother," Walter explained. "I would be closer to farmers who might take in Jews. She had a list of twenty-one people. Actually, it's the main reason I'll stay on in Ede."

"Did she also tell you those are my relatives and my parents' friends? I begged her. I am deeply touched. Thank you."

"Do you have any contact with your mother?" Walter asked.

"No. I don't want to jeopardize the situation. I wonder, can you do me a favor sometime? As a minister, it would be easier for you to visit Hendrik's farm. I'm anxious to know how she and David are doing."

"Once I'm moved in, I will," Walter said.

Walter had lived at Kasteel Koppelburg barely a week when Anna showed up. She'd called him at the parsonage and asked if he would meet her at the station. He'd trucked her on his bike through the woods, her legs dangling off one side of the baggage carrier she sat on and her hands holding firmly onto his waist. When he led her into the salon, the baroness exclaimed, "Anna! Since you became a student in Utrecht, I've had more surprise visits from you. I am delighted, but I am equally suspicious. I don't think I am the only reason for your coming."

Anna laughed. "Blame it on the war, Oma. I hope to God you're the only one who's suspicious. I came to bring the new Kennkarte. Nerve-racking! This was my first experience as a courier. Truly, I thought every German soldier I came across looked through me and knew what I carried."

She sat down on the couch next to her grandmother and leaned her head into the older woman's bosom. The flaming wood in the fireplace crackled and sent glowing particles up the chimney. The baroness put her arm around Anna's shoulders and stroked her hair. "The war is bringing changes into our lives," she said after a cozy silence. "Quite insidiously."

"I know. I thought I would be studying medicine in Utrecht. I am. But my conscience is pulling me into other directions, if you know what I mean."

"Yes. Do your parents have any inkling of this? Your mother visited a week ago, but we didn't discuss the war."

"No, I haven't told her. Nobody outside of you, Walter, and the Group of Eight knows anything about what we do. I think it's safer that way."

"I agree," Oma said.

Walter marveled at the complete trust between these two women. They treated each other as contemporaries. In what kind of incubator had this relationship been hatched?

Walter and Anna left for Hendrik's farm after tea. Bertien was in the yard, cleaning out a milk can with soap and water before the next milking. Anna introduced Dominee Vlaskamp, and Bertien took in the new man in the neighborhood with poorly hidden curiosity. News traveled fast here, even with farms spread out over hundreds of acres. Hendrik and Bertien belonged to a more orthodox church, but they'd already heard of Dominee Bosma's troubles, and about the new minister living in the castle out of regard for the poor minister's wife with young children.

They were invited inside, where they found Mrs. Timmermans sitting at the kitchen table with a little girl in her lap, guiding the girl's hand, awkwardly clutching a pencil, over a sheet of paper. A box with coloring pencils stood close at hand. The domestic scene looked as natural as a grandmother entertaining her grandchild. Walter was struck. He'd imagined her tucked away somewhere in a closet, out of sight.

"Hello," Anna said, careful not to call the woman by her real name. "You look very cozy."

Mrs. Timmermans had been forewarned of their coming. Oma had sent over a worker to Hendrik with a message in a closed envelope. A stranger would come to visit with Anna. Not to worry about it. Yet a flicker of fear showed in her eyes. She remained seated, as if letting go of the little girl would render her vulnerable.

"This is Dominee Vlaskamp, a good friend of Dirk," Anna said. "He is the temporary pastor of the Remonstrantse Kerk in Ede. Dominee Vlaskamp stays with my grandmother."

The woman's eyes lit up.

"Good afternoon, Mevrouw," Walter said, stepping up from behind Anna. "I bring you greetings from Klaas."

Mrs. Timmermans, soon to be renamed, put the girl on the floor and came to him with an outstretched hand. "How nice to meet you. Please tell me Klaas is well."

Walter didn't know if Bertien knew Klaas was her son. He chose his words cautiously. "Klaas asked me to say hello and to tell you he's doing a lot of drawing."

"Is he one of your pupils?" Bertien asked Mrs. Timmermans.

"Yes, he is, and a very talented one. Please give him my regards. Tell him I am drawing too, as you can see." She reached for the piece of paper on the table and held it up. "Right, Annie?"

The girl pulled at her dress. "Ouw," she cried. "Me too!"

Bertien scooped up her daughter and told Anna that *Ouw* stood for *Mevrouw*.

"Bless you. That's a beautiful name," Anna said. "Talking about names. I've brought some important documents. Instead of No-Name, you are now Geertrui van Es. Your son is Tom Velder." She pulled up her coat and undid some small hooks inside the coat's lining. She'd sewn them into the hem. Out came a light silk pouch. Geertrui fingered the Kennkarte gingerly.

"I know how much work went into this," she said, "A lot of careful work. I can't thank you enough, Anna. It feels very reassuring."

Anna asked Bertien if they could see the living situation for Geertrui and Tom. They entered a room off the kitchen that was probably only used for weddings, baptisms, and funerals, the only room with a carpet and upholstered chairs. Bertien moved a picture aside on the wall and reached for a tiny knob behind it. When she pulled on it, a flat door that looked like part of the wall, covered with the same flowery wallpaper, gave way to a room. The only source of light was from above, where a roof tile had been removed and replaced with a thick pane of glass. It was a very small room. On opposite sides were fold-up beds behind drawn curtains. They could be taken for shelves. Leaning against the third wall were two wooden chairs. There was no other furniture, just a small trunk. Walter assumed it held personal belongings of mother and son.

There wasn't the slightest hint this room was in use. Walter thought of the clothes he'd left hanging on the chair in his room at the castle; his toothpaste and brush on the table next to the sink. It wasn't messy by any means, but if the Gestapo opened the door of his room, they would know at once someone had slept there recently. It must take extreme care not to leave a trace of life. For a teenager to live this way must be hell.

Bertien said they had performed one drill. When Hendrik saw a visitor coming, whoever it might be, he was to go to the kitchen door and ring the brass bell. That gave the son, now called Tom, time to hide in the haystack and his mother to get into the little room, which she could close with a latch on the inside. It took barely two minutes. They reasoned that even when Bertien was working in the vegetable garden, Geertrui could take care of the hiding procedure herself when she heard the loud brass bell ring. The little girl always stayed with her mother.

"You've thought this all through," Anna said. "I am impressed. But what happens if Geertrui is in the barn and can't make it to this room?"

"Then she has to flee into the potty place at the end of the barn and stay there till we tell her to come out." Bertien looked pleased and smiled. The smile of an angel, Walter thought. It would take many more angels like her to hide the hunted.

Anna was quiet on the way back to her grandmother's. It was clear she wrestled with the reality of what it meant to be a Jew in hiding. They walked at a slow pace, avoiding the hardened ruts left by wagon wheels.

"How long?" she finally said. It was more a cry of agony than a question.

"As long as it takes to wear down the Germans."

"That can't come too soon, as far as I'm concerned. The thought that people like Geertrui and Tom have to live like this … I just can't stand it. What if it takes more than a year?"

Walter didn't answer. It was unanswerable. They stood at the side of a pasture. Two black ponies stopped their grazing and ambled over to the barbed wire fence. Anna stooped to pick some late autumn grass and held it out to them.

"I have a problem," she said as she scratched the forehead of one of the ponies, "and I wonder if you can help me."

"What's your problem?"

"Something weird is going on in the house in Utrecht where I live. Things aren't the same after the summer. I have a feeling the couple is hiding something from me." She told Walter of the remodeled room she wasn't allowed in, and of things in big bags being carried in, and a stranger coming and leaving with goods, and money being exchanged. It had happened a couple of times since she'd come back from vacation. "It's all very circumspect. I'm suspicious they're involved with the black market. And I don't want to be caught in the middle."

"Were you happy living there last year?" Walter asked.

"Oh, yes. They're very nice people. Good people, I thought. Betty is a retired governess with solid recommendations. That's how my mother found them. Jan still works."

"Have you told them you are hiding Jews?"

"No, of course not!" Anna looked at him, shocked.

"Then maybe they are doing something similar. Be charitable. These are strange times. The Germans may regard what the Underground does as illegal—and you are now part of the Underground—but we call it patriotic. As it says in the Bible: 'Judge not and thou shall not be judged.'"

"Now I feel like a fool," Anna said.

"You're not a fool. You're cautious, and that's not a bad thing. Be vigilant, but don't jump to conclusions too fast."

That night at the supper table, Anna asked her grandmother if she could think of more farmers like Hendrik who would be willing to hide one or more Jews.

"How many do you have in mind?" Oma asked.

"Around fifteen, but it could be less. Some of the Jews don't think it's necessary to hide. My friend Emmy tried to convince a couple, but they said the Germans wouldn't do a thing like that."

"If it hadn't been for Dirk, I would now be on a train to God knows where," Klaas said. "Dirk had to convince me. It seemed so totally incredible."

"Good thing he did," Oma said. "Klaas, let's look at the register of farmers tomorrow morning with Walter. Their histories will come back to me when I see their names in print. Then Walter can visit them on my behalf and see if they are willing."

Walter knew he was not only a stranger in these parts. He was a minister from a different Protestant strain than most farmers here. He prayed for courage and a hefty dose of good luck.

CHAPTER SEVENTEEN

Anna – Winter 1943

The year 1943 started out with temperatures below the norm and piles of snow that didn't want to melt. Housewives stood in line for food stamps with admirable persistence on poorly shoveled sidewalks, their feet frozen through their well-worn shoes and socks. A year earlier, Anna had also slogged through deep snow on the day she'd met Carla and Dirk for the first time. She didn't get to see them as much these days, as they had entered the hands-on phase of their medical studies, but the Group of Eight met at least once a week. Walter Vlaskamp had worked miracles. At least fifteen Jews surrounded Oma's place in a wide radius, and the Group of Eight had to find ways to provide them with false IDs and food stamps.

Anna's cheek scraped against a rim of ice on her pillow, and her breath rose like a plume. Before going to bed, she'd turned off the gas stove. There were too many stories about people found dead in their bedrooms because of gas leaks. She shifted under the sheets to find the warmest spot, and fought with the knowledge she would have to get out of bed right away and wash with icy water if she were to make it to anatomy class. She pulled the blanket tightly about her and dozed off. Images, thoughts, and fears scrambled into a weird scenario: Dirk was on a train with stolen food stamps. A man grabbed his coat and reached into its pocket. Dirk slapped him in the face. A Gestapo opened the compartment door and grabbed Dirk by the lapels of his tweed jacket, dragging him into the hallway. She yelled, "Dirk, no!" and kicked the soldier in his groin. Another soldier opened the exit door and threw Dirk off the train. "Dirk," she shrieked, and started to jump after him. "Don't," he yelled on his way down to the bed of gravel beside the tracks.

She woke with a start and threw off her heavy woolen blanket. She felt clammy, and her mind was still in her nightmare. But a calm voice in the hall on the other side of her bedroom door said, "Don't worry. I'll take care of it." She could swear it was Dirk's voice. With the image of him being thrown off the train behind her eyelids, Anna grabbed her morning coat and yanked the door open. There, in the hallway, stood Jan handing Dirk a very large package.

"What's going on?" she almost screamed.

Jan and Dirk looked mortified, shocked by her sudden appearance. Anna stood nailed to the floor, staring at them.

"I—I thought you were in your anatomy class," Dirk stammered.

How could Jan and Dirk know each other? Dirk had never set foot inside this house. Did it have to do with IDs for Jews or food stamps? Not likely. They wouldn't be in a package that size or that heavy. Dirk looked at Jan. What were they up to? Her thoughts were in turmoil. Walter's words about being charitable came to mind, but they were overruled by dread. Were they in black-market cahoots? Well, the three of them couldn't just stand there.

"What's in that package?" she demanded.

"I can't tell you, Anna. Please don't make me," Dirk said.

Those words cut through her heart. They were hiding Jews, they were taking on all sorts of risks that involved others, and he didn't trust her?

After an awkward silence, Jan spoke up. "These are illegal newspapers, Anna. I knew Dirk before he knew you. We've been distributing these papers for almost two years so people can get news based on fact. We used to distribute them from my printing plant, but it got dangerous. That's why I made the hobby room, so I could distribute them from a safer place. The fewer people who know about this, the better the chance we can continue. I'm sure you understand."

Of course! Jan was a printer. She should have guessed. She'd always wondered how Jan and Dirk could know facts nobody else seemed to know. By saying he couldn't tell her what was in the package, Dirk had shown his loyalty to Jan.

"Yes, I understand," she said.

Jan nodded to both of them and went downstairs. Anna drew up her morning coat, and then she burst into laughter.

"What's so funny?" Dirk asked, setting the package on the floor.

She pulled him into her room and flung her arms around him.

"All this time I thought Jan was involved in the black market. All those packages, and different people coming to pick them up at all hours. And then you stood there! In my train of thought, you were one of the takers."

"That wasn't a clever conclusion for a smart girl like you, Anna."

"I'm sorry, Dirk. I owe you an apology. How can I repay you?"

He looked around and saw the unmade bed. Smiling, he eased her down on the heavy blanket she'd thrown aside only minutes before. She fell back with her head on the pillow. Dirk sat down next to her.

"Just before I saw you, I woke up from a nightmare," she whispered. "I dreamed that the Gestapo threw you off a train, and I was going to jump after you."

"That sounds more compassionate than accusing me of dealing in the black market."

"I'm sorry, Dirk. When I saw you with that package, I was filled with dread."

"Anna, listen to me. This war will test us again and again. Our own integrity is the only constant. That's our shield against the woes of this war. Have faith in me. You can always be sure of my love."

How could she have doubted him, even if it was for only one second? Dirk was a rock. She felt tears welling up.

"I love you, Dirk." She was going to say more, but he covered her body and kissed her wet eyelids.

On the morning of March 6, 1943, the newspapers came out with fat headlines: the commander of the Legion of Volunteers, General F. A. Seyffardt, had been assassinated during the night. He'd been at home, answered the doorbell, and was shot point blank. It was the first liquidation by the Resistance since the start of the war, and the German authorities suspected a student had done it. The Legion of Volunteers was made up of young Dutch citizens who sympathized with the Nazis and fought alongside German soldiers at the Russian front. Patriotic students loathed them, and didn't hide their loathing.

The Gestapo took revenge by holding *razzias* at universities. They randomly rounded up students, hauled them off in open trucks, and threw them into jail without charges. Of the group of Eight, all but Emmy had witnessed students being taken away from classrooms. They gathered at Carla's place in a state of fear and confusion.

"Otto was closest to the door," Herman said, "so he was the first one they grabbed. They simply pushed the professor out of the way. I was in the back row. They took three students from our class. We were all flabbergasted."

"I hope they won't keep Otto as long as they kept Walter last year," Carla said. She was pouring tea into mugs, but her hand shook, and she spilled some of it on the counter.

"I don't think so," Piet said. "This is a big show. They want to scare us out of our wits."

"Does anyone know if Otto had anything incriminating on him?" Anna asked. She finger combed her hair in quick, repetitive gestures.

"Not that I know of," Dirk said. "I hadn't given him the food stamps to give to Walter yet."

It was oppressively quiet in the room. Anna stared at the painting above the sagging couch. It depicted the cathedral in Breda before staging had enveloped it. The soaring tower dominated the canvas, but the colorful market below caught her eye. The orange zinnias, the ocean smell of fresh fish, the bench in the castle's park, Dirk's passionate kiss … Her heart leaped at the memory. Why was she thinking of this now? Dirk sat across from her, his long legs stretched out over the carpet. A hole in the leather of his right shoe was beginning to show. He'd walked many miles to protect Jews. Like Walter, he aroused compassion.

"They're shining a bright light on students," he said. "We'd better keep a low profile."

"And out of sight for now," Herman said. He looked genuinely frightened.

Anna remembered with a shudder the time, not long ago, she'd seen a German officer step out of the house across the street. She decided again not to mention it. Instead, she said, "Carla, how about if you come with me to my place and spend the night? That way the men can stay here overnight."

The three men looked at Carla.

"That's fine with me," she said. "We'll come back tomorrow with breakfast."

"I'll join you for breakfast and bring newspapers," Emmy said.

"In that case, you may have to evict us," Piet said.

Otto reappeared a few days later, thoroughly disgusted with the Germans, the Gestapo, and the treatment he'd received. Like Walter, who'd never elaborated on his time in Het Oranje Hotel in Scheveningen, Otto didn't provide much detail. Carla opened a bottle of red wine she'd saved for a special occasion, to celebrate his safe return.

"If it wasn't for wanting to get my degree, I would get myself to England right now," Otto said. He jerked his head to push back his persistently falling forelock.

"That would be a hazardous undertaking, Otto," Herman said.

"There's more honor in climbing the Pyrenees to get there, than succumbing to brutal treatment in a concentration camp," Otto shot back. "I heard stories you wouldn't want me to repeat."

"Here, take another sip of wine," Carla said, and refilled his glass.

Otto looked at her with obvious affection. "You know what a man needs!" he said. Carla blushed.

"Our friend General Rauter is stocking up on hostages," he continued. "He ordered thirty of them to be executed in revenge. But the fact remains, it was the communists who were behind the murder of Seyffardt, and it was a student who fired the shot. That was my bad luck."

"Let's hope they'll leave us alone for a while," Piet said.

But the Germans didn't. They had a plan for students that created a watershed moment.

CHAPTER EIGHTEEN

Anna – March 13, 1943

I t was an odd sight, a large group of students seemingly frozen in place, staring at a bulletin board in the university's hall. Anna and Carla worked their way to the front. A posted message from Reichskommissar Seyss-Inquart ordered all students in the Netherlands to sign a declaration of loyalty. Students were to promise not to engage in plots against German occupiers, and to obey all orders and laws. Without a signed declaration of loyalty, a student was not allowed to attend classes.

They read it twice. It was Saturday, March 13, 1943. They were given until April 10 to sign the declaration. Twenty-seven days. The Group of Eight, perplexed and furious, gathered at Carla's place.

"Loyalty to the German Occupation?" Otto yelled. "Are they crazy? I have only one loyalty and that is to my queen and country."

"I thought the razzias were enough punishment for Seyffardt's murder," Piet said. "How strict do you think they'll be?"

"Germans are punctual," Dirk said. "They're like terriers when it comes to executing orders. *Ein Befehl ist ein Befehl.* An order is an order. Hitler has manipulated his people with that mindset. Look at what he made them do to Jews."

"Germans may have that mindset, but we don't," Carla said. "What kind of laws and orders will we have to obey?"

The words on the bulletin board began to sink in. Meanwhile, Carla brewed surrogate coffee, and they formed a circle on the floor, their fingers clamped around warm cups.

"What if we all refuse to sign?" Herman said. "What consequences would that have?" He leaned against the couch with his left arm around Carla's knees.

"I'm sure they've a plan already in place," Anna said. "They're not short on ideas when it comes to revenge."

"Never mind what the punishment will be," Dirk said. "It's the principle that counts. Let's think about that first. How will it make us feel to obey every rule and order the Germans come up with?"

He didn't press further. Dirk would never sign a piece of paper that would force him to be loyal to the Nazis. That was clear to Anna. Despondency hung over the room.

A few days later, obstinacy replaced despondency. The university's administration took a stand. "Sign the declaration," it urged. "It will be the only way to obtain your degree." But the student leadership reasoned differently. It issued a directive: "Don't sign! Whoever signs will be considered a deserter."

The Group of Eight got back together. "Consider this," Herman said. "What if their orders include enlisting in the German Army? We'll end up on the Russian front, side by side with that despicable Legion of Volunteers. Or, what if they tell us to work in their factories? If we sign that piece of paper, we'll have to go."

"Usually, when you sign a document," Piet said, "you have a pretty good idea what you're getting into, or what you'll get out of it. This feels like signing your life away."

"You well might," Herman said. "Trouble is, you might lose it either way."

"I'll let my conscience be my guide," Dirk said. "I would rather lose my life than sign." It didn't sound like a casual, top-of-the head remark.

Anna sank deeper into Carla's old couch and listened to the agonized chatter. She was also a student. The *Verordnung* couldn't be read as if it only applied to males. It stated "every student." If she wanted to become a doctor, she would have to sign. The muscles in her neck and shoulders tightened. The Germans weren't likely to send girls to the Russian front, she told herself. What could they have in mind for women? What should she do? Not sign and go back home? That would be bitter. It would be a cruel defeat of her ambitions. But what would signing say about her as a human being? That she allowed her ambitions to overrule patriotism? Could she live with that decision the rest of her life? Her desire to become a doctor tugged at her, but Dirk clearly didn't let that stand in his way. She heaved a sigh. Deep down, though, she knew what to do.

"To sign or not to sign," she said, after the chatter died down. "It's a moot point, really. Here we are, committed to hiding Jews. How could we possibly promise loyalty to the Nazis? We have already blatantly disobeyed the law. What kind of foolish hypocrites would we be?"

The Group of Eight made a collective decision. They refused to sign. April 10 came and went. Only 2200 students signed. Over 12,000 did not, among them 1800 girls. The Germans extended the deadline to the end of April. Scared by rumored threats, another 1500 students signed the loyalty declaration. What would the Germans do against the 75 percent of all students in the entire country that refused to sign? That question was on everyone's mind.

General Seyss-Inquart answered with a swift decision. He ordered the objectors to present themselves immediately at the *Arbeitseinsatz* bureau in Ommen, halfway to the German border. If they didn't show up, he promised the Gestapo would go after them.

The next hard choice was whether to show up at that German Bureau of Labor or to go "underground."

Faced with empty classrooms and out of sympathy with their students, all universities in the land decided to close their doors. General Rauter, the feared police chief, now had the task of rounding up thousands of stubborn young Dutchmen. The order was not aimed at female students.

Anna went over to Carla's place the day after the university closed. It felt like coming home from a funeral. Gone was the electric atmosphere, even as the familiar scent of cigarette smoke and beer hung in the curtains. The echo of male voices rang in her ears. *This part of my life is over,* she thought. While Carla brewed surrogate tea, Anna walked aimlessly from one end of the room to the other, her mind drowned in melancholy.

Carla held out a cookie jar. Anna reached inside, and instead of pulling out a wafer, she came up with a small triple-folded piece of paper beneath the top layer of cookies.

"What could this be?" She handed it over.

"No idea," Carla said, and carefully unfolded it. She frowned. "You'll have to help me figure this out."

"What does it say? Do you know who it's from?"

"I can only guess."

They looked at the scribbles. It had clearly been written in haste. *From now on, when you listen to Radio Oranje on the BBC and you hear these words,* Geef Carla een zoen, *you'll know I made it.* It was signed with the letter O.

Give Carla a kiss?

Anna looked up. "That's got to be Otto. Did you know he was in love with you? I always thought he had his eye on Emmy."

Carla's face reddened, and she looked away. "He never said anything, but I sensed he liked me. I have to admit, I like him too."

"Oh, my God, Carla. Let's figure this out."

"Do you remember," Carla said, "when he came back from the police station? He was very angry with the Germans. He said to Herman that if it weren't for wanting to get his degree, he would go to England. I guess he figured he might as well leave now."

"It sounds that way. It's like a tsunami came over us and swept all the men away," Anna said. "When I biked over, I saw only old men in the street."

Carla walked over to the counter, got the teapot, and refilled their cups. As she sat down again, the weight of her body shifted the couch pillows, and Anna rolled toward the middle against her. They sat in silence for a while with their arms around each other, struggling with the same questions.

"Have you heard anything from the boys?" Carla asked.

"Not a word. Do you think Otto went over the Belgian border alone?"

"I can't imagine Piet or Dirk taking that step. Herman maybe."

Anna chuckled. "Do you have more than one cookie jar?"

Carla threw back her head and laughed. She couldn't stop laughing. Tears streamed down her cheeks. It was infectious, and Anna joined in. They laughed until they forgot what they were laughing about. Carla got up to fetch a handkerchief.

"Oh, Lord, this is ridiculous," she said. "I like both of them."

"Time will tell which one you love," Anna said. "The war may give you plenty of time to sort that out."

"You know, I've always wondered how Dirk and you could be so sure of each other, in such a short time. In a flash, really."

"Neither one of us was looking for it. It just happened. I was drawn to him from the moment he stepped into this room. Hard to explain."

"You're lucky," Carla said, which made Anna wonder again if she'd snatched Dirk away from her. If so, Carla had been mighty fair about it. She had never dared ask Dirk why he came to Carla's room that snowy day. It was too risky. The fabric of a budding love is fragile and tears easily.

"There's a flip side, Carla. Now, I'm worried sick. Where is Dirk? What's he up to? You know as well as I do, he's not going to sit by idly. Can you imagine him hiding in a closet in his parents' attic?

He'll do something, and it will be dangerous."

She got up and walked over to the window. She wanted to shake off a creeping fear, but it had the opposite effect. A German staff car turned into the street and stopped in front of the house across from Carla's. The swastika sign on its bumper triggered an acute panic.

"Carla, come here." Her voice was hoarse. "I've seen that car before. Several times, actually."

The heavy oak door of the patrician home opened. An officer of high rank walked out with a leather briefcase under his arm.

"My God, I never knew that," Carla said. "Why didn't you tell me before?"

"I didn't want to scare anybody. There was no reason to. Now, it's different. I'm afraid for the boys. They should not come here."

The officer—this time without an ankle-length coat over his uniform—settled in the backseat. Who else over there could be spying on the houses on this side of the street? Goose pimples crept up her arms.

They returned to the couch. Carla had lost color in her face. "If I stay here, I will create a trap for Dirk, Piet, and Herman."

"We have to make some radical changes," Anna said. "The university is closed. So, what do we do? Go back home?"

"That feels like defeat. I love my parents, but what am I going to do in Breda?"

"And what am I going to do in Arnhem?"

They sat quietly. Carla drummed her fingers on her thigh.

"You know," she said. "The university isn't the only place we can study. We could become accountants!"

"Can you think of something more exciting? Our neighbor at home is an accountant. My brother nicknamed him The Pencil because he always had a pencil behind his ear. The dullest man I know."

"We could become nurses. They just might love to have two medical students for nurses."

"Hmmm. Interesting idea," Anna said. "But the first thing we should do is put out a note to the boys not to come here. Do you have their addresses?"

"Yes, I can come up with those. But we have to make sure they can find us. If not here, where?"

"How about giving them my address? Better yet, why don't I ask Jan and Betty if you can move in with me till we find out if we would be accepted at a hospital that trains nurses? What do you think?"

"Would they take me in?"

"Let's go find out."

They put on their coats and got on their bikes. Spring was trying to make its way past the bitter winter. The trees stood out like skeletons against a restless gray sky, but the tulips were ready to bloom. A faint promise of changing seasons briefly lifted Anna's spirits.

They found Betty in the kitchen dressed in a rubber apron with her hands in a washtub. She was about to lift it onto the gas stove to boil the laundry. Anna and Carla took the handles of the heavy tub and placed it on the burner for her.

"Do you remember my friend Carla Vlaskamp, Betty? She stayed overnight once."

Betty asked Carla if she was related to Dominee Vlaskamp, whom Anna had worried about so much. It made for a good introduction. Betty knew why Walter had been arrested. These days it was important to find out what "side" a stranger was on. Carla passed the test without uttering a word.

Betty took off her apron and invited them to the living room. They filled her in on the situation of the university closing and finding out that an SS officer lived across from where Carla rented a room; and how anxious they were that "the boys" might walk into a trap if they came to her door, since that was the place where they always met. Betty sat with her hands folded in her lap and listened quietly, settling their roiled mood. When they were done talking, she asked if they'd thought about what could be done.

"We want to stay in Utrecht," Anna said. She told of their half-baked plan to become nurses. They still had to investigate how to go about it. Meanwhile, could Carla stay here with her?

As she talked, Anna realized she was making far-reaching plans without consulting her parents, but she couldn't bring herself to ask them for their advice. The memory of discussing her future with her mother two years ago was still fresh in her mind. She didn't want to go back in time, especially not about becoming a nurse. At twenty-one, she could set her own course. And she would.

Betty told Carla she was welcome to stay if she could make do with sharing Anna's room. It wasn't big, but it would give them time to figure out what to do next, she said.

When Jan came home from work, he found Carla and Anna in the kitchen peeling potatoes and carrots. A worried look crept over his face, and Anna hurriedly told him the university had closed. He frowned.

"Where is Dirk?" he asked, ignoring Carla's presence.

"I wish I knew. This is Carla Vlaskamp, Jan."

He shook her hand absentmindedly and moved on to the living room. He seemed more relaxed later at the dinner table.

"I take it neither of you signed that loyalty declaration?"

"That's right. Dirk didn't sign it either. We haven't seen him or any of the boys we know since they were told to go to Ommen. We assume they all went underground."

"That's pretty serious," Jan said.

Anna understood his worry. He depended on daring young men. From now on, he might have to depend on daring young women. As Anna saw it, their immediate future as couriers was set.

Jan brought a cot into Anna's room. It shrank the room to half its real size.

"You know," Anna said into the dark that night, "you could have stayed in your comfortable room downtown. All we had to do is let the boys know they should not come there."

"True," Carla said. "But it didn't seem like the same room anymore. Not without the boys and not with a high-up officer across the street. Most of all, it feels a lot better to be together."

"I agree," Anna said.

CHAPTER NINETEEN

Dirk – Early May 1943

Dirk didn't have a doubt in his mind about what he would not do. He would never give the people at the labor bureau in Ommen the pleasure of seeing him appear at their desk. Instead, he decided to risk taking a train home and have a talk with his father. The Gestapo could not possibly arrest thousands of students in one day, even in a few days.

He ran into Otto at the station. "Where are you going?" he asked as they strolled over to the ticket counter together.

Otto stood still for a moment and whispered, "To England."

Dirk was not surprised. Otto was a man of action. Simply waiting for the war's end — to sit it out in somebody's basement or attic — was not his way. If it took a fight to set his country free, he would join the ranks, preferably with a weapon in his hands. Dirk had considered that route as well, but rejected it. To leave it to Anna to take care of the Jews, to let down the people who bravely hid them, no, that would be less than honorable. There was plenty to do right here and now.

"Maybe I can help. Buy yourself a ticket to Den Haag," Dirk said.

Otto looked him in the eye and nodded.

Dirk weighed if he should take Otto straight to his father's office, but that was like putting two white eggs in a coal bin. The numerous Nazis in the immediate area would take one look at two strapping young men like Otto and himself and send them off to a labor camp. Better to go home.

The kitchen smelled of vinegary sauerkraut. His mother was mashing boiled potatoes in a large pan with the full force of her slender arms. She stopped to embrace her son and shook his friend's hand. His father didn't ask for an explanation when he found a stranger sitting next to his son at the dining room table. Otto was accepted as a matter of course, and the conversation was kept neutral. It must happen all the time, Dirk thought. Otto's presence gave him a peephole into how his parents' life had unfolded in wartime. They didn't ask unnecessary questions. They drew their own conclusions, always vigilant.

After dinner, his father invited Dirk and Otto to his study. He chose a pipe from a small rack on the wall and stuffed it with tobacco, taking his time doing it. He leaned back in his leather chair and looked directly at Otto. The neutral tone of the dinner conversation was dropped. Mr. van Enthoven zeroed in on their new status: students turned out on the street.

"Are you a medical student as well?" he asked.

"I am studying veterinarian medicine, Mijnheer."

"You were, but no longer," Mr. van Enthoven said. His eyes followed the smoke that curled up from the pipe's bowl. "This goes for both of you. What are your plans?"

"We refuse to go to Ommen," Dirk said.

"Of course. That's the first step. What's next?"

Otto took out a pack of cigarettes from his breast pocket and asked if he could smoke. Mr. van Enthoven pointed at his own pipe and smiled.

"For some time I've wanted to go to England," Otto said, "but not until I'd finished my studies. Now the decision has been made for me. I want to join the army. Hiding is not for me."

"Where do you live? Are your parents aware of your plans?"

"My parents live outside of Rotterdam. My father owns a shipyard there. He builds river barges. But I haven't been home since the university closed."

"I see. Wouldn't you rather join the navy? You must have spent your youth on the water."

"When the war started, I was called up for service in the army. Since the fighting was over in five days, the experience was brief, of course, but it taught me a few things about battle. And I don't think it will be the navy that liberates Holland. The Allies will need Dutch boots on the ground when the time comes."

"Good point. So, you want to get to England. Have you thought that through? How will you get there?"

To Dirk, the conversation sounded like an interview. An interview for what? he wondered. His father never lacked a purpose or a plan.

"The honest answer is no. I know I will have to go through Belgium, France, over the Pyrenees, make my way to Portugal, and hope to catch a ship to England. I know the way, but not the means."

"Do you have connections to the Underground?"

"No, sir, I don't."

"You won't get very far without them, Otto," Mr. van Enthoven said. He relit his pipe and puffed hard to keep it going. "What's your plan?"

"I want to seek contact with the Underground."

"Hmm, you seem to have a clear head. I can help you, if you promise to carry out orders."

"That's what it's all about, it seems to me," Otto said. "Take orders and give orders. All at the right time."

"That's the idea." Mr. van Enthoven leaned forward in his chair and lowered his voice, although, as far as Dirk knew, there was no one in the house he couldn't trust. "I need an important message to go to England. Do you think you could take that on?"

Otto didn't hesitate. "Yes, sir."

They spent the rest of the evening developing a plan.

A steel barge lay moored in a backwater harbor of Rotterdam, ready for a trip to Maastricht to take on coal from the mines in Holland's most southerly province of Limburg, which hung like a sack from the other provinces, fitting narrowly between Germany and Belgium. The skipper stood on the gangplank and took off his flat cap when he saw two young men approaching. Like himself, they were dressed in heavy corduroys and black wool sweaters.

"Welcome aboard, Otto," the skipper said. "Ready to sail?"

"We're ready if you are," Otto said. "This is my friend Henk." He pointed to Dirk, who'd been given a new name and a new ID. They tossed their duffel bags onto the deck.

"Come meet the wife," the skipper said.

Underneath the pilothouse were living quarters, cozy with white lace curtains and red geraniums in the windows. A middle-aged woman stood behind the sink in the galley, washing dishes. She turned around and wiped her hands on her apron.

"Hello, Otto," she said. "This your friend?" She shook Dirk's hand. "Welcome. Coffee?"

It was a cool morning, and it felt good to hold a hot mug. It might be spring, but biking through a heavy fog had chilled them to the bone.

"You can sleep in the bow," the skipper said. "There's coal dust, but it's safer. We'll take off in half an hour."

"We'll help you," Dirk offered.

"Not now. Don't show your face on deck. The Germans are a suspicious lot. They're forever expecting an English submarine to turn up in the harbor. Anything that looks out of the ordinary raises their curiosity. And I suppose you don't want to call attention to yourselves."

The skipper and his wife left the living quarters. Dirk looked at Otto. "Don't tell me this woman is going to send this ship sailing down the river?"

"That's precisely what she will do. Typically, a man-and-woman team operates a barge this size. It's their home, their job, their life, all in one."

Dirk walked over to a porthole, pushing a geranium pot out of the way so he could watch. The skipper loosened the ropes front and back, quickly walked up the gangplank, and pulled it up. Then he climbed to the pilothouse and took over the steering from his wife. The diesel motor roared, and Dirk could feel the ship pull away from shore. A shiver traveled through its rump as it was made to change direction, the stern now pointing eastward. Dark water reflecting the gray sky churned into bubbly circles below the porthole. Gradually, a devastated cityscape came into view. Hitler's infamous bombardment had turned the once thriving harbor into a sad heap of rubble. A single church tower dominated the city's broken skyline — the last man standing.

"When I see this," Otto said, "I am doubly motivated to get to England."

Dirk nodded.

The barge picked up speed, leaving the harbor behind. Dirk joined the skipper in the pilothouse. The displacement of water rippled over low grassy banks. Farther back, dikes protected the hinterlands from flooding. The pastures were divided by *sloten*, narrow canals that regulated the water level with help from windmills. They acted as natural fences. Cows and sheep weren't tempted to jump over water to graze on the other side. The landscape gliding by was familiar from the biking he'd done as a teenager, but it looked different seen from a ship. How bizarre that instead of studying medicine, and just as he was putting dry science into practice, he was to sleep in a dusty coal bin on a barge. The recent turn of events was unsettling. Covert work might be more thrilling than studying medicine, but the day the university closed, his dream of becoming a doctor had gone up in smoke. In the dirty smoke of a world on fire.

The Nazis were now in control of his future. The choices they offered ranged from becoming a laborer to joining the ranks of able young men in hiding, forced to waste the formative years of their lives. What was to become of a country that sidelined its upcoming generation? Instead of a healer, he was invited to be a laborer in a war machine that spewed bullets, guns, and tanks. His anger at the Nazis had evolved from their treatment of the Jews to enfold his future as well.

His mother had understood his rising anger. Her reasoning was not unlike the advice the baroness had given Anna. "What are you ready to defend, Dirk?" she'd asked. "Compassion led you to medicine, I know, but you can turn it into passion for your country. It might help you swallow this bitter pill of losing your right to study. Turn your anti-Nazi feelings into pro-Dutch defense. Our country has a long history of fighting for freedom. You know that."

It was good advice. He was all for fighting for freedom. He just wished it hadn't been such an abrupt transition from medicine to full-time Underground work. What he was asked to do on this trip required skill and more risk than he'd taken before.

It gave him comfort to watch the skipper turn the wheel this way and that. It was busy on the river, and the man was agile in setting his course. With enviable self-confidence, he evaded other barges. A curved pipe hung from his lips, and with a graying beard of about two inches in length, he looked the part of the quintessential sailor.

"How long have you known Otto?" Dirk asked.

The skipper, whose name was Arnold, said, "For as long as he's lived."

"So, you know his family well."

"For sure. Good people," Arnold said.

"Interesting that Otto chose to become a vet instead of a shipbuilder, like his father."

Arnold's eyes were on the river, his hand on the wheel. "His older brother is the one interested in his father's business. Otto was always busy with animals, inseparable from his dog. He had rabbits and goats as well. A quiet kid. Went about his own business."

"Is it safe yet," Dirk asked, "to go on deck and get a breath of fresh air? We could scrub or do something useful." He didn't have a handy vocabulary when it came to parts of a ship.

"This is a busy area," Arnold said. "The whole seaboard is under German scrutiny, and we're not far enough inland. For now, I wouldn't go on deck till it's dark."

Dirk maneuvered down the narrow staircase to the living quarters below. The skipper's wife had poured Otto a cup of coffee, and she stood with the blue enamel coffee pot ready to pour one for Dirk. When Otto asked when they would anchor, and if there would be a post office there, she said it wouldn't be till they'd gone through the lock at Andel.

Dirk and Otto climbed on deck at dusk and sat down on the bulkheads over the hold.

"Why are you so anxious to find a post office, Otto?"

"When I came home, I found a letter from Carla."

"From Carla? What did it say?"

"She said we should not come back to her place. A high-up Gestapo officer lives across the street, it turns out. Carla moved in with Anna after they watched him being picked up by a staff car."

"That's sweet. They want to protect us."

"Didn't you get a letter from Anna? Carla said they were warning Piet and Herman as well."

"That probably arrived after I left Den Haag to come to your parents' home. Actually, I don't even know if Anna has my parents' address."

They dropped the subject. Otto took out a cigarette and lit up. In their black sweaters and black slacks, they blended in with the black paint of the barge. The days were lengthening. It had been a long wait for the day to turn into dusk.

"I should have brought more than one book," Dirk said. "I don't know about you, but I don't find it easy to be cooped up. It really gets to you."

"I'd already noticed that when I crammed for exams. Sitting in a chair with a book under my nose was not something I enjoyed."

As darkness fell, the barge moved at a slower pace. They walked over to the bow, where Otto lifted a hatch. Using a narrow rope ladder, they found themselves in a small area partitioned from the large hold. Otto turned on his flashlight, and they saw that Arnold had put their duffel bags on the berths. Steel was all around. Dirk ran his finger over the edge of what was to be his bed and it came up black. He was not fussy by nature, but studying his finger, he wondered what an X-ray of his lungs would look like if he spent too much time in this dark hole.

"I'll take the upper," Otto said.

They didn't bother putting on pajamas. Dirk took off his wool sweater but kept his slacks on. A small package his father had handed him when he left home to join Otto in Rotterdam sat in his right-hand pocket. It contained microfilms of German fortifications in and around Den Haag. Their order was to get them into the hands of British Intelligence. Otto knew something needed to be passed on, but not what and how. Dirk had decided to hang onto the package till they made contact. If something happened before they got to Maastricht, he'd rather be the one to get caught. Arnold's assessment of Otto was reassuring, yet he might buckle under pressure. Dirk didn't want to put his friend in that position.

The pitching of the barge as it cleaved its way through the river brought him closer to sleep than he'd expected. He worried about Anna, but the gentle rising and falling of the bow smoothed the sharp edges of his thoughts. He drew the rough blanket tightly around his body and pretended it was Anna. A deep sleep came over him.

Arnold had to switch the barge from one river to the next before he could get on a straight course to Maastricht. Dirk was in the pilothouse when a rather ugly medieval castle came into view.

Arnold didn't take his eyes off the busy wide river while he pointed out that they had passed Slot Loevenstein.

"The man who built that castle had a good head for business," he said. "Three provinces and two rivers come together here. He raised a toll for every ship that needed to pass by."

"It looks more like a prison than a castle," Dirk said.

"It was used for that too. Remember the story of Hugo de Groot?"

"Yes, the famous philosopher. He escaped from there in a book chest."

"Yes. Something to remember," Arnold said. "These days you have to think of ways you can dodge General Rauter's henchmen."

Dirk laughed, but he stored the hint, wondering if he'd ever have to use it.

When they arrived at Andel, Arnold maneuvered his barge into the lock chamber and waited for the water to rise before he could lock out on the other end. He and the lockmaster had gotten to know each other over the years of Arnold sailing back and forth between Rotterdam and Maastricht. The two men chatted, but the lockmaster had bad news. All Dutch soldiers who'd been released by Hitler as prisoners of war after the fighting was over in 1940 were ordered to present themselves for work in Germany. He said 200,000 men would have to leave their current jobs and trade them for working for the enemy.

From one lock to another — there were eight to go through — they formed a picture of what was going on. At an important factory — Stork in Hengelo — 3000 workers walked off the job in protest, soon to be followed by 4000 at nearby factories. This news went through the country like wildfire. A strike! Not only factory workers were affected by the new order, but farmers as well. They were furious and dumped gallons of milk into the canals — the milk that would otherwise be exported to Germany. Thousands of gallons turned the canals' water white. Miners in Maastricht refused to go down below. In anticipation of the transport of these many workers to

Germany, the Underground blew up the rails in key places. General Rauter ordered his infamous SS Police Regiment Todt to occupy the Stork factory in Hengelo with instructions to shoot anyone.

It went from bad to worse. Radio employees had gone on strike as well, but people didn't need the German-controlled distribution radio to spread the news. Stories flew around the country, as if on the wind. The strike emboldened even children to go into the street and sing outlawed patriotic songs. This could not last. General Rauter found himself without the tool of the radio to put the fear of God into the population. Instead, he ordered his troops to shoot and kill without giving prior warning wherever more than five people congregated.

"Not over their heads," he was reported to order. "Shoot to kill."

Otto and Dirk overheard the conversation. They praised themselves lucky for the coincidence that this strike and the brutal reaction to it happened while they were on the river, out of reach.

Arnold moored his barge in the small harbor of Maasbommel. It wasn't more than a cluster of houses, but it had a post office, a grocery store, and a small café. The town itself was further inland. Otto went off to mail his letter to Carla, the skipper's wife did her grocery shopping, and Arnold went to the café. Dirk joined him. It was a brown café with a veil of cigarette smoke, like the one in Amsterdam where he'd met the mystery man who'd given him identification cards for Daan's mother and brother. The men at the bar were burly. They could be farmers or ditch diggers. Arnold seemed to know them all, and it appeared to Dirk as if they had been waiting for him. They turned from their barstools and moved to a table. When Otto came through the door, Arnold introduced him and Otto by their newly acquired names, Henk and Ralph. He emphasized the fact they were both students.

The men seemed in a surprisingly good mood. With glee, they told of having gone over to the town hall of a nearby town that morning. They'd asked to see the mayor, a notorious Nazi sympathizer. They'd taken the portrait of the national NSB leader,

Anton Mussert, off the wall and smashed it over the mayor's head. Then they took him to the canal, threw him in, clothes and all, and told him he could come out if he removed his NSB insignia. He obliged, and the men fished him out of the canal's milky water.

Dirk wondered what they thought they'd accomplished with this prank. It was a clear sign of frustration. If the population was treated to random shootings and executions of innocent people, then the least they could do was dunk a traitor and make him look like a fool. Their anger had bubbled up like fizz in a soda bottle after a good shake.

From boisterous laughter, the conversation got serious. Arnold told them Ralph and Henk were on their way to St. Pietersberg in Maastricht. The men nodded. They seemed to know what that meant. Enough said.

It didn't take Dirk long to figure out that these robust men had formed a KP, a *Knokploeg.* A KP was a group of men that would fight its way into a municipal administration building to steal sheets with food stamps. These were then handed over to the Underground, who in turn got them to people who hid Jews. The groups had sprung up spontaneously in different parts of the country, and worked independently from one another. Dirk was familiar with their existence through his father, and lately had been on the receiving end of food stamps for the hidden Jews around the castle in Ede.

The man who looked to be the leader, based on age and physical strength, told Arnold he would have a good catch for him on his way back to Rotterdam.

"When do you expect to come by here again?" he asked.

"If we can hold to our regular schedule, we'll be back in ten days," Arnold said.

"I wouldn't count on it," another said. "There's trouble in Maastricht. The miners are on strike. It depends on how long they'll hold out. There's no telling how long this strike will last."

Otto looked over at Dirk and gave him a baffled look. Dirk

wondered how much Otto knew. Did he realize he was sharing the table with a KP? Was he worried about the miners' strike? Had he known about Arnold's involvement with the KP? Back when his father had asked Otto outright if he had connections to the Underground, Otto had answered with a firm no. Going to Maastricht had been his father's idea, but Otto had come up with the thought of traveling on Arnold's barge.

The meeting broke up. Otto, Arnold, and Dirk watched the men mount their bikes and go on their way. As dusk fell over the fields, they soon changed into large shadows.

"Those are some brave men," Arnold said.

That night, Dirk asked Otto if he'd known that Arnold was involved with the KP.

"Not at all," Otto said. "I hadn't seen much of him after he stopped working at the shipyard and bought his own barge. But am I surprised? No. He's one of the most unperturbed men I know. I trust him. I've known him all my life. That's why I thought of him to get us down to Maastricht."

At the fourth lock on the way, Arnold told Otto and Dirk to hide in their bunks down below. He had seen German soldiers several times before at that lock, and with the strike going on, they might be jumpy. He was right. While the barge was in the lock's chamber, waiting for the water to rise, Otto and Dirk overheard two soldiers talking to the lockmaster. When the water rose high enough, they jumped on board. Dirk could hear boots strike the deck. Loud voices ordered the skipper and his wife to come out on deck and open the bulkheads. They sounded like barking dogs. Apparently, Arnold came down and did as he was told. He started opening those closest to the pilothouse. Dirk heard footsteps coming closer, and through a narrow crack he could see the sweep of a strong lantern rake over the partitions. Instinctively, he pulled back his head. The footsteps of the soldiers sounded distinguishable because of the steel heel-protectors on their boots. Dirk could swear he heard the *squish* sound of Arnold's rubber boots overhead on top of the round lid that gave way to their bunks. He released the breath he'd been holding.

The footsteps receded. Commands were shouted to open the pilothouse. It took an eternity before they heard the voices again on deck. Since they'd gone through locks before, the sounds of locking out the other end were familiar. The barge's motor revved up, and Dirk felt the barge plowing down the river. After a long while, the skipper's wife came over and lifted the lid.

"You can come out now. We'll have some bean soup," she said. "Nothing much happened. But they took a smoked ham I had hanging in the closet. They asked me where I got it. I lied. God forgive me. A farmer had handed it to me behind the grocery store. Farmers are not allowed to sell outside the official market, you know. All the meat has to go to Germany. Oh, well, those young jerks are probably having a good meal of it. It would have gone well with the bean soup!"

She gave a short laugh. Dirk admired her. The woman knew how to swallow a loss.

They neared Maastricht without further incident. Arnold called Dirk and Otto into the pilothouse to strategize about how to get them from the harbor to the St. Pietersberg.

"You'll have to be extra careful. I don't know if the miners' strike is still going on, but we've seen how jittery the Germans are."

"Is it far from the harbor to the St. Pietersberg?" Dirk asked.

"It depends on where I let you off. The caves are south of the city. If I can get you off near the second bridge, you can walk it. Where I load coal is farther down the river, but that would be a long walk. Better keep it short. Once you're at the caves, you don't have to worry. No German dares to enter the caves. They don't get near that place."

"Will we look suspicious carrying our duffel bags?" Otto asked.

"Maybe."

"I will leave mine on board," Dirk said, "because I'd like to hitch a ride back to Rotterdam, if that's possible, Arnold?"

Arnold gave Dirk the address where he would moor the barge.

On the morning of the designated day, the skipper's wife served a hearty breakfast with eggs she'd kept hidden from the soldiers.

"I've enjoyed your company," she told them. "It gets lonesome down here. Take good care of yourselves. *God zij met U.*"

It was dark when they got to the bridge. Arnold slowed the barge and steered it close to the shore. He cut the motor. Otto threw his duffel bag on the grass. The barge lay still. Otto jumped off. Dirk followed. They hid under the bridge, behind its underpinnings.

Arnold waved from the pilothouse and gave a thumbs-up. The sound of the diesel motor revving up echoed against the bottom of the bridge. The barge slowly pulled away.

Otto picked up his small duffel bag and looked over at Dirk. "Let's go," he said.

Chapter Twenty

Anna – May 1943

The ding-dong of the doorbell startled them as they sat with their freshly brewed cups of surrogate coffee in Betty's living room. Anna glanced through the gauzy curtains and observed a man waiting to be let in. His fedora was pulled deep over his forehead, and he stared down at his shoes, as if he didn't want to be recognized. After Betty unlocked the front door, they strained to hear the voice in the narrow hallway.

"Doesn't that sound like Herman?" Anna said.

Carla opened the door to the hallway on impulse. "Herman! You found us." She threw her arms around him. Betty offered to make a fresh cup of coffee.

"You got my letter," Carla said as they entered the living room. "Was it in time? We were afraid you and the others would come to my room. Can you imagine how shocked we were when we saw a Nazi come out of the house across the street?"

"Thank you for the warning." The tone of his voice was slow and dull.

"We dashed over here," Anna said. "Now we're trying to make plans for doing something other than studying medicine."

He didn't react. She'd never seen Herman this way. Slumped in his chair, his eyes cast down and without their usual gleam, he looked the picture of a beaten man.

Betty came in with a steaming cup of coffee, placed it on a side table, and quickly withdrew, conditioned by years of moving discreetly around people engaged in conversations that were not her business. Herman took a sip.

Finally he spoke. "I haven't heard of women being sent off to labor camps. You study medicine. Not veterinary medicine. You're lucky."

"How can that be lucky?" Carla asked.

"Some medical students will be allowed to work in hospitals."

"What do you mean, some?"

"You have to be in your fourth year of medical studies to qualify."

"That means you and Dirk can work in a hospital, Carla," Anna said. Carla let herself fall into a chair, dumbfounded. "You must be kidding, Herman."

"So, where does that leave you, Herman? What are your plans?" Carla asked.

"I feel as if my life was never more than a house of cards, and then it got knocked over in one blow. As a first move, I went home to hide. Maybe I would live in the cottage on the lake in Loosdrecht. I just didn't know. Then General Rauter proclaimed he would imprison parents and confiscate their property if their sons went into hiding. That changed things. My parents are well-off. This last news scared them. Me as well."

"So?" Carla asked.

"I figure the Germans will find us eventually, anyway. They're already conducting razzias in Rotterdam and Den Haag. A van gets parked at the end of a street, and they go house to house to round up anyone who's hiding. Jews, students, laborers ducking work in Germany, people involved in the Underground. You name it, they grab them all."

"Don't tell me you're going to present yourself at an Arbeitseinsatz bureau?"

Herman cringed. He stared at his big hands. Anna imagined them examining a cow or running down a horse's leg. Carla's sharp tone had cut through him. Her lips were pressed into a tight line; her cheeks had turned bright red.

Before Herman could answer, she said, "My God, Herman, I hope you will think this through some more. What if the Germans are just threatening? "

"And what if they're not, Carla? I would hate to be responsible for getting my parents in jail. Or have them turned into paupers. That thought is unbearable to me."

It was on Anna's lips to say, "But how about your own life? How about your principles? Work willingly for the enemy? How could you?" But she kept it to herself. She wondered if her own parents, had she been born a boy instead of a girl, would hold their belongings in higher regard than their offspring. And what about Oma, who lived in a castle and hid a Jew? She had a whole lot to lose, including her life. Herman was in obvious turmoil. How far should they push him in the opposite direction? A decision either way would have huge consequences. But Carla didn't let it go at that. While Anna debated what her responsibility was toward a good friend, Carla came out strong.

"Herman. Listen to me. There are more angles to this. You will have to work for the enemy, and not in the best of circumstances from what I've heard." Her voice was rising. "Does that prospect jibe with your patriotic feelings?"

"Tell me what I can do for my country while I'm hiding in an attic somewhere." It was a taunt.

"You could come out of hiding once in a while, help the cause of hiding Jews and keeping them alive. Blow up a bridge. There are myriad ways to obstruct the enemy."

"I'll leave that to others. For me the overriding factor is that I want to protect my parents. We know what General Rauter is capable of. He doesn't hesitate to throw people in jail. Or, as we saw with the Jews, take all their belongings. How does that compare with the dubious success of me blowing up a bridge?"

"Don't you want to take any risks?" Carla shouted. At least she was kinder than calling him a coward to his face.

"I am taking my risks by going to the Labor Bureau, aren't I? As you said, I will not live in the best of conditions, and I don't know for how long. I am making this choice to protect my parents."

Carla sighed and slouched in her chair. "I guess that's for you to decide," she finally said. "Each of us has to come to terms with how much we're willing to sacrifice to rid our country from oppression. The question is, 'What is dearest to us?'"

Those last words filled the room with a dreadful silence. The conversation had come to this weighty moment. Listening to their sparring, Anna wondered if preaching ran in the Vlaskamp veins. She'd never seen Carla so feisty and righteous. But Herman's jaw was set, his mind made up. There seemed nothing they could do about it. He got up to leave. The nearly full cup of coffee stood on the side table. The clock on the wall ticked louder than ever as each of them stood, not knowing what to say or what to do. Anna furiously searched her mind for a luminous idea that could thwart Herman's decision at the last minute, but she couldn't come up with it. He'd rejected working for the Underground. Protecting his parents and their fortune was what he considered important above all else. He would be at the mercy of the Nazis, but so were they all, whether they worked for them or against them.

"Well, I'd better go," he said, and grabbed his hat from the back of the sofa. "It may be a while before we see each other again."

Carla stepped forward and gave him a firm hug. "Take care of yourself, Herman. You can still change your mind, you know. Please stay in touch."

He didn't hug her back. He turned around, pushed his hat down to his ears, and left the room in long strides. They heard the click of the lock and his fading footsteps in the street. Betty came back into the room and noticed the cup of coffee.

"What happened?" she asked.

Carla burst into tears. Betty reached out and pulled her to her bosom, adding Carla to the list of children she'd consoled over the years. Through sobs and tears, Carla told her Herman was making a terrible mistake.

"I can't believe this is happening," she said. "I always thought he would put his country above all else. But, oh, no, he's putting his family and their possessions first. That's what he will defend! I feel terrible. Why couldn't I change his mind? He's walking into a horrible trap."

Betty offered her a handkerchief. Carla wiped her tears and sat down. Anna's mind flashed back to Loosdrecht, where they'd stacked their right hands in solidarity. Had they been naïve? Less than a week of isolation and fear had knocked the starch out of Herman. What about the rest of the Group of Eight? Where was Dirk? Not a word from him yet. Otto was presumably on his way to England. And what about Piet? And Emmy? A tremendous desire to go to Ede and talk to Oma and Walter surged. There was no hurry about getting into nursing school. That could wait. First, she had to see if they weren't leaving Walter in a lurch. How could they keep the Jews around the castle alive without help?

The next day, she and Carla went to Ede. Walter would meet them at the station. There were noticeably fewer young men on the train. That portion of the male population seemed to have fallen through a trap door. Gone. Farther away from Utrecht, Anna saw a few. Maybe it was not totally impossible for Dirk and Piet to travel on public transportation.

Carla, next to her, stared out the window and looked glum. Her pain was palpable. Herman, the happy-go-lucky man who'd been so much fun to be with, had turned his back on a promise to help Daan and his family survive. Worse to Anna's mind was the reason for it.

Walter stood outside the station with a little boy at his side whom he introduced to them as Bram.

"Do you have two sisters?" Bram asked, looking up at Walter.

Walter laughed. "No, this one is my sister," he said, pointing at Carla. "But I might just as well call the other one my sister too."

"So, you do have two sisters," Bram said triumphantly.

"All right, I have two sisters."

Anna hooked Carla's arm, while Bram sought Walter's hand. Together they walked toward the parsonage. The boy's mother met them at the door.

"Mevrouw van Staveren is here, Walter," she said. "I let her into your office. I hope you don't mind."

"Not at all," Walter said, and excused himself to go upstairs.

Ruth said she had a pot of tea ready for them and led them into a sunny dining room. Two little girls sat in a corner surrounded by toys; one still a baby, the other a toddler. French doors gave way to a garden filled with red tulips and tender green shoots on low shrubs. Anna had prepared herself for a clouded household. After all, the reason Walter was in Ede was because the resident pastor was in a sanatorium with a dreadful disease. She'd expected his sad absence to permeate the atmosphere, but there was no sign of it. Instead, the warmth of the domestic scene was striking. The eldest of the two little girls ambled over to her with a teddy bear, which she put in Anna's lap with a look of expectation. It took Anna off guard. Growing up in a household with a much older brother and no other siblings, her experience with small children was nil. How did one engage a three-year-old? But some hitherto hidden maternal quality rallied. She took the little bear into her hands and rubbed its fuzzy coat against her cheek. The girl laughed, her eyes filled with mirth.

"What's its name?" Anna asked.

"Floris," the girl said, and leaned into Anna's knees.

She pulled her into her lap, surprising herself. "And what's your name?"

"Emily," the cuddly thing in her lap said. "And that's Lideke.

She's just a baby."

Anna intercepted Ruth's look while she held Emily. Her smile was captivating. No wonder Walter had decided to live elsewhere. It would not be hard to fall in love with this woman. The warmth of the home she'd created, the adorable children, Walter had foregone it all and traded it for an old castle with an old woman at the helm.

A while later, Walter entered the room, and Bram immediately ran up to him. Anna projected the scene onto Dirk, and felt the jab of not knowing where he was and if such domestic bliss would ever come their way. *Bury that thought. There is a war going on.*

Upstairs, in the pastor's study, both Anna and Carla were stopped in their tracks by a reproduction of Rembrandt's *The Good Samaritan* on the wall.

"Walter, what did you think when you first entered this room and saw that picture?" Carla asked her brother.

"I thought it was an omen."

"That sermon you gave changed my life, and a few others' as well. As a matter of fact, it's the indirect reason we're here today."

In his quiet manner, Walter invited them to sit down. Anna felt like a congregant coming for spiritual guidance, and in a way that was the case, but especially for Carla. Seated behind his desk, he looked less like a brother and more like the preacher he was. He reached for his pipe and started filling it with tobacco from a leather pouch, waiting to hear what was on Carla's mind.

"The universities are closed, as I'm sure you know. Anna and I considered applying for nursing school, but then Herman dropped by and said that fourth-year medical students could work in hospitals instead of working in Germany. If true, that would be great for Dirk, and maybe for me."

Walter nodded.

"But this is not really the reason we came here today," Carla went on. "Actually, there are two reasons, and they're interrelated. We're wondering how we can provide food stamps for the Jews you've found hiding places for."

While Carla talked, Anna looked around the room and noticed the plants in the window. They were well cared for, like the children downstairs. Did Ruth come in to water them, remove their wilted blossoms and yellowing leaves? She couldn't imagine Walter doing it. They must have stood in the window when her husband was still behind his desk. Doing small chores for his plants might be a way of keeping his memory alive. Anna wished she had something that belonged to Dirk she could nurse while he was away doing God knows what.

"We haven't heard from Dirk and Piet since the university closed," Carla said. "We suspect Otto is on his way to England. And here comes the real reason I'm here. Herman is presenting himself at the Labor Bureau! Can you believe that? I am sick about it. He says General Rauter is threatening parents of students who hide, that they might actually have to go to jail and have their possessions taken away, like they did to Jews."

Walter put down his pipe in a large ceramic ashtray. He moved from behind the desk and hauled his chair next to theirs.

"I can see that upsets you."

"I blame myself for not talking him out of it, but I couldn't think straight. I was so angry with him. It seemed cowardly and unprincipled. He turned defensive and left angry."

"Why did you think it was unprincipled?" Walter asked.

"I think a twenty-two-year-old man should want to defend his country against an aggressor and put the common good above his earthly goods. Even above protecting his parents. Any man who goes to war leaves his parents behind, for heavens sake! Hiding means you can work underground and obstruct the enemy. But go to work for him? Producing bullets that kill your own people? No, that's not in my book of principles."

"The Nazis are playing on man's worst instincts," Walter said. "Money is a powerful drive. And for a young man to leave his parents in danger is an equally powerful motivation to do their bidding. But I agree with you. Herman did not make a heroic decision. Let's assume it wasn't the money that influenced him, that it was protecting his parents. Even then I think he made a mistake. Jesus made it very clear that a young man should leave his home and follow him 'to do the will of my Heavenly Father.' A story appears in each of the synoptic gospels that relates to this. His mother and his brothers were waiting at a gate and wanted to speak to him. But Jesus said: 'Who is my mother and who are my brothers?' He looked at the circle of people around him and said: 'Whoever does the will of God is my sister, my brother, my mother.' So, the Bible is very clear on that issue."

"I have to confess," Carla said, "that I always thought it rather impolite of Jesus to leave his family standing at the gate."

Walter chuckled. "Jesus wasn't teaching good manners in that story. 'Go out and do what's important' is more like it. As long as what we do is right in the sight of God."

"There's the rub," Carla said. "What is right and who is right? The one who defends his home and hearth, or the one who defends his country?"

"Do you have doubts about that, Carla?" Anna asked. She'd been quiet during the dialogue, admiring Walter's calm reaction. Brother and sister had different temperaments.

"Good question," Carla said. "I respect and love my parents. They brought me up to be patriotic and to respect our queen. So, I suppose it follows that working for the Underground is the right thing to do."

"Everything in life is debatable," Walter said. "Yet, there are underlying truths we can't get around. Justice is one of them. Instinctively, we reach for truth, but at the same time, we have to deal with our other instincts: self-defense, greed, and power. Time and again, we wrestle with being pulled in opposite directions. I wager that Herman was at odds with himself, or he wouldn't have left in a huff."

"I was angry with him, but I am also angry at myself." Carla leaned forward in her chair and balled her hands into tight fists. "Why couldn't I change his mind? How can I forgive myself?"

"Once you forgive Herman for making his decision, you can forgive yourself. He made a choice, right or wrong, wise or unwise. You have to respect the path he chose, even if you do not agree. You did the right thing by challenging his decision. Now, you have to pray for him."

Ruth offered her bicycle to Anna, and Carla hopped on the baggage carrier of Walter's, who said he had to go home to the castle anyhow. The three of them took off to see Oma. The way she was seated, leaning into Walter's back, Carla couldn't see what was ahead of her, only trees on the side of the path. She was obviously surprised to see a castle when Walter stopped.

"Are we at the right place?" she asked.

"Yes, we are," Anna said.

"You never told me more about your grandmother than that she was a neat lady and that you loved her."

"I was telling nothing but the truth. Let's go inside. I'd love for you to meet her."

They put their bikes close to the kitchen door. Mien was busy preparing lunch.

"Can you add two to the table?" Anna asked.

"Your grandmother will be happy to see you, Miss Anna. She's been fussing about what's been happening lately."

"That's unlike her. We'll cheer her up."

They left the kitchen for the large hall with its white marble floor and gallery of ancestral paintings. Carla wanted to take it all in, but Anna hurried her along. She turned the brass handle and opened the salon's tall mahogany door. The late morning light gave the large living room a cheerful aspect in spite of the heavy, dark curtains. Oma stood near the window, rearranging red tulips in a crystal vase.

"Anna, my dear," she said. She walked over to give her

granddaughter a warm hug. "I am so relieved to see you. Are you all right?"

"Not to worry, Oma. I'm fine, and I would like you to meet my roommate, who happens to be Walter's sister."

Oma reached out her hand. "How delightful. What is your name?"

"Carla Vlaskamp."

"I am about to have lunch. Would you all join me? Anna, ask Mien to add two plates."

"I already did," Anna said.

The baroness presided at the head of the dining room table and steered the conversation.

"The developments of the last few weeks are upsetting," she said. "I do not trust what I read in the papers anymore, but it's clear the Germans have crossed a line by forcing young men to work for them and forcing students to swear loyalty to rules they can't possibly obey in good conscience. Something very precious is being taken from us."

"Freedom!" Walter filled in for her. "The queen would agree with you. She strongly urges us not to work for the Germans."

A secretive smile played around Oma's lips. She evidently was aware of Walter's news source, which could be no other than the broadcast on Radio Oranje via the BBC.

There was a knock on the door. When it opened, Daan filled its frame. Carla gave a cry of surprise and made motions to run over, but Anna gently pressed Carla's knees down in the chair and whispered, "He's Klaas now."

Daan lit up when he saw Anna and Carla.

"Excuse me for being late for lunch, madam," he said. He walked around the table and warmly embraced Carla. "Great to see you. How are you?"

"You seem to know each other," the baroness said.

Anna hastened to fill her in. "Oma, remember I told you about the Group of Eight? Carla is one of them. We always met at her place in Utrecht."

"I see. Now I know four of the eight. Will I get to meet the other four?"

"Not likely," Anna said. "At the moment, only the three of us here at your table are aware of each other's whereabouts. The group is made up of three women and five men. We haven't heard from Dirk, Otto, and Piet for over a week. Emmy went home, I think. Herman showed up yesterday to say he was going to work in Germany. We're still reeling from that."

"He did?" Daan said. "What made him do that?"

"General Rauter threatened parents of hiding students, he told us. They could be relieved of their money or be jailed. Herman didn't want to run that risk."

Daan looked stunned. He seated himself in the empty chair next to Walter.

"God, I hope not every student feels that way. Unbelievable! It would be easy to say, to each his own, but we're in a war."

The baroness changed the subject. "Tell me, Carla, are you aware your friend here has a different name now?"

Carla looked flustered. "Yes, madam, I know his new name is Klaas. Please trust me. I will never call him by any other name until the war is over. When he left last August with Anna and Dirk, I knew he would be Klaas from then on, but I had no idea where he was headed until now."

"This Herman you just talked about," the baroness said to no one in particular. "Does he know anything about Klaas? He sounds like a weak link in your chain."

"All he knows is that Klaas disappeared," Anna said.

"Good," Oma said. "It seems to me the Germans are stepping up their retaliatory measures. I hear they've already taken hundreds of hostages. The strike is a very serious development. Well, we can spend our time commiserating, but that doesn't do any good. Everyone around this table has made the choice of obstructing the enemy. We're in equal danger. I beg you not to be overconfident."

By asking four well-placed questions, the baroness got the complete picture of the Group of Eight. At the same time, she established equal footing when it came to resistance to the enemy, and she assumed the role of councilor to boot.

It was quiet around the table. Klaas—his name was now firmly established in everyone's mind—made up for his late arrival and lifted a slice of bread from a silver basket and spread butter over it. He asked Walter to pass a platter with ham slices, elegantly arrayed by Mien into a fan-like pattern. As he pried the top one loose, his mind didn't seem to be on the task. He told them Janus had chatted with the *postbode* that morning. The man had pointed at his mailbag and commented there was more mail to deliver at the farms these days.

"I don't know what Janus's conclusion was," Klaas said, "but I can tell you what mine is. I think we have to tell family members of the people we're hiding to stop corresponding, or the *postbode* will start wondering. We have to act fast."

They decided Walter should write a letter to the effect that correspondence had to stop. It couldn't be sent out by mail, of course. That would only add to the problem. The letters had to be hand-delivered. Since Anna and Carla were now on permanent vacation, they could take on the job.

That evening, Walter wrote the letters on his church's stationery. Klaas pointed out the farms involved on a large map of the area— easy to remember for Anna, as she was very familiar with the lay of the land around Kasteel Koppelburg. Walter had persuaded several of his parishioners to provide hiding places as well. Those addresses were closer to town and not necessarily farms. Anna stuffed the letters into her leather bag.

CHAPTER TWENTY-ONE

Anna – The Next Day

Anna and Carla walked out of the castle's gate into a splash of early sunshine. As Oma's Welsh ponies spotted them, they whinnied and raced up to the fence. Across the road, tiny shoots of wheat poked their heads through the tilled soil, a hopeful sign for a plentiful August harvest. Anna inhaled the spring fragrances that wafted through the air. Any other year, on a different page of history, it would have made her heart sing.

Carla was quiet, though the ponies running alongside the fence amused her. Last night, they'd talked till early morning with Klaas and Walter about their uncertain futures, so closely linked to the fate of the *onderduikers*. The word *onderduiker* literally meant "dive under water." The word had become part of daily parlance. It stood for any person who had good reason to stay out of sight of the Gestapo. It was illegal to hide, and it was illegal to care for one who was hiding. And caring for them meant providing money and food. How to get those things to them was the challenge, and they agonized over a strategy. Walter didn't know how long he would remain in Ede, though it was looking as if it might be for some time. Dominee Bosma's condition was not improving, and Klaas's life was on hold. All he could do was wait for the end of the war; Anna and Carla had no clue what they would be doing the day after tomorrow.

Hendrik's farm was first on their list. Roaming chickens greeted them in the farmyard, and Hendrik waved from a strawberry patch with Daan's brother at his side. Anna pulled the cord of the brass bell by the kitchen door. She didn't want to frighten Bertien, who might be alarmed by Carla's presence. Nothing happened for a few minutes. The door opened a crack.

"Miss Anna! It's you."

"I didn't want to scare anybody, Bertien. We're on a mission. This is Dominee Vlaskamp's sister."

They followed Bertien in. Little Annie sat in a highchair coloring a perfectly drawn horse. A box with coloring pencils stood on the table in front of an empty chair next to Annie's highchair.

"We have a letter for you," Anna said, and picked one randomly from the stack in her bag. The envelopes were not addressed. As she was about to hand it over, the bell rang. Bertien scented trouble and motioned Anna to put the letter back in her bag. She walked up to a window that looked out on the yard.

"The inspectors," she said. "Hendrik rang the bell."

Inspectors made random visits, she explained, to make sure no cows or pigs were sold to the black market. Each farmer was allowed to raise only one pig for their own use.

"Are those inspectors Germans?" Anna asked.

"Might as well be," Bertien said. "They do the snooping for them. That's how I look at it. I don't trust any of them, tell the truth, but they don't get further than the barn. I don't offer them coffee." She laughed. "But would you like some?"

Daan's mother didn't come out of hiding while they drank their coffee. There was no need to tell Carla that Daan's mother was hiding there. Dirk had frequently pointed out that you can't be hurt by what you don't know. Yet, it felt weird not to. On the way out, Anna turned toward the strawberry patch to say hello to Hendrik.

Tom Velder was still at his side, leaning on his hoe. The inspectors had left.

Back on the road, Carla said, "That teenager doesn't look like a typical farm boy to me."

This stupid war pinched relationships, Anna thought, and she felt conflicted. Carla went on to point out the reasons why she thought the way she did. The way he leaned on his hoe, the intelligent expression on his face, something about him, she didn't know exactly what. Carla was too smart to be fooled for very long. Anna weighed her options. They were in this enterprise together.

"Would you be shocked if I told you Tom Velder is Daan's younger brother? I rang the bell to warn Bertien. Daan's mother was hiding inside."

"My God! I had no inkling anybody was hiding from us. What courage those people have. I figured some of Daan's relatives must be in this area. Still …"

"Please be careful with this knowledge. Only Oma, Walter, and Hendrik know that Geertrui van Es is Daan's mother. Even Bertien doesn't know. She hasn't met Daan. So act as if you've never heard this information."

"You have my word."

They walked on. The sun was rising higher in the sky where birds flew to and fro, fetching bits of twigs and straw to build nests high up in the trees. Anna saw that Carla couldn't keep up. She looked tired. The emotions of the last few days were taking a toll. Herman's decision had shocked her. The castle had floored her, and now, being confronted with the reality of hiding Jews, her energy was fading. Anna decided to spare her the strain of covering a lot of territory, and suggested Carla take a nap. Carla eagerly accepted and turned back to Koppelburg.

Wherever Anna rang the bell or knocked on a door, it took a while, but she was always let in. Miss Anna was well known around here. By now, she'd made a half circle. The church tower was in her sight, and she was ready for a coffee break. Her next address was on the other side of Ede.

But a cup of coffee was not in store. A Gestapo van at high speed appeared around the bend and came to an abrupt halt in the yard of the last farm down the road. Four soldiers, their guns drawn, rolled out of the van. An officer stepped down from the passenger seat and slammed the door shut. Two more soldiers jumped out of the back of the van. In no time, the farm was encircled. The officer walked up to the kitchen door and, when it didn't open immediately, he had a soldier break it down by the force of his body and a hard kick of his boots. Anna hid behind a tall shrub. Through the branches, not yet dressed with leaves, she could make out what was going on at the other end of a plowed field that separated her from the spectacle that quickly unfolded. Three men, who looked to be of different ages, came out with their arms raised, each with a soldier behind his back and pushed forward by the barrel of a gun. The officer came out the door last. In a loud voice that carried over the field, he gave orders to line them up behind the barn.

Anna closed her eyes. "Oh, God, help!" she whispered.

Three shots.

When she dared look again, the three men had fallen to the ground. The officer gave orders to get back into the van. As quickly as they'd jumped out of it, the soldiers piled back in. The driver was still behind the wheel. The officer took his seat next to him.

She heard a loud tire squeal.

Anna's heart was beating furiously, her mind racing. A strong impulse to go over to those fallen men overtook her. She ran through the field to the back of the barn where the men lay in pools of blood. They had been shot in the back of their heads. She kneeled down and searched for a pulse on the closest victim. Their bodies were still warm to the touch, but their hearts had stopped beating.

Her mind flashed back to the start of the war, when she was in the hospital with a broken leg. Through the window she'd watched wounded soldiers being brought in on stretchers. She'd reacted to that horrible scene with a strong desire to become a doctor. Nothing had seemed nobler than to have the know-how to fix those bleeding, broken soldiers. And here she was: a second-year medical student with the very same desire, but there was nothing she could do.

The sound of voices and wooden shoes hitting the cobblestone path alongside the barn came closer and closer. Anna steeled herself not to cry. She was still holding the wrist of what looked like the youngest of the three victims, when a woman in a long black skirt with a colorful apron over it appeared around the corner. She gasped, put her hand to her mouth, and let out a wail that would haunt Anna for a long time to come. Soon, a throng of neighbors stood around in heavy silence, looking in horror at the bodies.

Anna got up and went over to the first woman to arrive at the scene.

"I happened to walk by and saw all that happened," she said. "I'm a medical student." She took the woman's hand in her own. "I am so sorry. But I'm afraid I cannot do anything to bring them back. They died instantly."

The woman looked at her in a daze. "God have mercy," she said.

Another woman—this one younger—worked her way up to the front. She fell at the feet of the youngest of the victims and started to cry uncontrollably. She could be his wife, Anna thought. The people around her stood bolted to the ground, unable to digest this sudden horror. Anna went over and put her arm around her. She did no more. What could she say? She stayed kneeling beside her till an older woman in the crowd stepped forward and put her hand on the woman's head.

Anna got up. There was nothing more to do here. She was a stranger among grieving people, who must know why these men were killed. This was not the time to ask questions. She snuck away without saying who she was, and nobody asked.

Chapter Twenty-Two

Dirk – May 1943

Otto had carefully studied the area's map before embarking on the trip to Maastricht. He knew the road names and how they connected like the lines in the palm of his hand. Arnold had dropped them off at the Blekerij. At this point, the Maas River suddenly enlarged to twice its width. Otto crossed the street with the purpose of someone who knows his way. Their clothing was black as the night and their faces dark from coal dust, blending them with the pale shadows of a quarter moon. It helped that the streetlights weren't lit.

They moved in spurts, hugging the brick walls of tall warehouses that lined the bank. It being after curfew, there was no sign of human life. A dog barked. Dirk prayed it wasn't on the loose to create a spectacle while they surreptitiously crept along the street. Gradually, they covered more ground, bringing them closer to their destination. Dirk had the name of a café in his pocket. It's where they would make contact with the local Underground.

Before reaching the Glasisweg, they heard the rumble of a truck coming from behind. They ducked into a gap between two warehouses before it came around the bend, pressing their backs against the side of the building. The dimmed lights on what turned out to be a German Army patrol wagon were directed down the road, away from them. They soldiered on, turned inland, and left the city with a sigh of relief. Limburg's undulating landscape offered cover with lush growth and winding paths.

It was past midnight when they spotted Café Sjans. Dirk had been instructed to ring the bell at the back. Through a small window in the upper portion of the door, he saw the light of a lantern approach through a narrow hallway. The man holding onto it was the size of a child. He looked into Dirk's face and waited for a signal. Dirk held his father's passport picture against the glass. The man nodded and opened up.

"Your names please?"

"Henk, and this is Ralph," Dirk said, pointing at Otto.

"Welcome. My name is Max. You must be hungry. I'll make you an *uitsmijter*."

They followed the dwarf-like figure into the kitchen. He turned on the gas stove and produced four eggs, slices of ham, cheese, and bread. In no time, they sat at a crude wooden table with more delicious food than they'd seen in quite a while, though the skipper's wife had fed them adequately.

"You'll need a little sustenance for the next leg of your trip," Max said.

"How long is it from here to *de grotten*?" Otto asked.

"The way the crow flies, it isn't far. But under German scrutiny, it is like the way a turtle crawls. I would say about two hours. I'll be your guide." He put on a dark jacket that fell to his knees in front, but only to his waist in back. A hump took up the extra length. They set out on the Luikerweg toward St. Pietersberg, hugging the right-hand shoulder where the underbrush was dense. No one spoke.

St. Pietersberg was the highest point in the entire country. Around 1700, a mighty fortress had been built on its top to protect Maastricht from invaders, who crossed this narrow part of Holland to get from Germany to Belgium and vice versa. They had done so for centuries, including the present one. The fortress provided a marvelous view of the city below, but Otto and Dirk would not get to see it. They were headed to what was underneath the mountain. Max led them to a small door hewn into the side of the mountain and opened it with a key. They stepped from darkness into darkness. A light switched on, and a man came forward, stepping down from a hole in the wall. The guard recognized Max.

"You know the way," he said, and didn't even ask who his companions were.

By the light of a lantern, the beige walls came into view. Max told them there were over 20,000 of these tunnels. A scary thought. How would they keep track of the many left and right turns they took in this maze? Dirk wondered. Their footsteps sounded hollow against the limestone quarry walls. Already, the Romans had cut blocks of *mergel*—marl—to build the city of Maastricht. Dirk had never been underground, leave alone walking such distances, yet he didn't feel claustrophobic. He'd expected it to be a lugubrious experience, but the stone's delicate beige color wasn't gloomy.

Finally, they reached a wide area where several tunnels came together. It had the feeling of a marketplace. The surprisingly high ceiling diminished the people who'd gathered there in small clusters. Overhead lights threw sharp shadows on the rough floor. Without a way to tell if it was night or day, Dirk wound his watch so he wouldn't lose track of time.

Max headed for a small group of men who were talking in English and smoking cigarettes. Otto's eyes went longingly to the open pack one of the men held in his hand, its brand name Players prominently displayed on top. Otto's look was intercepted, and the man offered him one.

"Not your last English cigarette, you hope," Dirk said to Otto.

"On your way to England?" the stranger asked.

"Yes," Otto said, and struck a light. He inhaled the first drag and held it for a few seconds. "When I taste this," he said, "I wish it wouldn't take so long to get there."

Max introduced Dirk and Otto without revealing the names of the three Englishmen. There was some polite inquiry about their barge trip, which they seemed to know about, and Dirk told them what was happening above ground, like the strike that was costing lives and the refusal of students to sign up for labor in Germany. A few other things came up in the course of the conversation, enough to satisfy the three men that Dirk and Otto were probably the ones Dirk's father had alerted them about.

"Now that you have made contact," Max said, "I will show you a place to rest. I know you haven't slept for a while."

It was true. They'd been going on adrenaline for over twenty-four hours. At the mention of rest, Dirk felt all energy flow out of his body. They agreed to meet at the same place at noon.

"Rembrandt lives here," Max said when they passed a heavy vault-like steel door set in cement blocks.

"Sorry, what did you say?" Dirk said.

"This is where his famous *Nachtwacht* painting is stored. They rolled it up. Before the war started, the government decided to keep it safe from bombs. The Germans would love to put their hands on it. They plunder art in all of the countries they occupy. And I bet they know where this Rembrandt is hidden, but no German, high rank or low, dares to venture here. Many other famous paintings from the Rijksmuseum are stored here as well."

In his sleep-deprived state, Dirk felt like he was walking in a huge cathedral. The ceilings were high, intriguing drawings were carved into the walls. On the way, he observed a man chisel the likeness of Queen Wilhelmina into the marl. Dirk shook his head, as if to remind himself that standing up for queen and country was the reason for this weird adventure. With that noble thought, he fell down on a straw mattress in the corner of a small side tunnel. Otto, lying beside him, fell asleep the instant he felt the straw underneath him. It didn't take long for sleep to overtake Dirk as well.

He didn't know how many hours had passed when Max shook him hard.

"I didn't think you'd get up by yourselves," he said.

They felt disoriented, but the sight of the short man with the bulge reminded them they were many feet under the ground.

The three Englishmen stood waiting for them at the same spot as before. It was time to negotiate. Otto had a favor to ask and Dirk had a favor to give.

The tallest of the three addressed Dirk. "I understand you have something to hand over to me."

"That depends," Dirk said.

"Oh?"

"Can you describe what it is you expect from me?"

The man ran his right hand over the stubble on his cheeks, and a worried look spread over Otto's face. Dirk had never told him what he carried in his pocket.

"Give me a good reason," the man said.

"I want to know whom you represent," Dirk said, and planted his feet firmly on the uneven ground. His father's words rang in his ears: "Don't give it to anyone who's not a member of the SIS. That's the British Intelligence Service." When Dirk asked how he could know for sure whom he was dealing with, his father had shown him a small enamel button with an emblem. In the center of a green background sat what looked like a black mole. Very small and very appropriate for a secret agent.

The Englishman studied Dirk's face. Dirk, in turn, searched the man's eyes, which were the color of his own. Hazel. He wondered if what he saw in them—passion, scrutiny, intelligence, power— was a roadmap into the man's character. Under any circumstance, it was a good idea to evaluate a stranger, but during a war it was crucial.

The man turned the lapel of his well-worn tweed jacket to show a tiny green button with the black mole. "Will this do?" he asked.

"Yes. That will do it," Dirk said, and instantly felt much lighter. He reached inside his pocket and produced the tightly wrapped package with the microfilms.

"Here are the films," he said. "Now I wonder if you could do something to help out my friend."

"I am trying to make my way to England," Otto said.

"To do what?" the Englishman asked.

"To join whatever army will take me."

"Do you have any contacts?"

"No, I don't yet. I was hoping to make some here."

The Englishman gave him the same once-over he'd given Dirk. Otto's big-boned frame would give any wrestler pause. The man reached for his hand and said, "We'll take you with us. We'll leave when the sun sets."

Dirk looked at his watch. It was three o'clock.

"That will be around eight thirty then," Otto said.

"Yes," the Englishman said. "I will look for you here at that time. Rest up while you can."

Back on their straw mattresses, Dirk and Otto didn't fall asleep right away. From now on their paths would go in opposite directions, and both pointed to unknown territory. Either direction would confront them with the enemy.

"What are your plans?" Otto asked. "Back on the barge and then what?"

"First, I will report to your parents and mine. Second, I need to find Anna. And I don't know what the third thing will be exactly, other than working for the Underground."

"When you find Anna, you'll probably find Carla as well. Tell her I'm on my way to England and not to worry. I will be back in uniform."

Max woke them up just before eight. Otto grabbed his duffel bag and together they walked over to the "marketplace." The Englishmen were waiting.

Dirk grabbed Otto's hand. "Farewell, my friend. Give my respect to her majesty."

Otto smiled. "Hold the fort," he said, and followed his guides.

CHAPTER TWENTY-THREE

Anna – May 1943

Anna rushed back to the castle, haunted by the images of the killing and shaking all over. Oma sat in her chair by the window, her fingers laced in her lap, like a mother who waits for her children to come home from school. She was quick to pick up on Anna's mood.

"What happened?" She rose from her armchair and put both her hands on Anna's shoulders.

"Something awful, Oma," Anna said, haltingly and on the brink of tears. "I watched three men being shot by the Gestapo."

"Shot? Why? Who were they?"

"I don't know why and I don't know their names. It was at a farm close to town. I saw it all. I ran as fast as I could to see if I could help, but there was nothing I could do. The men were killed instantly. Women came out of the farm after the Gestapo left. It was awful."

"Oh, my dear." Oma stroked Anna's hair. "Let's sit down."

She rang the bell and asked Janus to bring coffee.

"You don't have to tell me what you saw. No sense bringing those images back to your mind."

"Thank you. I'm used to seeing blood, but I'm not used to violence. That part was very upsetting."

Janus brought in a tray with two cups, a creamer, a bowl of sugar, and a silver coffee pot. To watch Oma go through the ritual of pouring coffee, done in graceful, deliberate motions, calmed her overwrought mood. It brought at least some sense of normalcy to a day of stupendous injustice.

The news of three men being shot flew around Ede on wings, like a butterfly touching down briefly and then lifting up to find the next flower. The local Gestapo chief issued a statement. "Communist elements among farmers are responsible for unrest and strikes in the area. We have eliminated the known communists." This vague statement appeared in the newspaper. Ede's citizens read it in disbelief.

On the same day, similar atrocities happened in several other places around the country, but the public was kept in the dark about them. General Rauter allowed only local press to publish such news. Radio and national newspapers were expressly forbidden to carry it.

Walter came to dinner with the names of the people shot and the reason for it. Farmers had been meeting at Aad van Gelder's farm to decide how long they could resist delivering milk to the co-op. They weren't of a mind to send their strong young men to work in German factories. They were needed on the farms. They believed in the strike, but for how long could they throw away milk? There had been other men at the meeting besides the three unlucky ones who were killed. Those had fled in a split second to whatever hiding place they could find. Aad van Gelder was one of the victims. A Nazi sympathizer had tipped off the Gestapo.

The mood around the dinner table at the castle was timorous. When Carla found out what happened after she'd left Anna to go and take a nap, she was mortified. Dangers lay in wait like poisonous snakes in tall grass.

"A few things have become crystal clear today," the baroness said as she put down her knife and fork. "The Gestapo has no qualms twisting the meaning of the word *justice*. To execute three men without due process, guilty or not, is a serious breach of the rule of law. Another unfortunate discovery is that there are traitors among us. But let us not forget that people with immeasurable courage outnumber them. The lesson of today is: proceed with caution."

She picked up her knife and fork to continue eating.

"May I ask for a moment of silence for the victims and their families?" Walter asked.

They stopped eating and bowed their heads. "God, receive these brave men in your endless mercy. We pray for their families, and we ask for courage to continue our work. We depend on your guidance as we walk this difficult path. Remind us not to repay hate with hate. In Jesus's name, Amen."

"Thank you, Walter," the baroness said.

"What do we do next?" Anna asked. "The risks are clearer than ever. Can we get around them?"

"Around them? We'll have to face them," Carla said.

"Before anything, we have to define our mission," Walter said. "By now, the Jews have either been taken to concentration camps, or they've managed to find a place to hide. The next wave of onderduikers will be men who refuse to work for the Germans. Their number will grow. They will need hiding places, food stamps, and money. Do we want to take them on?"

"This is like the moment at the lake in Loosdrecht, when we heard Klaas had been summoned by the Nazis," Carla said. "We rallied then and we can do it again."

"I agree," Anna said.

"I am eternally grateful," Klaas said. His face was flushed as he leaned forward to give emphasis to his next words. "But I am also extremely frustrated. All of you around this table are taking risks on my behalf and that of many others. It is hard to watch and not be able to take part in the effort to help. I've been thinking," he continued. "Since the Group of Eight has lost its male members, the brunt of the care now falls to Anna and Carla, and maybe Emmy. That is hardly fair. I am dying to jump in and help. I don't need to tell you that I have blue eyes and curly blond hair. The Gentile blood in my veins speaks louder than the Jewish blood. It's helped me so far. Don't forget—I got away with studying at the university for two years while Jews were barred."

Before anyone could react, the baroness looked over at Klaas and said, "I can see you have a plan. What would it take to accomplish it?"

He was ready with his answer. "I need to have a job description—a title, if you will—so I can prove I am needed, like Walter, who as a minister won't be asked to work in Germany. And if that isn't enough, I could try to get a doctor to give me an *Ausweis*. A sympathetic doctor could give me an exemption on the basis of some condition that would make me a poor candidate for hard labor. Like chronic back pain. " He smiled. "Or flat feet."

It was quiet. The daring plan needed time to sink in.

"When you came here, Klaas," the baroness said, "I told Hendrik that you were my new secretary to help out Mr. van Dijk. He is getting on in years. Since that is quite obvious, I could officially make you assistant estate manager and tell Mr. van Dijk that he is to teach you everything he knows. Of course, this way you put yourself at risk even more. I'm sure you realize that."

"That is very generous of you, madam. I accept your offer."

Anna weighed how this might put Oma at risk. She could say she didn't know Klaas was Jewish at the time she hired him. Would the Gestapo accept such an excuse, if it came to that? It seemed doubtful, yet she wouldn't dissuade her grandmother. She was immensely proud of her.

Mien came in with a bowl of fruit. Anna watched her grandmother struggle with peeling an apple. Her fingers couldn't get a good grip on the small knife. Finally, the apple got sliced into quarters—easier to peel that way. Anna took a good look at Oma's fingers. They were slightly disfigured and knobby. She'd never noticed that before. It jolted her. Oma was getting older. Maybe, she should spend more time at the castle. Never mind pursuing a degree in nursing. Had she ever wanted to become a nurse?

"I feel the energy in this room to go ahead with our mission," Walter said. "Even if it gets more dangerous. Am I right?"

Everyone nodded, including the baroness.

"All right. Then we have to make a plan." His leadership was instantly accepted. Just like Dirk's, Anna thought. "These are the phases we have to cover." He ticked off getting hold of valid ration cards as number one. Second was transporting them from their place of origin to the castle. Couriers would be needed in both cases. A dangerous job. The ration cards needed to be distributed to the onderduikers around Ede. And new addresses had to be found to hide more of them.

"How shall we divide the tasks?" Anna asked.

Dirk was the one with the KP contact, the Knokploeg that stole the ration cards. If only he would show a sign of life. Walter offered to convince more people to hide onderduikers. Carla and Anna said they would be couriers. Klaas could do the local distributing.

The baroness looked around the table and smiled. "My part will be sitting back and watch all of you scurry around." But then she turned serious. "And I will pray for you and feed you."

CHAPTER TWENTY-FOUR

Anna – May 1943

Carla and Anna separated at the railroad station. Anna took a train to Utrecht. Carla took a train to Breda to talk things over with her parents.

The minute Anna stepped into Betty's house, she could tell something had happened. Betty didn't act like her composed, cheerful self. A seldom seen frown marked her forehead. When they sat down in the living room, she told Anna of a visitor she'd received the night before. It was the *hospita* of Piet. Piet was missing, she said. His mother had called to find out where he was, but she'd told his mother she didn't make it her business to know what a renter did with his time. Yet, she hadn't seen him for a few days. His mother was frantic because she'd heard the Gestapo had randomly picked up students from several universities and brought them to Vught. Chills went up Anna's spine. Piet sent to a concentration camp?

"Why did Piet's landlady come here?" she asked.

Betty explained that the woman had found an opened letter with Betty's return address on it when Piet's mother had urged her to search his room for clues. It was the letter warning him about not coming to Carla's room anymore.

"What makes it worse," Betty said with tears in her voice, "just this morning, it came over the radio that thirty of those students have been executed."

Anna froze. Where was Dirk? Did his parents know? Should she call? Dirk had never encouraged her to meet them. She didn't even know his address in Den Haag. But she could find out.

"And what makes it even more cruel," Betty went on, "no names were given."

"Did the woman leave an address for Piet's mother?" Anna asked.

"I have a phone number."

Anna gathered her wits and got on the phone. A wary voice answered. Anna explained she knew Piet well and wanted to help find out what might have happened to him. When was the last time his mother had heard from him?

Piet had called right after the university closed, his mother said, saying he would come home as soon as possible, but he first had to pick up some papers he'd worked on with a professor. His mother also shared that she'd put in a call to the camp in Vught, but that hadn't turned up anything. No information would be given out. Since Assen was a long way from Vught, Anna offered to go there right away and get the names of the students held there. She avoided the word *executed*. That would be cruel. Besides, she wasn't able to get that horrible word over her lips.

Back at the station, a train was about to leave for 's-Hertogenbosch. Once there, she changed trains. Vught was the first stop. Its station looked small and deserted. There seemed to be only one way to get to the camp, and that was on foot. She started walking without a sense of direction. A teenager gave her a troubled look as she asked him for the way to the camp. Did she really want to go there?

His startled reaction confirmed the rumors she'd heard. This sleepy little town had the only SS concentration camp in northwest

Europe in its perimeter. To be sent to Vught meant there was only a slight chance you would make it out. Bad things happened there. When the Group of Eight embarked on their path to resistance, they'd thought they knew the risks they were taking. Since she'd witnessed the raid in Ede, and now was on her way to find out what might have happened to Piet, the risks were set in high relief. Dark shadows clouded her mind.

She came to De Loonse Baan, a country lane shaded by tall trees and lined by widely spaced homes. Once she left them behind, there was an open field of heather. With a heavy heart, she made a right turn onto the Lunettenlaan. The evidence of a concentration camp came into view. Strands of heavy barbed wire interconnected tall concrete posts, the kind that never rot. They lined both sides of a moat. Watchtowers stood spaced at half-mile intervals. Escape was not an option here.

Anna took a deep breath as she approached the entrance where two SS soldiers stood guard in front of a one-story brick building that looked more like a farm than a prison. A long boom, painted in white and red sections, separated her from the courtyard, where a soldier walked with two Doberman pinschers straining on their leashes. Her skin felt prickly all over. But once this far, she had no choice but to walk up to the guard. She took a straightforward approach and asked for information about a student. This didn't seem to surprise the soldier. He pointed to a door into the building, and, when she stepped inside, she understood his lack of surprise. In a hall bigger than she'd thought possible from the outside, three SS officers sat behind a long table, facing an agitated crowd of parents. What had happened to their sons? Anna was the youngest person by far. This exclusivity made her feel nakedly unprotected. Without a plan on how to proceed, she stood nailed to the floor behind the angry parents in the back of the hall.

All eyes were on the officers. Nobody paid attention to her, but an officer to the left side of the long oak table made eye contact. Anna didn't know what to think or feel as he came closer, slowly advancing along the brick wall. Now he stood in front of her. She recognized him in a flash. He was the officer she'd shared a first-class train compartment with almost two years ago. Same blue eyes, same young face.

In German, he said, "Fraulein, what brings you here?" She even recognized his voice from when he'd offered to bring down her suitcase. His was not like the barking voice she'd despised in Ede at Aad van Gelder's farm.

"I am worried about a student friend of mine. He disappeared suddenly. I was told he might be here."

He studied her face as if to verify she was indeed that girl from the train. "What's his name?" he asked softly, almost in a whisper.

"Piet Zandberg," Anna whispered back.

"Stay here. I will check."

He walked back slowly to the table with the three officers, who looked older and of higher rank. He hailed a sergeant from behind and spoke into his ear. The man abruptly turned and disappeared through a door behind the wide table. Anna trembled. The officer kept checking if she was still at the same spot. She didn't dare take one step forward or backward.

The sergeant finally returned with a piece of paper in his hand. The young officer traced it with his finger. At the bottom of the page, his finger stopped. Z for Zandberg, she thought. He looked over at her, handed the paper back to the sergeant, and walked toward her as slowly as the first time.

Anna tried to read the clouded expression on his face. Either Piet was held here, or—God forbid—he was dead.

"Piet Zandberg ..." He hesitated. "Are you his *liebchen*?"

"Yes," Anna lied. If it took a lie to find out the truth, so be it. Dirk would forgive her.

"Fraulein, I am sorry to tell you this, but he was executed this morning. He refused to report to the Arbeitseinsatz."

Tears sprang into her eyes. Piet was dead. Wiped from the earth. How could this be? Something snapped deep inside her, creating a fault line in her heart that could rip apart at any time. Through her tears she saw empathy in the young officer's face. This made the news almost worse. How could Hitler have enticed this seemingly decent man to become involved with something so inhumane and abhorrent?

He looked back at the long oak table. Anna followed his glance. The senior officer seemed to focus on them.

"I have to go back," he said. He hesitated. "I'm sorry to give you this news." He turned and walked back as slowly as he'd come.

Nothing would be gained by staying. She could have asked about Dirk, but thank God she hadn't. One death was enough. This way, she could still nurse the hope Dirk was alive.

She walked out the door in a daze, past the guards, automatically putting one foot in front of the other. She hardly saw the road in front of her. Through her tears, the barbed wires got distorted into fractured lines, as if she were looking through a kaleidoscope. There was only one sharp image before her: Piet, the way he'd stood by the side of the lake in Loosdrecht saying he was sorry, but he didn't have the courage it would take to hide Jews; Piet with his likeable baby face, who had shown the courage to say no to working for the enemy. The notion that life was totally unpredictable came like a hammer blow to her mind. She mocked herself for once actually believing she could determine her own course through life.

How long it had taken to walk back over the Lunettenlaan, she didn't know. She looked at her watch. Close to 7 p.m. Twilight was setting in. The weariness from having been on the train all day crept into her body. Getting back to Utrecht before curfew was out of the question. The realization sent her into a tizzy. She didn't know anybody in Vught. For lack of a better plan, she kept walking. Her options were few. Actually, there weren't any. She trudged on. Thatched roofs on the houses farther along the way reminded her of the farms around the castle, but the castle was far away, unreachable. She'd never felt this forlorn in her entire life.

Through the window of a home with less of a setback from the road than its neighbors, she noticed a woman sitting at a table, reading a newspaper. By impulse, she walked up to the front door and rang the bell. A small brass nameplate beside it read G. J. van Mourik. A woman looked at her through a small window in the door. Then the face disappeared. After a few minutes, Anna saw a different face peeking at her. A latch was undone, and the tiny window opened.

"*Wie bent U?*"

"My name is Anna Smits. You do not know me, but I need help."

It was quiet. The little window was still open. She was being measured.

"All right, come in," the voice said, and the door opened slightly. Anna remained standing, afraid a step forward might be interpreted as threatening.

"I came from Camp Vught," she said. "A friend of mine was executed."

As she said this, tears sprang back into her eyes. They were noticed. The door opened wider, and the woman made a friendly gesture for her to step inside. She was led into a large room. An open newspaper lay on a wide desk.

"How can I help you?" Mevrouw van Mourik asked. She proved to be a good listener, and didn't once interrupt the stream of words that came out of Anna.

"You can stay here overnight, if that helps. Would you like something to eat, my dear? You have been on trains all day, it seems."

It was true. She hadn't eaten anything since she'd left the breakfast table at Oma's place, and even that had been in haste to catch the train to Utrecht with Carla, all of which seemed ages ago. Mevrouw van Mourik produced a cup of tea with a large cookie on the side. "Here, take this while I ask Hilda to warm up some soup for you."

She disappeared. Anna looked around. Through French doors

at the other end of the large room, she could see a well-tended garden. Blue and yellow irises poked their heads above a low brick wall that enclosed a wide terrace. Rustic wooden chairs stood waiting for company. Who would fill them on a sunny afternoon? The house breathed a lived-in atmosphere, yet there was no sign of life other than that of Mevrouw van Mourik and, evidently, a maid in the kitchen.

The door to the hallway opened, and Hilda invited her to the dining room where a plate of steaming soup and a bowl of sugarcoated strawberries awaited her.

"Do you live here alone, Mevrouw van Mourik?" Anna asked, though she couldn't imagine that was the case, judging from the six chairs around the dining room table.

"I do, at the moment. My husband is at the same place you just visited."

Anna bolted upright in her chair. "Oh, no! That's terrible."

"Yes, it *is* terrible. He is held hostage. You probably know what that means?"

"I do," Anna said, but she didn't reveal how she'd learned that terrible truth when her mother's cousin had been executed. As in the conversation with Piet's mother, she didn't want to utter the word *executed*.

"My husband is president of the supreme court of the Provincie Noord-Brabant," she said simply.

That explained it. The Nazis preferred high-profile men as hostages. They were good bargaining chips. How unbearable it must be to know that your husband was just two miles down the road and at the mercy of the enemy. Anna tried hard to hold back welling tears.

"My dear," Mevrouw van Mourik said, "I don't want to burden you. We live in strange times."

"In brutal times," Anna burst out.

Mevrouw van Mourik looked over at her. "Yes, brutal and unjust. I struggle with the irony of the injustice done to my husband, whose life's work is bringing justice."

It was one thing to be told you couldn't attend university, quite another to be locked up without due process and be used as a chip in a dangerous game. The unfairness and the anxiety of what might happen to her husband were chiseled into the woman's face. Anna marveled at her composure.

"My two sons also studied law. At your university, in fact," Mevrouw van Mourik went on. "The eldest finished before the war started, the youngest two years into the war. Like their father, they're not able to practice their profession. They went underground."

Anna couldn't remember a day in which she'd heard so much bad news.

"Come, you must eat some of that soup. Hilda puts God knows what in it, but I can guarantee it's nutritious. You need strength. We all do."

"You are strong, I can see," Anna said. "What keeps you going, if I may ask?"

Mevrouw van Mourik folded her hands and stared at them for a while. She didn't seem like the kind of woman who would give a flip answer. Dusk fell outside, and the world narrowed to just this room and the two of them at a table meant for six.

"We can't give up. Ever. We must endure."

"What gives you the strength to endure?" Anna asked, hoping she wasn't too forward.

"In the end, the good in humanity will prevail. I strongly believe that. That is not to say it won't take many lives and horrible destruction. Victory never comes without sacrifice. But Hitler will eventually run out of support. His promises are hollow and false, and he will fail his people. What helps me to endure most is that I know my husband is a man of faith. He will bear the burden. Besides, there is nothing I can do to change his plight. So, I place my worries in God's hands. He is my rock."

"I think I'm here for a reason," Anna said. "Thank you for giving me two kinds of nourishment."

The bed in the guest room was comfortable, but it didn't induce sleep. Anna twisted and turned under the heavy linen sheet, her mind alive with scary images and existential questions. Piet, who'd started the day inhaling the sweet air of spring, was now dead. He would never take another breath or utter another word. All because the last words he spoke were, "No, I will not." The thought that up the road two Doberman pinschers could tear a prisoner to shreds and nobody would lift a finger to stop them haunted her. Innocent people, like Judge van Mourik, lay on a cot over there, looking at the stars through tiny windows, knowing that miles of barbed wire would ensnare them if they tried to break out of their misery. Without viable options, how could they survive? Was there really a God who looked over them? She hadn't seen any sign of him in Camp Vught. The only ray of light had been in the eyes of the young German officer. Was that the way God worked? Was that enough to slay the devil that had taken up residence in that forsaken place?

She fell asleep without answers.

CHAPTER TWENTY-FIVE

Dirk – Early June 1943

The street swayed under his feet, and Dirk decided to push his bike instead of mounting it. After weeks of constantly adjusting his balance on the barge, he didn't trust himself.

He pulled the bell on the house he'd left three weeks ago with Otto. A maid opened the door and ushered him into the living room where he found Otto's mother. Perched on the edge of her chair, she listened to him with every muscle taut in her body. She had been in on the plans, so he felt safe telling her about meeting the British agents.

"Will he make it, Dirk?" she asked, her anxiety clear in her hushed voice.

"I'm confident he will. It's a roundabout way to get to England, but these agents are very competent, and they have many contacts on the way. He's as safe as he possibly can be."

"How will we find out if he got there?"

"Listen well to the BBC every night. Messages are passed on in code on Radio Oranje. When you hear, *Geef Carla een zoen*, then you'll know he made it."

"Carla? Who's Carla?"

"She is one in our group of friends in Utrecht. All students. We always met at her place."

"Oh, I see."

Dirk could see she was curious, but she didn't ask for more. Just as well. He wouldn't have known the answers. Otto had only slipped him the code for the BBC at the last moment without explanation. But he could guess.

He started on his way to Den Haag, this time *on* his bike, taking back roads he remembered from the time his family tried to escape to England. In his corduroys and skipper's sweater, which no longer looked brand new, he belonged to the landscape. It didn't surprise anyone to see him biking along, not even the German soldiers patrolling here and there. Dusk had set in by the time he reached Den Haag. His family had just sat down to dinner.

"Surprise, surprise." His sister was the first to see him standing in the doorway. He seated himself next to her.

"How did it go?" his father asked.

Dirk showed the index and middle finger of his right hand in a V sign, a gesture he'd seen Churchill do in a picture in an illegal newspaper. It was enough of an answer to satisfy his father.

His mother produced a plate and cutlery and dished him boiled potatoes, green beans, and carrots. "Sorry, no meat today."

He inhaled the food, but he was as tired as he was hungry. He couldn't wait to fall into a soft bed. Sleeping on a hard cot in a tiny space hadn't been like the hardship people in prisons endured, but today the thought of sleeping on a mattress and in pajamas seemed like the height of luxury—and he didn't even feel guilty about it. In the morning when he took a bath, the water turned black and the coal dust he'd accumulated left a dark rim in the bathtub. Even his hair looked a shade lighter.

At breakfast, an envelope leaned against his teacup. He looked at the date on the stamp. It had been mailed from Breda two days ago. It was from Carla. It gave no news of anybody's whereabouts. She only asked if he would get in touch with her. He looked up her parents' telephone number. Her mother answered. She remembered him well, she said, and got Carla on the phone.

"Hi Dirk!" Carla's cheerful voice boomed over the line. He imagined her standing in the sunlit living room with the modern paintings beckoning from the white walls.

"Hello, Carla. I got your letter. What are you doing in Breda?"

"Regrouping."

"Where is everybody?"

"Not in Utrecht, as far as I know," Carla continued in a lower tone. "I assume you're in Den Haag, since you apparently got my letter?"

"Yes. Got here last night. Do you know where Anna is?"

"I can only guess. When I called her two days ago, Betty said she'd gone to Vught."

The mention of Vught stuck like a fishbone in his throat. He couldn't speak. Carla filled the void. Piet had been missing. He'd not come to his parents' home in Drente as planned. There was a possibility he'd been picked up like several hundred other students and brought to Vught. Anna had gone to find out if he was among them.

"Good God," was all he could say. Anna had guts, but this was overdoing it. Vught!

"Do you know anything about Otto?" Carla asked.

"You don't have to worry about him, Carla. He's well on his way. He asked me to say hello to you." Knowing that she lived across from the police station, he didn't elaborate. You never knew how telephone lines could get mixed up.

Carla switched subjects. "Herman has gone to Germany to work."

"No! You must be kidding."

"I wish I were. He said he was afraid his parents would end up in jail and have their money taken away. Apparently they're well-off."

Dirk gulped for air. "Any more bad news?"

231

"Everything is fine in Ede. Anna and I went over. We know Emmy is in Haarlem, but we haven't heard from her yet."

Dirk didn't tell her what he'd done since the university closed. Neither did she ask.

"You know, Dirk," she said, "Herman told us that as fourth-year students, we don't have to do labor in Germany. We can work in hospitals."

"Are you sure? That sounds pretty fantastic. I'll have to check that out."

When Dirk went back to the breakfast table, he asked his father about it. Yes, they could work in hospitals, but in Germany, and most likely near concentration camps. Not an attractive alternative to staying underground and doing resistance work.

Dirk felt a strong urge to get himself to Utrecht. The thought of Anna in Vught haunted him. Calling the castle would only upset the baroness. Better talk to Betty. If he could get a job at the University Hospital that would fall into the category of "exempt from labor" in Germany, he could stay "above ground" and do resistance work. His father encouraged him to try that.

Dirk didn't mention Anna as the primary reason for his hasty departure. He got back on his grandfather's upright, taking back roads once more and praying that his father's fedora, pulled deep over his forehead, made him look older. Older than twenty-two anyway. How long would he be able to pull off this charade?

He found Betty home. Jan came in from work later in the afternoon. They filled him in on what had happened in the time he'd been gone from Utrecht in more detail than Carla had been able to do over the phone. Still … where was Anna? She'd left two days before. Not a word from her since. Maybe she'd gone to the castle instead, but usually she called.

Betty, the keen observer, noticed Dirk looked tired. She offered to let him sleep in Anna's room. If she was planning on coming home, she would have called by now. He accepted gratefully. Pushing the heavy bicycle over dikes and dirt roads had tired him out. He went upstairs and pulled on the pajamas Jan lent him.

He looked at the pictures Anna had pinned on the wall next to her pillow. A family photo taken before the war: her mother chic, beautiful, and surprisingly vulnerable somehow; her father the way Dirk remembered him from the lunch at their home: intelligent and calm. The older brother might be a rebel, he thought, judging from the glint in his eye. And Anna, still young, already showed self-confidence, the way she freely looked into the camera's lens. She had inherited facial features from each parent: the light-colored blue eyes from her mother, the determined mouth of her father. A framed picture of the baroness riding sidesaddle made him smile. Even at that young age, she looked every inch the impressive woman he'd come to admire.

Dirk felt enveloped by all that was Anna. He forced himself not to think of her in imminent danger. He traded his fears for good memories, such as the way they'd sat in the grass at the edge of the river, telling each other about the start of the war. Her grandmother lived among farms, she'd told him. That was how she knew about chickens. She'd left out some important details! The moment he'd walked into Carla's room on that snowy day more than a year ago, he'd fallen in love with her.

It was still light in the room when he woke with a start. Where was he? What was happening? Something moved over his hair. He tried to raise his head off the pillow, but a hand pushed him back. He opened his eyes, and in the twilight he recognized Anna's face. Anna? Was he dreaming? She lowered her face and kissed him.

"Dirk! You're alive! Oh, my God!"

She was in tears. He'd never seen her cry. Really cry. He pulled her down and took her in his arms. She gave in and nestled her head close to his.

"Anna! Thank God you made it back."

There was so much to share; they knew they couldn't get it all out right away. Dirk pulled the blanket back and covered them both. Anna stopped crying and lined her body up against his. It would be the perfect prelude to an act they both wanted, but knew they should avoid. Dirk applied the brakes on himself, difficult as that was. He loved her too much to get her in trouble. This was one more example of how the war stood in the way of a normal life. The future was opaque. All he knew for sure about his future was that it would be filled with risk. At some point, he might have to turn himself into an invisible man. Death was a possibility.

"You better go downstairs, Anna. I will get into my clothes and join you."

She looked up at him. "Yes, you're right."

Betty had made tea and produced cookies. They sat around the dining room table.

"I don't know how to bring this news gently," Anna said, "but Piet is dead."

"Bastards!" Dirk put his head down and balled his hands into fists. "Piet of all people. He never lifted a finger to harm anybody."

"That's what makes it so hard. I still can't believe it happened, and I can't accept it."

They sat in silence for a while. Betty, the one to pass on the message from Piet's *hospita*, looked devastated. She brought out her handkerchief to wipe away copious tears. Jan stared at the cuckoo clock.

Anna told them how she'd found out, and how she'd spent the night in the home of a stranger.

"Did you spend two nights there?" Dirk asked.

"No. I wanted to come back here, but the train from 's-Hertogenbosch to Utrecht was derailed. People on the platform said it was sabotaged. I never found out if that was true. But there was a train going in another direction, to Arnhem, so I decided to go there."

"Have you contacted Piet's parents?" Dirk asked.

"No. I haven't been able to bring myself to pick up the phone. Besides, the telephone lines in Arnhem were cut, another act of sabotage. But I discussed it with my father. He suggested I go there in person."

"He 's right. You shouldn't do that alone, Anna," Dirk said. "That's a job for a minister."

"Do you think I should ask Walter to go with me?"

"Good idea. Ask him."

Betty suggested to Jan it was time to go to bed. She offered Jan's remodeled hobby room for Dirk to sleep in, since it was now curfew time. Jan would get a sleeping bag ready for him.

This was a new experience. He'd never spent an evening alone with Anna. At Carla's, they were always part of the Group of Eight. He sank down on the couch in the cozy living room and pulled Anna next to him.

"I've always tried not to ask what you've been doing," she said, "but three weeks was a long time to wonder if you were all right."

"Would you believe I was on a barge all that time?" Dirk said with a teasing smile.

"Oh, come on! Were you hiding?"

"No, Otto and I were on a mission. We had to get to a place where I could introduce Otto to British agents, so they could help him get across. The best way to get there was by barge."

"So, Otto is on his way to England? Why didn't you join him when you had the chance?"

"Would you have liked me to?"

"No, of course not! But I want to know why."

"Because I couldn't take you with me," he said, and pulled her closer. It was only partly a tease.

"I bet," she laughed. He knew she wouldn't ask any more questions. She had a proven record of leaving well enough alone.

"Do you want to know how Carla and I found out that Otto was on his way to England?" she asked.

"You knew?"

"Yes. I was over at Carla's the day after the university closed. She made coffee and offered me a cookie. I stuck my hand in the cookie jar, and a tiny piece of folded paper came out. The scribble on it said she should listen to Radio Oranje to find out if he'd made it to England. It was signed with an O."

"*'Geef Carla een zoen,'* right?" Dirk said.

"Yes. Did Otto tell you that?"

"He asked me to give that message to his mother."

"Were you as surprised as we were? Even Carla didn't know Otto loved her. At least, that's what we assume."

"Yes, I was surprised, but Otto is good at keeping things to himself."

He was more interested in what Anna had been up to while he was on the barge. After the university closed, she told him, the only decision she and Carla made was to abandon Carla's room. They contemplated becoming nurses. Meanwhile, they helped Jan distribute his illegal paper locally, but that was cut short after Herman showed up to say he was going to work for the Germans after all. Carla was so distraught, they went to see Walter in Ede and stayed at the castle.

"What are your plans now?"

"Vague is the best way to describe them. I only know what I don't want to do."

"Like what?"

"Become a nurse."

"Why not? It's an honorable profession."

Her body stiffened. "Oh, please. Don't say that. That's what my mother said."

"What do your parents suggest you do?"

Anna sought his hand, and in her firm grip he sensed her dilemma. She had gone straight to her father's office from the station, because she trusted he would understand her, and she'd been right at that. He totally supported her involvement in hiding and supplying Jews. The fact that the baroness was involved didn't surprise him one bit. It had made him smile. He'd even agreed that telling her mother all this would be a mistake. He knew his wife well. No sense making her nervous. But things became difficult during dinner. Her mother had, of course, read in the papers that all universities were closed. She suggested that Anna should come home. And if not that, she should become a nurse. It brought Anna back to the agonizing days of high school when she'd rejected the nursing profession in favor of studying medicine. The very suggestion had made her cross.

"But I couldn't tell her I had plenty to keep me busy and home was not the place to do those things," she said. She sounded exasperated.

"I can guess what those busy things are, but can you spell them out for me?"

"Yes, but only if you will give me an idea of what you will do with yourself till this war is over."

"All right. You go first."

She told him she'd given her immediate future some thought. Having Piet, Herman, and Otto out of the picture made her realize it was up to her to help Walter and Klaas with caring for the onderduikers. Somebody had to make sure they had food stamps, money, and whatever else they needed. She saw providing them as her responsibility. Also, Oma was getting older, and she wanted to watch out for her. All in all, she would divide her time between Ede and Utrecht.

"Your turn, Dirk."

"My hope is that I can get a legitimate job at the hospital. There is always work to do in the lab, and maybe I can talk my pathology professor into something with an important-sounding title so I can stay above ground. It will take some fancy footwork to get that done. I don't need to be paid. That's not the point. I need mobility."

Anna put her chin in the cup of her hand, and after a pensive moment said her father had told her of a good friend from his student days in Leiden who was director of the University Hospital in Utrecht. In fact, he was the one whose visiting card he'd given her when she'd first left for Utrecht. She could call him anytime, he'd said.

"Maybe he can help you, Dirk."

"Thank you, but I won't take you up on that offer. Call it pride if you will, but I want to get a job on my own steam. I don't want to be a protégé of the boss."

"I see. Well, then the best thing I can offer you is prayer."

They laughed and decided that was enough serious talk. It would be what it would be, but at the moment they were still together and without imminent threats. They fell asleep on the couch in each other's arms.

CHAPTER TWENTY-SIX

Walter – June 1943

Walter laid the telephone back in its cradle after he heard the click on the other end. Anna's pleading voice rang in his ears. Would he go with her to Assen to tell Piet's mother her son had been executed? He remembered Piet well from the day in Loosdrecht, less than a year ago. His hand had been in the pile of hands that guaranteed Daan's secret would stay a secret. And now this. Death by a bullet. Walter shivered. Carla's well-meaning friends had stuck their heads out against the organized brutality of the Nazis, and now one of them had paid for it with his life.

Of course, he would go with her. She was a courageous young woman, but this task was beyond her years of wisdom. He should at least share her burden.

There was a soft knock on the door of his study. It was Bram. Walter turned around in the swivel chair and opened his arms. Bram ran into them. As he smelled the boyish fresh-soap odor of his hair, his eyes filled with tears. Piet's mother, twenty-some years ago, had cradled her son just like this.

Bram looked up. "Are you crying?" he asked.

"No, I had a piece of dust in my eye," he answered.

"Oh."

"Can I help you with something, Bram?"

"Mother asks if you would like to have lunch with us. Would you?"

"I would like to, but I can't. Let's go down and I will talk to her."

After he excused himself, Walter put on a raincoat and got his bike. Bram walked him to the gate.

"Are you going away for long?" he asked.

"I will be back the day after tomorrow. Be good to your mother."

He took a train to Zwolle. Anna was waiting for him on the platform where a train to Assen was steaming up to leave.

"I made it by the skin of my teeth," Walter said, and opened the door of the only empty compartment he saw.

"I never realized how far Assen was from what we think of as the center of the universe," Anna said.

"I notice less evidence of the Occupation here." Walter took off his coat and put it overhead. "I saw fewer military. It's our coastline they need to defend. Well. Anyway. Anna, tell me how you found out about Piet."

After she told him the whole story, Anna said, "I hope you don't mind I begged you to come along, Walter. The very thought of having to tell Mevrouw Zandberg this awful news makes my heart sink to my toes. What can be worse for a mother than to lose a child? Especially her only child."

The train poked along stretches of green pastures and widely spaced farms. The rain splattered against the window, and the wind scattered copious amounts of drops over the dirty glass. Horses stood in the flat landscape with their tails to the wind, their heads cast down, waiting out the foul weather.

It was quiet between them for a while.

"There's no easy way to bring bad news," Walter said. "You can't spin a sudden death into a tolerable fact, especially not a violent one. You can't make it go away."

"Then what do you do?"

"It's more like what you shouldn't do. Pouring a waterfall of words over the head of someone who's dealing with a devastating loss is definitely not the best way. A professor in Leiden once gave us a proverb to meditate on. It has stuck with me ever since, especially this line: 'Don't sing songs to a heavy heart.'"

"Don't try to put it in another light? Is that what it means?"

"More or less. You can't wish a hurt away. In your profession, Anna, you will be constantly challenged to solve problems, to get into action, to *do* something. But there are times when action is not the solution. In this case, it is very tempting to shine a bright light into a dark corner, but that doesn't bring the bereaved any closer to acceptance."

At his urging, Anna had called Mrs. Zandberg ahead of their visit. When they arrived, Walter pulled the bell on a house in the middle of a row of red brick houses that lacked front yards. A maid opened the door. They were expected. Without asking any questions, she led them straight into the living room. The only light to counter the darkness in there was a floor lamp next to a mahogany fauteuil upholstered in a dark-green material. The floor-length curtains were drawn halfway.

Mr. and Mrs. Zandberg rose to greet them. Piet's father looked ready to hear whatever the news was. His mother rushed over to Anna and reached for her hands in a frantic motion. She probed Anna's face with feverish eyes while Piet's father made a gesture toward a couch. But before they could sit, the woman blurted out the question that was burning on her mind.

"What is the news?"

"Let's sit down first, dear," Piet's father said.

"No, I want to know. I have waited long enough."

Walter watched Anna struggle to find the right words, but was there a euphemism for a sudden death?

Horse's hooves pounded the cobblestones in the street with relentless regularity and broke the silence. Walter could hardly bear their jarring sound.

Anna took a deep breath. "Piet was executed four days ago," she finally said, her lips trembling. She gave it straight to the poor mother. Gutsy girl, he thought.

Mr. Zandberg slumped into a chair closest to him and brought his hand to his face. Piet's mother said nothing. She stood nailed to the Oriental rug under her feet. Then she spread her arms around Anna and sobbed uncontrollably. Walter put a chair next to Piet's broken father. He heard the wind whip rain against the windows, and somewhere in the house, a door slammed shut. Anna moved Piet's mother to the couch. The four of them sat in a circle. The invisible dagger, having cut the harsh news deep into these people's hearts, waited to be pulled back out. Walter thought of the images of Piet that surely must be racing through his parents' minds right now; a collage of pictures, dormant in their memory, of the various stages of their son's life, from birth through age twenty-three. He thought of Bram running into his arms that morning.

"Rejoice with those who rejoice, weep with those who weep," the Apostle Paul wrote in one of his letters to the Romans. The line came to his mind as he looked at Piet's slumped father and his sobbing mother, and he felt tears welling up. He didn't try to hold them back. Instead, he put his hand on the father's thigh and left it there.

"I got to know Piet," Walter began. "He was in my sister's circle of friends. You probably know he was working with their small group to hide Jews."

Mr. Zandberg nodded with his eyes closed.

"Piet was very honest. At their first meeting, he said he didn't have the courage to do that kind of work. But he overcame his fear."

Mrs. Zandberg pulled out a handkerchief and dabbed her eyes. "He was furious when our neighbors got hauled off to the railroad station. That changed everything for him."

Walter had provided an opening. Gradually, words came out. They asked Anna for details. She emphasized that Piet had died because he'd refused to go to Germany to work for the Germans. They said a prayer. Anna promised to visit again, and offered to help with the Jews Piet had found a hiding place for in their area. Though much more could be said, there was really nothing more they could do.

Walter knew how hard it was to bid good-bye to devastated people. He asked if they had family or friends who could come over. He was given a phone number, and he arranged for friends to come right away. A middle-aged couple showed up fifteen minutes later.

On the way back in the train, he and Anna sat in silence, each sifting through the words that had been spoken and the ones that had not been, because they were too painful to be said out loud. Walter thought of the other twenty-nine students who had been executed with Piet. Right now, twenty-nine couples, spread out over all of Holland, were struggling for an answer to why they had to lose their sons. Piet's parents had shown tremendous grace under the stress of first not knowing, and then having to accept an irrevocable fact, the death of their only child. He prayed others would find similar courage. It would be understandable if they railed against a cruel God. It might even help them. God could handle such venting and ranting. It was utterly human to want to put the blame somewhere, although the Nazi regime would be the logical place.

Anna broke the silence. "You've chosen a hard profession, Walter. In my profession, I will wield a surgical knife and hope for the best. What is *your* tool?"

"Listening."

"And that's all?"

"No, that's not all. I have the Bible."

Anna was quiet. The train rushed on. The storm had subsided, and a glimmer of sunshine fell over the fields.

"I don't know if I will ever have a faith like that."

"Faith is not a possession," he said. "It is an experience. God works in indirect ways. Whether you know it or not, Anna, God worked through you today."

She didn't answer, and he didn't push the conversation further.

When the train rolled into Zwolle, Anna said she wanted to visit her grandmother before going back to Utrecht. They changed platforms and took the train to Ede, where Walter had parked his bicycle. The back tire felt soft to his touch, so he filled it up with air, using the small hand pump fastened to the bike's frame. Satisfied the tire was now hard as a rock, he swung into the saddle; and as soon as he had momentum, Anna jumped onto the luggage carrier and held onto his waist.

The woods they biked through looked mysterious in the twilight. Wet leaves shimmered in the afternoon sunrays, while soaked tree trunks stood out like stiff sentries in dark uniforms. Closer to the castle, the woods thinned out. Walter liked the familiar feeling of almost being there. The beautiful building always sprang a surprise on him, seemingly rising up out of nowhere. But today he was doubly surprised. He stopped. Anna jumped off the carrier. In front of them was not only the castle. An imposing Mercedes-Benz with the Nazi standard on the fender stood parked in front with a chauffeur in uniform behind the wheel.

"Oh, my God," Anna said. "Not again."

"What do you mean?"

"When we brought Klaas here, that same car was parked in front. It belonged to the commandant of the military base in Ede. He came to order my grandmother out of her home. He wanted it for his headquarters."

"I remember you telling me about that."

"Oma got out of it by offering him her prize Oldenburg mare, because she'd found out he was a breeder. He took the mare and left Oma alone."

"That's quite a story."

"God help us, Walter. What if he has the same request today? She doesn't have another horse to give away. And what about

Klaas?"

"Anna, don't think of the worst scenario first. There might be other reasons for his visit."

She didn't look assured. With her eyes cast downward, she seemed to count every pebble she trod on.

They walked Walter's bike around the circular driveway to gain more time to let this unwelcome surprise sink in.

"Well, it's still my grandmother's house, so we can enter through the kitchen."

Mien stood with her back to the door. She was busy preparing a tray with tea and cookies for Janus to bring into the living room. She turned around to see who had snuck into her domain, and Walter saw horror in her eyes.

"I don't know what to make of this," she said. She gave a deep sigh and looked over at him. "Dominee Vlaskamp, do you know anything about this?"

"About what, Mien?"

"About this visit of you-know-who?"

"Not a thing, Mien. Did the baroness know she would have a visitor?"

Janus answered for her. "The commandant called this morning, asking if he could pay her a visit. Mien, is this tray ready to be brought in?"

Walter opened the door to the salon while Janus balanced the tray on the open palm of his left hand, accustomed to reaching for the doorknob with his right. Walter peeked inside and saw two people. The baroness sat on the couch across from the commandant, who was dressed in civilian clothes, looking totally relaxed. If Walter hadn't known the man was a colonel, he might have taken him for a good friend or maybe a neighbor. He briefly considered that possibility. But neither a friend nor a neighbor would show up in a car with a swastika flag attached to the bumper.

He stood back to let Janus put the tray on the table next to the couch. The baroness started to pour tea. When she noticed Janus didn't shut the door, she looked up.

"Walter! Please come in and join us for tea. Who is that with you?"

He stepped aside and let Anna walk in.

"Anna! My dear girl, it's you. What a pleasant surprise. Herr von Schloss, this is my granddaughter. You met her once before, I believe. And this is Dominee Vlaskamp, pastor of the Remonstrantse Kerk in Ede."

The commandant stood up and lifted Anna's hand. She looked flustered as he kissed it.

Mien had already put cups on the tray for Anna and himself, maybe as a safeguard to make sure the baroness wouldn't be alone with "that German." Once everyone was seated, the baroness reopened the conversation. Apparently, it had centered on the mare she had given to the commandant.

"She is a beautiful mover, Frau von Haersolte," the commandant said. Walter saw Anna wince at the German *von* instead of the Dutch *van*.

"Yes, my husband was very proud of her. He often said she was the best mount he ever had. But now I want to know what brings Anna here."

Anna fiddled with her necklace and hesitated. Walter wasn't sure she was going to answer. Clearly, a battle of opposing urges was going on. The baroness smoothly changed her role from hostess to grandmother.

"You seem distressed, Anna. Tell me, what has happened?"

She took Anna's hand. Anna's reaction to her touch was to break out in tears. An uncomfortable silence fell over the room. The baroness reached over and put her arm around her granddaughter. Walter held his breath. This was a situation he hadn't foreseen, but then, Anna had been under a lot of stress lately. Could he effectively interfere? Should he? He was lost for words. Not so the baroness.

"Something happened. You don't have to tell us, my dear. Here, take a sip of tea. It will make you feel better."

Anna wiped her tears and complied. Walter marveled at the baroness, who'd spared Anna the agony of having to come out with the truth, which, she keenly sensed, was not the kind of subject appropriate for the commandant to hear.

The conversation got back on track to neutral terrain—horses. Since Walter knew nothing about them, he let the horse talk fly by and sank back in his chair to observe the commandant. He was a handsome prototype of the Aryan race: blue eyes, blond hair combed back flat to his skull and parted on the right in a line so straight, you would think he'd done it with a ruler. He was no slouch, the way he sat upright in the fauteuil, though it wasn't a rigid posture. It just called up the image of a man completely comfortable in the company of formidable women like the baroness. Walter wouldn't be surprised if it turned out the commandant was a baron himself.

"Where did you take Tango?" the baroness asked. Tango had to be the mare.

"I shipped her over to my place in Oldenburg. She will be safer there. I have good hands to look after her."

He didn't say *home,* and Walter guessed that "my place" was bigger than an ordinary house.

"What do you have to keep her safe from?" the baroness asked.

"There is a scarcity. The cavalry is desperate for horses."

"I was appalled to learn about the carnage," the baroness said, "that took place when horses met up with steel tanks in Poland. No living being, be it man or horse, is a match for a hunk of steel."

The commandant was visibly taken aback, but he had good salon manners.

"Yes, that was unfortunate."

"Are horses still useful in warfare these days?" Anna interrupted. "What's a horse to do when face to face with a monstrous tank?"

Walter was glad to see she had regained control of her emotions, but her words had an edge.

"*Ach*, Fraulein, the answer is, nothing. But tell that to a cavalry officer!" He gave a short laugh.

"So, then, what are they used for, if they're not suitable for battle?" Anna pressed on.

"They're mostly used for transport, unfortunately." Herr von Schloss sighed. Walter saw a glimmer of humanity in his remark.

The baroness stepped in. "I am grateful you are protecting Tango from such a fate. She neither has the build nor the temperament to be turned into a pulling horse. But tell me, what do you hear from your family back home?"

It was a deft move away from warfare. The late afternoon sun threw low-slanting rays into the room. On the other side of the high windows, a fog lifted off the manicured lawn in back of the castle. It drifted westward, revealing the elegant carriage house in the distance. Walter saw the commandant's glance wander over the outline of the building that sported a shining weathervane in the form of a galloping horse on top of its cupola.

"Ach, gnädige Frau, looking outside at your lawns and stables, I feel the tug of my own place. I haven't been home since Christmas. What I hear from my family is that they miss me as much as I miss them."

"Did you join the army voluntarily?" the baroness asked.

"I come from a long line of military officers. When the German empire fell, there was not much appetite for war anymore. My father decided to devote the rest of his life to something he'd always liked better than his career as a general in the emperor's cavalry, and that was raising the famed Oldenburg breed of riding horses. After he died, I took over. But things changed drastically over the past decade. Here we are at war again!" He stopped abruptly.

Walter felt like saying, "Yes, we noticed!", but what purpose would that serve? Besides, he was a guest. The baroness should set the tone. Maybe she knew why this German officer was visiting her.

"It must have been hard for you to leave the breeding business in the hands of others," she said. "And it must be hard to find stable hands, since they've been forced to enlist in the army, I suppose."

Herr von Schloss sighed. Apparently, his hostess had hit it on the nail. He sank deeper into his fauteuil and stretched his long legs. He probably hadn't discussed the subject of breeding Oldenburg horses in a long time. Walter sensed his relief. This woman knew what he was talking about. At the barracks in Ede, there was probably little interest in his particular dilemma.

"Yes, that is indeed a problem. One that keeps me awake at night."

"I hope for all of us the war won't last too long, Herr von Schloss," the baroness said. "We will all be better off with a return to peace and life as we knew it." She made a gesture toward the teapot under the cozy. She was about to offer a second cup of tea, but in another sign of knowing his way around the rarified world of nobility, he politely refused.

The commandant got up. He thanked his hostess for the pleasant afternoon with a bow and a clack from the heels of his shiny shoes. The baroness stayed seated while Walter and Anna rose. Herr von Schloss reached for Anna's hand again and said, "I hope the reason for your tears will make a turnaround."

"That's a vain hope, Herr von Schloss," she said. "One of my best friends was executed in Vught three days ago. He refused to sign the declaration of loyalty."

The commandant had raised Anna's hand to the level of her waist. He stopped, held it there, and looked up at her. Walter wondered if he could see what *he* saw. Anna's light blue eyes had taken on the color of a frozen lake, its icy crust sealing off the bodies of her cousin, of the three farmers in Ede, and of Piet Zandberg. Forever.

A hush fell over the room.

"*My lieber Gott*, the SS. Please understand, Fraulein, that the Army and the SS are two entirely different institutions. But that is no solace to you now."

He kissed her hand and turned toward the door. Walter opened it for him and saw him to the front door. Before the chauffeur got out of the car, he said in a low voice, "Please thank the baroness for receiving me." He looked up and added, "Her granddaughter has every reason to be upset. *Grüss Gott.*"

The chauffeur raised his arm and gave the Heil Hitler salute before opening the door to the backseat. The commandant got in. The door slammed shut. Walter watched the impressive automobile navigate the circular driveway and disappear in the twilight of the oncoming night.

CHAPTER TWENTY-SEVEN

Anna – June 1943

Anna found a letter from Emmy when she returned to Utrecht. It sounded an alarm without explaining anything, but it was clear Emmy wanted Anna to come to Haarlem. There would be no time to settle back into her room.

Betty told her Carla had showed up to say she'd been accepted at the University Hospital as an apprentice nurse. And Dirk had found a job in the hospital laboratory, as he'd hoped.

"I guess *this* medical student's job is traveling on trains," Anna said with a laugh.

"You be careful now, Anna," Betty said. "The Gestapo is getting more aggressive. Carry your ID card. Jan says things aren't going well for Hitler on the Russian front. And you know what a cornered cat will do. He will scratch!"

Emmy stood waiting for her on the platform of Haarlem's railroad station with her bike in hand. Once outside the station, Anna jumped on the baggage carrier and off they went. She'd never been to Haarlem. The city she grew up in was old as well, but it showed in different ways. Arnhem was praised for its beautiful parks and its greenness. Haarlem was remarkable for its seventeenth-century architecture. While holding on to the belt on Emmy's dress and bobbing up and down over cobblestones, she took in the quaintness of an age-old market and the overwhelming size of the Gothic church in the center of the city.

Emmy pushed hard on the pedals. They'd hardly spoken a word. What dread was propelling her? She stopped in front of a home in a row of houses lining the river they'd already crossed several times in different places. It meandered through the heart of the city.

Anna dismounted and looked up at the tall façade, three stories high.

"This is my parents' home," Emmy said while she brought her bike into the wide entryway and leaned it against the fancy wainscoting. A door opened upstairs, and a man looked down over the bannister. "It's me," Emmy called up. The head disappeared.

"That's my father. He works at home when the court is not in session."

They climbed steep stairs to the top floor where Emmy's room was.

"God, I'm so glad you came," Emmy said as she shut the door. She threw her arms around Anna.

"What's going on? Tell me."

"It's about the couple I was supposed to find a hiding place for. Remember?"

"Yes, I do. Relatives of Daan. They didn't believe the Germans would ever move them from their home."

"Exactly. I had promised I would check back, so I decided to visit them after the university closed. They'd received the notice to appear at the station the day before. They were incredulous."

"And stubborn, I bet."

"Not just a little. But as you know, people who can afford to live in Bloemendaal are not stupid."

Anna nodded. In the days before the war, it was a given that people who lived in places like Bloemendaal had made their fortune elsewhere. Many had returned from the Dutch East Indies, leaving behind a lucrative career trading in sugar, tea, coffee, rubber, or oil. Bloemendaal was the paradise they'd dreamed about. It lay nestled behind the dunes that lined the Noordzee, a beautiful area for retirement.

"They weren't about to leave," Emmy said. "Mr. Hirsch said he'd heeded my warning and he'd done a smart thing. He sold his house to a man who'd worked for him on Java and who'd also repatriated. The understanding between them is that when the war is over, the man will sell it back to him. The house is divided so two families can live in it."

"Clever," Anna said.

Emmy sat on her bed, leaning against the wall. Anna looked around. She noticed a picture of the Group of Eight, taken while they were all in Loosdrecht at Herman's cottage. It was framed in silver and stood on the desk by the window. It showed Otto with his arms around Emmy's shoulders.

Mr. Hirsch had carefully choreographed his escape. He and his wife took a small suitcase each and sadly said good-bye to the neighbors on either side of their home and walked toward the station. Halfway, they removed the yellow stars on their outer clothing and took a sharp right into a stranger's yard. They hid behind the garage. After curfew started and it had turned dark, they left their two empty suitcases behind and surreptitiously crawled back home, hugging the gardens bordering the dark lanes. They reentered their home through a cellar window. A moonless sky that night was their good luck.

"My goodness," Anna said. "This sounds like an Agatha Christie novel."

"I called shortly afterward to see where things stood, but I could tell it wasn't the voice of Mr. Hirsch on the other end of the line. It was Albert, the man who'd bought the house from him. He didn't hang up on me. Apparently, he'd been told about me. He asked some pointed questions, of course, to make sure I was 'that girl.'"

"And 'that girl' has to deliver, I assume," Anna said.

"Right. And I have no idea how to deliver what they need. My God, Anna! I got into this because of the Group of Eight. I have no regrets, mind you, but I need help. Desperately."

"I can see that. They will need monthly food rations. Does Albert have a family?"

"Yes, a wife and three teenagers. Why?"

"That's good, or else the grocer might get suspicious when he shops for more than one man needs. Did the police ever come to check where Mr. and Mrs. Hirsch were?"

"Yes, but Albert told them they'd sold the house to him. He had the papers to prove it. They believed him and didn't do a house search."

"Lucky! The police came to Daan's house after they all fled. The place was turned upside down. His father's secretary told them that when she came back to work after the weekend, she'd found nobody home upstairs. She was taken to the police station, but they couldn't find anything against her."

"How are the others?" Emmy asked.

"I have sad news, I'm afraid." Anna took a deep breath. "Piet was brought to Vught. He was one of the thirty students executed there. You must have heard about that."

"Oh, my God, Anna. Please tell me it's not true. Piet! That's horrible. How could they? I read about the roundup in the paper, but no names were given."

Emmy got up and walked over to the window. She took the picture frame in her hands and stared at it. When she turned, tears ran down her cheeks.

"We will always be the Group of Eight," she said defiantly. "No matter how few of us will be left after this is all over."

"But Daan is safe," Anna said. "And Dirk is officially working in the lab of the University Hospital in Utrecht. Carla is there also as a nurse apprentice. Herman decided to go to Germany after all. And Otto is on his way to England. So now you have all the news."

Emmy hugged the picture to her chest and walked back to her bed. She sat hunched over. Anna couldn't think of anything sensible to say. Circumstances had pushed her into the role of messenger, and she hated it. But what she hated even more was that the horrors she'd witnessed — the murder of the farmers in Ede and then dealing with the execution of Piet — were building a dam around her heart. Hard facts shatter you and then they harden you. She could feel it happening. Bursting into tears in front of a German officer had been the turning point.

"That shouldn't happen again," Oma had told her afterward. "If you want to do this kind of work, you can't afford to break down. A smart opponent will pounce on his victim when he senses weakness. That goes for vultures and it goes for Nazis. You were lucky Herr von Schloss is obviously not a Nazi."

She was right, of course. She doubted Oma had even blinked when Janus had told her the commandant had come again.

"Why did you receive him, Oma? What are Janus and Mien to think of this?" Anna had asked her.

"My dear Anna, refusing him would have been the equivalent of slamming the door in his face. Better to hear directly from him in case he wanted to take over my home again. I'm glad I received him. He doesn't like what he has to do, but he has no choice. I pity him."

"*Pity* him? Oma, how can you pity any of *them*?" Anna had almost screamed at her grandmother.

"Any of them? No two people in this world are the same, Anna. You cannot measure all people with the same ruler. To declare all Germans ill-intentioned is a mistake. It pays to approach them first of all as fellow human beings."

Anna talked with Walter about it later. "Your grandmother is a practiced observer of human nature," he said. "She avoids judgment, but nobody can pull the wool over her eyes. She faced the possibility that her home could be taken from her, but she was rewarded for her courage. If it's up to the commandant, she will stay where she is. He needs her in other ways."

"*He* needs *her*?"

"The man is homesick. Your grandmother offers him respite. There are more castles and grand houses around here that he could demand, but the baroness is unique and he knows it. You should be proud of her, Anna. She has high principles. She's not going to allow herself to be used. What she gave the officer was not traitorous."

"Would you approach Hitler with the same goodwill?" she challenged him.

"Ah, now you are talking about a man who lives on the fringes of what is human. It's no wonder people came up with the concept of the devil. Since the beginning of time, every generation has had to contend with people who simply cannot be understood, and whose deeds we cannot condone. But that doesn't mean we shouldn't try."

"For how long do we try to understand them? "

"For as long as it makes sense. For as long as it fulfills justice."

Emmy straightened up, drawing Anna's attention. Emmy didn't look her happiest, but Anna couldn't help noticing how pretty she was. Everything about her was well proportioned. She was tall, slim, and naturally elegant with wavy blond hair she'd combed away from her face. Emmy was the kind of woman who turned heads.

"This is the time to think about whether you want to continue this work, Emmy. You could also spend your time reading French books, you know. You would be way ahead if and when the university reopens, which it must at some point in time."

"My parents would like that." It was the first time she had a smile on her face.

"Are they aware of your connection to Mr. Hirsch?"

"God, no! They would die if they knew. They don't sympathize with the Nazis by any means, but the idea of working for the Underground is far removed from their minds. They aren't risk-takers. My father is cautious by nature, and being a judge makes him even more so."

"And your mother?"

"You will meet her at lunch. You can decide for yourself."

Outside the door to the dining room stood an easel displaying a large reproduction of a painting. What it depicted stopped Anna in her tracks. She felt punched in the stomach by the face of a girl whose eyes had a hollow look and were out of proportion to her face. Her mouth was wide open. She was cast against a background of undernourished and distressed people. It was a horrifying scene.

"That face is hard to walk by," she said.

"I know. I can't wait till next Saturday when Mother puts up another painting."

"What do you mean?"

"Every week she chooses a painting for us to study, and we are expected to critique it. This painting is by Leo van Gestel. It portrays the refugees from Belgium in WWI. What do you think of it?"

"Frankly, it makes me cringe. I hope we'll never have to watch anything like that here. Our food is rationed, but we're not emaciated. It almost makes me feel lucky."

Anna was filled with curiosity about the woman she was about to meet. Anyone who put a painting like that outside the place where meals were taken had to be out of the ordinary.

Emmy's father was already seated. Anna's immediate impression of him was that of a wise owl. His horn-rimmed eyeglasses magnified his steady brown eyes, set in a serious face that didn't move a muscle as his daughter entered. He got up from the heavy armchair when he spotted Anna, and politely shook her hand and invited her to sit next to him. The table was set for five people, and a moment later two women came in. The young one looked like Emmy and was probably her sister. The other was unmistakably their mother. All three cast from the same mold.

"So nice of you to come," the mother said warmly, and shook

Anna's hand.

A lazy Susan at the center of the table was laden with jam, butter (or was it margarine?), and thin slices of cheese. A silver basket with bread slices was sent around the table, and soon everyone had a plateful.

"I almost feel like I should go and give what I have on my plate to the girl in the painting in the hall," Anna said.

Emmy's mother looked up. She was an attractive woman with delicate features. "Isn't that a gripping painting?" she said. "Actually, it's a charcoal, which is most unusual for Leo van Gestel. He worked mostly with paint in bold colors."

"He made good use of the charcoal," Anna said. "I don't know much about painting, but the color black seems very appropriate for the subject matter."

Emmy's mother reacted with animation. Her whole body seemed to respond to the prospect of discussing her "painting of the week."

"Charcoal is a difficult medium to work with," she said. "It easily smudges, and it doesn't adhere well. He used charcoal pencils that allowed him to make bold strokes, and paper with rough texture."

Emmy and her sister made faces at each other. They seemed to say, "Here we go again," but their mother ignored them. She was obviously onto her favorite subject.

"Do you paint yourself, Mrs. van der Linden?" Anna asked.

"No, I don't, but I am fascinated by art and the history of art. And I'm trying to pass this on to my children. With mixed results, I should say."

"What I react to when I look at a painting," Anna said, "is the story it tells and the message it sends. This charcoal screams hunger and injustice at me, and I think to myself, 'God, I hope we don't have to go through that agony again.'"

"Yes," Mrs. van der Linden said. "Isn't it amazing how he gets that across? I marvel at his technique. It isn't used that much anymore, but it goes back to 23,000 BC. Charcoal paintings were found in caves. Probably because it was the only medium available."

At that point, Anna completely understood why Emmy did not involve her mother in her concerns for Mr. and Mrs. Hirsch. This woman lived in a world of her own, a refuge from today's ugly realities.

"Mother," Emmy said, "Anna invited me to come with her to Utrecht. I am dying to go back to my alma mater, even if it's only for a few days."

"Do you live in Utrecht, Anna?" It was the first thing Judge van der Linden had said during the entire lunch.

"No, sir. My family lives in Arnhem, but I kept my room in Utrecht. I'm hoping to find work in the hospital, so I can keep my pulse on the art of medicine. It worked for our friend Carla." It was a lie of course, but she couldn't very well say she worked for the Underground.

Emmy sent her a grateful look.

The train back to Utrecht was crowded. The two wagons reserved for the German Army were scarcely populated. The others were packed, unlike the ones Anna had taken between Zwolle and Assen a few days ago. Emmy had brought a small suitcase. She placed it on the overhead luggage rack next to a large package that looked uncannily like the bundle Dirk had carried under his arm the time she caught him and Jan standing outside her bedroom. A middle-aged man was seated directly underneath it. In spite of the warm summer weather, he wore a fedora hat. Anna was intrigued and decided to keep an eye on the package. She could see it through the window of the compartment's door as she stood in the hallway.

At the next train stop, several Gestapo walked alongside the train. One of them entered the gangway where she and Emmy stood among the crowded passengers.

"Kennkarte!" he shouted.

Anna kept her eye on the man with the fedora. He had a physical reaction to the command, something like a quick cringe of his upper body. It confirmed Anna's suspicion.

People started to reach for their IDs. The man with the hat took out his ID and showed it to the Gestapo with his eyes cast down. The officer looked at it, was about to give it back, but turned it over and examined the passport picture. His eyes burned a hole in the man's forehead right through the visor of his hat, and Anna could feel her sweat glands start to work under her armpits. Emmy, next to her, was oblivious to the drama playing out so close to where she stood. The officer finally gave the ID back. Anna looked at the man and made eye contact. She raised her eyebrows and directed her gaze to the package. She could swear he knew what she thought.

The Gestapo had moved on by the time they approached Utrecht's station. Another middle-aged man, who also wore a gray fedora, worked his way through the crowded corridor. He stopped in front of the compartment where Emmy had placed her bag and tipped his hat to the man seated under the package. The seated man returned the greeting by doing the same thing, and then he slowly rose and prepared to leave the compartment. He did not take the package with him. Emmy reached for her suitcase and started toward the exit, as did everyone else. Anna lingered. The second man with the fedora immediately placed himself under the package in the brown wrapping paper. This train was destined for Arnhem.

Emmy called her from outside. She was already on the platform. The first man with the hat was long gone when Anna stepped down from the train. She was sure she had witnessed the transfer of illegal newspapers.

"What took you so long?" Emmy asked.

"Nothing," Anna said. "You're just faster than I am."

CHAPTER TWENTY-EIGHT

Dirk – June 1943

Dirk took his new white lab coat out of the closet in the laboratory and chuckled to himself. A white coat was far better than striped prison pajamas, the kind worn in concentration camps. It was better than workman's clothes while digging trenches, and better than sweaty clothes while hiding in an attic under a hot tiled roof without a window to the world. No. Looking like the doctor he'd hoped to be one day was infinitely better. Realizing his good luck had put him in a good mood, he decided to get a cup of tea before starting a day of peering through a microscope at slides of human tissue. This was his second day on the job. The head of the lab had not asked any questions and had hired him on the spot. If his coworkers were suspicious, they didn't show it. Who knew? Some of them might be there for the same reason. If the war taught anything, it was to avoid asking questions. These days, only the Gestapo or people in the NSB asked pointed questions

He had changed his false name back to Dirk, but it had taken a bit of doing, because his old ID showed *student* as his profession, and that wouldn't do. Now, if he got stopped to show his Kennkarte, he could point to his job at the hospital. His father had helped by appealing to the man Dirk had met in Amsterdam, who had taken care of the IDs for Daan's parents and brother.

The hospital was a maze of hallways. On the first day, he'd walked by a room where people were drinking tea. He found his way back there and looked through the glass window that was part of the door. Three nurses looked up when he knocked. Dirk opened the door and asked if he could join them. In the same breath, he added an explanation, well aware that the professional distance between physicians and nurses was as wide as the North Sea.

"I'm working in the lab," he said. "I noticed you were serving tea here, and I'm dying for a cup."

"Come in," one of them said. "I am Sister Bertha. It's surrogate tea, of course, but not the worst kind."

She poured him a cup, inviting him to sit down, and asked his name.

"Dirk van Enthoven. This is my second day."

She looked at him as though she felt she should know him from somewhere, but he couldn't think of any place or occasion where they could have met. If so, he would have remembered her, because she was a very good-looking woman with striking blue eyes below her starched nurse's cap.

Bertha introduced him to the other nurses, who looked older, or perhaps they looked older because they were tired after their night shift. He apologized for interrupting their conversation. It was about the price of meat.

"The small roast I bought last week," one of them said, "was so tough, my family complained. If you don't marinate it for twenty-four hours, you can't chew it. But I don't always think ahead to do the marinating overnight."

"Let's face it," the third nurse said. "The best meat goes to you-know-where. Maybe what you ate was horsemeat."

"There aren't that many horses left for the meat market," Bertha said. "Besides, the idea of eating part of a horse revolts me."

"It was a busy night," the oldest-looking nurse said. "Some wounded policemen were brought in. They were in terrible shape."

"Policemen?" Dirk asked.

"Guards at the prison. It was stormed. One guard was killed. We got the wounded ones. The Underground does their work under cover of the night. We seem to be busier at night than in the daytime lately."

Dirk didn't want to be pulled into a conversation about the Underground's work. He got up and thanked Bertha for the tea.

"Come again, Dr. van Enthoven. The teapot is always filled," she said.

He winced at the "*Dr.* van Enthoven." Amazing what a white lab coat did to a nurse who knew the hospital hierarchy only too well. It wasn't surprising, really, in a country that had boasted over ten political parties before the war. So much of life was compartmentalized. Its society resembled a neatly organized sewing box. Everything was tucked in its place. What would it look like once the Nazi yoke came off?

After the day's work, Dirk biked over to Jan and Betty's house. The person he hoped to see opened the door and fell into his arms.

"Anna! You made it back. How is Emmy?"

When she heard her name, Emmy stepped forward.

"Hi Dirk. Congratulations on your new job."

"Thank you. It beats worrying, if you know what I mean."

They walked through the kitchen to the tiny backyard to soak up the late afternoon sun. It still sat high enough in the sky to peek over the tiled roofs of the houses in the next street over. Two wooden benches on the stamp-sized lawn invited them to sit down.

The hinges on the gate squeaked as Jan opened it to get himself and his bike inside the garden. Dirk helped him ease it in and undid the leather straps on the baggage carrier. Jan lifted off a large package bound in canvas and quickly ran it inside. It was accomplished before he realized he had company.

Betty came out with a jug of orangeade. Or at least it looked orange.

"Well, I see we have company," Jan said when he returned.

Emmy got up and introduced herself, saying she was a friend of Anna and Dirk. In his own quiet way, Jan looked keenly at the stranger in his backyard before stepping up to shake her hand.

"Dirk, I see you got your harem back," Jan said. "Betty tells me Carla is also in town."

Dirk smiled. "And all without my doing, Jan."

The sun dropped down, and a sudden shadow stole the color from the bright red poppies in the border. Voices traveled over the fences left and right. It was a nice summer evening that was best spent outside, but it wasn't long before the curfew and flies chased them back inside. On the way in, Jan whispered to Dirk, "Is she one of us?"

"Not to worry," Dirk whispered back.

They all sat close together in the small living room. The heat had built up through the day, but Jan closed the windows all the same.

"This is what I heard today," he said. His hushed voice got everyone's attention.

"The Nazis think they've found a way to cripple the black market. Raw materials and scarce food go for unheard amounts of money, and they have difficulty tracing it. The black market is huge. And, of course, it cuts into what they want to take out of our country. So, they have decided that as of the end of next month, all one thousand and five hundred guilder bills will be declared invalid." Jan reached for his pipe in the small rack behind his chair.

"Invalid?" Dirk said. "Can't a black marketer go to any bank and change his thousand guilder bills? How will that help them trace the money?"

"A bank won't serve him. They will send him to the tax office." Jan stuffed his pipe from a soft leather pouch.

"Oh, that's clever," Dirk said.

"Why is that clever?" Anna asked.

"Because people will have to justify the amounts of large-denomination bills they want to exchange," Jan said.

"At least that's one thing I won't have to worry about," Emmy said.

"Me neither," Jan said. "But think of the Jews, who fled with whatever they could carry. Not just jewels or gold, but large-denomination bills."

Dirk needed a moment to absorb the information Jan had plunked in their midst. He saw trouble ahead.

"A Jew can't very well ask the farmer who's hiding him to go to the tax office and break down thousand-guilder bills," he said.

"That's right," Jan said. "They'll ask the farmer how he came by that amount of money."

The smoke curling up from Jan's pipe was dark gray and smelled less than sweet. Dirk wondered where it came from. Not from the East Indies. And, knowing the kind of man Jan was, certainly not from the black market. Clever people didn't just make surrogate tea and surrogate coffee. They apparently also concocted surrogate tobacco.

"How about the people in small villages that hide Jews?" Betty said.

"Same story, I'm sure," Dirk said.

"Do the Jews *need* the money?" Emmy asked.

"They certainly do," Anna said. "They can't expect their hosts to pay for their food and whatever else they need. I don't think people hide Jews as a way to make money, but they shouldn't get into debt over it either."

"We'll have to find a way to help them," Dirk said. "It will be a delicate task. If anything can foul up relationships, it's money."

"I'll have to tell the people I'm responsible for," Emmy said. He'd never seen her with such a troubled look on her face. "I wouldn't know what to do if they asked me to change their money. And whom else could they ask?"

"Don't worry yet, Emmy," he said. "We'll come up with something."

But he didn't know what that something would be. His father might have some advice. There was just over a month left before those hefty denominations turned into worthless paper.

The front door bell rang; it was Carla. Her appearance created immediate pandemonium. The room burst at the seams with exclamations of joy. Jan and Betty stood back and smiled as their home suddenly resembled a noisy student club. They seemed to love it. Dirk thought back to when he first met Jan. It was about two years ago, when he joined a small group of senior students who were determined to correct the misinformation the Germans sent out through the media. Their illegal newspaper was titled *Feiten* (Facts). Jan had been roped into doing the printing. Dirk was the only student in the group not born and raised in Utrecht. The others had known each other practically since kindergarten, but Dirk was useful to them because of what he knew through his father, though he had only obliquely let them know who his source was.

Carla had a way of instantly becoming the center of attention. With her twinkling eyes and engaging smile, she drew people into her magnetic field. She didn't have to force herself. It came as natural to her as singing did to a bird. There had been a time when he was totally enamored of her. Then Anna walked into his life. Anna had disarmed him, the way she didn't pretend to be anything other than the person she felt she was. Most importantly, he'd sensed compassion and depth in her.

"Dirk," Carla said to him, "I hear you met Bertha at the hospital."

"Do you know her? Did you drink tea with her?"

"I've been drinking tea with her for as long as I can remember."

"Explain," he said in surprise.

After Carla told him that Bertha hailed from Breda, he understood why the woman had reacted to his name the way she had.

"She's a top-notch nurse," Carla said. "Everybody loves and respects her. I'm in a class she teaches. Such a funny feeling! We used to play hide and seek as kids."

Dirk was intrigued. He wanted to get to know this woman better. A week later, he ran into her in the hospital's library where she sat at a wide mahogany table, rifling through a medical journal.

"*Dag*, Dr. van Enthoven," she said with a smile that had a tinge of amusement.

"Please call me Dirk. I think we have more in common than we knew when we first met."

"So I found out," Bertha said. "Your name sounded vaguely familiar to me. Now I know why." She looked around to make sure they were alone and the door was shut. "You did a great thing for Walter, and I'm going to be so bold as to ask you if you could help me with an endeavor I'm involved in."

"I will, if I can," he said.

The endeavor was mind-boggling. It was as bold as it was compassionate, and Dirk knew, before she finished explaining, that he wanted to be a part of it.

"How can I help?" he asked.

"We need money and ration cards."

"I'll try. Is this library a safe place to communicate with each other?"

Bertha got up from the desk and walked over to a bookcase. She reached up to the top shelf and picked out a leather-covered book from a row of similar ones.

"Appropriate, don't you think?" she said.

Dirk took it from her. It was heavy and dusty, written a century earlier in German by a professor in internal medicine. The pages, as he leafed through them, showed signs of age and smelled musty. Not exactly a contemporary textbook.

"Let's pick page 177. We can leave messages there," he said.

"There's one more thing we need," Bertha said. "And that is prayer. Lots of prayer."

"I will get on my knees and say my prayers before I go to bed."

Bertha looked at him. "I thought only us Catholics got on our knees."

Dirk chuckled. "Some circumstances bring Protestants to their knees."

"And the same God looks down on us and loves us all." Her voice had a wistful quality to it. She sighed and turned toward the door.

"By the way," she added, "the head of the laboratory is in on all of this. If you need to be absent for a day, he will understand."

She opened the door and left him standing with the heavy book in his hand. He put it back on the shelf, returned to the lab, and prepared a slide for the microscope. He tried to concentrate on the magnified white cells he had to count, but his mind was on what he'd just heard. The scope of Bertha's undertaking was sinking in. She and others had saved over six hundred Jewish children and hidden them. They needed to be cared for. The childrens' parents had willingly handed them over to brave volunteers, who had stationed themselves close to the Schouwburg in Amsterdam, since Jews from all over the country were brought there before being put on trains to the camp in Westerbork, and from there to Germany or Poland. Or to hell, for all he knew.

He had a hard time focusing on the slide. The cells seemed to move; they were as hard to count as fish in a tank. When they turned into a complete blur, he realized he was looking through his tears. Instead of white cells, he saw a young child's hand leave the tight grip of its mother, who had to decide in a flash what would be better: to leave her child behind with a stranger or to take it onto a train that led to a dark and terrifying future. He couldn't begin to gauge the pain in that moment of choice. Where was God in this? He'd posed that question many times before, but never with such immediacy. What was to become of a child who knew his mother had deserted him? Who would forever be waiting for that mother to return? And would God comfort a mother whose heart was broken when she stepped onto that train? It was the most cruel and unnatural thing he could think of, to separate a mother from her child.

Walter once told him that God didn't orchestrate these horrific events. God didn't punish people. Right now, Dirk was too overcome with sadness to believe that. It was easier to get mad at God, to vent his anger at the fact that the Nazis could get away with their unscrupulous behavior. The God in the Old Testament could do all sorts of spectacular things, like parting the Red Sea. Couldn't he send a bolt of lightning on Hitler and strike him dead? It was not a logical thought, of course, because if God did not punish people, he would not strike Hitler dead either.

He lifted his head from the microscope and wiped his eyes. Reality returned. Men in white coats stood to the left and right of him, peering through microscopes. The head of the lab walked around and looked over their shoulders. He gently touched Dirk's elbow and said, "I'd like to see you before you're done."

When the clock struck five, Dirk walked over to Dr. Hamel's office.

"Please sit down, Mijnheer van Enthoven."

There was no one else in the room. Dr. Hamel was seated behind a small desk in the small and sober room. Dirk estimated his age to be in his late forties. He was good-looking and came across as an affable man.

"I understand that Sister Bertha talked to you and that you are willing to help us."

"I'll do what I can," Dirk said. He was surprised the man came so quickly to the point.

"As she told you, she is part of a group that has taken on responsibility for the care of young children."

"Yes, that's what she told me. I am in awe."

"You should be. She has undertaken a huge task. Remarkable. As you can imagine, it takes money to keep these children fed and clothed. And we don't know for how long. It would be of tremendous help if you could provide ration cards and money. If you need to take time off to accomplish that, I will make that easy for you."

"Thank you, Doctor. I will need some time to find sources, but I think I can."

"I wish you luck. Let me know how you're faring and how I can help you."

Dirk fetched his grandfather's bicycle. It had been a momentous day. His immediate fury at a God who allowed a man like Hitler to devise a sick system of persecution had abated somewhat. Maybe God showed his hand in people like Sister Bertha and Dr. Hamel. Dirk would rather be on their side. On the side of a merciful God.

The next day, he borrowed Anna's bicycle, since the Germans weren't interested in women's bikes. It would get him to Den Haag faster. A conference with his father was in order. Three problems needed to be resolved, and his father came up with solutions to each one. To get fl.1000 bills cashed into smaller denominations, he advised to ask big businesses like furniture stores that routinely handled large amounts of cash to break them down for Jews as a favor. To obtain ration cards, he should ask Arnold, the skipper, to talk to the Knokploeg he'd come across on his way to Maastricht. Knokploegen were all over the country, and regularly raided offices that gave out the ration cards. As for the money needed to feed and clothe the children, he gave his son fl.1000 in one-hundred guilder bills.

"You'll have to go begging for the rest," he'd said. "Or better yet, find a way to raise money."

Two days later, Dirk was back at work. He stuffed an envelope with his father's gift between pages 177 and 178 of the German textbook. On the outside he wrote: "A first contribution."

CHAPTER TWENTY-NINE

Walter – Summer 1943

Walter played with his pencil, twirling it around the way he used to in grammar school when he lacked the answer to a question. That usually had to do with math. Today, it had to do with numbers as well. A project Dirk and Carla had got involved in needed money. They'd asked him if there was a way he could raise funds from his parishioners. He twirled his pencil some more. The answer didn't come to him right away. As a minister, he was used to encouraging his parishioners to be generous. It was not his favorite aspect of being a pastor, but a necessary one. The church building needed to be kept up and heated, as well as the parsonage. The custodian received a minimal salary, and the minister's wife and children received support. There wasn't much left over for himself, but he was young and didn't have a family. And the baroness had graciously waived any form of rent. But how should he approach the congregation for donations if he couldn't tell them what it was for? He was not absolutely sure his church was void of Nazi sympathizers. It was a strange time to live through as a preacher. His task was to relate the Bible to contemporary issues, but he had to constantly tiptoe around hard truths for fear of being misinterpreted or overinterpreted. He had been too direct in his sermon in that small town outside Utrecht. He wasn't sorry about it, but he'd learned a lesson.

The Bible lay on his desk. He picked it up and leafed through it for inspiration. His gaze fell on the third chapter of Peter. "Finally," he read in verse 8, "all of you have unity of mind, sympathy, brotherly love, a tender heart and a humble mind." That verse would be a good basis for a sermon on giving.

His sister had been pushing him hard on trying to raise money. Did she realize she was opening a wound? The confluence of circumstances was as amazing as it was unsettling. Was this God's design to bring Bertha back into his life? He didn't really believe God ordained such meddling in love affairs, but it was hard to escape the thought that it wasn't just coincidental that both Carla and Dirk worked at the same hospital where Bertha was apparently a star. It was no surprise to him that she had thrown herself into helping protect Jewish children. She'd never lacked courage or compassion. Like a spider, she wove a web and hauled people in. Not to devour them, but to protect them, and—yes—to use them for a common purpose. He was in her web again.

There was a shy knock on the door. He didn't have to ask who was on the other side.

"Come in, Bram," he called out.

"How did you know it was me?" Bram asked. He held something in his hand.

"You have a special way of knocking. And you are special," Walter said. "I see you have something to show me. What is it?"

"Don't touch it! It's a little bird."

"Did it fall out of its nest?" Walter peeked into the small opening Bram's fingers created. "I think it's a robin."

"I'm going to put it in my room, Dominee Vlaskamp." Bram was glowing like a ninety-watt bulb.

"Maybe we can find its nest and put it back," Walter suggested.

"No! I want to keep it. It's mine."

"We don't own God's creatures, Bram. Little birds need to be with their mothers in a nest, like you need to be with your mother in a home. Birds and other beings don't belong in cages."

"No!" Tears were forming in Bram's eyes. "My room is not a cage," he said. "I will feed it."

"With what? Do you know what little birds eat?"

Bram was stumped.

"Their mother brings worms to their nest," Walter said.

"Worms?" Bram made a face.

"Yes. Mothers know what's good for their babies. Your little sister Lideke gets a bottle of milk and you get oatmeal. Your mother taught you how to walk, and the robin's mother will teach this little bird to fly. That's what mothers do."

Walter convinced Bram to go downstairs with him. They looked into the garden and saw the nest under the eaves of the garage.

"Look how beautifully the mother made that nest," Walter said. "See the pieces of straw she wove together with bits of clay?"

A fiercely chirping bird tried to drive them away by diving repeatedly at them. The mother robin didn't want anybody close to her nest. Walter took the baby bird from Bram's hands and reached up to place it back in the nest. Bram ran to the house, scared off by the aggressive mother robin. Walter waited from a distance to see if the robin went back to her nest. The smell of human hands might turn her offspring into something strange that she didn't want to take care of any longer. He turned away, not wanting to know how it would end.

Back at his desk, he picked up his pencil with a heavy heart. To take a child out of its nest was an unforgivable sin, and the urge to find it a new nest was understandable. Laudable even. Wasn't that what God commanded? Yet … would the child become like the robin that fell out? Unwanted and unloved forever, even if its mother returned to it after her own hardships? And worse, could the child ever love its parents again? These were depressing thoughts. How many would return, and what from? He wanted to turn away from answers he feared. The end of the war would undoubtedly provide them.

Walter let out a deep sigh and started to write his sermon. He would raise as much money as he possibly could, and he would tell the congregation that suffering children needed help. No need to call them Jewish.

A few days later, he met Anna at the castle. She looked thinner than he remembered, but she was her usual animated self. He joined the baroness, Klaas, and Anna for dinner. Mien had made a creamy vegetable casserole with fresh carrots, green beans, onions, and spinach from Hendrik's garden. Meat was scarce. After Janus left the room, Anna told them what Walter already knew. She was on a mission to raise money.

"Dirk and Carla are working with a nurse who's saved Jewish children. Right now, her group hides more than six hundred of them."

"My goodness!" the baroness said. "What an undertaking."

"Yes," Anna said. "Some of them are patients in the hospital. They're not sick, but it's a way to hide them."

"Where are the others?" Klaas asked.

"Placed with families all over. An old friend of Carla's from Breda is the nurse at the center of it. It takes a lot of people to keep it going."

"And money, Carla told me," Walter said. "I've been thinking of a way to raise money. I wrote a sermon for this coming Sunday that appeals for donations to children in need as a result of the war."

"How will that money be spent?" the baroness asked.

"For food, clothing, false IDs, transportation, because new hiding places have to be found when there's a threat of betrayal," Anna said.

"It must be near impossible to hide a young child that doesn't understand what is at stake," the baroness said. "When a family adds a child to its household, how does it explain a new face at the table? What do the neighbors say? Oh, dear, what a mess Hitler has created."

"I was a new face at the table once," Klaas said. "I never found out what the neighbors thought."

"You fit nicely into a useful job," the baroness said. "Otherwise, the neighbors might have raised their eyebrows."

A moment of silence passed in which Janus took the plates away. "I have an idea," the baroness said. "We could make raising money fun. We all need a little cheering up."

"Fun?" Anna dropped her fork on her plate. "Fun? What do you have in mind, Oma?"

"We could give a performance here at the castle. It's been a long time since we used the ballroom. Let's dust it off and fill it with merriment!"

Klaas, Anna, and Walter looked at each other. Did they hear that right? A performance? Performing what? The baroness inclined her head back and looked at the ceiling with closed eyes. "Ach," she said wistfully. "We used to have chamber music concerts; balls, of course; and even a theater group in the ballroom. It's the perfect place to do something special that would lift everyone's spirit."

Walter tried to imagine what she could have in mind. God forbid she would make them perform a play. Even though people maintained that a good minister should be a good actor, he didn't see himself in, let's say, a Shakespearean role.

"I was talking to my cousin the other day," the baroness went on. "She said her daughter is studying ballet at the Arnhem Conservatory. That's nearby. She is young. Fourteen, I believe, but apparently extremely talented in ballet. Wouldn't it be fun to see if she and her classmates would come over and give a performance?"

"Maybe," Walter said, "I should wait with giving my sermon until we get this organized, so I can invite my parishioners to the performance."

"I will get in touch with Ella," the baroness said.

The plan took shape quickly, and a date was set for a Saturday afternoon in early September. A hustle-bustle atmosphere settled over the castle. Klaas marshaled workers to do the heavy cleaning of the ballroom, which hadn't seen such activity in years. Windows were washed, gilded mirrors and chandeliers carefully dusted, and a strong smell of floor wax permeated the hallways. Walter borrowed chairs from a restaurant that used to host big affairs but lacked customers these days. And the baroness traveled to Arnhem to confer with the director of the conservatory about a recital of dance and music that would be appropriate for the size of her ballroom. She later confided to Walter that the director hoped the performance would be for the benefit of Jewish people. When she'd looked surprised, he explained that in his profession, one couldn't help notice the disappearance of some of the best performers of classical music. She'd agreed and confessed that indeed she was raising funds to protect Jewish children. He was delighted.

The baroness didn't want to hear about selling tickets. People should give what they could afford. There would be a silver plate at the door to discreetly receive donations. Walter and Anna worried about the number of people that might show up, well aware that the Gestapo didn't allow more than five people to assemble at any given time at any given place.

"This is not a meeting," the baroness retorted. "This is a performance. With a bit of luck, the Gestapo won't find out. And what would be the worst thing that could happen? They might take me to court! That's all."

After Walter's sermon, the performance at the castle became the hot topic among his parishioners. Of course, they would give money for such a good cause, but having a chance to go inside the castle was a magnetic incentive.

The day of the performance arrived under a clear blue sky. Walter opened the blinds in his bedroom and surveyed the recently cut wheat fields. Short yellow stubble stuck up through the soil. He'd preferred looking out over golden stalks that waved in the wind, pointing in the same direction, except where a deer might have tunneled through on its way to escape.

Anna went over the list of tasks that faced them before the performance could begin. Hendrik had been engaged to hitch up his workhorse to one of the castle's wagons and fetch the performers and their musical instruments from the railroad station in Ede. Janus and Klaas would set up chairs in the ballroom. Mien was told to polish a large silver tray to a radiant shine. The chambermaid prepared a room where the performers could change into their costumes.

Walter and Anna watched Hendrik pull in at noon. Janus helped nine young people, five girls and four boys, down from their high perch on the wagon and handed them their luggage and instruments. A middle-aged gentleman in a black suit appeared around the bend. He had preferred to rent a bicycle and peddle behind the wagon, he told Walter with an amiable smile. He was the director. He asked Walter to show them the ballroom. The girls giggled when one of them curtsied in front of the floor-to-ceiling mirror. The director told them to hurry up and get changed. He seated himself behind the piano, and had three of the young men take out their violins and tune them. The fourth took out his flute. Dissonant sounds and an occasional flourish on the flute gave Walter butterflies in his stomach.

He joined Anna at the front door to greet neighbors and parishioners, who began to arrive on foot and on bicycle. Bertien walked up, dressed in the local costume with a starched lace cap, and smiled shyly at him. She certainly didn't need to add any money to the tray, he thought. She'd done her duty, and might even have to pay for it with her life. Yet she put a shiny guilder on it.

Little Bram ran up to him with outstretched arms, his cheeks flushed with excitement. His mother couldn't hold onto him. Walter picked him up.

"Do you live here, Dominee Vlaskamp?" he asked.

"My bedroom is here, Bram," Walter said.

"Can I see it?"

"Later. Hello, Ruth. Glad you could make it." He was aware of Anna's probing look. "Anna, you must remember Ruth."

"I certainly do," Anna said. She took the ten-guilder bill Ruth held out to her and placed it on the silver tray. "Thank you very much, Ruth. That is very generous of you."

Ruth smiled. She was such a lovely woman, Walter thought, and looked away.

The ballroom was filled to capacity. The silver tray was filled to the top. The young men had completed their tuning and sat waiting behind music stands with sheets of music on them. There was an air of expectance.

Moments later, the baroness walked in, a stunning appearance in a pearl-gray ankle-length dress that looked deceivingly simple, decorated with an unpretentious diamond brooch that matched her earrings. Soft light from the windows reflected in her silvery-gray hair. Admiring whispers rippled through the room as she walked to the front and faced the audience.

"I would like to welcome you all to this special occasion," she said in her sophisticated, confident voice.

Walter watched from his second-row seat between Bram and Ruth. He knew what it felt like to face an audience. The baroness would make an excellent preacher, he thought. He waited for the next sentence, but it didn't come. The baroness's gaze focused on the entrance, and Walter saw a flicker of fear in her eyes that he'd never seen there in his entire acquaintance with her. Or was it surprise? The director seemed to be equally taken aback. The students, holding their violins, showed plain angst. Walter turned to see what they were looking at. There, in the splendor of his Wehrmacht uniform, stood Herr von Schloss. Walter turned back to look at the baroness. She had regained her composure.

"Herr Commandant," she said. "You have arrived just in time to be treated to a marvelous performance by young students of the Arnhem Conservatory. But before I invite you to come and sit here in front with me, you have to do one thing."

All heads turned.

The commandant took a few steps forward. "What is it I have to do, gnädige Frau?"

"I ask that you, like everyone present here, make a donation to help children displaced by the war."

There was a brief moment of indecision. The confusion among the guests was palpable. The commandant looked around. "Ach so," he said. He reached for his wallet and produced a fifty-guilder note. Anna walked over to him with the silver tray. He recognized her. He looked at the tray and added his donation to the impressive pile. Walter felt something had to break the tension. He clapped his hands, and Bram immediately imitated him. Soon the room was filled with the sound of clapping hands.

The baroness walked up to the commandant, who looked flustered. Walter thought he'd probably realized he had no choice but to give in to this woman he plainly admired. After he was seated in the front row, the baroness faced her audience again and picked up the thread of her interrupted welcome. She emphasized the generosity of the conservatory to give this free performance and thanked the audience for theirs.

"The war has changed many lives," she said, "especially the lives of children who have lost their parents."

She left it at that and gave a signal to the director that the show could begin. He got up from his piano seat.

"I thank Baroness van Haersolte for the opportunity to perform in this beautiful room. My students will dance a part of Tchaikovsky's *Nutcracker Suite* called 'The Waltz of the Flowers.' Of course, we lack a full orchestra and a full-sized stage, and I ask for your indulgence, but I am sure you will enjoy this adaptation of the original."

He went back to the piano and gave a sign to the flutist. Walter was seated behind the baroness. When he put Bram on his lap, she turned around and smiled at the boy, and then took a quick look at Ruth, the way Anna had done. It put him in a different light, he realized, to have a child in his lap and an undeniably good-looking woman at his side. It might arouse the wrong conclusions. Too bad, if it did.

The flutist started with a lively rendition of what normally would have been played by at least three trumpets. Walter banned the memory of a full orchestra with tubas, saxophones, and cellos from his mind and concentrated on the young flutist. A side door opened. Five girls tiptoed in on their satin toe shoes, wearing short taffeta skirts over white leotards and tight-fitting bodices. Colorful flowers—real or silk, Walter couldn't tell—had been worked into their hairdos. It was a tender, refreshing sight. The violins started in. The director softly set the right tempo on the piano.

"*Bezauberung,*" he overheard Herr von Schloss whisper to the baroness.

What enchanted the commandant were the movements of the young girls, who effortlessly danced from one side to the other, executing classic movements like pirouettes and promenades.

One girl stood out. She had a petite frame, delicate features, and a demure expression. Walter couldn't keep his eyes off her. There was something unusual about her. What was it? She performed a solo, doing the difficult arabesque, balancing on one leg while her arms took on various poses. It was breathtakingly beautiful. Then he saw it. Her eyes. They were brown and almond shaped, set at a slightly upward angle.

"Who is she?" he heard the commandant ask.

"She is a distant cousin of mine," the baroness said. "Only fourteen years old."

"Remarkable," he whispered.

They took in over a thousand guilders. Afterward, the baroness invited the commandant to have tea with her. Walter asked if she had found out why the commandant had come.

"That's why I invited him to have tea. I wanted to know," she said. "He'd heard rumors by way of the Gestapo that something was going to happen at the castle."

"That's concerning," Klaas said. "Who would have told them? Who's spying on us?"

"We'll probably never know," the baroness said. "It may have been an innocent remark they picked up on. The important thing is that the commandant told them he would go and see for himself. Things might have gone quite differently otherwise."

"Thank God for the commandant," Anna said. "You were right to have received him a few weeks ago, Oma."

"He seemed to enjoy himself immensely," Walter said.

"Indeed. He was quite taken with the performance, and he especially liked my cousin. He asked her name. I gave him her pseudonym, Edda van Heemskerck. Her real name is Audrey Hepburn, but she doesn't want to call attention to her British name. Her parents are divorced. She lives with her mother in Arnhem."

"She was outstanding," Walter said.

They all agreed.

CHAPTER THIRTY

Anna – Fall 1943

Emmy had told Mr. Hirsch that fl.500 and fl.1000 bills would soon be worthless. This unexpected move by the Nazis seriously jolted him. As Jan had correctly guessed, he had taken many fl.1000 bills out of his bank account at the start of the war. What to do? Asking his former employee, who now shared his home, to go to the tax office and exchange them would raise suspicions. Also, Mr. Hirsch hadn't lived long enough in Bloemendaal to befriend shopkeepers, who handled enough cash so that a few extra fl.1000 bills would not look out of the ordinary if they tried to exchange them. But, as it turned out, Mr. Hirsch had more than a few. He was a wealthy man. He was wringing his hands in despair. The only one he could turn to for help was Emmy. He called her his angel.

Emmy asked Anna for advice. Anna turned to Jan, who knew a man who worked at a large department store. He would ask him if he could break some of those large bills. The man obliged, but said he could only do a few one week, maybe a few more the next week. One of the students Dirk had published the underground newspaper with had an uncle with a pharmacy. He could take care of a few. Three here, five there, bit by bit Emmy broke down eighty large bills over the course of several weeks, and accomplished the feat just a few days before the new rules would be implemented.

To transport those eighty large bills from Bloemendaal to Utrecht, she had stuck them in her bra. Divided over two breasts, it hadn't looked too much out of the ordinary. But bringing them back in many smaller bills was a different matter. What once fit in a large envelope had become a pile. Emmy was anxious for Anna to share the responsibility, although Anna wasn't eagerly jumping to the task. But she worried about Emmy. The last time they'd been on the train together, Anna had seen that Emmy wasn't a keen observer. The exchange of the large package next to her own suitcase had completely escaped her. Emmy seemed oblivious to things Anna had developed a sixth sense for.

Fortunately, one of Betty's many gifts was sewing. She divided the fl.100 guilder bills into small packets. The idea was to make small sacks of a light material and attach them to the insides of Anna's and Emmy's skirts, but there were too many. Either they had to make several trips, or they had to come up with another thought. Since the year had progressed to the fall, it was not unreasonable to wear raincoats. Betty sewed larger pockets to fit between the outer coat and the lining. She made them oblong with divisions so the bills wouldn't bunch together.

"Betty, you've done an amazing job," Emmy marveled.

"Thank you. I've never handled so much money in my entire life, " Betty said. "Now, you girls be careful with that precious load."

They got on the train and then on a bus from Haarlem to Bloemendaal without a hitch. Nobody asked for a Kennkarte anywhere. It was a lucky day. They walked from the bus stop through lanes with gorgeous homes and well-tended gardens, filled with tall dahlias and pink phlox. No two houses looked alike. Innovative architects must have had a field day in this neighborhood. Anna chuckled at the thought that she was surreptitiously carrying the stuff that made living in homes like these possible. What she hid under her coat was probably only part of Mr. Hirsch's fortune. He might still have interests in the Dutch East Indies, and she imagined his wife bejeweled with pearls and diamonds he could trade.

A little window in the front door, like the one of Mevrouw van Mourik in Vught, squeaked open after Emmy pulled the bell. Suspicious eyes raked her face for clues.

"It's all right, Albert. It's me, Emmy, and I brought a good friend. Please open up."

The air in the upstairs room was stale. With the fragrance of blooming phlox still in her nostrils, Anna was overwhelmed by what it must mean to be holed up, to not be able to throw open the windows, to take a stroll in the garden. Mr. and Mrs. Hirsch sat at a large table. Each of them had a deck of cards in hand; each played a game of solitaire. Enough light came through the slightly opened slats on the blinds to create a pattern of stripes on the tablecloth. Anna estimated their ages at around sixty, although their pale complexions made it hard to judge, especially in contrast to Emmy's sunburned face.

"Well, there's my angel," Mr. Hirsch said. "How I have looked forward to seeing you and finding out if you had results."

For good reason, Anna thought, when somebody you barely know walks off with your fortune.

"I see you brought someone," he added.

She wondered what she could say to make him comfortable with a stranger barging into his hideout.

"I'm so pleased to meet a relative of Daan Timmermans," she said. "I am Anna Smits. Emmy and I are both students in Utrecht and good friends."

"Daan?" Mr. Hirsch looked up. "Do you know him?"

"Yes, very well. I saw him just a few weeks ago. He is safe and happy."

Emmy took off her coat, held out her hand for Anna's, and

placed them on a chair.

"Here is your money."

They looked baffled. Two raincoats to replace fl.80,000?

"This is not a joke," Emmy said. "I'm sorry it took so long." She lifted up the outer material of the coat and reached inside.

"Dear God," Mrs. Hirsch said. She stroked the bag Emmy pulled out like a baby.

"How did you do it, Emmy?" Mr. Hirsch asked. He gleamed.

"A lot of people stuck out their necks for me, Mr. Hirsch," she said. "Store owners, a pharmacist, an accountant. It was amazing. But it took a lot of time to find them."

"I am very grateful. Please sit down, both of you, and we can share some really good old-fashioned tea."

Emmy asked for scissors and undid Betty's careful sewing. A pile of fl.100 bills grew on the table. It dwarfed the pile on the silver tray after the performance at the castle.

"Mr. Hirsch," Anna said as he organized the money into neat rows, "we are involved in hiding Jewish children who would have been transported to Westerbork if it hadn't been for volunteers taking them in."

His wife looked up. "Westerbork? Where is that?"

Anna could not believe her ears. "It's a holding camp in Drente," she said. "From there, people are shipped to Germany or Poland."

"I never heard about that," she said, and looked like she meant it. Here was the ostrich Emmy had described to them earlier.

"Well, the unfortunate truth is, it happens every day. Volunteers offer to take the children and hide as many as they can. By now, over six hundred have been spared a concentration camp."

There was silence in the room.

Anna understood how terribly hard it had been for Emmy to convince this couple of hard facts. Like Emmy's mother, who also ducked an ugly reality by creating a world of her own, they ignored and denied the daily news.

"As you can imagine," she added, "it takes more than a few

people to hide six hundred children, and it takes a lot of money."

Silence.

"Innovative ways are used to raise money to keep the children fed and clothed," she went on like a terrier that wasn't letting go of a bone. "Artists are giving secret performances in private homes. I attended one a few weeks ago. It raised over fl.1000. But since we don't know how long this war will last, it's obvious we will need more."

Silence.

Mr. Hirsch didn't stop counting his money. His wife watched him and kept busy by turning her diamond ring round and round.

"Do you have children?" Anna asked.

"No, we don't," Mr. Hirsch said without looking up.

"But I'm sure you realize how important it is to keep these children out of the hands of the Nazis. Would you be willing to make a donation?" There. She'd said it.

Silence.

The heap of bills sat in the middle of the table like an unmovable mountain. It pulled all eyes, but no tongues. The mountain could only be moved by compassion. So far, nothing she'd said had stirred her hosts. Was not having a child enough of an explanation for this lack of empathy? She could understand Mr. Hirsch would not fork over all his money to a complete stranger. She wasn't looking for that.

"Could you give us a piece of your thinking on this, Mr. Hirsch?" Emmy asked him.

Anna wished she could shake off the heavy silence like drops of water from an umbrella after a drenching rain. The quiet street below didn't offer any distraction. It was almost a relief to hear the teakettle scream insistently in the nearby kitchen. It forced Mrs. Hirsh out of her chair as she hastened to stop the sound. Any noise would be a giveaway. Running a tap, flushing the toilet were things they did only at night.

"Is that why you brought your friend, Emmy?" Mr. Hirsch said when his wife returned to the table.

"No, it wasn't. I needed her help to transport all this money. She was willing to share the risk. A girl my age with that amount of money would be very suspect."

"I see."

"Mr. Hirsch," Emmy said, "you can fully trust us with whatever donation you are willing to give. After all, you trusted me with fl.80,000 a few weeks ago. And here we are, bringing it back to you. We are trying to find places for these children. People are taking enormous risks for them. They may have to pay for it with their lives. And, as a matter of fact, so may Anna and myself."

Emmy was building a head of steam, and she let it escape by saying it as it was, just as she had during their discussions about whether or not to sign the declaration of loyalty.

"You have to understand, ladies," Mr. Hirsch said, "that even though this may look like an endless amount of money to you, it is all my wife and I have to fall back on. As you said yourself, we do not know how long this war will last."

Emmy was ready with a retort. "We're not asking for all of it, or even half of it. But this is to protect your own people! If so many are willing to risk their lives for them, out of sheer compassion and principle, don't you want to contribute to their care, in whatever amount?"

Good for her, Anna thought.

"No!" Mr. Hirsch shouted. He went over to a desk, took out a large attaché case, and stuffed the entire loot into it. He slammed it shut and snapped the latches in place.

Anna shuddered. Emmy turned red. She got up abruptly—it almost threw her chair over—snatched the raincoats from the table, and reached for the doorknob.

"Come on, Anna, we have nothing more to discuss here," she said.

"Wait a minute," Mr. Hirsch said. "Don't desert us!"

"I beg you pardon?" Anna said, as livid as Emmy. "You have

just deserted six hundred children! Jewish children. Why should we take responsibility for you if you don't take any for them? Goodbye, Mr. Hirsch." She followed Emmy out the door, down the staircase, and out to the street before Albert could utter a word.

They walked briskly without speaking. Anna couldn't think. The street became a blur of bricks, trees, and flowers. Her heart was beating wildly in her throat. Emmy's long legs took giant strides, and by the time they turned the corner of the long lane, she was out of breath.

"Slow down, Emmy."

Emmy halted and looked at her. "*Die rotzak!*"

That word had crossed her mind as well. Mr. Hirsch deserved it. He had shown a dark and selfish side of his character.

"Yes," she said. "I feel offended and disgusted."

They sat on the bus and in the train in silence, both churning the images of the day.

"How did it go?" Dirk asked when they entered the living room where Betty and Jan were waiting for them.

"We got the money there," Emmy said.

"But you don't look too happy, Anna," Dirk said, and got up to give her a hug. "What happened?"

"I lost my temper. Mr. Hirsch said he couldn't afford to give a donation to save the Jewish children. Can you believe that? He said he didn't know how long the war would last. I almost shouted at him. I couldn't stand it. He turned his back on the future of his race."

"Did you say that to him? In those words?" Dirk asked.

"Close to it. I asked him to help protect the children and that they were his own kind. But he swiped all the money off the table, put it in a suitcase, and shouted no. That's when we left."

"Oh, dear," Betty said. Jan raised his eyebrows.

Anna sat down on the couch and put her head in her hands. Dirk walked over and sat next to her.

"How do you feel about it now? And how about you, Emmy?

Will you go back to them?"

"Yes," Emmy said. "I won't leave them in a lurch, but I need some time to cool off."

"You know," Anna said, "Just because we all feel so badly for what the Nazis are doing to the Jewish people, that doesn't mean you have to forgive them for everything they say or do. On the way home, though, I wondered what Bible verse Walter was going to put in front of me."

"How about what the Apostle Paul wrote to the Romans?" Dirk said. "'Repay no evil with evil, but give thought to do what is honorable in the sight of all.'"

Anna groaned in response. "Sorry, but I do not feel that what I said and did was evil. I think I spoke the truth: you have to help your fellow men, and in this case your fellow children."

"Paul probably wouldn't be quoted so often if it were easy," Dirk said, "but you have a point. I love you for standing up for what you see as the truth, and—" Loud wailing sirens overwhelmed his voice.

"*Lucht alarm*," Jan said. "Get to the cellar. Quick."

On her way to the cellar, Anna saw the sky eerily lit up through the small window above the front door. Searchlights crisscrossed the sky.

The five of them crammed into the tiny cellar space where they could barely stand up straight. Jan dropped his shoulders to fit in. Dirk pulled Anna to his chest, and Emmy sidled up to Betty's comfortable bosom while airplanes screeched overhead. Then ... a loud explosion. The house shook right down to its foundations, and the cellar wall vibrated. Anna held her breath.

"That was close," Dirk whispered. "Are they mistaking us for Soesterberg?"

Nobody answered. It was a logical conclusion. Soesterberg was the airport fourteen kilometers from Utrecht. Finally, the siren gave its safe sign. The house was still standing when they got back upstairs except for a few broken windows. But they smelled smoke.

Jan opened the blackout curtain over the kitchen window just enough to see the sky filled with a hellish yellow light and dark smoke billowing from behind a row of houses close by.

"Something happened." He was about to open the kitchen door and dart outside, but Betty reminded him it was curfew time.

At the crack of dawn, he was out the door. He came back with the news that the airport had been the real target of British bombers, but one airplane had been hit by German anti-aircraft fire and came down in flames a few streets away. Two homes were burned to the ground. The pilot was dead. So was an elderly couple that hadn't been able to get out in time.

It wasn't their first bombardment, but it was the closest. Later in the day, when Anna looked at the piles of rubble, she remembered what Mevrouw van Mourik had said: "Hitler will lose the war, but it will take many lives and much devastation."

Betty removed the pockets for the fl.100 bills from the raincoats and replaced them with ones that could hold the larger illegal newspapers. Each pocket held a packet of twenty, and two packets per raincoat. Jan used very thin paper and the letter size was small.

Anna and Emmy were halfway through delivering the newspapers the day after they'd delivered the money to Mr. Hirsch. It made for awkward bicycling. The four packets were to be delivered at four different addresses. As they came to the site of the burned homes, they had already delivered two, the ones in Anna's raincoat.

They were ready to get back on their bikes when an *overvalswagen* rumbled down the street, blaring a loud siren. Soldiers jumped out. Rifles in hand, they quickly blocked both ends of the street. The crowd of curious onlookers that had gathered in front of the sad pile of rubble tried to disperse. A young man darted across the street, but he was grabbed before he could slip into a small grocery store.

"Kennkarte!" a Gestapo officer yelled at him. The man, who

looked like Dirk's age, stopped and handed over his ID. Moments later, he was shoved into the back of the canvas-covered truck.

Emmy still carried two packets of illegal newspapers inside her raincoat. Beads of sweat were forming on her forehead.

"Do you have your ID on you?" Anna asked her. Emmy nodded. At that moment, Anna remembered with an electrifying shock that she'd forgotten her own. How could she have been so stupid to leave the house without her pocketbook! *Quick! Think!* She broke out in a prickly sweat.

"Emmy, let's not stand together," she said.

"Why?"

"Never mind why. Please do as I say. You'll understand later."

Emmy moved away with the bike she'd borrowed from Betty. A Gestapo officer was working his way through the crowd, shouting for Kennkarte. When it was Emmy's turn, she reached into her pocket and handed hers over. He looked at it briefly and motioned her to walk on. She obeyed and moved to the other side of the street. Next was an old woman. The Gestapo hardly looked at her ID. They wanted to catch men, not old women. Now it was Anna's turn.

She took a deep breath. "I forgot to take my pocketbook with me. I left it at home."

"Dummkopf!"

His blue eyes glared at her from under the black visor on his officer's cap. He was right. She was an idiot. Her palms turned sweaty, and she felt unsteady on her feet. This was a tricky situation, but at least Emmy was cleared.

She knew what was coming and braced herself. While the officer hailed a soldier to come and take her away, she quickly handed her bike to a middle-aged woman next to her. "Here take my bike. I live on the Van Swindenstraat. Number 134."

The woman obliged. Anna didn't care if she ever saw her bike again. Better in this woman's possession than the Gestapo's.

A soldier pushed her forward with the butt of his rifle and heaved her into the truck. She looked back at Emmy, who stood stiff as a broom next to Betty's bike, fear clearly written on her face.

It was dark inside the truck. A young man, eighteen years old at the most, offered her a seat on one of two wooden benches.

"Do they send women to work camps?" he asked.

"I hope not," Anna said. "I didn't have my ID on me."

A canvas curtain was lowered from the outside, and the truck started moving. There were no windows for light to come through.

"Where will they take us?" the boy asked.

"To the police station," a voice in the dark said. "They'll sort us out and send us on from there."

Every turn the truck made sent them bumping into one another. There was no telling which street they were on. Darkness enveloped Anna. She shuddered at the thought that came to her, that she was inside a coffin on her way to her last resting place. Better to consider the real situation she was in. She would have to give her name and address, the ones on her ID. Would the Gestapo go out and ransack Betty's house? There had been a pile of newspapers still lying on the floor in Jan's so-called hobby room when she left with Emmy. God only knew what else might be in that room. A hidden radio? *Emmy, get over there. Hurry up! Warn them!*

The truck stopped, and the canvas backing was rolled up. They were at the central police station.

"Oh, boy, here we go," the eighteen-year-old said with a quiver in his voice.

Anna touched his arm and squeezed it lightly. "Don't be afraid. There's light at the end of every tunnel."

She was really talking to herself, but he gave her a grateful look, jumped down on the pavement, and reached for her hand as she tried to get off. They were herded inside. She had correctly guessed she was the only woman in today's catch, and a Gestapo officer — the one who'd arrested her — immediately pulled her aside. She was brought to a small room decorated in Spartan taste. The bare walls, a depressing color gray, evoked a dreary, rainy day. A steel desk with two straight-backed wooden chairs facing it stood in the center. She waited. A middle-aged man in a Gestapo uniform sat behind the desk in a comfortable chair, studying papers.

"Sit," he said after a few minutes of her standing there.

The room was stuffy. She had no need for her raincoat, but the last thing she wanted to do was take it off.

"*Persoonsbewijs.*"

"That's why I am here. I left my purse at home."

"Your name?"

"Anna Smits."

"Your address?"

"Van Swindenstraat 134."

"Do your parents live there?"

"No. I rent a room there."

"Why?"

"I study medicine."

"The university is closed. Why are you still renting a room? Where do your parents live?"

"In Arnhem. But I have applied for nursing school. I am waiting to be admitted." That was a lie, of course, but what else could she say?

"What do you do in the meantime?" He gave her a sharp look while reaching for a pack of cigarettes. He took one out, lit it, and took a long drag, all the while keeping his gaze on her. She willed herself not to look away. A trickle of sweat pearls made its way down between her breasts.

"I study. The fact that the university is closed doesn't interfere with learning. That way I will be ahead when it opens again. But I also help my landlady and stand in line to get food."

"Interesting. Very interesting. We will look into that."

He reached over to press a bell. A young Dutch policeman came into the room.

"Take her to cell 15," the officer commanded. He looked back down at the papers in front of him. He was done with her.

"But why?" Anna said. "I just forgot my *persoonsbewijs*. It's at home!"

He looked up from his papers and gave a sign to the policeman by pointing to the door with his thumb. She was handcuffed and led through long corridors until they finally reached a row of cells. The policeman unhitched the bundle of large keys that hung from his belt and opened the door of number 15.

"Does everyone who doesn't have their *persoonsbewijs* on them get to spend time in jail?" Anna asked as he inserted the key. He stopped and looked at her. His young, boyish face seemed out of place above the black uniform. Was serving in the police force a way for him to escape working as a laborer in Germany? He didn't look much older than the boy she'd just shared the bench with in the overvalswagen. He hesitated for a moment.

"That depends on who you know," he said softly. He turned the key and opened the door. Before she stepped into the unappealing dark space, with its concrete floor and brick walls and with four other women inside, Anna thought, *I know Dirk van Enthoven.*

CHAPTER THIRTY-ONE

Dirk – Same Day

Dirk stood behind his microscope, ready to insert a slide, when Bertha surprised him by walking into the lab. This was not her territory. There had to be a special reason, and his mind went on alert. Just in case he wasn't the one she was looking for, he kept concentrating on positioning the glass slide. From the corner of his eyes he followed her around the room until she came to a stop. He felt a tap on his shoulder.

"Do you have a minute to come out?" she asked.

They walked into the hallway and down to Dr. Hamel's office.

"My God, Emmy! What are you doing here?" Dirk exclaimed when Bertha opened the door. He didn't have to wait long for an answer.

"The Gestapo took Anna."

"What?"

"We were at the bombed house. They blocked the road. They checked people's IDs. I still don't know why they took Anna. We were delivering papers. We had delivered the ones she carried. I still have mine. That's why I didn't go back to Betty's. I thought the police would go to her house right away. Besides, I wasn't sure I could find my way back there. I knew how to get to this hospital and warn you."

Dr. Hamel sat behind his desk. When he heard Anna's name mentioned, he looked up. He knew Anna had successfully organized the charitable event at the castle that had made a huge contribution to the Jewish Children Fund.

"Feel free to go and do what you have to," he said to Dirk.

"Thank you, Doctor."

Bertha stayed behind in Dr. Hamel's office as Dirk took Emmy by her arm and practically pushed her out the room. His mind raced with different scenarios. Why had Anna been taken and not Emmy? How fast would the police check on Jan and Betty's home?

"Emmy, do you still carry those papers on you?" he whispered. She nodded.

They walked down a long dark corridor, part of the bowels of this large university hospital. The laundry and linen dispensary were somewhere around here, he remembered from his earlier wanderings to get his bearings of the place. He had an idea.

"Take the papers out and I'll get rid of them," he whispered.

Emmy quickly undid the buttons inside her raincoat and handed the papers to Dirk, who held on to them as if he were carrying medical records. Footsteps sounded from behind, but they turned into another direction, down another part of the complicated maze of corridors that reminded him of the caves in St. Pietersberg. They came upon a huge canvas bag on wheels, bulging with soiled linens. He looked up and down the narrow corridor, separated the top layer of linens, and stuffed the papers underneath. He led the way back to the main entrance where Emmy had left Betty's bike. After he fetched his own, they raced through the streets of Utrecht to Jan and Betty's. Out of breath, he rang the bell. Surprise and fear swept over Betty's face when she opened the door.

"What happened?"

"We got stopped by the Gestapo," Emmy said. "They took Anna. I don't know why."

"Quick," Dirk said. "Let's see what we should hide."

Betty stepped aside to let him run up the stairs. He opened the door to Jan's hobby room. The newspapers Emmy thought might still be on the floor weren't there. He tried to look at the room the way a suspicious Gestapo officer would. From the stories he'd heard, they didn't stop at anything. Nothing was sacred or respected. They would take a bayonet and ram it through anything they thought might hide something or somebody. He knew the forbidden radio was behind a panel in the wall. Jan had effectively divided the room in two. Behind the false wall were his small printing press and a radio-receiver installation. It was craftily done. Even as he tried to look around with the mind of a Nazi, he couldn't see anything that roused his suspicion. Satisfied, he went back downstairs. Betty was in the kitchen brewing surrogate coffee.

The bell rang. She put down the coffee pot and went to the door, opening it up a crack. He fully expected the Gestapo to be there. They'd had enough time at the police station to find out where Anna lived. But to his surprise, a woman was at the door.

"I am returning a bike," she said simply.

"Please come in," Betty said.

"Thank you," the woman said. "What shall I do with the bike?"

Dirk stepped forward. "I'll take it and bring it around to the shed."

"Can I serve you a cup of coffee?" Betty asked. "I was just brewing some. Surrogate, of course."

"That would be lovely," the woman said. "I have to admit, I am a bit shook up." Her hair was graying at the temples; her eyes signaled intelligence. Fine wrinkles around them made Dirk think she liked to laugh a lot. But she wasn't laughing now.

"Could you tell us what happened?" Betty asked. "We know the Gestapo took the girl that owns the bike. But we don't know why."

"She told the Gestapo she'd forgotten her pocketbook. She couldn't show her ID."

"Oh, so *that* was it," Emmy said.

"He called her *Dummkopf.* He turned to get a soldier to take her, and that's when she quickly handed her bike to me and gave me this address. I pretended it had been mine all along, so they wouldn't steal it."

She took a sip of coffee. "I went home right away to tell my son to hide. They're combing the neighborhood for young men, you know." She looked at Dirk. "Be careful," she said to him. "But then, I thought you might not know what happened. So, I came over first thing."

"Thank you so much," Betty said. "Anna rents a room here, but she feels like a daughter to me."

"We live in crazy times, don't we?" the woman said to no one in particular. "Let me give you a warning." She leaned forward in her chair. "My husband is in real estate. He says something very suspicious is going on. The Germans are buying homes in several neighborhoods. They put civilians in them as spies. It's a means of surveillance. He said the other day they trapped someone by giving false information to a neighbor, like it came from the Underground. That person acted on it, and next thing, that person was taken into custody. If you can't trust your neighbors anymore, my God, then what are we coming to? So, if you see new people move in a house close to you, you have to be careful. It gives me a creepy feeling that it has come to this."

Although he trusted the woman instinctively, Dirk thought it best to be careful with his words. "Well," he said, "maybe this will all be over soon. I don't think the war is going too well."

"Have you heard that the British took Sicily?" the woman asked. Her look of dismay lifted. She could only know this from a clandestine radio. He already knew about it, but he wasn't going to say so.

"No, tell us. That's interesting."

"Never mind where I heard that," she said with a secretive smile. "Of course, Sicily is a long way from Utrecht, but if they have a foothold on the Continent, at least there's hope."

"We won't tell anyone we heard it from you," Betty said with a laugh. "It helps that we don't know your name. And we probably should leave it that way. As you say, these are dangerous times. But, believe me, you can trust us."

The woman got up. "Thank you for the coffee. You seem like good people. I hope Anna will come back to you soon. Now, I'd better go on my way. I have quite a hike ahead of me, and I want to be sure to get home before curfew. Till better times," she said as she walked out the door.

Emmy had gone upstairs, found Anna's pocketbook, and handed it to Betty, who rummaged through it till she found the infamous ID.

"Here it is. Now, what do we do with it?"

Dirk looked at the picture, and a shiver crept down his spine. He'd hardly had time to let the thought of Anna being in the hands of the Gestapo sink in. *The bastards!* He had to get her out, and quick. But how? When Walter had been taken to the Utrecht police station, he'd tried to get him out. To no avail. Walter's was a different situation, though. He had angered the NSB official with his sermon.

"You'd think it should be as simple as going up to the Gestapo and saying, Here is the ID you were looking for," he said. "Let's think this through before we make a tactical mistake. What do you suppose they could accuse her of?"

"Let's think about why having an ID is important in the first place," Betty said. "They want to know if you are Jewish, for one."

"True. Another is to see if she is suspected of illegal activity," Dirk said. "They probably have lists they can check her name against."

"Would she be on a list of suspects?" Emmy asked.

"Not likely. Unless they found out she raised money for the Jewish Children Fund."

He paced the small living room. Was there anything they could catch Anna on? She'd carried many ration cards for the Jews that were hidden around the castle, as well as Jan's illegal newspapers. But she'd always gotten away with it. Or had she been under surveillance?

"I'm going to go back to the lab to talk to Dr. Hamel. He seems like a man with many connections in important places. I'll leave the ID here in case the Gestapo comes and looks for it."

He biked fast. He knew every street, every house he passed, but the world felt like a different place. The nice lady, who'd been honest enough to bring Anna's bike back, was right: the world was rapidly becoming hostile. Without Anna, it would be a barren place. He'd always been ready to defend his country, but ever since he'd met Anna, his priorities had shifted. He was propelled by a deep desire to bring back peace, to retain freedom, to restore this country to a place he could start a life in, to raise a family in with Anna. If God was testing his love for her, he had succeeded. A future without Anna wasn't worth living.

The lab was closed, but Dr. Hamel was still in his office.

"What did you find out, Dirk?" he asked.

"Anna couldn't produce her ID because she'd left her pocketbook at home."

Dr. Hamel looked at his watch. "We're getting close to curfew time."

"I know. What should I do?"

As soon as he said it, he realized how he'd come to see Dr. Hamel more as a friend than a boss. The stakes they shared in the enterprise outside the lab had distorted their relationship of strictly employer and employee.

"If you present yourself at the police station," Dr. Hamel said, "you may not have the credibility you need to get Anna out, even though you would be absolutely right if you told the Gestapo she didn't do anything illegal or underhanded. At least, not anything they can prove."

"Yes. That's why I didn't go over there yet."

Dr. Hamel swiveled in his desk chair and opened a file cabinet behind him. He took out a folder. "Here, take this name and address. Jasper Bosch is a friend of mine, and he may be able to help you. Tell him you work for me. He will understand."

Dirk thanked him and got back on his bike. It was twilight outside, but that didn't mean anything. The curfew clock would start ticking at nine in the evening. It would run till four in the morning. He looked at his watch. It was half past seven. The address he'd been given was on the other side of Utrecht from where Jan and Betty lived. He had a vague idea which street it was on, and he prayed he wouldn't have to stop to ask for the way. Time was of the essence.

When he reached the house, a woman came to the door. He handed her the note Dr. Hamel had given him by way of introduction.

"Wait here a moment," she said. She opened the door and let him into the vestibule. He had the distinct impression she didn't want him standing in front of the house. For good reasons, probably.

It took a while, but finally a burly, tall man appeared. "I'm Jasper Bosch," he said. "Come in." He led Dirk up the stairs to a small room where two other men sat on the floor next to a radio.

"Radio Oranje will be on in a moment," one of them whispered, and put his index finger to his mouth in a sign for him not to speak. Dirk looked at his watch and realized that the daily broadcast over the BBC was about to begin. One of the men held a notebook and pen in his lap. Soon, the familiar first notes of Beethoven's Fifth Symphony sounded, and then a Dutch voice came on. The news was encouraging. North Africa was now free of Germans and Italians. The Mediterranean Sea had been cleared of enemy war vessels. The Germans had been halted in Russia. The news was followed by instructions for the Dutch Underground, given in code messages. The pen raced over the blank page of the notebook.

Then: *"Geef Carla een zoen."*

Dirk jumped. "My God! Otto made it," he exclaimed.

"Shhh," Jasper said. He gave him an admonishing look, but Dirk didn't care. Otto got to England! He was ecstatic.

The broadcast was over. The radio was carefully put away under a board in the floor, a rug pulled over it.

"Now, let's see," Jasper said. "You are Dirk and you need help getting somebody out of jail."

"That's correct. A woman in my group was taken in because she couldn't show her ID. She'd forgotten it at home. She was delivering illegal newspapers."

"You want me to risk my life because your friend forgot her pocketbook?"

Dirk realized how lame it sounded, but he decided not to take the bait.

"She had just finished delivering the papers, so she wasn't caught red-handed. She's invaluable to our operation."

"Has she ever been caught doing these valuable things? Could there be any surprises?"

"No."

"All right," Jasper said. He shifted his considerable weight in his desk chair. "I am a retired police inspector. I used to run that station and I know the people in it. Do you have the woman's ID?"

"No, I left it with her hospita. I thought they might come and look for it there."

Jasper looked at his watch. "You might just make it before curfew if you go and get it. I will meet you at five a.m. at the police station's side entrance."

He drew a blueprint of the station on a small piece of paper. He marked the side door with an X.

"Thank you, sir," Dirk said as he took the paper.

"Just call me Jasper. I'll see you later."

He beat the curfew by a few minutes. Jan, Betty, and Emmy were in the living room. He couldn't wait to tell them about Otto, but they jumped on him with questions.

"Where's Anna?"

"Still in the same place, I hope."

"You hope?" Jan said. He sounded almost angry. His tone made Dirk realize how much was at stake for Jan. He must have been shocked when he came home from a day's work to find out Anna had been taken by the Gestapo. Last he knew, she was delivering his newspapers. Dirk decided this was not the best moment to tell them the good news about Otto.

"I hope to get her out in a few hours," he said. "Can I snooze on your couch, and do you have an alarm clock? I have to be at the police station at five. Oh, and I need Anna's ID."

They didn't ask any more questions.

It was still dark when Jasper Bosch arrived at the side door of the station. Dirk was already there and had been for five minutes, wondering how he would explain himself to anyone who saw him and asked what he was doing there. Thankfully, that didn't come to pass. Jasper reached inside his pocket and took out a key. He winked at Dirk and smiled. "The only thing I didn't return. It comes in handy sometimes."

Dirk followed him into a hall. They walked to a desk where a clerk in a Dutch police uniform was having a hard time staying awake.

"Hey, wake up, mate," Jasper said. He gently shook the man's shoulder.

"Oh, good morning, Inspector."

"Look on your list and see if you see the name Anna Smits. She's held here by mistake."

The man did as he was told. "Here it is. Anna Smits. No Kennkarte. Cell 15."

"Good. Here is the ID they were looking for. Make a note of it and mark her entry with 'Released.'"

The man again did as he was told.

"If there are any questions," Jasper said, "tell them they can go to her address and they can verify it, if they care to. Now, it would be nice if you could let her out. She's been here long enough for just not having her ID on her."

"As you say, Inspector," the sleepy clerk said. He got up and fetched the guard from an adjacent office.

"Get Anna Smits from cell 15," he told the older guard, who also recognized Jasper, but didn't say so for some reason.

Dirk was in awe. Could it be just this simple? Jasper read his mind while they were waiting in the hall. "Trust is a beautiful thing," he said. "But it only works if it's backed up by truth. Anna is not guilty. That can be proven. Strictly speaking, the Gestapo had no business locking her up."

Moments later, Anna stood before him, ready to shout his name, but Jasper put his fingers to his lips in a sign for her to be quiet. She understood. The three of them quickly walked to the side door.

"Don't thank me," Jasper said. "I will call you when I need you." He got on his bike and disappeared.

"Quick, Anna, let's get out of here," Dirk said, and got on his bike. Anna jumped on the baggage carrier and held onto him tight. The world looked a lot brighter. Anna was safe. Otto was safe. The Germans and Italians had been beaten out of Africa; the Allies were putting boots on the Continent. The Russians were standing fast. Yes! There was hope. Maybe the hinge of fate was turning.

CHAPTER THIRTY-TWO

Anna – April 1944

Anna noticed a hint of green on the trees outside the window of her room in the castle where she had been staying since being let out of the police cell. The severe winter was finally over. Mother Nature had shown little compassion the past few months. Mounds of snow had become the other enemy as fuel supplies matched the drop in temperature, and food got scarce. People began to wonder how they would survive if rescue didn't come before the next winter. Nobody had expected the war to last this long. It was now springtime in 1944, and no end was in sight. Allied troops moved north through Italy at a snail's pace. Chasing Hitler out of the countries he had so blithely invaded proved to be an inch-by-inch operation. The Nazi-controlled local radio spoke only of victories—their own—at the eastern front, but listening to the names of Russian towns and cities in the broadcasts made sharp minds wonder if the front was moving westward instead of eastward, as the Nazis would have them believe. The Soviets had retaken their ground and gained some. And Churchill was making good on his promise to avenge Hitler's Blitz on London by sending large bombers over the North Sea on their way to Germany's industrial cities.

In the late afternoon of a day in April, Anna stood with Walter and Klaas on the upstairs balcony of the castle, hoping to catch sight of the planes. Occasionally, the setting sun broke through the clouds and lit their aluminum wings. Like migrating geese, they flew in perfect formation. It was an exhilarating sight, until one bomber veered from its squadron and suddenly went down in a rapid descent. Stiff with fear, they watched as parachutes unfolded and crewmembers dangled in the air. The wind drifted them toward the woods close to the castle. The plane burst into flames. Like a pig at slaughter, it made a screaming sound as it plummeted to the ground. A large column of smoke rose, and they covered their ears as the bombs, meant to fall on Germany, exploded. It was hard to tell exactly the place it had come down, but one thing was certain, there were Allied crewmembers close by, and the Nazis would go on a relentless hunt.

The next morning, Anna opened the window and inhaled the moist early-morning air. A million dewdrops, reflecting the rising sun, covered the lawn, turning it into a brilliant sheet. It was a peaceful scene, but it didn't reflect her mood. Walter and Klaas hadn't said so, but she was sure they'd gone on a rescue mission last night.

She poured water from a jug into the porcelain basin next to it and splashed it over her face. A tired face looked back at her from the mirror. Worry about what the Nazis might do to the airmen, or to anyone trying to rescue them, had robbed her of a sound sleep.

She sat at the breakfast table among five empty chairs. It was still early. Janus poured her a cup of tea. He asked if she knew a plane had come down. She said yes, but where?

"On the west side of Ede, Miss Anna."

That was the side he lived on. Every morning he biked over to the castle to serve breakfast, and went home again after serving dinner. He was the only member of the staff to do so. Mien and the chambermaids slept in the servant quarters.

"Was it close to your home, Janus? Did it do damage?"

"Yes, it was close, but it landed in a field. There's a big hole there now. Three windows in my house broke. My wife was very frightened."

"How about you? Weren't *you* frightened?"

"Well, yes ... I heard glass shattering everywhere." He was quiet for a moment. "Would you like some breakfast, Miss Anna?"

She said she would wait. She wasn't hungry.

"On my way over," Janus said, "I saw soldiers in the woods. They are looking for the pilot."

"Do you know if they found any? We saw three parachutes coming down."

"Someone said they found two."

"I think I'll go for a walk, Janus, and get some fresh air."

The ponies ran alongside the fence and whinnied to get her attention, but she paid them no heed. Fear crept over her as she sidestepped the ruts in the road. She told herself to be calm. If she found what she expected at Hendrik's farm, she needed to keep her wits about her.

Tom Velder waved from the strawberry patch. She pulled the rope of the brass bell outside the kitchen door. Whoever was inside must have seen her coming, because the door opened immediately. Walter stood in the doorframe.

"How did you know I was here?" he said.

"I had a hunch. You weren't at the breakfast table, and you're usually the first one there."

He led her into the kitchen, where all chairs were taken. She recognized every face but one. Klaas sat next to his mother. Hendrik was at the head of the table with Anneke on his knee. The face she didn't recognize belonged to a man in a foreign uniform that was badly torn. He had scratches on his face, and blood had seeped from under his hair and drenched his shirt collar. Somehow she had expected this, but it still gave her chills to see the reality of what it meant to be ejected from a plane.

"Klaas and I found this man sitting on a tree limb," Walter said.

"What happened to his parachute?"

"It got hung up in the tree, so we cut it loose from the branches and buried it under a pile of leaves."

"Good thing," Anna said. "Bertien, can you give me some water and a towel? This poor man will be a sitting duck for some eager German soldier if we leave the blood all over him."

Now that she knew what she was dealing with, a burst of energy rose in her. She wasn't a doctor yet, but she knew enough to clean wounds.

Bertien pumped a gush of water into a kettle at the soapstone sink and placed it on the woodstove, which had been fired up to take off the early morning chill. In English, Anna told the stranger to take off his jacket, shirt, and tie. She asked for scissors, or better yet, a razor. Bertien produced iodine and clean towels. Hendrik rummaged in an emergency kit he kept in the barn.

"Do you hurt anywhere?" Anna asked.

"Mostly my head and my chest," the stranger said. "I hit a branch when I came down."

She pulled up his eyelids to look at his pupils with a flashlight. He didn't have a concussion. She asked him to stand up and felt his ribcage. He winced as she pressed her fingers on his side. There wasn't much she could do for his ribcage. Broken or bruised, ribs had to heal by themselves.

"Do you mind if I cut some of your hair so I can see the wound?"

"Go ahead."

She aimed the scissors at the blood-soaked blond hair and exposed a three-inch long gash. It needed stitches. Should she try to sew it up with an ordinary needle and thread? The risk of infection was obvious. She rejected the idea. The best she could do was remove the hair around it with the razor, clean the wound, and put the iodine to it. She created a wide path and tightly taped the sides of the wound together. It wasn't pretty, but it was the best she could do.

"I'm sorry, but you'll have a bald spot on your head."

"My battle scar! Nobody will believe I was in the war if I come home without one," the airman said. He had an accent that made her think he wasn't from England.

"Are you American?"

"Yes, ma'am. I'm from Texas."

"Welcome to Holland. We'll take good care of you."

He gave her a grateful smile and held up his arms full of scratches. She treated those as well. The man was stoic throughout.

"Now that I have painted him all over with iodine," Anna said in Dutch to the others in the room, "what's the plan?"

"Tom is on the lookout for German soldiers," Walter said.

"It'll be too late if he sees one." Anna finger-combed her hair in a quick, jerky motion. What were they thinking when they brought this airman to a place where Jews were hidden?

"We have no time to lose," she said. "Janus told me the Germans already found the other two. On his way over, he saw soldiers in the woods. We know they won't find anybody in those woods."

Hendrik jumped to his feet. "Bertien, go get some of my clothes, used ones. Quick!"

When Bertien returned with an armful of clothes, Hendrik told her to bring the stranger to the one-holer in the back of the barn and have him exchange his uniform for the farm clothes. He passed Anneke to Walter's lap and told Geertrui to hurry up and get to her hiding place. Anna saw the same flicker of fear in Geertrui's eyes that she'd seen on the train on their trip from Den Haag. Dark rings lined her eyes. Living in the shadows had marked her face.

Anna followed Hendrik into the barn. The airman came out, looking uncannily like a Dutch farmer. With the uniform draped over his arm, Hendrik walked to the hooiberg. Through the small barn window, Anna watched him stuff the uniform deep into the haystack.

The kitchen bell rang. She quickly pushed the airman back into the one-holer. "Stay here and don't make a sound. Sorry for the bad smell."

"They're coming this way," Tom Velder shouted.

Anna swiped the bloody scissors from the table and shoved them into the barn's emergency kit. Bertien picked up the bloody towels, shirt, and tie, opened the stove, and threw them in the fire. The distinctive smell of burned fabric filled the kitchen. She took a pan holder and held a match to it. After it burned a black hole in it, she put out the fire with water and placed it near the woodstove.

Klaas stood at the window, his eyes glued to the road, constantly shifting his weight on the balls of his feet. He'd taken a huge risk. For as long as she'd known him, he'd counted on his non-Jewish looks and his good luck. But this time, there was more at stake than just his life.

"Three of them," he whispered.

She peered over his shoulder. Three soldiers came into view, moving slowly like menacing cats on the prowl, their rifles pointing down in attack mode with bayonets attached to the ends of the barrels. The blades flickered in the early sunrays with every step they took. A cold hand gripped her heart as her breath caught in her throat. Never in her life had she felt so threatened. This could be the end for all of them. The thought pushed her into action.

"Klaas," she said, "go hide with your mother, or we'll have a lot of explaining to do with all of us being here."

He looked at her with pursed lips. His clenched jaw was proof of a fierce inner struggle. Was he going to give in to someone else's fears?

"Hurry up! Do it!" She gave him a shove.

Bertien overheard them. She opened the door to the front room and knocked on the wall.

"Open up, Geertrui. It's me."

The two of them pushed an unwilling Klaas into the hiding place. Bertien hung the framed picture back on the papered wall with trembling fingers, but she made sure it looked undisturbed.

One of the soldiers walked up to Tom in the strawberry patch. With biceps bulging under his shirt and leaning on his hoe, Tom looked every bit the farmer he pretended to be.

"Keep your cool, Tom," Anna said under her breath as she watched from the kitchen window. Tom reached into his back pocket for his ID. Another soldier approached the hooiberg and jammed his bayonet into the hay at random. Hendrik ambled over and started a conversation, distracting him from further exploits, but now the soldier walked toward the kitchen door, hailing the third one to join him. They didn't bother to ring the bell. Instead, one of them kicked the door in with his boot. The insignia on his tunic indicated the rank of sergeant.

"We would have opened the door for you," Walter said in German.

"Let's not get fresh," the sergeant said. "Who are you?"

Before Walter could answer, Bertien said, "He is our minister."

"Kennkarte," he bellowed at Walter. Annie was still sitting in his lap.

While Walter searched for his ID, the sergeant shouted at the women, "The airman. Where is he?"

"We heard explosions," Bertien said. "The minister came over to see if we were all right. We haven't seen anybody we don't know." Bertien told her lie with a straight face.

Walter's ID was handed back without comment.

"Search the barn," the sergeant commanded the soldier.

He looked around the kitchen. His gaze fastened on the cellar door. He opened it, looked down, and saw jars with canned vegetables. Next to it was a door to the one and only bedroom in the farmhouse. He opened that door as well and looked under the bed. Finally, he pushed hard on the door to the front room, as if someone on the other side would push him back. Anna followed his movements step by step. He seemed interested in the pictures on the wall. He turned around and faced her.

"Anyone hiding an Allied pilot will get the death penalty. You know that, don't you?"

"Yes, I know," she said.

"What is this smell? Something burning. Not wood. What is it?"

"I burned my pot holder just before you came in," Bertien said. She held it up.

Little Anneke looked up at the stranger from Walter's lap with her innocent blue eyes. He came over, stooped down, and patted her cheek. She smiled at him. He smiled back. His hand went into the pocket of his tunic and came out with a candy in a colorful wrapper. Anneke studied it, but she didn't make a motion to accept it.

"*Nicht scheu sein,*" he said, and put it in her little hand. A broad smile spread over Anneke's face. The sergeant melted before their eyes.

Abruptly, he turned on his heels.

"*Auf Wiedersehen,*" he said, and went out the door.

They heard the soldier, the one who'd inspected the barn, say, "*Nichts.*" Nothing.

The sergeant hailed the third soldier and they continued their search down the street to the next farm. Hendrik rushed in. "Quick! Call the neighbors. Warn them," and left again.

She assumed this meant the neighbors were also hiding Jews. The rush of adrenaline sprang on her tongue. Her heart was pounding in her chest so fast, she thought it might leap out of her bosom. The sudden ending to the ten minutes of panic left her speechless. Little Anneke had brought the sergeant to his senses. But that was probably not the right way to describe his sudden change of mind. If he had been sensible, he would have looked a bit harder for an airman on the run. It was more likely the sentimental aspect of the German two-sided character, the side that falls for the innocence of a small child, that had caused this unexpected ending. A picture of Hitler pinching the cheeks of a *Madchen* came to mind, and there was even a movie of Hitler feeding a deer. Hitler, of all people! The monster that caused the death of thousands of blameless people!

She plunked down in a chair next to Walter. "Why did you bring the airman here and not to the castle?"

"We didn't want to hide him at the castle without permission. Your grandmother doesn't deserve such a risk."

"Neither do Hendrik and Bertien."

"True, but Hendrik was in the woods with us. It was getting close to daylight, and we had to hurry. It was Hendrik's idea to bring him here."

"But you know we can't keep him here."

Bertien started a pot of coffee and took out bread from the cupboard. It was breakfast time. Hendrik and Tom kicked off their wooden shoes outside the kitchen door and brought the smells of hay and manure with them. Tom checked at the window to see how far the soldiers had gotten down the road.

"They're coming out of the Willes farm," he said. "The soldier asked why I wasn't working in Germany. I said I suffered with asthma. Thank God he didn't ask for proof. But I made a show of coughing."

"I'll get the man from Texas," Anna said. "He must be anxious to get out of the one-holer. Really! Why was the one-holer overlooked as a good hiding place? Was it the smell?"

"I tossed a pile of hay in front of it," Tom said. "It sits kitty-corner from the end stall, and that's where the bull stands."

Hendrik rescued Geertrui and Klaas. The Texan cast such longing eyes at the bread and the coffeepot that Hendrik suggested they say a prayer of thanks and eat before hatching a plan.

They weighed their options. The Germans would be all over the place looking for him. He'd have to be kept hidden until they could produce a false ID. Then he could be handed over to the Underground. A long, arduous trip was ahead of him through Belgium, France, and Spain to get him back to his base in England. Strangers along the way would risk their lives to provide safe houses.

Walter finished his cup of coffee and pushed back from the table. "It seems to me the castle must have a nook somewhere that is hard to discover. But we can't do it without asking the baroness for permission."

"I know the stables from one end to the other," Hendrik said. "There are good hiding places there."

With that in mind, Anna went back home, and going home meant going to Oma. Hadn't it always been that way? Her most precious childhood memories were of summer days at the castle, riding a clever Welsh pony, visiting with the farmers, climbing cherry trees, and listening to stories at Oma's knee. Now that she was here as an adult, she saw qualities in her grandmother she'd sensed as a child. Oma deftly navigated the minefield of dangers the war had wrought. She effectively stood up to the bullies of this world, and she did it with grace.

As Anna neared the castle, the ponies signaled danger. They galloped in their paddock, their tails held high, and then stopped abruptly, snorted, and turned around to face the danger. What they were pointing at were soldiers with rifles crouching around their run-in shed. A lorry was parked in front of the castle. More soldiers jumped out. Anna hastened to the breakfast table.

"Anna, my dear, good morning," Oma said, looking up from behind the local newspaper. "I hear we have some excitement in the neighborhood."

"Excitement is an interesting word to use, Oma, when a plane burns up and bombs explode. I watched it happen yesterday."

"Yes, I heard some commotion. Janus tells me three airmen came down in parachutes."

"That's right. And one is on the loose. At this very moment, Oma, soldiers are surrounding your home to look for him."

"I see. Well, I suppose it's a logical place to look for someone who's in need of a place to hide."

They walked over to the salon, to Oma's favorite place by the window with a view of the meadows and the stables.

"Oma, I know where the third airman is. He is not in or around the castle."

"That is good to know."

"I don't think it will be long before the Germans will come and demand to search inside."

It was a good guess. Minutes later, Janus came in to say that Herr von Schloss asked to see the baroness. In his Wehrmacht uniform and with an adjutant at this side, he clearly was on a mission.

"*Entschuldigen,*" he said without coming over to kiss her hand. "I gave orders to search your home and your grounds."

"You have my permission, Commandant, though that's not what you're asking for. You can go anywhere you think you need to go."

"Thank you," the commandant said, and turned on his heels with a clack of his riding boots. He returned an hour later, again with his young adjutant.

"I have to ask you some questions. Are you hiding an enemy of the Reich?"

"How do you define an enemy of the Reich? There are people under my roof who are not necessarily enchanted by your Reich, Herr Commandant."

"You must understand I am looking for an Allied pilot who was on his way to bomb the Reich." Herr von Schloss looked exasperated. Obviously, his soldiers had not turned up what he was looking for.

"Nobody knocked on my door to ask for protection. If you do find the pilot on my property, he would be here as an uninvited guest."

"I see," Herr von Schloss said. "There is a death penalty for anyone aiding the enemy. I thought I should warn you about that."

"I appreciate your forthrightness," Oma said.

He hesitated a moment, but turned to leave. The young officer followed him out the door. Two minutes later, he was back without knocking and by himself.

"Gnädige Frau, I am sorry to cause this trouble. My orders are to find the pilot, and if I don't, the Gestapo will be the next ones to search here."

The baroness looked at him. "I understand," she said. "Your prestige is on the line, isn't it?"

Herr von Schloss sighed. "There is so much I cannot say. But you read me well. Please know that I have protected you and will continue to do so. You take risks with the young people that surround you. Don't tell me you don't. I know that. Be careful."

Anna sat at the edge of her chair. How would Oma react to this allusion?

The baroness got up from her chair. She took the commandant's hand in hers, a reversal from the *kuss die hand* he had practiced on her several times.

"Herr von Schloss, I thank you for your courtesy." She smiled at him, and he smiled back. Then he left.

"Is he in trouble, Oma?"

"I think little love is lost between Herr von Schloss and the SS people. He is old school, and the SS is not populated with gentlemen. He is an unhappy man, caught in the middle."

"Oma, if you had to choose between the fortunes of Herr von Schloss and those of an Allied pilot, what would you do?"

Oma sat back down and folded her hands. Anna heard commands being shouted, doors slamming, and motors revving up. The war had come to the castle's front steps. Oma rang the bell for Janus and asked for coffee. Only after she'd poured a cup for Anna and herself, and Janus had returned to the kitchen, did she react to the transparent question her granddaughter had put to her.

"Where is the pilot, Anna?"

"Hendrik, Walter, and Klaas found him. They didn't want to bring him here without your permission, so they brought him over to Hendrik's farm. I was there when three German soldiers came looking for him. They didn't find him, thank God."

"That's a dangerous situation. It won't be easy to hide a foreigner on a small farm."

"Exactly. Hendrik says he knows of a hiding place in your stables nobody can ever find. I came to ask if you would allow him to hide the pilot there."

Oma got up and walked closer to the window that looked out on the courtyard in front of the stables. "It would be unfair," she said, "to ask Hendrik and Bertien to take the risk any longer. They obliged me when I asked them to hide Jews."

She turned around and faced Anna with a faint smile playing in her remarkable light-blue eyes. "The ponies would like some company, I'm sure. They seem terribly lonely with the empty box stalls around them. Hendrik is no fool. He's worked in the stables since he was a boy. If he can find a safe way to get the pilot there, then he has my permission. The SS be damned."

It took Anna by surprise to hear her venerable grandmother use such a word.

"I'm sure we can come up with a way to get him over to the stables safely," Anna said. "He is from Texas, but he looked every inch a Dutch farmer after he put on Hendrik's farm clothes. And he is blond. I know! I cut some of his hair because he had quite a large wound on his head."

"I always knew you would make a good doctor, my dear."

Anna embraced her grandmother and took off for Hendrik's farm, where it was business as usual. Hendrik and Tom stood in the field, preparing the soil for seeding. Bertien was busy pouring fresh milk into tall canisters. German soldiers with guns and bayonets had hardly interrupted the everyday rhythm of their farm life. Hendrik and Bertien lived with the dictates of nature. A cow with swollen tits needs to be milked, and when spring is in the air, it's time to seed.

"Miss Anna, please go inside," Bertien said. "They're waiting for you. I will call Hendrik."

"Should I ring the bell?"

"No. They've had enough scares to last them a whole week."

When Hendrik came in, Anna didn't waste precious time. "The commandant showed up at the castle with an aide and soldiers. They searched the castle, inside and out."

"That figures," Walter said.

"Herr von Schloss warned that the Gestapo might repeat the search if the pilot wasn't found. Oma agreed that hiding him in the stables was the best solution, as long as Hendrik could assure her it was a safe bet the Gestapo would never be able to find him."

How to get him to the stables without being detected? Klaas suggested that since the Texan lived on a ranch, he could ride a horse over. They all laughed at that idea. "With *klompen* on his feet?" Hendrik asked. But it prompted them to give the Texan a lesson in walking in wooden shoes. He practiced in the barn, looking as unbalanced as a toddler, but he got the hang of it.

"It's my turn to bring the milk to the *Melk Centrale* in Ede this morning," Hendrik said. "My route passes the castle before my first pick-up farm. I can drop him off and show him where to hide."

"Doesn't that look suspicious, having a passenger?" Walter asked.

"He looks like my cousin in my clothes."

Hendrik hitched up his horse to the wagon while the Texan loaded it with the heavy canisters of milk in spite of his sore ribcage. He got aboard on the open-ended backside and let his feet with the wooden shoes dangle.

Hendrik parked the wagon close to a small door in the back of the castle's stables and told his horse to stand still and wait for him. He led them through a center aisle lined with box stalls made of solid oak and with impressive ironwork. The last time Anna had been in there was as a child. It had always been filled with the sounds of whinnying and hooves impatiently pawing the floor. Now, she was struck by the silence. The painful silence of vanished glory.

Hendrik took them to an ornate tack room, where several saddles rested on brass brackets, bridles hung on the wall, and the smell of glycerin soap was pervasive.

"Who takes care of these saddles?" she asked. "They still look in fine shape."

"My cousin. He takes care of the ponies and cleans tack when I ask him to."

"Won't that be a problem?"

"No. It's spring and the ponies stay out in their run-in stables. He won't know the difference."

He removed a large leather harness from a paneled wall. A tiny piece of rope stuck out that Anna didn't even notice until Hendrik pulled hard on it. A piece of the paneling gave. He caught it and moved it aside.

"This is where harnesses used to be repaired when carriages were still in use. My cousin doesn't even know it's here."

She stuck her head in. It was like a large walk-in closet, the length of the wall. A narrow window sat near the ceiling. A bucket with odd-sized pieces of leather stood in a corner, and tools lay on a narrow table, ready to be picked up again. Hendrik pointed at a rack with horse blankets.

"Tell him he can fold and spread them to make a bed, Miss Anna."

She translated the instructions and told the Texan she would be back with food. Hendrik showed her how to fit the panel back. It fitted into a groove at the bottom and snapped in place at the top. The harness was as heavy as the panel, but she managed to hang it up and cover the wall. Back outside, the horse stood where Hendrik had left him.

For the next two days, she brought meals and English books through the back door at sunup and sundown. The pilot's resilience was impressive. He'd made himself comfortable on a pile of horse blankets. She checked his head wound. It was healing well. Now, all he needed was a false ID, and he could leave on the next leg of his odyssey.

Of course, the Germans couldn't find the pilot. They combed the area, but nothing turned up. As the commandant had predicted, the Gestapo was disgusted.

They were certain they could do better than the Wehrmacht, and on the third day after the plane fell out of the sky, they took over the search. Their suspicion fell on the castle. A Gestapo officer walked up to the door, pushed Janus aside, and barged into the salon, where, as usual, Oma sat in her favorite chair by the window, Anna at her side.

"Where's the pilot?" he barked.

Oma got up and walked over to the officer. "That's a good question," she said.

"The commandant did a search here," the officer said, "but it cannot have been very thorough."

"I told the commandant he could look anywhere he needed to on my property. As far as I know, he did."

The officer took off his leather gloves and slapped them into his left hand.

"Didn't the commandant visit you here several times before?" He took a step forward. The top of his cap, which he had not removed, reached no higher than Oma's nose.

"Yes, he has," she said. "Never on my invitation."

Oma was playing for time, Anna knew. Was the Gestapo accusing her of corruption? Or was this insinuation aimed at Herr von Schloss?

"Has the commandant ever asked you for favors?"

The baroness was ready for him. "No, unless you consider serving a cup of tea a favor."

"Do you have anything to hide?" It sounded more like a threat than a question.

"Nothing and nobody," Oma said. "No airman or pilot has asked me to provide a hiding place. You may search wherever you want." The baroness pulled herself up, which made her look even taller in front of the officer.

"We'll see," he muttered, and left.

Moments later, the castle was overrun with soldiers. Anna had sat nailed to her chair throughout the tense conversation. A rivulet of sweat ran down the back of her neck. After an hour of listening to commands, doors slamming, and boots marching through the halls, the officer walked back into the living room. The baroness put down the book she was reading and looked up.

"Well, did you find the missing pilot, officer?" she asked.

He was visibly annoyed and not about to admit defeat.

"We found a young man who should be serving in the Arbeitseinsatz. We arrested him."

"Arrested him? Klaas Voorne? He is my manager and he has an Ausweiss. He is absolutely essential to me. If you take him, you're chopping off my right hand."

"He's played games with the rules. He is a strapping twenty-two-year-old, and he should be working for the Reich. Flat feet are no excuse."

Anna jumped up and practically screamed, "You can't do that."

The officer let out a sarcastic laugh. "Ach so!" he said, and turned and strode out of the room. Anna ran after him. There was Klaas, standing in the hall, held by two soldiers. His luck had run out. The officer gave a command, and he was led toward an overvalswagen parked outside. Klaas turned around to look at her.

"I'll see you after the war is over," he said. "Count on it."

After the door slammed shut, she gave the officer a dirty look and ran back to the salon.

"They've taken him, Oma! He's gone."

She fell on her knees in front of Oma's chair. A dam was giving way in her soul. A dam she had thrown up against the everyday anxieties the war caused. Her thoughts turned dark with a hate she'd tried so hard not to feel, because hate was a poor master, she knew, and it wasn't what had propelled her into illegal activities. But the thought of Klaas being sent to a concentration camp was like stepping over a threshold into a state of hate, despair, and disgust. When she lifted her head, she noticed her tears had darkened Oma's skirt.

"This is a very unfortunate outcome, isn't it?" Oma said while she tenderly stroke Anna's hair. "We've saved the pilot, but now

Klaas is taken. But think of it this way, Anna. Even if we hadn't hidden the pilot, the Gestapo would have come here looking for him anyway."

She didn't respond.

"And the other thing to keep in mind is that Klaas was not taken as a Jew but as an able-bodied man. That will make a big difference in the way he will be treated. A work camp is not the same as a concentration camp, as I understand it."

Anna didn't want to think of what would have happened to Oma if Klaas had been identified as a Jew. She also didn't want to think about how she was going to tell Geertrui that her son had been taken away by the Gestapo.

"What could we have done differently, Oma?"

"In ordinary circumstances, we could have prevailed with reason and made a case for how essential Klaas is to running the affairs of the estate. But we do not live under our own rules of behavior. This SS officer had to come back with a trophy so he could outdo the commandant. It makes no sense, but that's the tragedy of this war. A madman, who is devious enough to convince others to execute his sinister schemes, governs us. I am not telling you anything you don't already know, but it is different when it is brought to your doorstep, isn't it?"

Anna straightened up. "I feel terrible for Klaas. My God, what is going to happen to him? It can't be good. It makes me sick to think of him digging ditches for the Moffen."

Oma sighed. "Let's go out for a walk, Anna. We need some fresh air."

She fetched her walking stick and once outside, stepped onto the path that led by the ponies. In passing, she rubbed their foreheads. To Anna's surprise, she kept walking past the paddock, deftly picking her way over the ruts in the road. Soon, they were close to Hendrik's farm. Bertien was outside with little Anneke.

"How she has grown," Oma said. Anneke looked up at the strange lady with a disarming smile. "I would like to go inside,

Bertien, if I may?"

Bertien turned shy. Oma put a reassuring hand on her arm. "I just would like to talk to you about something, if you don't mind."

They went inside. Geertrui sat at the kitchen table and was truly shocked to see the baroness walk in. She got up and nervously straightened her wool sweater.

"We have met before, but you may not remember me," Oma said, and reached for her hand. "I am Anna's grandmother."

"How do you do, Mevrouw van Haersolte?"

"Please sit down. I am bringing you some news about Klaas. It is not good, but it could be much worse."

Geertrui sank back into the kitchen chair. "Oh, no."

"The Gestapo came looking for the missing pilot. You may be aware a plane came down and he parachuted out. Well, they have not found the pilot, but they came across Klaas."

Geertui was unable to speak.

"They arrested and took him."

Anna thought Oma was being too direct, but how else was she going to tell this mother her son was now in the hands of the Nazis?

"As I told Anna, the bright side to this sad turn of events is that Klaas was taken because in the eyes of the SS, he should have reported to the Labor Bureau, even though he had an Ausweiss. He was *not* taken for any other reason. They will put him to work, but they won't send him to a concentration camp. That I am sure of."

Anneke was in Bertien's arms, but as soon as she was put down, she ran over to Geertrui and crawled into her lap.

"I see you have made a friend," the baroness said. "Life has hidden blessings, doesn't it? Klaas was a blessing to me. I will miss him. But I am absolutely convinced he will return to us."

She turned and headed for the door before Geertrui could react.

That evening, when it was time to bring food to the Texan, Anna noticed one of the saddles was missing in the tack room. She removed the heavy harness and opened the panel.

"Hi there," the Texan said as she stepped into what she still thought of as a closet. She put a small canvas bag with his supper on the workbench. It had some bread in it with slices of ham she'd spared from her own lunch, and a thermos with coffee. It was all she could offer. Fresh fruit was not in season.

"I had a few scares," the Texan said. "This morning I heard footsteps and shouts outside. It sounded like German. And then the sounds were on the other side of this wall. Two men were shouting at each other. They were very close to the wall, and I heard a thud, then the sound of boots that scurried away."

"Ah! I bet they fought over who would get the saddle. One is missing. The Germans are stealing us blind. If they like it, they take it."

"What was going on this morning?"

She had decided not to tell him they took Klaas. It would just make him feel bad, and it was not his fault.

"The Gestapo came looking for you. They left disappointed."

He unwrapped the sandwich.

"Do you mind telling me a few things?" he asked as he munched on the sandwich. "When I parachuted down, I saw a castle below. Do these stables belong to that castle?"

"Yes, they do."

"And who are you?"

"My name is Anna."

"Do you work at the castle?"

"Yes, I do."

"You seem well educated. You speak English. You read good English books."

"Thank you," she said. She changed the subject. Giving her full name was the last thing she should do. "Now I have a question for you. When will this war be over?"

He stretched his legs out over the folded horse blankets and leaned against the wall. What age would he be? Late twenties? A blond beard had begun to show on his cheeks, which hadn't seen a razor or a washcloth over the three days since he'd taken off from an airfield in England. He was the first American she'd ever met, and his laid-back demeanor intrigued her.

"They're working at it," he said. "It takes a lot of manpower to set Hitler back on his heels. My country is shipping tanks, trucks, planes, and troops. England is like an anthill, crawling with Yankees."

"That's good to know. But the end can't come soon enough."

"Yeah, it must be tough." He took a swig from the thermos. "Hitler may think he's smart enough to win the war, but we have a general who's a lot smarter."

"Who's he?"

"General Dwight Eisenhower. I think he will win the war for us. They made him the Supreme Commander of the Allies, and I'm proud to say he's an American."

Anna drank in his optimism. Things were happening on the other side of the Channel.

"Do you think your general can outfox General Rommel?"

"Sure!" the Texan said with a broad smile. "It's hard to beat American ingenuity. You'll see, once we set foot on the Continent."

"I can't wait. That will probably be on our coast. At least, that's what the Germans expect. They've turned our coastline into one continuous fort with bunkers and landmines."

The Texan took another swig of coffee, or what passed for it. "We'll step around them carefully," he said. He wiped his mouth with a khaki-colored handkerchief. "You'd better go, Anna," he said, pointing at the small window. "It's getting dark, and I bet you don't have a flashlight."

She got up from her crouched position. He had a point. It was hard to put the panel and the harness back in place in the dark, and it was downright spooky to find her way through the deserted stables without the help of a flashlight. And there was only a sliver of a moon in the sky to help cross over to the back of the castle.

"When you see Hendrik," the Texan said, "thank him for emptying the potty. The smell in here was getting very ripe."

Anna had a hard time falling asleep after that visit. The sure knowledge that a total stranger was locked up, night and day, in nothing more than a big closet was more than a bit unsettling. She was totally aware that she was responsible for his survival. And what if he were discovered? They would all be dead.

Something else kept her awake. His bearded face, his muscular body, his easy ways, and his optimism played hide-and-seek with her mind. Or was it her heart? She didn't want to admit it, but this stranger intrigued her.

The next morning, she lingered after he opened the canvas bag with the breakfast she'd brought. He immediately went for the coffee thermos.

"What kind of breakfast do you have in Texas?"

"On the ranch, we have fried potatoes, a couple of fried eggs, bacon, and cornbread."

She reached into the bag and took out the boiled egg she'd snatched from the kitchen table behind Mien's back. To get her hands on an extra portion was not easy. Food was getting scarcer by the day.

"What's a ranch like?" she asked while peeling the egg.

He told her about herding cattle over a large area and spending days in the saddle.

"How ironic that you should be hiding in a stable," she said, and handed him the egg.

The picture he painted of the vastness of his father's ranch put her grandmother's castle and environs in a new perspective. The way he talked about his country made it sound like the horizon was so far away, it was unreachable.

Again, he admonished her to go back before the sun came out, but she had one more question.

"Would you write your name and address in this book? I will remember on which page I can find it after the war is over. For now, I will put it in the bookcase in the library. Nobody will find it. There are hundreds of books there."

"Okay," he said with a smile. "But then you will have to give me your full name, so I can find *you* if I make it back to the States."

"Just remember Anna. It is too dangerous to give you my full name."

He understood. She handed him *The Good Earth* by Pearl Buck. Before she could read what he wrote, he slammed the book shut and handed it to her. As she looked up to thank him, he took her head in both his hands and gently placed a kiss on her forehead. She could feel herself turn bright red. He let her go, reached for the canvas bag, and said, "You'd better go now."

She did as she was told.

Before the day was out, the Texan had left. Walter had produced the crucial ID he needed to get him on his way back to England, and Hendrik had taken him to his next stop, wherever that was. They informed the baroness that the pilot was safe. The castle's history had been enriched by an intriguing story of escape, Walter told her. The baroness smiled.

Anna sat on her bed that night with Pearl Buck's book in her lap, and drank in the words the Texan had left for her. This was what he wrote: *To my guardian angel, who did more to save my life than I can know. But what I do know is this: she is loyal, courageous, smart, and beautiful. Thanks for the hardboiled egg! Jack Foster. Fair Weather Ranch, Barksdale, Texas.* She felt like a smitten sixteen-year-old. Would she tell Dirk about this incredible episode? How she had been touched by this man's optimism, his careless courage, his stamina, his "take it as it comes" attitude? He'd been a totally different kind of a gentleman than she had thus far encountered. He could have taken advantage of her. But he hadn't.

She put the book under her pillow. Tomorrow, she would put it in her grandfather's library, on the top shelf, where it came from. Maybe, after the war was over and she was married to Dirk, maybe even had a child, she could go back and reach for it, knowing that this too had been part of the war experience.

CHAPTER THIRTY-THREE

Dirk – May-June 1944

Dirk swung his legs over the side of his bed. It really was Anna's bed. He had taken over her room at Jan and Betty's after he helped her escape from the police bureau in Utrecht. There had been no repercussions from that daring deed, but it seemed safer for Anna to go to the castle. That was before Christmas, and now summer was around the corner.

Dirk felt as if he'd stepped into another life. Being a student was a distant memory. His friends were in hiding. Anna was unreachable. Sometimes, when the separation got the better of him, he opened the armoire to inhale the scent of her clothes. Even after all these months, her distinct perfume clung to the blouses and skirts that hung neatly in a row, waiting for her return.

He opened the window to let in fresh air. In spite of an upside-down world, Mother Nature remained true to the rhythm of the seasons. Late-blooming tulips replaced early-bird daffodils, and the stamp-sized lawns below looked ready to be clipped. A housewife hung laundry in the backyard of the third house to the right. He waved at her as she pinned a towel to the line. She waved back. It was her husband who'd surprised him a week ago by unexpectedly jumping like an agile cat into his room by way of the open window. He'd negotiated the gutters on the connected roofs to escape the Gestapo officers looking for him down below in the street. Sharing an enemy made for strong bonds.

The previous night, they'd shared a new kind of scare. Trusted neighbors in the corner house of the street had called Jan on the phone to warn that the Gestapo was coming down the street in a truck with an antenna on top. Dirk called his new acquaintances right away. Jan had turned off his radio and pushed it back in its hiding place. It was a new peril. The Gestapo had come up with a way to detect radios tuned to the BBC. At the time of the daily Radio Oranje broadcast in the evening, they drove around the city in that special truck. Frightening stories of people being dragged into the street and taken prisoner were making the rounds.

Dirk washed up, shaved, and got dressed. He tightened his belt an extra notch. He was losing weight at the rate of about one notch a month. Food was getting scarce. Poor Betty stood in line for hours to get groceries. Last Saturday afternoon, in the pouring rain, he'd offered to do the shopping for her. The line was long. The grocer's wife let people in only one by one. She looked like a battleax, tough and incorruptible. Only once during the four hours he stood there did she allow an older woman, who was near fainting, to get ahead. By the time he came home, he was soaked through and had a deepened appreciation for what it meant to be a housewife these days.

As he prepared to leave the room, he glanced at the mirror. Small pictures sat stuck in the rim of the frame. He'd added Anna's passport picture to her collection. As he stood looking at it, his gaze drifted to a business card below it. It had been there all along, but today it stood out for some reason. He unstuck it from the frame and studied the name. Dr. Alexander Boot.

My God, that's the medical director of the University Hospital where I work. Anna had once referred to him as her father's good friend from his student days in Leiden. He put the card in his wallet. It might come in handy someday, even though when Anna had offered to ask this doctor to get him a job, he'd refused the intercession. That was a year ago. With the red-hot irons he had in the fire these days, he could foresee a situation that might require someone with asbestos hands to save him.

At the laboratory, he took his spot behind the long counter, positioned a slide under the microscope, and went to work. He trained his right eye on the engraved lines that created squares, and randomly picked one square to count the white cells within it. He had to come up with a number and be sure about it. Somebody's treatment depended on it.

When he was done, he straightened up and turned his neck from left to right to get relief from bending over in one position. It wasn't what he had imagined when he enrolled in medical school. His dream had been to become a *huisarts*, to deliver babies at home, to listen to people's problems in his office, to treat and prevent illness, a life filled with action and satisfaction and good deeds. But here he was peering through a tiny hole, looking for signs of malaise in people he didn't know.

He picked up the next test tube and prepared a slide with a tiny drop of the blood in it. The name of the patient: Frits Nolen. Diagnosis: Leukemia. Age: 9. He'd seen that name before. The admission date was listed as 3/4 -1944. Once a week, Dirk examined his blood, and each time the white cell counts were normal. It was none of his business, of course—Frits Nolen was not his patient—but he couldn't get it out of his mind that there was something unusual about this sequence of negative tests. Did his doctor have the diagnosis wrong?

At lunchtime, he decided to walk over to the children's ward. He kept on his white coat, which provided him access to almost any place in the hospital. No questions asked. Frits Nolen was in the third bed in a row of seven. Dirk walked over slowly, taking in the sight of young children in white pajamas under white sheets in high white tubular-framed beds. Frits sat upright with his legs dangling over the edge. His curly dark hair sat like a black cap over his very pale face. The chart attached to the foot of the bed listed Dr. A. Boot as his physician.

"Dag, Frits, how are you?"

The boy looked at him without saying a word. There was weariness and fear in the way he sized Dirk up. Putting together the repeated negative blood tests and the features in the boy's face, with the low inset of the ears and the pronounced nose, he suddenly understood he was dealing with one of the children Sister Bertha had saved from being put on the train to a concentration camp. This boy wasn't here because he was sick. This boy had to hide an essential fact.

"I am the one who does your blood tests, Frits, so I thought I would come over and say hello."

Silence. More suspicion.

"I am a very good friend of Sister Bertha. Actually, I am probably one of her best friends."

A flicker of interest came into his eyes.

"Do you have enough books to read?"

Frits pointed to a stack on the stand next to his bed.

"Do you know how to play chess?"

Frits shook his head.

"Would you like to learn?"

He shrugged.

"My grandfather taught me when I was your age. It's an interesting game. Well, anyway, I have to get back to the lab now."

When he reached the exit, he turned around and noticed the boy was watching him. Dirk waved, but Frits didn't wave back.

That evening at dinner, he asked Jan if he had a chessboard and pieces.

"Sure I do," Jan said. "Want to play? I would have asked you before, but I didn't know you played chess."

"I haven't played in ages, but I need to bone up on the rules before I teach a nine-year-old patient."

"Not an easy game to learn when you're sick."

"This one is bored silly. He needs to keep his mind busy."

Over the next few days, Jan regularly beat Dirk at chess, but the rules were beginning to come back to him. On Saturday afternoon, he went into town to buy a travel-sized set and a rulebook. He biked over to the hospital and went to the children's ward in his street clothes. It was visiting hours. Family members surrounded the children's beds, but it was quiet around Frits Nolen's bed.

"Dag, Frits. Remember me? I wore a white lab coat the last time we met. I forgot to tell you my name. I am Dirk. I brought you a present." Frits took it from his hand. "Go ahead. Open it up. It's yours."

A wooden box appeared. Frits lifted it up. The pieces inside started to slide and made a rattling sound.

"Can you guess?" Dirk asked.

"Chess?"

"That's right."

"I don't know how to play, and I don't have anybody to play with."

"How about if I teach you? Since I work in the lab, I can come over during my lunch hour and we can play."

Frits opened the box and took out the pieces. One set was carved from black ebony, the other from ivory. They were small but beautiful.

"There's a book with it, so you can study the rules. I hadn't played for a while, and my neighbor beat me badly last night."

A bell rang to signal the end of visiting hours. Dirk got up to go.

"Thank you, Dirk," Frits said.

When Dirk came back a few days later during his lunchtime, Frits sat in a chair next to his bed with the chessboard spread out on the covers and his nose in the rulebook. The pieces were arranged in the correct order. Had Frits been waiting for him?

"Dag, Frits. *Hoe gaat het?*"

The boy looked up. "*Goed,*" he said in a dreamy voice. "I'm trying to understand this game."

"Are you ready to play?" Dirk asked. Being spoken to in full sentences was encouraging.

"Who made up these rules?" Frits asked.

"I don't think anybody can answer that for sure. They say the game started in India, way back in the seventh century. Later it traveled to Spain."

"Maybe Saint Nicholas brought it to Spain."

"Well, that's possible," Dirk said. "The good bishop still brings good things, doesn't he? So, why not chess?"

Dirk reached into his pocket and came out with something he hid in his fist. It was a silver guilder with the likeness of Queen Wilhelmina on one side, a strictly forbidden item. He opened his fist slightly. Frits giggled when he recognized it.

"I will flip it. If it lands with her face up, then you can have the ivory pieces."

He threw the coin up in the air over the bed, and it landed with Her Majesty's face up on the white blanket.

"Oh, that's good," Frits said. "I was hoping I would get the white pieces."

"Why?"

"I want to have the white queen. I named her Wilhelmina," he whispered.

"I think you figured out the game, Frits. Queens are powerful. I'll be back tomorrow, and you can have the white pieces."

The next day, Frits was waiting for him with the chessboard all set up. Dirk asked if he had named any of the other pieces.

"Shhh," Frits said. "I named the black king Hitler."

"Then I hope you beat me in our first game," Dirk whispered back.

They played till lunchtime was up. Day after day, Dirk returned to play chess. Frits had asked if he could always have the ivory pieces to play with and Dirk the ebony ones. He continued to give names to the pieces. The two ebony bishops he called Himmler, who was head of the SS, and Goebbels, who was head of propaganda. He didn't have a name for the ebony queen. Hitler wasn't married, he said. The ivory bishops became Churchill and Roosevelt. The ivory knight was General Montgomery, and the ebony knight was General Rommel. He seemed well informed for his age.

"Did you name the pawns?" Dirk asked.

Frits shrugged.

"Pawns are important too, you know."

"No!" Frits shouted at him. A nurse bandaging a patient in the next bed straightened up and looked alarmed. Frits had his head down on his bed, next to the chessboard. Dirk put his hand on his shoulder and let him be. After a while, he said, "Ready to go on with the game? You're in a good position to win."

Frits briefly raised his head. "Tomorrow," he said.

"All right, tomorrow."

The next day, Dirk saw the board had been wiped clean. They got busy setting up a new game. After Frits finished placing the larger pieces, he picked up one ivory pawn. "This is my mother," he said without looking at Dirk.

One by one, he picked up the white pawns. "This is my father, this is my grandfather, and this is my grandmother, this is my other grandfather, and my other grandmother."

He placed each one carefully and lovingly on the board. When he was done, he looked at Dirk through tears.

"And the black ones?" Dirk asked. "Who are they?"

"The bad people who're out to get my people."

Dirk's own eyes filled up. Frits had figured out that his people were pawns in Hitler's game. He felt a tremendous urge to lift the boy up and take him into his arms, but he put his hand on his shoulder instead. He didn't want to attract attention. His coming over every day was already raising some eyebrows with the other boys.

"Let's play and get that black king," he said.

Afterwards, instead of going back to the lab, he went to the library where he'd met Sister Bertha — Carla's friend from Breda — a year ago. He gambled she might be there. She was the one person he dared to tell about Frits. His gamble paid off. Bertha sat at the wide oak table behind a pile of books, preparing a lecture for apprentice nurses. Dirk took a chair next to her, put his elbows on the table, and his head in his hands.

"I hear you're helping Frits," she said.

He looked up at her, and was impressed with her beauty and compassion all over again.

"Yes, he's a very special boy with amazing insights. He got the better of me today. What worries me is that someday some visiting parent, who might not be a patriot, will figure out why he is here."

"That's the risk we take. It happened once, but we got the girl out before the police came looking for her."

"I don't think I could take it if that happened to Frits."

"It's dangerous to attach yourself to these kids, Dirk."

"That may be, but is it any more dangerous than a host of other things I do that are illegal, like raising money for you? Do you have a home to place him in? I assume he's here temporarily."

Bertha didn't have a home for Frits. It was getting harder and harder, she said, because so many people were looking for hiding places. Not just Jews. She didn't know when and where she could place him.

Dirk walked back to the lab to work, but he couldn't concentrate. It was not the kind of work that could be done with only half his mind on it. So he quit. He walked aimlessly through the halls. For as long as he'd known Bertha, he'd understood that she was engaged in a risky business. The children she protected were safe only up to a point. Now that Frits had put a face on the undertaking, an ice-cold hand gripped his heart. He walked over to the office of the hospital's medical director and asked to speak to him. It was urgent, he told the secretary. While he waited for admission to the inner sanctum, he took out the visiting card he'd tucked in his wallet, ready to present it if the situation called for it.

"Good afternoon. What can I do for you?" Dr. Boot said from his position behind a large desk. He was a middle-aged man with a benign smile. Dirk took an immediate liking to him. His keen eyes and mild manner put him at ease.

"Thank you for receiving me," he said. "I am Dirk van Enthoven, a fourth-year medical student, who has been sidelined to the laboratory here after the university closed. I have analyzed the blood tests for your patient Frits Nolen. I realize he is in the hospital for other reasons than the stated leukemia diagnosis. I got to know him well."

Dr. Boot interrupted him. "Yes, Sister Bertha told me you introduced him to the game of chess."

"He is a smart and sensitive boy, and I got rather close to him."

"I can see how that might happen."

"I'm worried about him. What if someone becomes suspicious? What if a visitor turns out to be an angry NSB and gets the Gestapo involved? I would like permission to take him out."

Dr. Boot got up and walked around his desk. He put his hand on Dirk's shoulder in a gentle gesture. "You are a good friend of Anna Smits, aren't you?"

Dirk was speechless.

"Dr. Hamel told me you raise money for this cause," Dr. Boot continued. "And I thank you for that. When I heard that part of it was raised at Kasteel Koppelburg, I saw a connection through Baroness van Haersolte to Anna Smits, who is the daughter of a good friend of mine. I understand she also studies medicine in Utrecht."

"Yes, she does. Or rather, she did." Dirk practically stammered. He didn't have to use the visiting card after all. "Anna lives at the castle these days. It's where I thought I would bring Frits."

Dr. Boot took his hand off Dirk's shoulder. "We live with the threat of being found out all the time. That's nothing new, but now that the Nazis are beginning to lose the war, they get more agitated.

And as with everything else, the NSB falls in line with them."

"I just have a terrible feeling of foreboding, Dr. Boot."

"Are you sure you want to take this on, Dirk? Have you thought this through? It's no small matter to hide a Jewish child, no matter how well intentioned you are. And are Anna and her grandmother prepared to deal with this?"

"I think I can speak for them. They are both brave and compassionate women."

The doctor smiled. "I believe you. Still, I think you need to discuss this with them. I can write a discharge note, but we have to be sure this will work out for all parties involved. Report back to me if and when you're ready to set things in motion."

Dirk couldn't believe what had just happened. The hospital's director had known about him all along. He should contact Anna right away. Dr. Boot was absolutely correct that he shouldn't just show up on the castle's doorstep with a Jewish boy in tow.

He left Dr. Boot and walked over to Dr. Hamel's office to ask if he could use his phone. Dirk was careful with his words, aware that his call could be tapped—always a possibility.

When Anna came on the phone, he told her to listen carefully. "I'm coming over the day after tomorrow. No, not by train. I'm coming on my bike and I'm bringing my nephew with me. He's ten. And I would like him to stay with you and Oma. His parents can't take care of him. Yes, you're right, he's a patient here. Nice boy. Ask Oma if that's all right with her, and if it is, give me a call back. My number is 20-56689. I'll be here another hour. I love you!"

Anna was a superb listener. She understood. Within the hour, she called back and said Oma would be delighted to receive them. He gave a sigh of relief. His heart filled with boundless love for both Anna and her grandmother.

Now he had to figure out the logistics. On his way out, he stopped at the children's ward. It was afternoon visiting hours. The large room was wrapped in a hushed atmosphere. He took in the scene. It was quiet around Frits, but the new boy in the bed next to his had visitors, a man and a woman, most likely his parents. They seemed to carry on their conversation in a whisper. Dirk again experienced a strong feeling of foreboding as the patient pointed at Frits. The man—he assumed it was the father—turned to take a look at Frits. Dirk decided not to go in and visit for fear his conversation would be overheard. This was not a good time to tell Frits he was going to take him out of the hospital. As he prepared to leave, the man turned and looked in his direction, letting his glance travel over the row of white beds. It stopped and rested on Dirk, who felt an electric current zip through his body, from top to toe. His mind instantly dressed the man in an NSB uniform.

Nothing of substance had happened, but Dirk felt jolted by fear. He had to get Frits out of this place as fast as possible, like first thing tomorrow morning. He decided to leave early on the bike Anna had left behind. Germans were less interested in confiscating ladies' bikes. With Jan's help, he tied a pillow onto the baggage carrier and clamped two small bars on both sides of the back wheel as foot rests. Betty asked a friend with an eleven-year-old son for some clothes. She also produced a rucksack.

Dirk was at the hospital at seven o'clock and went directly to Dr. Boot's office. Dr. Hamel had already informed the doctor that Baroness van Haersolte had agreed to take Frits Nolen. The discharge note had been written. The ID was on his desk.

Dr. Boot handed him the documents. "Be careful, Dirk. Tell Anna I would like to meet her someday."

It was busy in the children's ward as nurses performed their early-morning routines. The head nurse regarded him with a look of understanding when he handed her the discharge note and the rucksack with clothes.

To prevent the patient in the next bed from listening in, Dirk had written a note for Frits: "Shhhh. I will take you to a safer place. Shhhh." He handed it to him.

Used to keeping important secrets, Frits looked up and nodded. He reached for the drawer in his nightstand, took out the chessboard and the box with the chess pieces, and handed both to Dirk.

In a loud voice, Dirk said, "All right, Frits, put on your slippers and we'll go and get this test done. It won't hurt. I promise." He walked Frits over to the nurses' station. The head nurse stood waiting with the rucksack. She showed Frits to a near bathroom and told him to change his clothes and leave the hospital pajamas on the floor.

Frits came out looking very different in clothes that were on the roomy side, but with eyes that stood out like stars in his pale face. The nurse held out her hand, but he reached up and hugged her. Then he put his hand in Dirk's.

"Where are we going?" he asked.

"I can't tell you yet. Let's just say we're going on a family visit."

Dirk put the chess game and board in the rucksack, fitted its straps over the boy's shoulders, and led him down the hallway to the front door. When Dirk opened it, Frits abruptly stopped and took a moment to drink in the fresh air with his nostrils wide open.

"This will be a long bike ride, Frits, and you may be uncomfortable. Are you up to it?"

"Let's go," Frits said, his eyes still shining like stars.

They were lucky with the weather. The leaves on the trees looked like adolescents, full grown and green. Biking by an apple orchard once they were out of the city, Dirk noticed their blossoms had turned from promise to substance. He wondered what it all looked like to Frits. This boy, whose arms he felt around his waist, would be seeing the world anew, finding himself in a reality that to Dirk felt closer to God than to the world the Nazis had tried to create to their own liking.

He didn't have to look at a map. How many times had he pedaled to the castle since he met Anna? He was longing to see her. She was his reason for trying to stay alive in spite of the risks he took. Probably the biggest risk of all was putting a Jewish boy on the back of this bike and turning Anna prematurely into the mother of a nine-year-old.

Betty had put some sandwiches and a water bottle in the rucksack. When they got hungry, they ate and rested by the side of the road.

"Are you sore?" Dirk asked.

"Yes, a little," Frits admitted. "Do we have much farther to go?"

"We're halfway. Can you do it?"

Frits rubbed his behind and laughed. "You wouldn't leave me here, sitting by the side of the road, would you, if I said I couldn't?"

"Never!"

"I know that you can't tell me where we're going, but can you please tell me just a little bit? That way I can try to picture it. I want to think about happy things."

"Well, when you get there, you'll think you've landed in a fairy tale. You're going to a building that's bigger than a house, but don't worry, it's not a hospital. It has a forest on one side and fields on the other."

They heard a rumble. A German patrol car came around the bend. Frits's pale face turned chalk-white. Color slowly returned to his cheeks after the patrol car continued on without stopping. Dirk picked up his bike from the roadside, and Frits slid his arms through the straps of his rucksack.

"If it's like a fairy tale, then maybe I'm going to a castle," he said.

"That would be something, wouldn't it? While you look at my back for the next two hours, you can dream about going to a castle. All I can say is, you're onto something. It's a beautiful place."

Frits's eyes turned dreamy. "Maybe there's a princess in the tower. Remember the fairy tale with the spinster?"

Dirk laughed. "She won't stay a spinster for long if I can help it."

They continued on their way over back roads and through small villages. Dirk looked back once in a while to be sure Frits was all right, and every time he got a smile. But when they passed the barracks in Ede, he felt the small arms tightening around his waist. German soldiers marched in the courtyard with guns on their shoulders. How could Frits *not* panic? He let go of the handle with his right hand and squeezed the hand that tugged at his jacket.

"Don't worry. We're almost there." He remembered how it had frightened Anna when they biked by the barracks with Klaas in tow.

It was midafternoon when they entered the lane that led to Kasteel Koppelburg. He stopped and lifted Frits off the bike.

"We have to limber up a bit. We don't want to waddle in like ducks when we say hello to people, do we?"

"Are we close?" Frits asked.

"Really close."

Tall oaks lined the lane. They walked in filtered sunlight under a canopy of leaves. When they got closer, they stopped as an iron gate came into view. Frits looked through the stiles.

"It looks like a castle, Dirk."

"That's exactly what it is."

"Is it close to where I'm going?" He got very excited.

"This is where you will live till the war is over."

"I will live in a castle?" Dirk felt a clammy hand slide into his.

They walked on through the open gate. Once at the front door, Dirk pointed at the large brass knob of the doorbell. "Pull on it, Frits. Really hard."

Janus appeared. Dirk noticed he'd lost weight, but he was still his solemn self. Frits looked diminutive in the grand hall with its marble floor and staid portraits on the walls, but the look in his eyes was huge. The wide door to the salon opened. The baroness sat in her favorite place by the window.

"Dirk, how nice to see you again! It's been a while. I've asked Janus to tell Anna you've arrived. A day early! I see you've brought a friend with you."

She reached out to Frits. "What is your name?"

"Frits Nolen." He stepped forward, hesitantly, and shook her hand.

"*Welkom*, Frits. I hear you will stay with us. I'm so glad you were well enough to get out of the hospital. Let's have some tea. You had a long trip."

Anna burst into the room and made a straight line for Dirk. She flew into his outstretched arms, and they stood like that for a moment, oblivious of their surroundings. He let go, took her hand, and pulled her over to where Frits was standing.

"Frits, this is Anna. She will be taking care of you."

The fear and suspicion were back in his eyes when he stepped forward to shake her hand. "Dag," he said, but it was immediately followed by a question. "Aren't you staying, Dirk?"

"I have to get back to work, but you can be sure I will come and visit as often as I can."

Anna went down on her knees and took Frits's hand. "I'm glad you came. We'll have a good time. There's a lot to do here. A castle is a fun place to live in."

"Does it have a tower?" Frits asked.

"Yes, it does. But there's a lot more than a tower."

Dirk understood the magnetic attraction of a castle to a boy who'd spent months in the same bed and a long day on the back of a bicycle.

"Would you like to go and explore while we talk?" he asked.

"What if I get lost?"

"Just avoid going up any stairs," Anna said. "You can't get lost on the first floor, because every hallway leads back to the front door."

Janus came in with the implements for serving tea. He pointed at a silver bowl. "Mien thought your nephew might enjoy some fresh strawberries, Mr. van Enthoven," he said. "She just picked them."

The baroness situated herself behind the large tray. She put a dollop of whipped cream and a spoonful of sugar on the strawberries and handed the bowl to Frits, who—it was obvious—hadn't seen anything this good to eat in ages. In no time, his face was smeared with white from the cream and red from the fruit. The baroness laughed at the sight of him and offered a napkin.

"Now that you are fortified," Dirk said, "you can go and explore. We'll come looking for you in a while."

Frits took the hint and left the room. Maybe, just to be sure he would be able to find his way back, he left the door ajar.

Dirk brought Anna and her grandmother up to date and explained what had motivated him to bring Frits, and a day early at that. They were in the middle of discussing how they would deal with his presence when, suddenly, the baroness raised her hand to have silence. Music flowed in from down the hall. Anna got up. Dirk followed her. The door to the ballroom was wide open. They stopped and peeked in. There was Frits sitting on the stool behind the grand piano. His fingers flowed over the keys with his eyes closed.

Dirk looked at Anna. "That's an early Mozart piece," he whispered. "I know. I had piano lessons."

Frits stopped abruptly. "Hmmm," he said to himself. "This piano needs tuning."

"Well, then we'll have to see to that," Anna said.

Frits looked up as if waking from a dream. "Do you have sheet music?" he asked.

"I'm sure I can dig up some. We'll ask Oma."

"Is Oma the lady who gave me the strawberries? Is she your grandmother?"

"Yes, she is. You can call her Oma too, if you want."

He immediately withdrew into himself. His right hand touched the ivory keys of the piano and he rubbed them softly. Looking straight ahead, he said, "I already have two grandmothers. One I call Mutti. The other I call Meme, because she is French. She taught me to play the piano."

It was a delicate moment, transparent with affection and agony. Anna let some time go by before she said, "You can call her whatever you want, Frits."

"I'll think about it," he said.

That evening, when it was time to go to bed, another bridge had to be crossed. Frits clearly expressed what he thought of sleeping alone in a room in a castle. It apparently loomed large in his mind, and he didn't hesitate to show his fear.

"Dirk," he said, "I want to sleep in your room tonight."

"That's up to Anna," Dirk said, but he understood he'd become Frits's safe anchor. It would take time for him to feel the same way about Anna.

"I had an extra bed brought to my room," Anna said. "So, you can both sleep in my room tonight, and I will sleep in a guest room."

Standing at the foot of the staircase, ready for bed with Frits at his side, Dirk put his arm around Anna and whispered in her ear, "Some night, God willing, we will sleep in the same room."

She turned and kissed him passionately. He remembered that kiss all the way back to Utrecht the next day.

CHAPTER THIRTY-FOUR

Walter – June 1944

Walter stepped into the kitchen where Mien was peeling white asparagus. With a very sharp knife, she created paper-thin curls that landed on the kitchen table like curly hair on a hairdresser's floor. Mien was always busy putting together meals from ever diminishing supplies. She had a chef's gift for invention, and the loyalty of a devoted servant.

"Dag, Mien, I see you are preparing for a special meal. Asparagus, no less. What's the occasion?"

"We have a new member in the family, Dominee. While you were away for the weekend, Mijnheer van Enthoven brought his nephew over from the hospital. He looks awfully pale. He needs good healthy food."

"Well, if anyone can fatten him up, you can, Mien."

"I'm trying, Dominee Vlaskamp. It's a good thing we have our own vegetable patch."

It was striking that Mien referred to Dirk's nephew as a new member of the family. That could only mean one of two things: she considered Dirk van Enthoven a member of the family, or she considered everyone who had found shelter under the baroness's roof a member of the family. How old was Dirk's nephew? he wondered.

It was late afternoon. He should go straight up to his room and unpack his bags after his trip to Breda, but curiosity got the better of him. He knocked on the door of the salon. The baroness was not in her usual place by the window. Instead, she sat at a small table across from a child that didn't look old enough to be a teenager. A chessboard was between them, and they hadn't heard him come in. Walter stood back and took in the scene. Never before had he seen her play chess, but here she was, brooding over a chessboard.

The two chess players were in deep concentration. Walter studied the new addition to the family. Mien was right. He had an unhealthy pallor, yet he didn't look sickly. Whatever ailed him that put him in the hospital was not obvious.

It would be better to leave and not interrupt the game, but before he made it to the door, the baroness called him back. "Walter, did you have a good trip? Come and meet Frits."

He turned to greet her.

"Frits, this is Dominee Vlaskamp. He also lives with us."

The boy was too polite not to get up and shake hands, but poorly hid his annoyance at the interruption. Or was it evasion? Walter wasn't sure how to interpret the weariness in the brown eyes that stood out in his pale face. He was used to the open, happy smile of Bram.

The baroness filled the awkward silence. "Frits just came out of the hospital. The doctors prescribed fresh air and fresh food for him. So, what better place than Koppelburg?"

"I agree. There is no better place to recover. I'm glad you came, Frits, because I saw in the kitchen that Mien is preparing asparagus for tonight, and I love asparagus. How about you?"

Frits shrugged. "I never had it before."

The lack of enthusiasm puzzled Walter. How could he engage him? Best to let him go on with the chess game.

He excused himself and went upstairs. Janus had already

brought his bags to his room. What young minister had a butler carrying his luggage? For most people, the war meant a step down in one way or another, except maybe if you were a member of the NSB, but for him it had been a step up from his bohemian student life to putting his head down on a soft pillow in a castle. There had been a lot of questions to answer when he'd attended his mother's birthday party. They had come like rapid fire. Why didn't he live at the parsonage? What was the condition of the minister he was substituting for? How did he get along with the minister's wife and her children? At times, he felt like a witness in a trial.

Below his window, Anna walked over the lawn toward the kitchen door with a basket of strawberries. She was a busy woman these days. After Klaas was taken by the Gestapo and never heard from again, she took over his job of running the estate with the help of old Mr. van Dijk. The one huge advantage she had over Klaas was that she could freely move around the countryside. As she conducted business with the farmers, she also dropped off food stamps and money for the onderduikers.

There was a knock on the door. It was Anna. This was out of the ordinary.

"May I come in, Walter?"

He freed the chair of his suitcase and offered it to her.

"You know Dirk brought Frits," she said, coming right to the point. "I thought you should know he is not his nephew. He is Jewish. One of the many children Sister Bertha saved. She had put him in the hospital because he was about to be betrayed in the home where he had been placed. Dirk got close to him while he was a patient. He brought him here because he foresaw a second betrayal."

"He just brought him here?"

"No, he called the night before." Anna laughed. "He's not *that* bold, Walter."

So that was it. A Jewish child. It explained the boy's reticence.

"It will take some time to make him feel comfortable with us. Dirk won him over by introducing him to chess."

"Thank you for informing me. It would be easy to make a dreadful mistake."

He continued unpacking. His father had slipped in a can of really good pipe tobacco. Had he saved it from before the war? If he had got it on the black market, it would have cost him a mint.

It was good to have been home, but also stressful. Carla had a knack for dragging Bertha back into his life. His sister may not have intended it, but the results were the same. Every time she reported on Bertha, it brought back the pain of an unresolved issue. And recently, that issue had become entangled with current events. He could no longer treat his love for Bertha as something of the past, an episode he should forget, emotions he should bury. Because of circumstances beyond his control, Bertha was brought into the present, and the arrival of Frits rendered it even more acute. Hearing about how Bertha nobly saved Jewish children from sure misery fired up the dormant flame and raked up feelings that had settled at the bottom of his soul. Mistakenly, he thought he'd adjusted to the immovable fact that Bertha was a Catholic and he was a Protestant. In the straightjacket of a strictly divided society, there was no wiggle room to overcome such a distinction.

To complicate matters further, he worked in the home of a minister who was dying, while the man's good-looking wife and their three adorable children saw him increasingly as the man of the house. He wouldn't be human, he repeatedly told himself, if he weren't attracted to Ruth. It was a dual agony. Ruth was as untouchable as Bertha.

His bags were empty, everything neatly put away. He stretched and leaned out the open window. The sun was low in the sky, but not ready to give sway to the night. The sun never seemed to be tired. She would shine, disappear, come back, and follow her course faithfully and perpetually. The stars were never tired; the moon was never tired. Maybe it was just the human race that tired itself out, wasting itself on senseless wars, on chasing idols and goods, giving in to hate and forgetting about love.

He wondered if having thoughts like these meant he was depressed. He encountered parishioners with depression daily. Like Mrs. Dorsman, who was overcome by the strain of four years of German Occupation without any sign of liberation. The good woman had plenty to worry about. Her husband, an officer in the Dutch Army, had been taken to a P.O.W. camp a year ago, along with all other Dutch officers, when Hitler decided he wasn't going to play nice any longer, afraid officers left at home and unemployed might organize against him. Her student son worked in the Underground and had gone into hiding; she didn't know where. Right now, her teenage daughter was in the hospital with serious blood poisoning. Food and money were in short supply. And then there was the prospect of another harsh winter without enough fuel.

What had she done wrong to deserve such misery? she asked him. Like Job in the Bible, she thought she'd done everything right in her life, yet the notion that the righteous will flourish and the wicked will wither was also powerful in her belief system. If your life wasn't going right, then it was your own fault. Fix it!

Walter had told Mrs. Dorsman he didn't believe in a God of wrath who arranged for human misery that left people feeling guilty and inadequate. He believed in a God of love. Things happened randomly in the universe, and God was there to help us get through it all with an invisible hand.

He sighed. It was easier to lay down laws to live by and boundaries to live within. There were no set ways to teach how to experience God. Only metaphors. It took faith and trust and acceptance to be open to God's presence. Words only went so far. They helped to *know* God, but to *feel* God came through the human touch and the human deed.

He'd stood next to Mrs. Dorsman in a very dark moment, when the doctor informed her about the severity of her daughter's blood poisoning. It was life-threatening, he said. Together, they'd walked into the hospital room, where a middle-aged nurse threw her arms around Mrs. Dorsman when she saw the fear and shock in her eyes.

She showed the mother how to cool the girl's fevered forehead. As Mrs. Dorsman wiped the sweat off her daughter's face with a wet washcloth and softly talked to her, Walter had seen the pent-up tension flow out of her body.

He pulled back from the open window. Tomorrow, he should go to the hospital and see how Mrs. Dorsman and her daughter were doing. Outside, the leaves on the tall beeches whispered in a gentle wind, their tops illuminated by a lowering sun. Roaming chickens were heading for their pen to roost, and Walter knew that within the next fifteen minutes, Janus would be tolling the dinner bell.

The chairs around the dining room table were made of heavy, carved oak, and their seats were wide and upholstered with blue velvet. Frits was seated on a stack of pillows, and looked like a little prince out of a fairy tale. How would his tale develop? For Walter, this was the start of the story. For Frits, it was the umpteenth chapter, preceded by being born into a Jewish family, maybe chased out of Germany by the Nazis, coming to free Holland, then persecuted again till he was saved by Bertha, and again by Dirk. Some day his story would be told in detail. For now, the words were too painful, the memories too raw to dig them up. Walter decided to take Frits at face value. There was no greater disservice he could do this boy than asking for the details of his life. Frits had to put the past behind him, at least for now. He'd started the next chapter, a blank page with the heading: At the Castle.

Janus served the baroness white asparagus from a large platter. She lifted two hard-boiled eggs, doused them with melted butter, and arranged them along the tall stalks.

"Frits," she said, "this is a very special meal, because you may eat it with your fingers. Even the queen eats asparagus with her fingers. You mash the eggs with the melted butter and you heap it onto the spear. Look!"

She had mashed the eggs while she talked and raised the spear in the air, dangled it over her mouth, and bit off a chunk.

"That's how you do it," she said with satisfaction.

350

Frits's eyes stood out big and wide in his pale face. He wasn't sure what to do, and waited for others to take the lead. Anna was first. Walter followed. Frits looked at three adults holding long white stalks in the air, dangling them, and biting them. He erupted in laughter.

"You all look funny," he said.

"I'm sure," Anna said. "Now let's see you do it."

In the middle of this performance, Janus came in and whispered into Walter's ear. Walter asked to be excused and followed him out.

"What's going on? Is something wrong?" he asked.

"I've just heard that the Allies have landed on the French coast, Dominee Vlaskamp. I couldn't contain myself."

"What? Are you sure? Oh, my God. That's the best news I've heard in years."

"Hendrik came over to tell us. He heard it over the radio himself."

Walter slapped Janus on the shoulder. "Thank you, Janus. I can't wait to tell the others."

He went back inside and blurted out the good news. "The Allies have landed on the French coast!" he shouted unceremoniously.

The three at the table dropped the asparagus back on their plates. The long-awaited big news needed a moment to sink in. Frits was the first one to react. He jumped off his pile of pillows, stumbled to the floor, and then jumped up and ran circles around the table. He stopped in front of Walter, who lifted him up.

"How soon will they be here?" he asked.

"Not tomorrow and not the day after tomorrow, Frits. They have hard work ahead of them." He put Frits down. "They have to push the Nazis all the way back to Berlin."

"That is amazing news, Walter," the baroness said. Her face was flushed with excitement. "France! That's a big surprise. I always thought they would land on the beach of Scheveningen."

"I wonder where exactly they landed," Anna said. "We will have to find a map and then we can follow them. But there's one thing you have to promise me, Frits. You may not tell anybody about this news, because we're not supposed to know it."

"Yes," Frits said. "Nobody is supposed to have a radio, right?"

"That's right."

They were too excited to stay at the table. The baroness took them to the library and found an atlas. They gathered around it. She traced the coastline from the top of Holland, along Belgium and France to the south.

"The coast of France can be forbidding, especially in Normandy," she said. "I can't imagine they would land there. Calais would be easier and closer to us."

"Who knows what surprises still await us," Anna said.

CHAPTER THIRTY-FIVE

Carla – August 1944

What would be the smart thing to do? Stay in Utrecht and finish the nurse's training, or go to her parents' home in Breda? How fast could the Allies make their way north to Holland? And what if they veered eastward to Germany first? If they fought their way on a straight line through Belgium, then Breda could be the first city liberated in Holland, since it was just a whisker away from the Belgian border. After that, the rivers might stop them. The Rijn, the Maas, and the Waal were mighty rivers, hard to cross. They separated the northern provinces from the southern ones. Utrecht was situated north of the rivers. Breda was to the south of them.

Carla visited Dirk at Jan and Betty's on a Sunday afternoon in August, and took her dilemma with her. They sat in the backyard where Betty had started a small vegetable garden. Lettuce, spinach, onions, Brussels sprouts, and potatoes covered every available inch of soil.

"I didn't know you had a green thumb, Betty," Carla said.

"Neither did I, but working the soil takes my mind off the things I can't do anything about."

"I'll give you a happy thing to think about, Betty," Dirk said. "The Allies are close to Paris. Hitler must be getting nervous."

"Oh, my God! Hitler in a nervous state!" Jan said. "We know he is a poor loser. He will lash out in revenge, and at who else but us?"

"How fast do you think the Allies will move our way?" Carla asked. "We're in the middle of August. It's been two months since they landed in Normandy."

Nobody had an answer to that question.

"Dirk, I came for advice. I wonder if I should head for Breda. It would mean giving up my nurse's diploma, but I really want to be with my parents when the war comes close. Breda is a military city. The Germans are dug in there. You can bet they'll put up a fight. I don't see myself sitting here in Utrecht while worrying about them down there. What do you think I should do?"

"How important is it to you to get your nurses' diploma?"

"How important is it to you to be a lab technician the rest of your life?"

Dirk laughed. "Well, I think you've answered your question, Carla."

"Do you think Bertha will mind if I step out of her program? She depends on her students for taking care of the patients some of the time. We cover several shifts."

"You have an advantage here. Bertha is your childhood friend. Ask her."

A few days later, Carla got up her courage and went looking for Bertha before classes started. But when she looked through the window of Bertha's office door, instead of seeing Bertha, she saw members of the Gestapo opening desk drawers. They were rifling through her papers. She gasped and abruptly turned away. She ran down the hall, almost blindly finding her way to the lab where Dirk was just putting on his white coat. She pulled hard at his revers.

"Dirk! The Gestapo! They're in Bertha's office. Where is she?"

"Oh, God!" Dirk whispered. "I don't know, but let's look in the library."

They ran through the corridors. It turned out to be a good bet that she might be in the library. She sat at the large table in the middle of the room, dressed in her nurse's uniform, engrossed in a textbook.

Dirk walked over and put his hand on her shoulder.

"Bertha, take off your cap. We're getting out of here fast."

She stared at the two of them. The calm look in her eyes told Carla that Bertha had fully anticipated the possibility of this moment. She took off her cap and followed them out into the hall. It being early in the morning, the hospital was just waking up with people taking up their various posts. The three of them didn't look out of the ordinary. Passing through poorly lit hallways without speaking, they finally got to stairs that led into the cellar. Dirk seemed to know exactly where he was headed. A shiver ran down Carla's spine as he stopped in front of the heavy door of the morgue.

"Bertha," he said, "the Gestapo are in your office at this very moment. I have long thought they might catch up with you someday. I discussed that possibility with Dr. Boot, and he gave me permission to hide you here, if necessary."

Bertha stood perfectly still for a moment, taking it in.

"Do you have a key?" she asked.

"Yes. Dr. Boot gave me one after I came back from taking Frits. He thought it might be useful for both you and me."

"You have this all worked out, I see. Carla, how did *you* get in on this?"

"I went to your office and saw the Gestapo going through papers in your desk, so I got Dirk."

As he took the key out of his pocket, Carla wondered if he'd carried it with him every day, just in case. Clearly, he lived from minute to minute with the threat of the Gestapo getting wind of their joint effort of hiding Jewish children and raising money for them.

Carla took a deep breath as Dirk opened the door, and she closed her eyes before she dared look inside. When she opened them, she saw three stretchers with outlines of human bodies under white sheets. Tags with names were attached to their big toes sticking out from under the covers. It was a damp place with concrete walls and a flagstone floor.

"Just promise me one thing, Dirk," Bertha said. "Get me out of here as fast as you can."

"I'm going to Dr. Boot's office right now to get him to notify the undertaker."

Carla's eyes widened. She understood. There was only one way to get Bertha out of this place, and that was inside a coffin. *Lord, have mercy.*

Dirk helped Bertha onto a stretcher, found a sheet, and threw it over her.

"We'll dispense with the toe tag," he said.

"Prepare the undertaker. He might jump when I move," Bertha said, her voice muffled by the sheet over her.

"I'll stay with you, Bertha, until the undertaker comes," Carla said.

"I'm going straight to Dr. Boot's office," Dirk said. "I want to get there before the Gestapo come knocking on his door."

He left. Carla knelt beside the stretcher with her knees on the cold stone floor. She computed that at the most ten minutes had passed since she'd caught the Gestapo ransacking Bertha's office. And it had looked like they'd barely started.

"How do you feel under there?" she asked.

"Shhhh," Bertha said. "Let's not wake up the neighbors."

Carla pulled the sheet back from Bertha's face, and they giggled.

"That was quick thinking, Carla. Thank you for saving me."

"I was going to tell you that I want to go to Breda before the fighting starts there. Bertha, do you think they will find anything incriminating in your office?"

"Some records of funds we raised are in Dr. Hamel's office. I was always careful not to leave names of people in my desk."

They heard noises outside the door. Carla put the sheet back over Bertha's face. The heavy door opened. She recognized Dr. Boot. Two men, who wore black suits and black gloves, followed him in. They blended well with the macabre surroundings. Dirk must have informed Dr. Boot about her presence in the morgue, because he didn't seem surprised to see her. He asked her to identify the body to be taken out. Without uttering a word, the stony-faced men carried the stretcher with Bertha on it out the door and disappeared down the hall. Dr. Boot closed the door behind them and turned to her.

"Thank you for saving Bertha," he said. "Dirk would like you to get your bike and go to the undertaker's. This is the address. It's not far from here. Then he said for you to bring Bertha to Jan. I assume you know who that is."

Carla nodded.

"The Gestapo are still looking for Bertha inside the hospital. The quicker you can get her to Jan's house, the better. Thank you!"

He opened the door and walked with her down the hall, up the stairs, and back into the world of the living.

She needed street clothes. Biking through the streets in her uniform might arouse suspicion. And what about Bertha? She would need some clothes as well. She raced up to the nurses' living quarters, flung her uniform in a corner, put on some clothes, and stuffed an outfit for Bertha into a bag. At the last moment, she remembered to take her ID card.

Wherever she looked in the hospital, there were soldiers in green uniforms. Asked where she was headed, Carla, on a sudden hunch, said she was a visitor headed for the children's ward. She was let through. Once there, she sought out the head nurse to warn her, but Dirk had been ahead of her.

"Don't worry, Carla. We're safe."

That, at least, was a relief. When Carla was on duty on the children's ward, as part of her rotating schedule, she'd been aware of a boy named Frits. A quick look into the ward assured her he was no longer there. Bertha must have found a safe home for him.

Now she was in a hurry. She slipped by the guard outside the hospital and found her bike. The undertaker was just a few blocks away. One of the men who'd wheeled Bertha out of the morgue opened the door and recognized her. She handed him the bag with clothes and said she would wait for Bertha to change into them. Hardly five minutes passed before Bertha appeared in an outfit a bit too small for her, but it would do. She handed her uniform to the undertaker to discard it or burn it, whatever. She wouldn't need it for a while, she said. The man nodded somberly and took it from her hands. Carla decided that anything an undertaker did, he did it somberly. Or did he flip a switch from sad face to happy face? Would he make love to his wife, if he had one, with that somber face? What a miserable profession! She wanted to get back outside, into the brilliant sun, and wipe away the morbidity of the past hour.

She got back on her bike and pushed it off hard from the sidewalk to get some speed. Bertha jumped on the baggage carrier. The morning was still young, and city folks were busy finding their place in the daily order of things. Men, the ones that hadn't been rounded up to work in Germany yet, opened their stores. Housewives already stood in line at the grocery stores. Carla positioned herself in the middle of other bikers, blending in with the workforce. Farther from the city's center, the traffic thinned out, but they made it to Jan and Betty's without incident. Out of breath, Carla reached for the doorbell and blessed Betty for opening right way, and, for that matter, for being home in the first place.

"This is Bertha," she said, but she didn't have enough breath to say more.

"Dag, Mevrouw," Bertha said to Betty. "An hour ago I was a corpse, and now I am born again."

"Excuse me? You look troubled. Sit down. Tell me what's going on."

They told their story.

"Is Dirk safe?" Betty asked.

"I believe he is," Bertha said. "There was nothing in my office to incriminate him or anyone else."

They decided to stay out of sight in the dining room and kill time by playing mindless card games, just in case the Gestapo might find a shred of evidence that could lead to Jan and Betty's home.

At five-thirty, Dirk's tall frame filled the kitchen door. Jan was close behind, just like on any other workday. The Gestapo had stayed in the hospital for hours, Dirk said, but left empty-handed. They'd come to the lab and demanded to look at medical files, but Dr. Hamel told them that he wouldn't give access to patients' histories. That was against the law and against his oath. They'd tried hard, but finally backed off.

"Thank the Lord for Dr. Hamel," Bertha said. "Things might have gone differently if it weren't for his unperturbed demeanor."

Betty prepared a meal for the five of them from produce in her small garden.

"What's the next step?" Carla asked.

"Get a new ID for Bertha," Dirk said. "As soon as I get it, Bertha, I suggest you get out of Utrecht. They obviously found reasons to go after you."

"Do you want to go to Breda?" Carla asked. "We could go together."

"If the Gestapo can't find me in Utrecht, they'll try my parents' home."

"You could stay with *my* parents."

"Across from the police station? Thanks for the offer, but I'd better stay away from Breda."

"I have an idea," Betty said. "It seems to me that every time someone needs to be hidden, you bring them to Ede. First it was Klaas. Then it was Anna. And just the other day, it was Frits."

Ah! Carla thought. So, that's where Frits went. Betty had a point. The castle was out of the way. It wasn't a logical place for the Gestapo to look for Bertha. There was only one problem with this plan. Carla's brother Walter. There wasn't any way she could think of that Dirk would know that Bertha was the love of Walter's life. When her family had been together for her mother's birthday, a few weeks earlier, Walter had tried to steer her away from mentioning anything at all about Bertha, as if hearing her name cut straight into his heart. And what Bertha's feelings were, she had no idea. Bertha might not even know Walter was in Ede.

"That's a great idea," Dirk said. "Remember the money that was raised with a ballet performance, Bertha? That was in the castle that belongs to Anna's grandmother. Anna is there now and she could use some help."

"Me in a castle?"

"It's a great place to hide. As soon as we have your new ID, I can bring you there. I know all the back roads."

He made it sound as if this was now decided and ready to be executed. What should she do? This was too delicate a matter to discuss at the dining room table in front of people Bertha hardly knew. The war fostered common cause in many instances, but matters of the heart were not among them. Neither did she want to put a spoke in Dirk's wheel. Should she stay quiet and let events fall into place willy-nilly? Would Walter be forever mad at her if she didn't prevent Bertha from coming to the same place where he was boarding? Was this fate?

"It's almost eight o'clock," Jan said. During the entire meal, he'd had his eye on the cuckoo clock. "You can all come up and listen to Radio Oranje."

They spread out on the floor in Jan's hobby room as he rolled out the secret radio and tuned in to London. What would the news be today? It had taken the Allies over two months since they landed in Normandy to work their way up north. It was slow going to beat the Germans back. Forward and backward. Carla prepared herself to hear more of the same. When the familiar voice of the newsreader intoned that Paris had fallen into Allied hands, she gasped and was about to scream, but Dirk quickly put his hand over her mouth. "Not yet, Carla."

Paris! The City of Light. She remembered a picture in the newspapers of Hitler dancing a little jig with an arrogant, self-satisfied smirk on his face when his troops captured Paris in 1940.

"They're on a roll," Dirk said. His hazel eyes burned with excitement. "If this keeps up, they'll take Belgium in no time. This is the best news I've heard in years!"

He stretched out his long legs, crossed his arms behind his head, and stared at the ceiling.

"Carla," he said. "You may want to get yourself to Breda right away. The trains are still running, and you can make it over the Moerdijk Brug to Noord-Brabant. Bertha is sitting right next to you. She can give you permission to check out of the nurses' diploma program. You should consider a quick exit."

"Bertha, what do you think? Should I?"

"I wouldn't give it a second thought, Carla. Go!"

She slept on it, on the floor of Anna's room with Bertha alongside in Anna's bed. They talked about how they felt about leaving Utrecht, the city they'd pinned their hopes on, for Carla to get a medical degree and for Bertha to pursue a career in nursing. They cursed the Nazis.

Bertha asked what the castle looked like, and what were Anna and her grandmother like? Anna and her grandmother were down-to-earth people with a lot of class, Carla said. The castle and its environment were peaceful and beautiful. It was the perfect place to hide. Bertha would love it.

Was this the moment to tell her that Walter also lived there? Was it fair to let her walk into the castle and find Walter? Was there an alternative, a better place to hide? Bertha had to get far away from Utrecht. That was a given. Breda was out. The castle was perfect, and she could be a big help to Anna, who had her hands full with managing the estate, supplying the onderduikers with money and food stamps, and now apparently playing mother to a young Jewish boy as well. Her mind took a leap and landed on the side of transparency.

"Bertha, there is one thing you should know about the castle. Walter is substituting for a minister of the Remonstrantse Kerk in Ede. The minister has tuberculosis and is in a sanatorium somewhere. Walter let the minister's wife and her three children stay in the parsonage because she had nowhere to go. Her family is in the East Indies. But he didn't want to live there himself, so he is boarding at the castle. I just thought you should know that."

It was quiet, except for a constant drone overhead of bombers on their way to Germany, punctuated by bursts of anti-aircraft artillery from the nearby airfield in Soesterberg.

"Thank you for telling me," Bertha said at last. "I don't have to tell you the story. You were there all along."

Bertha was quiet again. After a while, she said, "These are strange times. It brings strangers together and, who knows, it may bring others back together."

Carla wondered if that's what she hoped for, and how about Walter? What would he want?

"In my view of life," Bertha went on, "there's always a reason for things, even if we cannot fathom why. Walter and I will have to figure out what to do with this sudden turn of events. I put it in God's hands."

"Dirk and Anna do not know of your connection to Walter," Carla said.

"Good. We'll keep it that way. Let's go to sleep, Carla. We have to be in shape for whatever falls our way. God bless you. You've saved my life."

Everyone was up early for breakfast. Plans, hatched during the restless night, were brought forward. Dirk would bring Carla to the train station on the back of his bike, hoping for a train to Breda. He asked her if she would make her bike available to Bertha as her getaway vehicle to Ede, as soon as he could get her a new ID.

Carla looked at the empty bowls of oatmeal on the table. A feeling of foreboding overtook her. The big rivers might separate them for a good long time. This could be a finite moment. The lure and promise of careless student days had been swallowed by the war. The Group of Eight was dispersed; one of them dead, two of them in German work camps, Otto unreachable in England. Only the three women of the group were footloose. And Dirk as well, of course, but for how long could he dodge the intensifying Nazi scrutiny? Everyone was in danger, including Jan and Betty, who still distributed illegal newspapers. She was overcome by a sense of loss, but she didn't show her dark feelings as she hugged each of them and cheerfully declared she would see them soon in liberated Holland.

A train was steaming up to go to Breda. All wagons, except one, were reserved for troop transport. German soldiers in combat gear were on their way to the southern front. The sight of them heightened Carla's keen sense of something big afoot. The faces under the square steel helmets showed the dread of the looming battle; a battle that might be lost. But Germans wouldn't be Germans if they couldn't yell out orders at the top of their lungs. The soldiers might look anxious, but their commanders were still whipping them up to fight for an ideology that had locked the Continent into a dead-end way of life for years. She was tired of the shouting. She was tired of the bullying. Deeply tired.

She wormed herself among the civilians to find a place in the overcrowded railroad car. The train pulled away, and the passengers rocked back and forth and into each other. The smell rising from their clothes was ripe. A bar of soap hadn't been seen in ages by most. *We've all turned into paupers*, Carla thought. In four years, this once proud country had been brought down, the shine of its civilized society coarsely sanded off. In dilapidated clothes, worn to a thread over bony frames, that's how they would greet their liberators.

After two hours of rocking back and forth, she could see the De Biesbosch come into view, the place where the North Sea, the Rijn, and the Maas Rivers came together. A terrifying flood in the year 1421 had inundated a huge area of land and changed it into a network of estuaries with interconnecting creeks, mudflats, and forested areas. It served as a sort of inland delta of the large rivers that fed into it, effectively separating the north of Holland from the south by a large margin. It was not far from Breda. De Biesbosch had always intrigued her, maybe because her father came from one of the small villages lining it. Some of her best childhood memories were of sailing with him on weekends. Since he'd been born on its shores, the intricate web of creeks and mudflats held no secrets for him. He'd grown up navigating a small rowboat through reeds and stands of willows.

She watched the glimmer of the water in the midday sun and the ripples of windswept waves. The uninitiated sailor could easily get lost in the maze of inlets and creeks. It was a haven for wildlife, and in these days of war, it was a haven for onderduikers as well, since no German patrol could hope to find its way back out. And rumors circulated in Breda that a large boat was moored somewhere in the middle of the wide, complicated expanse of the Biesbosch, and that the Underground had filled it with their prisoners, presumably traitors.

The train rumbled over the long bridge at De Moerdijk. A flat green landscape with modest farms and small villages unfolded outside the dirty train window. *I'm home,* Carla thought. *I made it back home.*

When the train approached the station, the buildings next to the rails looked charred and were surrounded by rubble. Carla gasped. What had happened to her city? Noting her horror, a man standing next to her said, "The Allies dropped a few bombs. They missed the station. They'll probably come back to finish the job."

"Why the station?"

"Troop transports."

The train screeched to a halt. The post office looked ravaged and helpless among the ripped-off chunks of cemented bricks and shards of glass that littered the street. So, this was what a bombed building looked like. What must those German cities look like after being bombed, week after week? God! Didn't she just get off a train with troops? She shivered at the realization of how fragile life was. She turned her back on the rubble and walked away, quickening her step through the park and past the castle, where German officers walked in both directions over the drawbridge, frenetic, running in and out, no longer the arrogant conquerors of yesteryear.

The tall, graceful spire of De Grote Kerk rose above the daily noises as a physical reminder of man's strongest aspirations: reverence for God and hope for humanity. Four years of Occupation under an ungodly dictator had shown humanity's underbelly, but it hadn't wiped out faith.

She reached inside the one piece of luggage she'd brought—a handbag—and took out the key to her parents' home. As she stepped inside, the antiseptic smell of her father's dental office stopped her, and she briefly leaned against the wall to savor the moment. Coming home felt like exhaling a long-held breath. Utrecht was behind her, at least for a while. Creating a circle of friends and turning her rented room into a center had all been a lot of fun. It had come easy to her. She'd been the hostess, and Anna and Dirk had been the pivot of the Group of Eight. She would be forever grateful that those two had taken the leadership onto their shoulders. To take responsibility for others' lives, to live without fear, no, she hadn't been ready for that, and she still wasn't. If it were otherwise, she wouldn't feel such relief in opening the door to the living room, such delight in seeing her mother sitting by the window, darning her father's socks.

"Moeder!"

The eternal word came out like a cry. The sewing fell to the ground as Carla embraced her.

"Carla! Darling! What brings you home?"

"I wanted to be here with you. Paris fell. It won't be long, and we'll be free."

Moeder was standing now. Her petite body no longer fit snugly in the before-the-war clothes, and her face was as pale as cream.

"Your father told me that news last night, but it hasn't sunk in yet."

"I was with Dirk and Bertha when I heard it. They thought if I wanted to be home for the liberation, I should get myself below the rivers. I was lucky to catch a train. It may have been the last."

"I'm overwhelmed. Funny. I've longed for the day we'll be free, and now I have to adjust. But I'm so happy you decided to come home."

Carla moved closer to the wide window. Their small city garden was not unlike the one Betty had cultivated into a source of fresh food.

"Moeder, it makes me hungry to look at that green lettuce."

"When did you eat last?"

"I had oatmeal at seven o'clock this morning."

They went straight to the kitchen. Moeder took out a loaf of bread—or what passed for it—and cut off a thick slice. They went to the dining room and sat down. Carla looked out the window at the police station.

"Moeder, how do you keep your sanity with that place across the street while you have two Jews under your roof?"

"To say it's easy would be telling a lie, but to say it's very hard is equally untrue. You do what you have to do."

"How are they?"

"You should find out for yourself. They would love to see a different face."

The next day, she carried a basket with a loaf of bread, some kind of margarine, two apples, an onion, and a healthy head of lettuce up to the attic. The couple—their names were Esther and Jacob—had been forewarned their hosts' daughter would make the next delivery. Once on the attic's landing, she looked around. The last time she could remember being there was with Bertha and Walter, playing hide-and-seek. In those playful days, the attic had been an open space with a lot of stuff, like antique furniture. Most of that stuff was gone, but the same suitcases were still jammed under the eaves. Her family hadn't gone anywhere for some years. A wall of crude planks faced her. A door had been set off-center from the landing.

No sounds came from the other side of the door after she knocked. She'd forgotten to ask if a special code was used, like two hard knocks followed by a soft one, or a secret whistle. She waited. Nothing. She rapped again, softly. She heard a slow shuffle.

"Hello. It's me, Carla Vlaskamp."

The door opened gradually, hesitantly. Through the widening gap, she looked into the hiding place her parents had created under the tiled roof.

"May I come in? My mother asked me to bring you this basket with food. You must be Esther."

The woman nodded and took the basket from her hand. The husband walked up to her. "Thank you," he said. In his firm handshake, she felt the hand of a carpenter, or maybe an engineer. "Please come in and sit down. We don't have company very often. Here, sit in this chair."

It was the one from her bedroom. She'd wondered where it had gone. Some of the furniture in the room had been her favorite pieces to hide behind while evading Walter and Bertha, like the wide chest of drawers with its elaborately carved feet.

"I'm bringing good news," she said. "Paris fell on the twenty-fifth of August."

"It has? Paris? That's fantastic," Jacob said, turning up the volume of his voice just a little bit. "Are things going in favor of the Allies, Carla? That's your name, right?"

"Yes, I am Carla, and I'm a good friend of Daan. One of you must be related to him."

"Yes, he's my second cousin," Esther said.

Carla decided not to tell her that Daan had been taken to a work camp in Germany.

"To answer your question, I came home from Utrecht because I wanted to be here for the liberation. Better to be south of the rivers, I thought. Radio Oranje tells us the Allies are making their way north fast. They'll be in Belgium in no time. You'll see."

They took the news as if it came through a muffled radio. Their mindset, like her mother's, was locked into assuming the war's end was a long way off. It was too risky to give in to good news. They might fall into a deep hole of disappointment. Better to mentally dig in for a long siege.

The following days, she kept climbing back up the stairs for more visits. At the end of the upstairs hallway was a heavy curtain, which hid winter coats and suits to give the impression of a storage closet. Behind the coats was the door to the attic. Every time she parted the heavy curtain, Carla wondered if people working in the police station could observe what was going on inside her parents' home. As a precaution, curtains had been hung in windows that had never had curtains before. Most of the activity across the street took place on the ground floor. Occasionally, she saw something or somebody move on the upstairs level. What would it take for the police to get suspicious that Jews were being hidden across the street? If the war years had proven anything, it was that many nosy people populated the world. When she expressed these concerns to her mother, the response was a shrug. "Carla," she said, "we take risks, and we live with them."

And that was that.

Carla felt the pull of the life being lived in the attic. She volunteered to bring the food upstairs from now on. She bought bright red dahlias at the market. At least flowers were still plentiful. She arranged them in a pretty vase, fitted them next to the bread and potatoes in the basket, and hauled them up the staircase, making sure to close the heavy curtain behind her and rearrange the winter clothes she'd pulled aside.

Esther's face lit up when she spotted the flowers. Holding the vase, she walked around the room to find the optimum place for it. The light in the white-walled room was indirect. It came from a skylight set high in the ceiling. Clouds passing overhead, framed by a dirty piece of window, were the only proof that they were still part of planet Earth.

"What good news are you bringing us today?" Jacob asked.

"That the Allies are making a run for Antwerpen. Vader says they're anxious to have a harbor closer to the frontline, now that it has moved northward so fast."

"That's exciting! You're sure, are you?"

"I'm absolutely sure."

"You know, Carla, I have to get used to thinking of Nazis as losers," Jacob said. "Ever since Hitler got it in his head to annex the countries circling Germany, he has been on a tear. He claimed he had to protect the German-speaking people in those countries."

"The Dutch aren't exactly German-speaking people," Carla said.

"True, but he didn't annex Holland. He occupied it. He wanted to be nice to you, because you belong to the Aryan race. Hasn't made much difference in the way you've been treated, right?"

"No, indeed. But what about countries like Poland and Hungary?"

"The Jews aren't the only ones Hitler wants to get rid of. He has a bone to chew with the Gypsies and the Slavic people as well. Somehow he wants them all to be removed from East and Central-East Europe. Whereto isn't clear. He hates the Polish people almost as much as he hates us Jews."

Esther had moved quietly around the room with the vase in her hand. She decided to place it next to what Carla assumed was their wedding picture. The petals of the dahlias reflected in its silver frame and gave it a pleasing red hue. Jacob had followed her around the room with his eyes. He was a tall and handsome man with expressive light brown eyes and a strong jaw, probably in his early thirties. Even in worn and rumpled clothes, he made a distinctive and solid impression.

"Are you and Esther practicing Jews?" she asked.

"No. Neither were our parents."

"But you're still considered a Jew?"

"Yes. Odd, isn't it? Hitler isn't concerned with religion. It's all about race. A Christian, as long as he practices the Christian faith, is called a Christian. If he stops practicing his faith, he's simply a citizen of whatever country he lives in. But that's not the case with Jews. A Jew is a Jew above all else, whether he practices Judaism or not. In Germany, a Gentile is forbidden to marry a Jew by law, if that Jew has more than one quarter of Jewish blood in his ancestry."

"Why?"

"Because the Aryan race has to stay pure. In Hitler's view, there is *das Herren Volk*, the Germans of course, and the rest are *Untermenschen*, which is the equivalent of rats, you might say."

"I hate that word," Carla said. "It is so demeaning."

Jacob sighed. He wrung his hands. She heard his knuckles cracking, as if he wrung someone's neck. If that reflected his state of mind, she couldn't blame him.

Esther came over and sat next to him at the table that served as counter, sink, and dinner table. If Moeder's skin color could be compared to cream, then Esther's was like parchment. She was petite and fine-featured. So far, she hadn't said more than a perfunctory thank you, but now she seemed ready to give vent to built-up anger.

"'Untermenschen,'" she said with poorly hidden scorn. "That word makes me feel like the equivalent of somebody's dirty laundry."

Jacob put his hand on her shoulder. "You're too pretty to be thrown into the laundry bin, Esther."

"As if good looks could save us! The Nazis are daily throwing thousands of Jews in the laundry bin, good-looking or not. You know that, Jacob. We are despicable. The scum of the earth."

He took her hand in his. "We're in nobody's laundry bin, Esther. Every day I'm grateful to Carla's parents that they took us in and take care of us."

Esther nodded, but she had tipped her veil of silence enough to bare her loss of self-esteem. What could be worse?

The last August days quietly ambled into the month of September, but once they got there, each day that followed was destined to make it into history books.

On the fourth day of the month, Carla's father issued an unusual invitation to his wife and daughter to come down to his dental office on the ground floor after dinner. He opened the glass door of a cabinet that displayed shiny instruments and shoved aside a sliding panel in the back.

"In case you ever wondered where I get my information," he said with a secret smile, "this is how. Today, I thought you should hear the good news yourself. Things are moving fast."

He turned on the old Telefunken radio that fit between the sliding door and the back of the cabinet. It was eight o'clock on the dot, and Carla recognized the BBC signal. Her father had guts to listen to the forbidden news while just a narrow street separated him from the very people who could throw him in jail for this transgression. Moeder reacted with characteristic sangfroid. She had probably guessed at her father's secret a long time ago.

"*Hier is Radio Oranje.*" The three of them crowded up to the radio. "Antwerpen has fallen into the hands of the Allies," the announcer said. "We have Professor Gerbrandy here in the studio to make a statement."

The Dutch prime minister, exiled in England, came on. With palpable emotion, he stated that Allied troops had crossed the Dutch border and reached Breda.

"What?" Carla cried out. "They took our city? Vader, can this be true?"

"My God, I have no idea, Carla. No idea at all," he said.

"I want to go up and tell Jacob and Esther."

"You won't do any such thing. We have to check this out first."

Her mind traveled back to sailing in the Biesbosch. Given to impulses, she would yank on the wrong winch, or throw the rudder abruptly in a different direction, and her father would sternly tell her who was captain. Even now—and never mind her four years of medical studies—he was still captain.

"How can we find out?" she asked.

"You won't like this, Carla, but we'll have to wait till tomorrow. The baker and the butcher will know. They're always the first to know. Unless you want to walk across the street to the police station and ask if it's true what you just heard over the radio."

"You're funny! All right, I volunteer to stand in line at the bakery when it opens tomorrow morning at eight."

She was the first in line at the bakery. After days of rain, the sun came out in full force, and it promised to become a warm and humid day. The street was quiet, and no Allied troops marched down it.

The baker, who'd known her since she was a little girl, put two breads in her canvas shopping bag. He bent over as she handed over the ration card and whispered, "They say Breda has been liberated, but I haven't seen it, have you? They also say German soldiers are deserting, and members of the NSB are packing their bags. Good riddance to them all. May they never return."

After she brought the breads home and shared what she'd found out, which wasn't much, she felt too restless to stay there. She needed to go on the streets and see for herself. Once in a while, a car with German military came by as she strolled down the Ginnekenstraat, looking at shop windows that had nothing new to show. People seemed to go about their business as usual. Children walked to school. Her excitement ebbed, and she felt betrayed. Vader had been right. It would have been premature and unwise to go tell Jacob and Esther about Breda's liberation last night.

She came to the bridge over the canal. A crowd of people was blocking the street. Men and women of all ages stood as if transfixed, staring ahead. But for the sound of shuffling shoes in the background, it was eerily quiet. Carla wormed herself to the front row. What she saw gave her a jolt. Bedraggled German soldiers in torn uniforms moved slowly down the street. The sight of them had rendered the onlookers mute, because it was beyond belief to see Hitler's proud, disciplined troops transformed into a miserable horde of beaten men. The snail's pace they set was a far cry from the vigorous marching exercises they had displayed in better days. What she looked at was a sad retreat. The spectacle of these exhausted, disheveled soldiers didn't invite taunting. They resembled a funeral procession more than anything, and you didn't laugh at a funeral.

The soldiers who had passed her in the Ginnekenstraat mingled with the onlookers. They looked bewildered as the stream of their beaten countrymen seemed without end. There were no generals to stop them. Their hero, General Rommel, had been seriously wounded in battle. It was all over, as far as these soldiers were concerned. They had lost their pride. They didn't care if they looked like scarecrows. They wanted to get back home, to the Heimat.

Carla stood as if nailed to the asphalt on the bridge, mesmerized by this wholesale mutiny. At a three-foot distance, she could smell their sweat and the stench of unwashed bodies. A sergeant, who seemed in better shape than many of the others, made eye contact with her. He stopped a moment and called out, "Come back tomorrow. It will be much better. The Tommies will be here."

His shout woke her up from the odd dream state she was in. Could the British troops be coming on the heels of this sad retreat? Her blood quickened in her veins. She turned abruptly and headed home. Moeder was on the phone with a friend in Rotterdam who wanted to know if Breda was indeed liberated. The news caused a great uproar, and members of the NSB were packing their bags. Rumors were flying. The Reichskommissar, Seyss-Inquart, had put his wife on a train to Austria. That was a fact.

Carla could not contain herself. The good news needed to be shared. She darted up to the attic. Jacob opened the door after her knock.

"I'm bringing more than a loaf of bread," she said.

"You look pretty excited, Carla."

"I am. Sit down. I am going to show you a movie."

Esther was stretched out on the bed. She rose slowly and walked over to the table where Jacob was sitting.

"I want you to see what I saw. Listen to my words. I'm counting on your lively imaginations."

"I'm all ears," Jacob said.

Carla painted the picture of what she had seen with such verve that Jacob and Esther were riveted, and Esther's lethargy evaporated. Their eyes could see tired horses pulling farm wagons filled with household goods, and women walking among the soldiers. Her images portrayed a soldier pushing a baby carriage filled with pots and pans, and another lying on a gurney in the back of a beaten-up Renault truck.

"My God, Carla," Jacob said. "What does this mean?"

"Remember you told me you couldn't imagine what Nazis would look like as losers? Well, now you know. I hope it means they're being driven out of Belgium and that our liberation cannot be far off."

But the liberation was not to come anytime soon. The prime minister had blundered. A patrol had crossed the Dutch/Belgian border by accident. A Dutch agent had met them and reported the incident to London, where the mood was filled with wishful thinking after the amazing advances made after the fall of Paris. The prime minister had overinterpreted the incident.

Mad Tuesday was not the end of the war. It was the beginning of the last phase of the war. Carla wasn't the only one in the country to go to bed that night thoroughly disappointed and deflated.

Chapter Thirty-Six

Dirk – September 1944

It had rained for three days. Betty's kitchen windows were steamed up, and all plants and bushes in the garden were dripping. As evening fell, the rain let up and a few sunrays cut through the mist. A change in weather was in the making.

Dirk climbed the stairs with Betty and Bertha for the daily ritual of listening to Radio Oranje. Jan had already tuned in. They were unprepared for the bombshell the prime minister dropped on them. Breda had been liberated. They were aghast. Eight days ago, Carla had left for Breda. It was hard to fathom it had taken only that short time for the Allies to get to the border, but it had to be true or the prime minister wouldn't have taken the unusual step of delivering the news himself.

"I should have gone to Breda," Bertha said.

"Wait! You may see the Brits here tomorrow," Jan said.

Bertha called her father in Breda. No, there was no sign of Allied troops yet, and German soldiers were everywhere. Nothing had changed. He didn't know what to make of it. If Breda had been taken, it had been without a fight.

Bertha's false identification papers were in Dirk's pocket. A courier had brought them up from Den Haag to the hospital. His father never disappointed. The next move was to get her to the castle, but he hadn't checked with Anna yet. He'd wanted to be sure he had Bertha's papers in hand before he called.

They were still at the breakfast table when the front doorbell rang. Jan let their neighbors in. The moment they stepped over the threshold, the house exploded with excitement. Had they heard the news? And did they know that the NSB family five houses down the street had fled at the crack of dawn? They weren't the only ones. All over the city, the NSB traitors were closing their homes and crowding the railroad station. And it was said that Dordrecht had also been liberated. In Rotterdam, people were rushing by the thousands to the city's approaches with armfuls of flowers to welcome the liberators.

Stories and rumors were flying. Dirk wasn't convinced they could all be true. Rumors at the start of the war had been equally irresistible, and many had failed the truth-test. He'd rather make decisions on rock-solid information. Giving into euphoria might be like stepping into a swamp of unexpected consequences.

After the neighbors left, he took Bertha aside. "I received your new ID. Let's think this through. There's a lot of misinformation out there. The Germans aren't going to lie down and be walked over."

"What do you expect to happen?"

"I expect that the liberation of the whole country will take a bit longer than people think. You've been lucky so far, but if I were you, I wouldn't push my luck any longer."

"And I cannot forever impose on Betty and Jan. They've been very hospitable. What is the plan, Dirk?"

"Let's take advantage of the confusion. The traitors are preoccupied with saving their hides. The Germans have other things to think about. This is the day to make your getaway. We have two bikes with pumped-up tires that should get us to Ede."

"It's Tuesday. You have to work."

"I'm sure Dr. Hamel will understand when I don't show up. I

told him that this was going to happen one of these days."

"You think of everything. I'll take you up on your offer. Shouldn't you call Anna? I feel uncomfortable just walking in and assume I'm welcome to stay."

"You proved this morning the telephones are still working, so I'll give it a try. It's hit or miss these days."

He tried, but it didn't work. It was a setback he'd half expected. What to do? One of these days, the Gestapo was going to catch up with Bertha. If they'd caught wind of someone hiding Jewish children, they were fanatic enough to pursue it. That would be bad for her, and equally bad for Jan and Betty, who'd hidden her. His intuition told him to trust the baroness to take on another onderduiker. And it was a lucky coincidence that Walter lived there also. He and Bertha had been childhood friends. Walter could speak for her. Dirk decided to take the chance. If it didn't work out, it would at least give them time to find another solution. And, who knew, maybe the rumors were true and the liberation was around the corner. Problem solved!

"I'm a light traveler," Bertha said as she prepared to mount Carla's bike. "I have no luggage beyond what I wear, and even that doesn't belong to me."

"You'll be grateful for the lack of luggage later in the day," Betty said. "It will be a humid one with the sun out after all that rain."

"Well, here we go! I'm leaving with a new name. I am now Sylvia van Tongeren. Next time I see you, Betty, I will be Bertha again."

Dirk swung his long leg over the luggage carrier of Anna's bike and was ready to kick off. He watched the jovial good-bye between Bertha and Betty. They'd become friends. How could they not?

The sun was generously pouring its light over the awakening city. Its rays bounced off the washed, clean windows. They stood out like bright mirrors and gave the brick houses a happy glow. The Germans might be super-organized, but the Dutch were super-clean. War or no war, they made sure their windows sparkled. And they were super gardeners, as well. Flowers were everywhere, and the prevailing color was orange. Orange marigolds, orange dahlias, a whole park filled with them, the same park where he'd sat with Anna while explaining how the movie *Eeuwige Jude* had been created to fix the Nazi mind on the unworthiness of the Jewish race. It had been one of Goebbels's more brilliant moves. It was painful to admit, but he'd been successful. Thousands of Jews had been carted off to Eastern Europe, and Hitler's minions hadn't shown any qualms about stowing them into cattle cars. They'd been effectively brainwashed to think they were transporting Untermenschen.

They biked by the closed university. A group of young teenagers—ones that hadn't been ordered to work in Germany yet—were playing soccer in the yard. He took a good look at them. They were lean but energetic in the way they tried to take the ball away from each other. What stopped him for a moment were the orange sashes they sported on their sleeves. Bertha saw it too. She raised her eyebrows. Surely, they would not have done this a week ago. Where did these sashes come from? Had their parents encouraged them? An air of daring had descended on the city.

Dirk breathed a little easier, relieved to get out of Utrecht without incident. He found the back roads he'd traveled with Frits. The fruits in the orchard they'd passed then had grown from little green balls to fully grown bright red apples. He was tempted to steal one. Not a good idea. They didn't need an arrest today for stealing apples.

At the halfway point, he stopped and placed their bikes in the berm.

"Frits and I took a break here," he said. "He knew he couldn't ask me where we were going, but could I give him just a little bit of an idea? So, I told him that he would think he'd landed in fairyland once he got there. Then he said that maybe he was going to a castle."

Bertha smiled. She took out the thermos with cold water from the rucksack, took a swig, and handed it to Dirk.

"I feel the same anticipation, but I know I'm not sent there by the wand of a fairy. I'm spirited there by the iron determination of a young man called Dirk van Enthoven."

Dirk smiled. This woman with her lovely straw-blond hair had done more to protect people than anyone he knew, with the possible exception of his father.

"If I have iron determination, then yours is made of tempered steel, Bertha."

He reached into his rucksack and produced pieces of bread with cucumber slices that Betty had prepared for them. They munched in silence, stretching their legs, comfortable in each other's company. It was a quiet back road with only two farms in the far distance. Occasionally, a few bikers came by. The humid air was filled with the smell of harvested fields, where waste from pulled-up potato plants were in a state of decay, signaling the end of summer.

"You must be looking forward to seeing Anna again," Bertha said as she pulled a blade of grass and sucked on it. "It's not easy, I'm sure, to carry on a long-distance relationship."

The casual remark caught him off guard. It was the first time his love for Anna was labeled with such a definitive term.

"Why are you surprised, Dirk? It's not hard to tell she's the glove that fits your hand."

"Are you clairvoyant, Bertha? You have never seen us together."

"I don't need to. I can tell from the trust you have in her from the decisions you make together. That's more convincing than any physical demonstration."

Dirk looked at his hand. A glove was a lovely metaphor for his bond with Anna, which amazed him every day he was lucky enough to wake up to sunlight. Her glove and his hand had become an instrument of sorts, a wonder of coordination in thoughts and values.

"It's funny, Bertha, but from the moment I met her at Carla's place in Utrecht, I knew she was the woman I needed in my life. I'll never understand how we knew that of each other."

"I am anxious to meet her, to put a face to the voice over the telephone."

"You talked to her?"

"Yes, at Betty's. She called. A lovely voice, full of concern for you and Carla, and smart enough not to wander off into dangerous territory in case the phone was tapped."

"To answer your question," Dirk said, "I'm excited to see Anna. I can't wait. We don't get to see much of each other. But then, maybe that's just as well."

He left it at that, and she didn't ask more. No sense elaborating on his pining for Anna. He felt it every minute of the day in every fiber of his body. It was an ache he tried to push away, but he wasn't very good at it. A love that could not be consummated was a hard thing to live with. It would be even harder if they saw each other every day. He could not guarantee that passion wouldn't get the better of him. But this damn war put everything in their lives on hold. Not their love, but their relationship, as Bertha called it. Their medical degrees were up in the air, and he often despaired if they would get their rightful turn at a normal life. It had become the returning, unresolved question he pondered every day. He looked over at Bertha, at this woman who was so brave and so frank, a stunning appearance with her unusual hair color, her deep-set blue eyes that looked out on the world with compassion and resolve. He guessed her age at just over thirty. Surely, men didn't pass her by without being attracted. What was her experience with love?

"Well, we'd better be on our way," he said. "We're in Maarsbergen, so we've covered eighteen kilometers. Ede is equidistant from here."

They biked through long stretches of fields and woods, a farm here and there, spread-out tiny villages that could hardly be called that. Evidence of a war that raged through the world was not part of this landscape. A military base was nowhere near, not until they came to the base in Ede where Herr von Schloss was the commandant. Dirk slowed down out of curiosity. The place looked sleepy. Even the guards in front looked a bit slumped. For whatever reason, the powers-that-be didn't need Herr von Schloss's troops to go and drive the Allies back to Belgium.

How many times had he stood in front of this gate with the coat of arms of Kasteel Koppelburg to bring someone in dire need of protection? He'd brought Daan here with Anna. The second time, they'd brought Daan's mother and brother. The third time, he'd come alone, on short notice, with a child. And here he was again, this time unannounced. Begging again.

He took his feet off the pedals and planted them on the ground for balance.

"This then is the castle," he said.

Bertha got off her bike and stuck her face in between the stiles of the gate to take a look. The lawn and circular driveway led her eye to the impressive building. Twenty-six shutters with triangular patterns in green, white, and red broke up the large expanse of the castle's front-facing walls.

"Fairyland indeed," she whispered.

They moved on to the side door of the kitchen.

"Mr. van Enthoven, that's a surprise," Mien said, and wiped her hands on her apron to greet him. "I can think of someone who's going to be very happy to see you."

"Who's that, Mien?"

"Your nephew, of course! Frits asks for you all the time."

"That's nice to hear. I'm flattered. I brought a guest, Mien. This is Juffrouw van Tongeren."

Mien probed Bertha's face and let her gaze travel over the tightly fitting clothes Carla had swiped from her own closet to replace Bertha's uniform. Mien was looking for clues. She was used to unexpected guests, and had developed a method for placing them on a rung of the social ladder. Her norms were set by the exposure to the castle where she'd served most of her life. But Bertha seemed to puzzle her. She couldn't reconcile the outgoing face with the awkward outfit.

"Frits knows this lady well, Mien. He will be very excited to see her."

Her face cleared. "Dag, Juffrouw van Tongeren. Welcome," she said, and she looked like she meant it. Frits had made a good friend in Mien.

"Is everybody home?" Dirk asked.

"All but Miss Anna and the dominee. And Janus just went on an errand in town."

They entered the marble-tiled hall. Bertha stopped to look at the gallery of ancestral portraits.

"Dirk, did you know, when you got here for the first time, that Anna had blue blood?"

"I didn't have a clue. None whatsoever. But, trust me, blue blood is not what she's all about. And that is true for her grandmother as well."

He knocked on the door of the salon and opened it a crack to peek inside. The baroness was sitting in her place by the window with an open book in her hands, as he'd expected. A small chair was drawn up close to her knees. She was reading Frits a story. Dirk gestured to Bertha. She studied the scene through the small door opening and listened to the distinct and melodious voice of the baroness. Dirk knocked again. Frits turned around. Immediate recognition sprang into his face. He tumbled out of his chair, crossed the room at a gallop, and swung his arms around Dirk's waist.

"Dirk! You came back," he said with a passion that betrayed his fear that people he loved might never come back.

"And I brought someone you know."

Frits let go of him, puzzled for a moment. Bertha without her nurse's uniform looked like a stranger to him.

"Dag, Frits," she said, and upon hearing her voice, he burst into a smile.

"*Zuster* Bertha!" He reached up to embrace her, and then took her by the hand and dragged her over to where the baroness was seated.

"Oma," he said, "this is *Zuster* Bertha. She is my friend."

"How lovely. What a wonderful surprise for you. Dirk, how are you? Anna will be so pleased to see you."

"I am well, thank you. I see you have become Oma to another person. May I introduce Sylvia van Tongeren? To Frits she is *Zuster* Bertha, but her name needed to be changed."

"Well, that introduction tells a story, doesn't it? Very efficient, Dirk. Welcome, Sylvia. Please sit down. You had a long bike ride, I'm sure."

Bertha walked over to the baroness, shook her hand, and said she was pleased to meet her.

"I assume you know Paris and Brussels fell," Dirk said. "It is even rumored the Allies reached Breda. It has put the NSB on the run."

The baroness smiled. "That's a good start."

A breeze mercifully moved the air through one open window and out the other on the opposite side. The heat of the day hung in the velvet curtains. Dirk's clothes stuck to his body, and he badly needed a splash of cold water. It had to be the same for Bertha.

Janus, back from his errand, came in to ask if he should serve tea, but the baroness instructed him to show the new guest a place where she could freshen up, and she asked Frits to have Mien set the table for two extra people.

"Dirk," the baroness said after they left, "I think you have something to tell me, and I guessed half of it."

"Yes, you probably did. Bertha is the one who saved many, many Jewish children like Frits. The Gestapo got on her trail. Ten days ago, Walter's sister Carla found two sergeants turning Bertha's office upside down. We hustled her out of the hospital. She's stayed in Anna's room since then. Today's turmoil offered a chance to get her out of the city. I brought her here because I couldn't think of any other place. I tried to call Anna this morning, but I couldn't get through, so I took my chances. I hope you'll forgive me."

"I see," the baroness said. She folded her hands and contemplated them. The late-afternoon sun caught the sheen of her gray hair and turned it into a silvery wreath. She must have been a beauty in her day. She was still very attractive. The strong architecture of her face and the calm, steady look in her eyes projected authority and a gentle power.

"As we saw with Klaas," she said, "there's no guarantee I can keep someone permanently out of danger."

"Let's hope the war isn't a permanent condition," Dirk said. "Who knows, this may be a moot point in a few weeks. But we cannot count on that, of course."

"My main concern is for Frits. How likely is the Gestapo to follow Bertha's trail? We raised money here for her organization, as you know. Could they discover a link?"

"There were no records in Bertha's office of either the children or of the donors."

He'd hardly finished the sentence when the door swung open, and Anna burst into the room with Frits close on her heels.

"Dirk!"

He jumped up, and she fell into his arms. Through her cotton summer dress, he felt her warmth, but also her ribs. She leaned her head into his shoulder and rested it there, as if letting go of pent-up worries, but Frits got impatient and tugged at her dress.

"Anna," he said, "Dirk brought my friend."

"A friend for you to play with?"

"Maybe chess. I don't know," Frits said. "She's a nurse."

Anna looked at Dirk. "A nurse? Is it Bertha? What happened?"

"That was a brilliant guess, Anna. Yes, it's Bertha, but with a new name. I introduced her to Mien as Sylvia van Tongeren."

Anna immediately turned to Frits. "You can keep a secret, right? From now on you must call your friend Sylvia. Can you do that?"

"Of course I can," Frits said.

Dirk believed him. This child had learned early on that names are only temporary in wartime. His birth name might be buried under a few others he'd been given since he'd let go of his mother's hand in Amsterdam.

"Where is Sylvia?" Anna asked.

"She's freshening up," the baroness said. "Would you have a change of clothes for her?"

Bertha reappeared in an outfit more suitable for her body. She looked refreshed, and answered questions about her work as a nurse.

Walter entered the room just before dinnertime, holding a bunch of orange marigolds in his arm. Frits ran up to him.

"Dominee Vlaskamp," he said, his voice high-pitched with excitement, "Dirk brought my friend. Her name is Sylvia."

"I want to meet her, Frits, but let me first give these flowers to Oma."

He started to cross the room, but then he saw Bertha. He stopped abruptly. They held each other's gaze long enough for the others in the room to notice that this wasn't a casual recognition. Dirk had never seen Walter flustered.

"B-Bertha," he stammered.

"*Nee, Dominee, haar naam is Sylvia,*" Frits said.

Walter's hand with the bunch of flowers dropped to his side.

"Bertha," he said again, ignoring Frits's remark, "how did *you* get here?"

"You might say the Gestapo chased me, Walter. How are you? I haven't seen you since you came out of prison."

"It seems I do not have to bother with introductions," the baroness said. "Please join us for tea, Walter. And I'm curious what the orange flowers signify."

It took him a moment to wipe consternation off his face. "May we soon see the queen back on Dutch soil," he said, raising the flowers. "The Allies have crossed the Dutch border. I have it on the best authority."

"Both Dirk and you give me the impression our liberation is imminent. Are you sure? Could that be right?" the baroness said. "If so, it would be cause for celebration, and I should have Janus venture into the wine cellar to see if we still have a decent bottle of wine to celebrate with."

"When I talked to my sister," Walter said, "she told me she'd seen an endless stream of defeated soldiers. And people all over the place are picking flowers to greet the Allies. What's most amazing, the Germans aren't stopping them."

They moved to the dining room. Janus had found a bottle of wine from before the war, and he ceremoniously as well as professionally filled a glass for each of the five adults. Dirk asked him to pour a few drops in Frits's glass of water as well.

"To queen and country, and to our steadfast hostess," Dirk said, and raised his glass.

The boiled potatoes and watery endives didn't complement the exquisite Bordeaux, but the prospect of an end to the war was enough to make them forget what they ate. The wine loosened tongues, and the baroness regaled her guests with stories about going horseback riding on the beaches of Scheveningen with a group of cavalry officers. She was riding sidesaddle, she said with a modest smile, but the officers couldn't keep up with her. "I was twenty," she added.

The mood around the breakfast table the next morning was decidedly less cheerful. News from Radio Oranje lacked further reports about the advance in the Netherlands. Walter called his parents. They told him the crowds had drifted home, because no Allied troops had shown up.

A sense of reality returned.

Sylvia should stay, the baroness decided. Dirk knew he had to go back. Food stamps and money had to be gotten to the people he'd helped hide around the castle as well as other places in the country. Jan needed help with the illegal newspaper. His father counted on him to carry out secret missions, like gathering information on German defensive positions. Dr. Hamel, who'd given him the lab job as a cover, was in on most of these activities. Dirk owed it to him to get back to Utrecht. But he worried about Anna. She'd lost weight and looked burdened. He'd felt ribs through her dress the few times they'd had an opportunity to embrace. He felt torn and heavy-hearted.

Anna went outside with him. The early sun brought color and warmth to the surrounding fields; another hot September day. Mien came out of the kitchen with sandwiches in his old rucksack. Frits followed with his water bottle.

Anna embraced Dirk, and he held her tightly.

"Those Allies better hurry up," he whispered in her ear.

"Have faith, Dirk," she said. "There will be an end to this. Take care of yourself. And always remember that you have all of my love."

He got on Carla's bike. When he came to the gate, he stopped to turn around and wave. Frits waved back, and Anna blew him a kiss. Every fiber in his body tugged at his heart, telling him to abandon his responsibilities. He had all he could do not to go back. But he didn't.

CHAPTER THIRTY-SEVEN

Walter – September 1944

Walter tossed and turned. Sleep wouldn't come. The images of the day piled on top of one another, like a deck of cards being shuffled. Images of people whispering to each other about the end of the war; of Ruth gathering orange marigolds in her garden; of telephone calls from congregants who wondered if he'd heard the good news; of German soldiers in the streets who looked strangely insecure. One image kept surfacing to the top of the deck until it wouldn't go away: Bertha, who'd appeared out of nowhere. Instantly, every reason why he'd fallen in love with her had jumped out at him. He'd often wondered if, over the passage of time, he'd turned her into a sort of deity. Not so. The images of the past and present overlapped and became one. She was a woman blissfully unaware of her own beauty. But her beauty was hard to miss. Her eyes, her hair, the peach-like quality of her cheeks, the ease and fluidity with which she moved, they combined to make her a feast for the eyes. And those were only the outward qualities. Bertha was more than the sum of good looks.

Walter got out of bed and wandered over to the window. Outside, light from the half moon turned the field into a faded black-and-white photograph. How would Bertha adapt to the quiet of the countryside? She was a city girl. Could he help her? Should he? She'd been remarkably composed when he entered the room, unlike him. But, of course, *she* had been prepared. Anna and the baroness obviously took a liking to her, and it didn't surprise him they'd offered her a place to hide.

He climbed back into bed, but the questions kept coming. She was here to stay under the same roof. How long before the liberation? *Dear God, what do you have in mind for me? For us? How do I interpret this sudden change in circumstance? Is it a sign? A sign of what?* He didn't know. He tossed and turned until daybreak. The only conclusions he came to were that he dearly loved Bertha and that he didn't know what to do about it.

Breakfast was over. Dirk was leaving. Anna and Frits were seeing him off. The ones left at the table with him were the baroness and Bertha. The baroness folded her napkin and got up.

"Walter, would you have time to give Sylvia a tour so she won't get lost? I know Anna will be busy, and I promised Frits to play chess with him."

She was a clever woman, and this was not the first time he'd thought so.

"Let's start indoors," he said, and opened the door to the hall.

He showed her the study with the antlers on the walls that had been Klaas's office and was now Anna's. Bertha walked over to the easel with an unfinished charcoal drawing and studied it.

"Who is the artist?"

"Klaas. Did Carla ever tell you about the Group of Eight? They gathered at her place. Dirk and Anna were a big part of it. So was Klaas. He was half-Jewish. The baroness gave him cover until the Gestapo took him."

Bertha looked shocked. "How?"

"They were looking all over for a parachutist. They couldn't find him, but they came across Klaas and asked how old he was, and said that at his age he should be working in Germany. They never found out he was Jewish."

The ballroom was next. Bertha let out a little cry of surprise and awe. The gild-framed mirrors reflected the early morning sun and lit up the room, turning the polished dance floor into a shimmering pool.

"This is where the money was raised for your organization. You must have heard about that. It was a stunning performance."

"Yes, I have, indirectly. Standing here makes those stories come alive. I was told the local commandant walked in on it and even made a donation. The irony of it all."

She walked around the room and couldn't avoid seeing her own image. He watched her from the center of the room. Their eyes met in one of the mirrors. A surge of love filled him. She turned around slowly. He walked toward her.

"The war makes so many things unpredictable, doesn't it?" she said, and reached for his hands.

"Yes," he said, loving the feel of her hands in his. "Who would have thought? Here we are in a castle, living under the same roof."

She steered the conversation into a different direction by asking if he had found fulfillment in his work as a minister.

"Yes, I have. That part of my life is fulfilled. How about you?"

"I love nursing. It suits me perfectly."

There was so much to say, but he was afraid to utter one word, lest it would lead to a place from which neither could retreat. She squeezed his hands, as if telling him that she knew exactly what he wasn't saying. He got hold of his surging feelings and let go of her hands.

"Well," he said, aware that his voice betrayed his emotions, "there is more to this place than the dancing hall. Let's go outside."

The sun was on its early ascent, and stood out in a clear blue sky with the carriage house silhouetted against it. The gold on the weathervane's galloping horse shone as brightly as an ancient Egyptian statue.

The door was unlocked. Cool and humid air mixed with the

intense smell of hay and manure, even though the box stalls hadn't been filled for several years now.

"As a little girl, I dreamed of having a horse," Bertha said as she inhaled the air.

"You never told me that, when you were that little girl."

"I didn't tell you everything, Walter! We shared other dreams, probably just as unrealistic as owning a horse."

"What are the dreams you made come true, Bertha?"

"Helping people, I suppose, trying to make them happy."

All but one, he thought, but he didn't say it. Instead he said, "We had that in common, didn't we?"

She looked at him and smiled. "Yes, we did."

They walked over the uneven brick floor of the center aisle and by the large box stalls.

"This is amazing. Everything about this place is amazing. It's like seeing a play about the turn of the century with the aristocracy at its center. When the baroness told us about riding horses on the beach with cavalry officers, it gave me an idea about the culture and times she was brought up in."

They walked on to the tack room. Saddles of various sizes were displayed along the wall on polished brass racks. Bertha stroked the sidesaddle.

"Imagine what it must have been like to have all this at your disposal," she said. "You can say to your stable hand, Saddle up my horse, or, Have the carriage ready at nine."

"A different time, a different use," Walter said. "A little while ago, this place was used to hide a parachutist. The one the Gestapo couldn't find."

"My goodness! That was a risky thing to do. They kill you for doing that. Did the baroness know? Did she approve it?"

"Nobody here would dream of doing it behind her back."

"No, I suppose not," Bertha said. "Dirk told me that blue blood was not all the baroness was about. When you see these stables, your first thought is that it takes privilege to have this kind of lifestyle, and it does of course, but I can see that Baroness van Haersolte rises above inherited privilege."

Walter ran a finger over the cantle of the sidesaddle and looked up at her.

"The French call it noblesse oblige," he said. "The privileged are obliged to help those less fortunate. Some do it grudgingly, as we all know, but a true aristocrat does it from the heart."

"How about a Christian heart, Walter? I've seen dirt-poor people give their last penny away. It doesn't take blue blood to follow Christ's example."

He could always count on Bertha to put him in his place.

Back at the castle, he took his bike to go to the parsonage and left Bertha to explore on her own. On his way through the woods, he looked in vain for Allied soldiers. Bram greeted him at the door.

"Dominee Vlaskamp, did you see English soldiers?" he asked.

"No, Bram. Not one."

"Oh."

Ruth stood in the hallway with her youngest in her arms. She looked tired and distraught.

"Walter, do you have a moment? I need to talk to you."

She told Bram to go play with his other sister and carried the toddler upstairs to the study that rightfully belonged to her husband. Subtle signs, like the pipe rack on the desk, told of a different occupant.

"I have received a call from the sanatorium. Frank isn't doing well at all. I don't know what to do."

"You should go there," Walter said.

"That's what I would like to do, but I'll have to find someone to take care of the children."

"There are plenty of parishioners who would love to help you out, or who could take the children for a day or two. We will solve this, Ruth. Don't worry."

She put Lideke on the floor. The little one put her arms around his legs, her signal to be picked up. He got the message and held her up high. It made her giggle. Ruth smiled, but he saw the black rings under her eyes. They were more pronounced than ever. She had lost weight since he first met her. Nobody gained weight these days, but some lost more weight than others. The healthy color in her cheeks had faded, and her arms were thin. He should ask Hendrik for a few eggs to bring tomorrow.

He went to work on the phone to find a member of the congregation willing to come in and take care of the children. He was not immediately successful, but he was sure he would have better luck tomorrow. The congregation he had inherited was compassionate. He stopped himself at that word. Inherited.

There was a shy knock on the door. It opened a crack, and Bram's face came into view.

"Dominee Vlaskamp, why didn't the English soldiers come?"

"I don't know, Bram."

"But everybody said they would. That isn't fair."

"Maybe everybody was wrong, and they weren't going to come."

"Everybody said my father would get better, but he didn't. They were wrong too."

He had come into the study step by step, and now he was standing next to the desk chair.

"Sometimes," Walter said, "people say that things will happen because they *want* them to happen. And you know, even if they don't happen right away, that doesn't mean they won't happen at all. Just not right now."

The explanation satisfied Bram for the time being. If the Allies couldn't make their way soon and if Dominee Bosma didn't get better, Walter would have to come up with very different explanations.

He swung by Hendrik's farm on his way back to the castle. Tom was outside, pulling onions out of the ground. He flung them into a wicker basket, and when it was full, he straightened up. His face was ruddy red, a striking contrast to Ruth's pale complexion. Tom had worked on the farm for two years now. They had changed him from a teenager into a man, and from a city slicker into a farmhand. Goebbels would be proud to use him as a prototype of the exalted Aryan race on one of his repulsive posters. So far, Tom had escaped the Gestapo's roving eyes.

"Hi Tom, anybody around?"

"Bertien is inside."

"I don't want to bother her, but I wonder if she might have a few extra eggs I could take to Mevrouw Bosma. She looked awfully pale to me this morning."

"I will get you some out of the hen house. I'm sure Bertien wouldn't mind."

It wasn't hard to tell where the hen house was. Several feathered creatures roamed the yard behind the barn. Tom stooped and went inside, reached under a brooding hen, and swiped her egg.

"You're robbing the cradle, Tom."

"That's my job, Dominee." They laughed.

He gathered another three and put them in his cap. "Here you are. You can return my cap another day."

Walter gingerly held onto the cap in one hand and the bike's handlebar in the other. He would ask Mien to wrap the eggs individually in newspaper and put them in a basket.

On his way to the castle's salon, the sound of someone playing the piano stopped him. He walked over to the ballroom. It could only be Frits. He marveled at the boy's self-discipline as he practiced scales, over and over. Standing before the closed door, he became aware of movements in the hall. He sharpened his ear. A German word was spoken. He stiffened and turned around. Janus was guiding the commandant, dressed in civilian clothes, toward the salon. But Herr von Schloss stopped suddenly. He veered to the left and walked toward Walter.

"*Gutten Tag,*" he said. "I hear someone play the piano. Could you introduce me to the pianist?"

It was a request from a man used to giving orders. How could he refuse? His imagination failed him. He felt miserably inadequate at protecting Frits. He saw no other choice but to open the door to the ballroom. There was Frits, seated behind the grand piano with his back to the door.

The commandant put his fingers to his lips in a warning not to say a word. He listened intently. Frits ran the same passage several times till he could do it without a mistake. Satisfied with his progress, he took up the piece he was practicing.

The commandant walked softly up to the piano and looked over Frits's shoulder.

"*Ach, Bertini. Das is schon, nicht?*" he said.

When Frits heard German spoken, he turned around with a quick jerk of his upper body, and a blood-drained face looked up. But Walter saw surprise as well. He'd probably expected a German in uniform.

"You play very well, young man," the commandant said. "I have played that same etude. Bertini was a wonderful French composer. How old are you?"

"*Tien.*" The question had been given to him in German, but he answered in Dutch.

"Do you have sheet music?"

Frits got up and opened the bench he sat on. He took out a sheaf of papers and showed it.

"*Wunderbar,*" the commandant said with a smile. He leafed through the bundle. "Ah! This is for four hands. *Quatre mains.* Have you ever played it?"

Frits nodded.

"I haven't touched a piano in a while. Do you mind if we play this piece together? That would give me great pleasure."

Frits took the sheet from his hand, placed it on the piano's music stand, and made room on the bench for the commandant. Color had returned to his face somewhat.

"I will play the lower hand," the commandant said, and seated himself on the left side of the bench. "You can play the upper hand."

Frits sat down on the right side of the bench.

"*Ein, zwei, drei,*" the commandant said, and Frits started to play. The commandant fell in with his part. They synchronized amazingly well.

Soft footsteps came from behind. The door of the ballroom had been left open, and the baroness entered with a look of both horror and amazement. Unspoken questions flew from her eyes. She and Walter observed the improbable scene side by side.

"*Feurig,*" the commandant said in the middle of a passage, and Frits responded by giving it more oomph. They kept on playing. When they'd come to the end, the commandant put his hand on Frits's shoulder.

"That was more fun than I've had in a long time. *Danke schön.*"

Frits nodded but didn't look up.

As Herr von Schloss got up from the piano bench, he noticed the baroness.

"Gnädige Frau, I apologize for not coming to greet you first. But hearing the piano being played was irresistible."

The baroness touched his elbow, turning him toward the door and guiding him into the hall. The tea was getting cold, she said. Walter went up to Frits and told him to relax and keep playing. He would be back to fetch him later.

Janus had brought in a tray with tea and biscuits. The baroness went through the familiar ceremony of filling the china cups, and Herr von Schloss sat across from her. He was the picture of salon correctness. His slacks neatly pressed, his shoes spit-shined, gold cufflinks peeking out from the sleeves of his impeccable suit jacket, his hair neatly slicked down.

"You are aware of recent movements on the war front, I suppose?" he began. It was a tricky question.

"I heard that the Allies had taken Breda," the baroness said, "and that people got excited, but it turned out to be just a rumor like so many others in wartime."

"The Allies have made progress over the summer," Herr von Schloss said. "After Paris and Brussels fell into their hands, it had a demoralizing effect on our troops."

"It's always nicer to be victorious."

"Indeed it is. The Allies have the momentum, and I wouldn't be surprised if they sprang an assault somewhere in Holland very soon. In that case, I may have to move my troops and get into the fight."

"That would be quite a change for you and your men, to go from being an occupying force to a fighting force."

"It would be."

"I hope and pray," Walter said, "that wherever the fight will be, it will be over fast and soon. That would be best for all parties involved."

In an awkward silence, the baroness reached for her cup of tea, and the commandant shifted in his chair. Walter watched a cloud drift over his face, leaving him with a brooding expression.

"I am an officer by profession," he said, "trained to defend my country. But these days, I wonder what I'm defending."

Walter was taken aback. Yet, he didn't doubt the sincerity of the surprising statement. Over the past year, he'd heard Herr von Schloss make several couched remarks that hinted at a difference of opinion with the Nazi regime.

"Deutschland is a great country," he went on. "But—dare I say it?—we have a leader with outrageous beliefs. What he does to people he considers inferior is disgraceful."

It wasn't clear what motivated him to unload these private thoughts on them.

"Yes," Walter said. "I find it hard to reconcile his attitude with my faith, which holds that all of us are God's children, regardless."

"Exactly. I was thinking about this as I was introduced to the young pianist just now."

The baroness put her teacup down and sat up straight, as if someone had shoved a plank behind her back.

"And what were those thoughts?" she asked, her voice taking on an authoritative tone.

"I thought to myself, what in God's name have we done to a nice talented boy like this, who is obviously Jewish and who understood every German word I spoke. My guess is that his parents fled Germany when Hitler came to power, and they came to live in Holland. How he came to be with you, I do not know, nor do I want to know. I understand and respect that you want to protect him from evil. So will I."

Walter let out the breath he'd been holding. The baroness didn't react immediately. What Herr von Schloss had discovered could result in her death sentence. All he had to do was go tell the Gestapo.

"Herr von Schloss," she finally said, "I share your desire to protect this sweet and talented boy. I do not know his history. Maybe his parents came from Germany, I do not know. What I do know is, he deserves to be alive."

The commandant nodded.

The next half hour was spent drinking another cup of surrogate tea, and the topic of conversation was the weather. What had been exposed didn't need further exploration. These two people now shared tightly held secrets. The baroness had bribed the commandant with a valuable steed. He had forewarned her about a raid of her property. He'd protected her when she held the concert with more people than assembly ordinances allowed. And today he'd given her the ultimate gift. He saved her from being sent to a concentration camp. At least for the time being.

He rose, looking trim and elegant as he stooped to kiss her hand.

"Gnädige Frau, you have been a marvelous hostess. I shall remember you as a wise and judicious woman. I admire your courage and I wish you well. May the war end soon. Auf Wiedersehen."

Walter got up and opened the door for him. A waterfall of music notes floated down the hall. Frits had advanced to a more difficult piece. The commandant stopped.

"Amazing talent," he murmured. "If I may give you a piece of advice, keep him away from strangers. It would be unfortunate if he were judged on his looks and not on his talent."

Walter nodded. He walked with the commandant to the front door, expecting to see the familiar Mercedes with the Nazi standard and a soldier behind the wheel. Instead, an ordinary car without recognizable insignia was parked outside. Herr Von Schloss got behind the wheel, started the motor, and waved at him. It was early afternoon. The sun was still high in the sky. Its rays shimmered in the left-side mirror of the commandant's car as he maneuvered it down the curved driveway. Walter waited till the car was out of sight and then turned back. Stepping onto the cool marble floor of the hall was a relief after the hot September sun. He absorbed the stillness and shook off the built-up tension from the last hour with its unnerving surprises.

Frits had stopped playing the piano. Walter found him still sitting on the bench, but he'd closed the keyboard. His folded arms cradled his head as he rested it on the cover. His reflected image in one of the tall mirrors stirred Walter's soul. This young boy carried a history only he knew. Where he came from, what had happened in his early years, those were secrets too painful to share. As the baroness had told Herr von Schloss: *I do not know if he came from Germany.*

Frits stirred and opened his eyes. He looked into the mirror, and when he saw Walter, he straightened up.

"Who was that man, Dominee Vlaskamp?"

"That was Herr von Schloss. He came to visit Oma. He's been here a few times before, but I didn't know he could play the piano. What do you think? Did he play well?"

"Yes. He played like my grandmother."

"The grandmother who taught you to play the piano?"

"Yes, but she is French, and this man is German. I didn't know Germans played Bertini."

"Well, you play Mozart, and he was Austrian and you're

Dutch."

"I am Jewish," Frits said. "You knew that, didn't you?"

"I assumed so."

"Because you can tell from my looks, right? Do you think the German man could tell?"

"Yes, he could." He walked over to Frits. He could feel the boy cringe under the hand he put on his shoulder.

"You are safe, Frits. Herr von Schloss will do you no harm. Soon, the war will be over. Until then, we have to make sure you stay out of the way of strangers. And by the way, if someone speaks to you in German, act as if you don't understand him."

Frits got up from the piano bench, put his arms around Walter's waist, and buried his face in his suit jacket. Walter stroked his curly hair while Frits held on to him for dear life and gave in for one small moment to fears and losses.

Later that day, Walter took Bertha for a stroll over the castle's grounds. Ripe apples and young mushrooms perfumed the air. They walked by the ponies and down the road. Hendrik stood in his vegetable patch, harvesting beans from stalks as tall as he was. He stopped and waved. Walter thought this might be a good time to introduce Sylvia. They walked over, shook hands, and Hendrik was told this woman was a guest at the castle and that she'd come to stay for a while to get away from the city. Hendrik nodded. He knew about people getting away from the city, and probably from the Gestapo as well. He didn't ask questions and gave them a jovial wave as they walked on.

A patch of beech trees provided shade and privacy. They sat down under the canopy of widespread branches where the ground was dappled with the moving shadows of their leaves.

Walter stretched out full length. Bertha sat down next to him and spread her wide skirt over her knees. The filtered light enhanced her beauty. It was unbearable to be this close to her and not know if something of the love they'd shared was still alive in her. He had to know. An overwhelming urge to touch her overtook his willpower. On impulse, he drew her to him. It took her by surprise, he could tell, and at first she held back and didn't allow her body to lean into his. He held her gently, and gradually she adjusted her position.

"Bertha, I love you," he whispered.

"I know you do, " she said, and rested her head on his chest.

"What I need to know is: do you still love me after all these years?"

"That's the easiest and the hardest question to answer, Walter."

"Try."

She lay still. He let her be. Whatever the answer, he needed to know to be able to go on with his life. She stirred and looked up at him.

"I haven't stopped loving you ever, Walter, and I have never loved anyone as I have loved you. It's as simple as that. What isn't so simple is that the world around us has changed in horrible ways, but in other ways it hasn't changed one bit. And that's holding me back from giving in to my true feelings."

He knew it was the wrong thing to do, but he couldn't help himself. He kissed her long and passionately. She slowly responded. There was no question in his mind that she needed this confirmation as much as he did. She buried her head in the fold of his arm and sighed.

"Dear God, what do you want us to do?" she said.

"I've asked myself the same question many times, but the answer I come up with each time is that I truly don't know."

"Do you think it's possible that after the war is over, the Catholic Church might change its restrictions?"

"That's possible. After all the suffering and destruction we've seen, some of those baked-in ideas may look less compelling. Maybe even to the Pope!"

Bertha laughed. "When Carla told me you would be at the castle, I told her I would put it in God's hands."

"That's safer than in anybody else's hands. Look, this is a time like no other. There's a brutal war going on. It may be over in a few weeks or it may last through another horrible winter. You are in danger. We could both be killed before all this is over. I think God favors people who truly love and honor each other. Let's take this day by day."

"Amen," Bertha said, and smiled at him.

CHAPTER THIRTY-EIGHT

Emmy – September 1944

Emmy stood at her desk and stared at a picture of the Group of Eight. Carla's brother had probably taken it. How healthy and tanned they all looked, except for Daan, who'd spent the entire summer inside. That sunny day was now two summers ago, at Herman's place in Loosdrecht.

She sighed. Where were they all? Dirk was the only male of the group still in Holland and free to move around, as far as she knew. Otto had apparently made it to England. The last time she'd seen Carla and Anna was in Utrecht, before Anna was brought to the police station. When she called to ask where Anna was, Betty hadn't given a direct answer. The only hint she gave was that Anna had left Utrecht for good.

She missed her friends and the common purpose. Living in her parents' home, she had to dream up a story to cover her tracks every time she needed to bring food stamps to Mr. and Mrs. Hirsch. Dirk had made sure she regularly received them. An invisible man, part of a local Underground group, faithfully dropped them off at a big pharmacy in the center of Haarlem. The pharmacist there was an amiable man with a keen sense of humor, who always had a joke to share while handing her the envelope. She'd begun to think of him as a good friend, and looked forward to her weekly visit. He was, after all, the only one who knew her secret. That was enough to think of him as a friend.

She rested her hand on a book with more than 1900 pages divided over 365 chapters. She had taken it upon herself to translate this tome to fight boredom, to keep her agility with the French language alive, and to satisfy her parents' curiosity about the time she spent in her room on the third floor by herself. The title in gold-embossed letters stood out on the leather cover: *Les Miserables* by Victor Hugo. It had seen the light eighty-two years ago, which was thirty years after the June Rebellion in Paris, the book's subject.

Although overwhelmed at first by its sheer size and the enterprise of translating it without the aid of a copy of a Dutch translation, she was getting intrigued with its message: a progress from evil to good, from injustice to justice, from falsehood to truth, from night to day, from corruption to life; from bestiality to duty, from hell to heaven, from nothingness to God.

Victor Hugo threw a blinding light on the darkest side of human nature, and in the process, he didn't lose his faith, in spite of steeping his mind in misery for years on end. His deep compassion for other people was palpable throughout.

There was a knock on the door. Her sister appeared.

"Liesbeth, what makes you climb up the stairs to the third floor?"

"I don't know. That's the honest answer. I feel at loose ends."

Emmy looked up at her sister, who was tall and slim like herself. Liesbeth, two years older, had decided against a university study after finishing high school. Their mother had wanted her to study the history of art, the very thing Moeder had wished for herself but couldn't do, because in her growing-up years, women didn't do that kind of thing. Straight from school, Liesbeth had gone to live with an Italian family in Florence until the threat of war drove her back home. Having been exposed to the epicenter of classical art, she was determined to try her own hand at visual art, and got an apprenticeship with an accomplished painter in Haarlem.

"How's your painting coming?"

"So, so." Liesbeth sighed. "It's easier to talk about a painting than to create one."

"And it's easier to translate a book than to write one from scratch."

Liesbeth fell on the bed and hoisted herself so she could lean against the wall with her hands behind her head. Emmy didn't know what to make of her sister's mood. Was she bored? Discouraged? Should she force it out of her? She knew how painful it could be to keep a secret.

"You know, Emmy, Victor tells me to make the subjects of my paintings more my own. He says I should put my heart and soul into it, never to think about what the critics will say. It should reflect your own joy or your own despair. To be a successful artist, you must feel deeply. The other day, he started a new painting, and he began by making the canvas almost entirely black. It was the day after his best friend got executed in the dunes of Scheveningen."

"All black! That reminds me of the reproduction Moeder put up of the starved Belgian refugees. My friend Anna was here, and she had a hard time with it."

"I remember," Liesbeth said. "All Moeder had to say about it was that it was done in charcoal and so on. She was more interested in the technique than the misery it represented. You and I have been brought up with an appreciation for the arts, but with a lack of compassion for what constitutes real life."

Emmy was stunned. She put her hand on Victor Hugo's book.

"Amazing that you should be taught by a man named Victor. You see this book? Victor Hugo wrote it, all 1900 pages of it. It deals exactly with that: compassion. Victor Hugo had it in spades."

Liesbeth leaned forward. Her blond curls fell to her shoulders. She pushed them away from her face.

"That's why I feel at loose ends," she said. "I feel conflicted. In the daytime, I hear about feelings, empathy, and that sort of thing. But at home those aspects are not discussed. Our parents live in an artificial world, Emmy. Maybe that's not true of Vader. I'm sure he sees a lot of real life from behind the bench. But he doesn't bring it home. Moeder has found a way to skip reality, especially the reality of war. The only aspect of war that seems to penetrate is the lack of food."

Emmy had never felt closer to her sister. They'd gone about making their lives in different ways, but they'd come to the same conclusion about their parents.

"Mother has chased 'Art' as an escape," Liesbeth said. "She has good taste. No question about that. She recognizes technique. But I'm not so sure she recognizes emotional content. Or the lack of it."

"Whoa, that's quite a statement. But I see what you mean. That's why it was so incongruous that she put up that painting of Leo Gestel's. Suffering and injustice stared us in the face for a whole week, for God's sake."

Liesbeth got up and walked over to the window. It was a bright September day. The red roof tiles on the houses glistened in the sun. She glanced at the picture of the Group of Eight and sighed.

"You must miss your friends. Do you feel sometimes like we're living in some sort of jail? Removed from our friends? All the men my age are either hidden somewhere or they've been taken to Germany, or they're dead. The war turns everybody into a victim of sorts."

She'd never seen her sister bitter. She wanted to help, to share how she had to play games with her parents, because she was convinced they wouldn't understand that helping Jews survive was a moral imperative for her. But she remembered how Dirk had warned not to involve others in secrets unless you absolutely had to. Liesbeth would be better off if she didn't know about Mr. and Mrs. Hirsch. So, she simply walked over and threw her arms around her sister.

Two days later, Emmy overheard the milkman say that strange things were going on. The sky over the big rivers was filled with hundreds of Allied planes, and parachutists tumbled down by the dozens near Arnhem. The Germans were getting nervous, he said. There was talk that people living close to the dunes had to evacuate, because there was going to be another invasion.

Emmy stiffened. She slipped out of the house, took her bike, and raced over to the town behind the dunes where Mr. Hirsch and his wife were hiding in their own home. Close to Bloemendaal, she saw posters tacked onto trees by the side of the road. Their message was that more than half of the village—the western part of it—was to be evacuated within three days. How much of those three days had already passed? She didn't have a clue. But Bloemendaal, usually a sleepy town, was bustling. Its residents were pushing anything with wheels that could salvage at least some of their belongings. The sight of a priest pushing an overstuffed baby carriage was as sad as it was comical. Two young boys pulled a raft on roller skates that was loaded up with household goods. She passed a horse and wagon with a piano on top. A handsome teenager stood at the keyboard and played the national anthem with a taunting grin on his face. He was lucky. No Germans were in sight.

Albert opened the front door cautiously. That wasn't unusual, but the disarray behind him was. Half-packed suitcases littered the floor of the hall.

"We're leaving today," he said.

"You and your family? Oh, my God. What about Mr. and Mrs. Hirsch? Do they have a place to go?"

"No. They hope *you* will know of one."

"Me? Can't they go with you?"

"We have to move in with my sister in Amsterdam. She has a family of her own, and she lives in a small apartment."

"When do you have to be out of here?"

"Tomorrow at noon, but we won't wait that long."

Emmy leaned her head against the doorframe. How was she to

come up with a new address? She slowly walked up the stairs while her mind raced in all directions. Albert and his family didn't want to be caught with a Jewish couple living on the second floor of their home. The quicker they left, the better for them.

She rapped her knuckles on the door—one long, two short, one long—and the door opened immediately. Mr. Hirsch greeted her with outstretched arms. His wife sat at the table, holding her head in her hands. She hadn't bothered to get out of her nightgown, and her hair was in disarray.

"Emmy, my angel, you finally came!" Mr. Hirsch said.

His exuberant welcome confirmed what Albert had said. Mr. and Mrs. Hirsch expected her to be their saving angel, again, who would miraculously whisk them off to another hiding place. She cringed. If only she hadn't heard the milkman spill the news of evacuation to her mother. She knew she had to pull herself together, but what she really wanted was to escape, to evaporate.

"You have to get us out of here," Mr. Hirsch said. His voice had changed from sugar sweet to commanding. "We have only one day left. I thought you would have come earlier."

"I didn't know what was happening until this morning."

"I know your father is a judge in Haarlem, and that you live in a big house on the Donkere Spaarne. I'm sure your parents would agree to take us in."

Lightning struck. An electric shock coursed through her body and mind. This was preposterous. Her parents? Who knew nothing about this?

"Mr. Hirsch," she said, "my parents don't even know you exist."

"Well, go home and tell them. And you can also tell them that I am willing to pay. You know better than anyone that I have a lot of money."

"My parents are not for sale, Mr. Hirsch. You can't bribe a judge."

His eyes narrowed. She had offended him.

"I have no intention of bribing anybody, young lady," he said.

"Please go home and ask your parents if they would take us in. We will pay for our keep. Unless you have another solution."

So, that's how he saw it. It was *her* responsibility to find a place to hide. But she did not have another place.

"Mr. Hirsch, do you realize what you're asking? The Gestapo will kill my parents on the spot if they find out."

Mrs. Hirsch hadn't said a word during this exchange, but Emmy had hardly finished her sentence before the woman started to sob inconsolably, a searing sound that cut through Emmy's heart.

"Do you realize now that we are desperate?" Mr. Hirsch said. "Please go home and tell your parents that our lives are hanging in the balance. By tomorrow afternoon, everybody in this house has to be out. Where do we go?"

"I—I don't know," Emmy stammered. "I really don't know."

"Go home!" Mr. Hirsch shouted.

Emmy trembled. "I will do what I can," she said, and turned toward the door.

"Your parents are Christians. They will help us," Mr. Hirsch called after her.

She closed the door and stood at the head of the staircase. The sound of Mrs. Hirsch's continued sobs paralyzed her. She gripped the railing. Her mind went blank. She had no solution.

Albert waited at the bottom of the stairs.

"He wants me to take them to my parents' home," she told him in a daze.

"Would that work?" Albert asked.

He wanted her to say she was going to take his old boss off his hands. It would make it a lot easier for him to leave with a clear conscience. She read that on his face.

"I doubt it, but I will try," she said. Albert looked uneasy.

"We have a long trip ahead of us," he said. "There may only be a few trains left that can take us to Amsterdam. I am responsible for my wife and children. We have to leave. I hope you understand."

She understood only too well. He had taken an enormous risk

by making the house-swapping deal with Mr. Hirsch and letting them stay under the same roof for two years. But now the Germans were closing in on them. Tomorrow, the Germans would walk in at noon and take over this house with everything in it. And if that included the Hirschs, Albert and his family had better be out of sight.

"Do what you have to do, Albert."

She got on her bike and started on her way home. Exactly a year ago, she'd walked through this street with Anna, when they'd brought Mr. Hirsch's fortune back to him inside their raincoats. The same pink phlox and tall dahlias graced the manicured gardens. Their colorful faces turned to the sun regardless of who lived in the homes behind them. Tomorrow, every house in this part of Bloemendaal would change hands. The civic rules that people had lived by, and that had always protected them, would evaporate overnight, replaced by the merciless rules of war and dictatorship.

Emmy gripped the handlebars of her bike till her knuckles turned white. Competing feelings of confusion and anger fueled her energy. Anger at the Germans, mixed with anger at Mr. Hirsch, who'd put the responsibility for their safety squarely on her shoulders. Had he ever taken responsibility for being Jewish? He hadn't cared one whit about the six hundred children that had been saved from a train ride to hell and were hidden at great personal cost to many noble souls. He'd not believed her when she first made contact and told him he would have to go into hiding. Oh, no, that wasn't going to happen to them! He treated her as if she owed him. She felt used. She'd been providing him with food stamps for two years. She'd risked being sent to a concentration camp by transporting his money. So had Anna. She'd literally kept them alive. Had he ever acknowledged that service?

The sound of Mrs. Hirsch's sobs rang in her mind like a blaring radio she couldn't turn off. She peddled faster to get rid of the sound till she was exhausted. The dunes were behind her now, and a greener landscape of meadows came into view. Down the road was a bus stop with a bench. She got off her bike and sat down, catching her breath. She needed to think. How did she ever get into this predicament? The sermon Dominee Vlaskamp had delivered two years ago had been so clear and undeniably logical. It had left no doubt about the duty to protect people against senseless racism. She had questioned at the time how a student could stand up against an armed Nazi, but Dirk had said that even though students didn't have guns, they had brains. And he'd been right. It hadn't taken a gun to provide Mr. and Mrs. Hirsch with food stamps.

Brains. Brains. She should use them. What were her options? Dirk was too far away to ask for help. A person she could trust, who did live close by, was Mr. Wets, the pharmacist. He was obviously connected, somehow, to the Underground. But was it fair to get him involved in this? To ask him to provide her with a name and address to hide a Jewish couple with less than twenty-four hours notice was unfairly pushing the limits of friendship. And just because he acted friendly toward her didn't mean he considered her a good friend, the kind you'd risk your life for. She rejected the option.

Her cotton dress felt damp and clung to her body. It was one of those warm September days that fooled you into thinking warm weather would last forever. The sun was as hot as on a midsummer day. The bus stop didn't provide shade, and the landscape was as flat as the sea. Better to get back on the bike and create some air movement.

The closer she got to Haarlem, the more she realized she had no other option than to do what Mr. Hirsch had commanded her to do. He might have foreseen that another hiding place couldn't be turned up within a matter of hours. And Albert must have made it clear he couldn't take them along. He had no power over Albert at this point. The house swap was a done deal. The only string attached had been that Albert would sell the house back to Mr. Hirsch after the war was over. With this last twist of fate, neither one would be the owner much longer.

Emmy resented the notion that Mr. Hirsch could have power over her. And what she resented even more was that he had succeeded. He had maneuvered her into going home and telling her parents that they should do their Christian duty and give shelter to a Jewish couple, even if they might end up in a concentration camp, like Corrie ten Boom and her sister and her father, who'd had the watch shop down the street from the pharmacy. One day they were gone, taken to het Oranje Hotel in Scheveningen. They'd hidden numerous Jews. Then they were betrayed. The ten Boom family had been a Christian pillar in the community, involved in many charities. They'd lived their faith. The thought gave her goose pimples. If she hadn't heard that sermon about the Good Samaritan and been stimulated by friends who'd shared the same experience, would she now be sweating over how to save a couple she didn't even really like or admire? Did she have the kind of compassion that Victor Hugo described in the book she'd steeped herself in for days on end, and that she had accused her parents of lacking? They declared themselves to be Protestant, but they didn't go to church. Mr. Hirsch had shouted at her that they were Christians. Of course, they would help. Would they?

She biked over the bumpy cobblestones of a small street that led up to De Donkere Spaarne. A quay where ships lay moored lined one side of the river. The opposite side was a wide street with patrician homes. One of those belonged to her family. Emmy stopped. She balanced one foot on the edge of the sidewalk and looked at the place where she'd been brought up, as if seeing it for the first time. Facing the river, the houses stood shoulder to shoulder. Some were tall and wide, others not. They had one thing in common. Each house was three stories high, but none looked alike. Bricks of different hues were used to differentiate between them. The gables were of various designs. Some windows were wide and tall, others had small six-over-six panes. But each house qualified as a patrician home. No wonder Mr. Hirsch thought there ought to be enough room in such a house to hide him and his wife.

She took a deep breath, kicked off from the sidewalk, and biked over to her home. She opened the heavy front door, lifted her bike over the stoop, and pushed it inside. Leaving it out was an invitation for theft. It made for a clumsy entrance to keep everyone's bike in the hall. More than once, Emmy had hit her ankle against a protruding pedal.

The house was quiet. It was late afternoon. She stood at the foot of the stairs, listening for a sign of life. She had no time to waste, yet she wanted to postpone the confrontation that was bound to come. She took off her shoes and walked up the staircase to Liesbeth's room. Without knocking, she opened the door. Her sister sat behind an easel. The light in the room was diffused by translucent gauze that Liesbeth had spanned over the windows. Moeder had objected, but Liesbeth had argued that for painting she needed indirect light. She'd won the argument.

"Hi Sis," Emmy said. "It's just me. I have to talk with you."

Liesbeth, dressed in a smock that looked like a modern piece of art for all the splotches of paint on it, moved her head to the side of the canvas on the easel.

"What about?"

"Hiding a Jewish couple."

"What?" Liesbeth put the brush down on the small table next to her and got up.

"I am in a very difficult situation, Liesbeth. It's a long story. A two-years-long story."

Emmy let herself fall on the bed and started to tell about the Group of Eight, Walter's sermon, how they all had gone out to find places where members of Daan's family could be hidden, and how that had led her to Mr. and Mrs. Hirsch in Bloemendaal.

"*Mijn God*," Liesbeth said. "And here I thought you just sat upstairs translating a French book."

"I divided my time between that and bringing them illegal food stamps. But now something awful has happened. The Germans want part of Bloemendaal evacuated. That's precisely where they live. They have to be out by tomorrow noon."

"Where will they go?"

"That's just it. They don't have anywhere to go, and they are counting on me to find them a place."

"Where?"

"Here … That was Mr. Hirsch's suggestion, and I don't have another one."

"You're joking, right?"

"I wish I were." She was close to tears.

Liesbeth dipped her brush in paint thinner and dried it with a cloth. She took off her smock and came to sit down on the bed. "This is serious. Are you sure you have no other options?"

"Yes. I'm only very indirectly connected to the local Underground group. Don't worry. I thought plenty about it on the way home. What do you think our parents will have to say about this idea?"

Liesbeth didn't answer right away. Emmy had never seen her sister look more serious.

"This is so ironic," Liesbeth said. "Just a few days ago, we were talking about compassion. Is some celestial body setting us up for a test?"

"If God is a celestial body, then maybe you're right. It could be the God I heard about in Walter Vlaskamp's sermon."

The room suddenly darkened. The clouds she'd seen moving in from the west blocked out the sun. The silver hand mirror on the chest of drawers instantly lost its luster.

"Did you say they have to be out by tomorrow noon? That's nineteen hours from now," Liesbeth said. She rested her head in her hands. "You will have to put that question to Vader and Moeder soon. They need time to make up their minds. It's either going to be a quick no or a long debate. Bring it up at dinner. I will help you to convince them."

Emmy recovered from her slumped position. Just the thought

that she could share and conspire with her older sister, who'd always been bolder, made the burden of keeping her secret a bit lighter. Together, they went down to the kitchen and helped their mother put a meager meal, fit for vegetarians, on the dining room table—boiled potatoes, endives in a thin white sauce, raw carrots on the side to provide roughage and vitamins.

Emmy went into the hall and beat the gong. No movement upstairs. She hit it again. The brass gong, made to look like a sunflower, had a deep sound that reverberated through the hallway and up the stairs. A door opened on the second floor, and she heard her father's footsteps. Her stomach did a flip. Could she convince him to take in a Jewish couple? He was a quiet man who lived behind his horn-rimmed glasses in a world of his own—the world of law and justice.

Walking behind him into the dining room, she noticed his once impeccable suit looked shabby, the seat of his pants shiny from wear. *He* didn't wear it out. The war did. It needed to be replaced, but that would not be soon.

With everyone seated at the table, she couldn't postpone asking the burning question.

"Vader, Moeder, I have something important to tell you."

"I hope it's something cheerful," Moeder said, "like the Allies have landed on the beach in Zandvoort."

"That would solve a lot of problems," Emmy said. "But right now I have to solve a specific problem, and I wonder if you can help me. I have to find a place to hide a Jewish couple."

The bomb landed, but it did not explode on impact. It was met with stony silence. The silence didn't last long, though.

"What in God's name did you get yourself involved in?" Moeder cried out.

"I've been helping a Jewish couple for as long as I've been out of college by providing them with food stamps."

"So, you are working for the Underground. Is that what you're telling us?"

"Indirectly, yes. One of the students in my group of friends — we call ourselves the Group of Eight — turned out to be half-Jewish, which the Nazis consider equal to a full-blooded Jew. We pledged we would help hide him and some of his relatives as well. And that's what we did."

"My God, Emmy, this sounds like a game ten-year-olds play. Hide and seek. Cops and robbers. Silly pacts sealed in blood. Hiding a Jew is not child's play," Moeder said.

Emmy felt the color in her cheeks rising to bright red. It wasn't from shame. Anger made the blood rush to her face.

"We are not playing games. And I am not a child anymore. It may seem that way to you, because Liesbeth and I still live at home, but that's only because the war keeps us here."

This was not going well. When asking for a favor, it wasn't smart to get angry. Liesbeth came to the rescue, amplifying what Emmy had just said.

"We are no longer teenagers, Moeder. We're in our twenties, and we have our own ideas. I, for one, admire Emmy for doing what she does. She cares."

Moeder looked like a frog, bulging with air, ready to blow up. She gripped the edge of the table, squishing the white tablecloth, and was about to say something, when Vader cleared his throat and, in his quiet way, asked, "Emmy. First of all, where does this Jewish couple live?"

"In Bloemendaal."

"Ah, that explains it, because now they're forced to move, right?"

"Tomorrow at noon they have to be out of their home."

"You ask us to help you. How can we help?"

"I am not part of the Underground here in Haarlem, Vader. I don't have any contacts. Since this came on so suddenly, I cannot go to my Group of Eight to ask for help. They're spread out all over the country after the university closed. I told Mr. Hirsch — that's his name — that I didn't have any options for him and his wife. Then he suggested that I ask my parents to take them in."

The bomb detonated.

"No, no, and no!" Moeder shouted. "You can tell them that, Emmy. No. This is the most ridiculous thing I've ever heard. How did you allow yourself to be involved in such a thing? You should have told this Mr. Hirsch that his request was unseemly, forward, and ludicrous."

"Now, now, Mildred, Let's not get ahead of ourselves here. We should make an informed decision."

"We have all the information we need," Moeder said, "more than enough to make a decision. If we take these people in, we will all end up in a concentration camp."

What Moeder said was not unreasonable. It was what Emmy herself had said to Mr. Hirsch.

"Can we please look at this in another way?" Liesbeth said. "Like from the point of view of Mr. and Mrs. Hirsch? Emmy told me that this couple managed to stay hidden on the second floor of their home, which they'd sold to an employee with the understanding he would sell it back at the end of the war. They've stayed hidden for almost two years. Can we show a little compassion for their predicament?"

Moeder sat straight backed in her chair, clasping her hands together and nervously twisting the diamond ring on her left hand. It brought to mind the diamond rings Emmy had seen glittering on Mrs. Hirsch's hands, all of them about twice the size of Moeder's more modest, solitary one. It suddenly hit her that these two women were worlds apart in style and background.

Vader asked where the employee, who'd bought the Hirsch's house, was going.

"He's probably already gone. When I left midafternoon, he said he was taking his family to his sister in Amsterdam."

"Why couldn't he take the couple with him?" Moeder asked.

"He has a wife and children, and he said his sister lived in a small apartment. He doesn't want to be anywhere near the house when the Gestapo comes to take possession of the place. He's hidden them for almost two years."

"And you want *us* to hide them, while this man was their employee and he's just taken off?"

Emmy sighed. Moeder's reaction, in all fairness, was not unlike her own had been when first confronted with the situation. Yet, it irritated her hugely that her mother only looked at it from her own point of view.

"Let me explain to you how I got involved. Then maybe you can understand where I'm coming from. Seven students and I went to listen to a minister, who was the brother of one of us. He used the parable of the Good Samaritan to make his point that we cannot look the other way when we know injustice is done. He put a question to us: Whom do you identify with? The robber, who takes away what belongs rightfully to another? Or the hypocrites like the priest and the Levite? Or are you the victim? Do you identify with the healer and the caretaker? Afterward, one of us said he was the victim. Right then and there, we decided that the rest of us should be caretakers. I could not see any other role for myself. I certainly didn't want to be a hypocrite."

The smoke had cleared from the bomb's detonation, but the debris was still smoldering. The Good Samaritan parable hadn't completely put out the fire.

"It's all very nice for a minister to stand in the pulpit and tell others what to do," Moeder said. "It's not that simple."

Emmy tried hard not to let her voice betray her anger. "If that's what you think, then let me tell you that the minister was taken away from the church — right before our eyes — by a high-up NSB man in uniform, who was in the congregation for the direct purpose of finding out what was preached in that church. Dominee Vlaskamp ended up in the jail in Scheveningen for many weeks. He's free now, but in spite of that, he continues to help hide Jews."

"That took a lot of courage," Liesbeth said, "for that minister to deliver a sermon with a traitor in uniform sitting in front of him. I admire his guts and I like his message."

The sound of forks and knives moving over the porcelain plates accentuated the silence of unspoken thoughts. But Emmy read her mother's mind. She saw a fat-lettered NO in the frown on her forehead. The facts were now established. She shouldn't embellish them to persuade her parents to take a huge risk. Either they took the Hirsches in, or they didn't. It was up to their level of compassion and courage.

"Let's look at the logistics for a moment," Vader said, the look in his brown eyes behind the horn-rimmed glasses steady and unflustered. Emmy imagined him in a black robe presiding over a court session, asking to-the-point questions.

"There are two practical things to consider. One is, how would we get this couple here? Second is, once here, where do we put them?"

"Alex," Moeder said, "you are not seriously considering this, are you?"

"The girls have spoken, Mildred, and the way I see it, this comes down to a moral decision. But before we make that decision, we have to think this through in terms of logistics."

Liesbeth and Emmy jumped in at the same time. Emmy would give up her room on the third floor, which had a bathroom next to it, and Liesbeth offered Emmy to move in with her.

Vader nodded. "Yes, having them on the third floor would keep them out of sight. God knows this house is big enough to accommodate a family of four as well as a couple. But how do we get them here?"

"The bus between Haarlem and Bloemendaal is still running. I don't know for how much longer," Emmy said.

"Good," Vader said. "Let's assume getting them here is no major obstacle."

This was too much for Moeder. She pushed her chair back and started to clear the dishes. Her hands trembled, and the dishes clattered on the sideboard.

"I think," Vader said, "that we should sleep on this. Tomorrow morning we will tell you what we will or will not do, Emmy."

He folded his napkin and fitted it into the silver ring with his initials on it, the customary sign that he was ready to retire to his study.

"Vader," Emmy said, "you realize, don't you, that the deadline is tomorrow at noon?"

"Even if you left now, Emmy," he said to her, "you wouldn't be able to get back and forth to Bloemendaal before curfew. It is better to use the evening to make a considered decision."

She should have known that judges didn't make snap decisions.

The next morning, she sat at the breakfast table early, waiting for her parents to show up. Liesbeth joined her. She said she would go with her to Bloemendaal.

Footsteps were coming down the staircase. Vader and Moeder entered and took their seats at opposite ends of the table. Moeder had dark circles under her eyes, and looked like she hadn't slept a wink. Vader didn't look any different from the night before.

"Let's get to the point," he began. "Your mother and I decided we couldn't turn our backs on this Jewish couple. We will provide them with a roof over their heads until you find another solution for them, Emmy."

"Thank you, Vader. That is very generous of you. Let's hope the Allies are on their way. Today would be better than tomorrow."

Moeder said nothing. She studied her fingernails. Her dish with oatmeal stood untouched before her. The mood in the dining room was heavy, and it got on Emmy's nerves.

"Come on, Liesbeth, we don't have a minute to lose."

They untangled their bicycles from other ones parked in the hall and carried them outside. The milkman had just stopped his cart—pulled by a harnessed German shepherd—in front of their house.

"*Goede morgen*, Flip," Emmy said. "What's the news today?"

He looked up and down the street. When he saw no one, he

leaned over and whispered, "Eindhoven was liberated yesterday."

Liesbeth jumped for joy, but Flip, who'd known her since she was a little girl, told her to stop and be careful. "There's fighting going on in Arnhem. The Nazis are upset. Watch out."

He walked up to the door and rang the bell. Liesbeth and Emmy got on their bikes and sprinted off.

Last night's clouds still hovered over the city, creating a gray dome. Without the sun, there were no shadows, no highlights, no colors. The river looked like an endless roll of steel, and the streets were quiet. Not many people were up and about. The city exuded anticipation. The German news service hadn't said a word about the Allies' surprising march through Belgium, but the people knew and were waiting, like expectant parents: When will the labor pains begin?

Emmy led the way. The bus to Bloemendaal passed them. That was a relief. Buses were still running. She shivered at the thought of having to put Mr. and Mrs. Hirsch on one. Would they be recognized as Jews? She shook off the thought. It was too scary to think about all the things that could go wrong today.

At Haarlem's city limit, German soldiers had thrown up a blockade in the road. Everyone was stopped and had to produce an ID. She never left home without hers after Anna had forgotten to take hers and landed in a cell at the police station. Every able-bodied man between the age of seventeen and forty-five was interrogated. Several were put on a truck, just as she'd seen happen in Utrecht. Finally, she and her sister were waved on. All in all, it took half an hour of their precious time.

It was after eleven-thirty when they finally came close to Bloemendaal. In the streets leading up to the Bergweg, there was a lot of activity in front of the homes ordered to be evacuated. Would they be in time?

They were not.

As they rounded the curve into the Bergweg, they saw several trucks parked in the road, and one was in front of number thirteen.

Emmy clamped her fists on her bike's brakes. Liesbeth screeched to a stop beside her. Neither spoke. They were thunderstruck. They were too late.

When she came to her senses, Emmy got off her bike and handed it to her sister. Her heart was beating in her throat.

"Maybe I can still talk to them," she said. "We can't just turn around and go home."

She walked the few steps to the small gate that separated the front lawn from the sidewalk. The front door opened. A German officer stepped out. He called to a fellow officer in the passenger seat of the parked truck.

"There were occupants upstairs. Take a look!" he yelled in German.

Emmy cringed. There, behind the officer, appeared Mr. and Mrs. Hirsch. A soldier stood behind them. Mrs. Hirsch was pushed forward with the barrel of his gun.

The officer in the truck came out and stood on the sidewalk, looking immensely pleased. He had seen right away that these were hiding Jews. Their looks had given them away. Germans had become experts at spotting them.

Emmy let out a shriek and clasped her right hand over her mouth.

The officer turned and looked up at her. "Do you know these people?"

She hesitated. "No," she said to the officer.

The other officer walked down the path. He looked at Emmy.

"Do you know these people?" he asked.

"No." It came out as a whisper.

Mr. and Mrs. Hirsch were shoved down the path toward the truck. They saw her. Mr. Hirsch made eye contact. It didn't last for more than a few seconds, but it seemed like an eternity. He did not say a word, but the look in his eyes told her all she needed to know: that he was devastated, that he didn't blame her, and that he wouldn't betray her.

The first officer asked her again, "So, you didn't know these people were hiding here?"

What should she say? What was to be gained if she said yes? This was a fait accompli. There was no opening for negotiation. She couldn't think of any argument that would change the officer's mind.

"No, I didn't," Emmy said.

She turned around, and she was sure she heard a rooster crow. Three times.

She retrieved her bicycle while Mr. and Mrs. Hirsch were shoved into the back of the truck.

"Let's go," she said to Liesbeth.

They biked away in a sprint, expecting to hear the truck behind them. When they reached the bus stop where Emmy had rested the day before, they were exhausted. No truck had followed them, but they were still jittery. Emmy plunked down on the wooden bench. Liesbeth leaned the bikes into each other so they wouldn't fall over and came to sit next to her. It was pleasantly cool. The gray clouds of the early morning were slowly dissipating.

"That was the worst moment of my life," Emmy said. "The look in Mr. Hirsch's eyes ... I don't think it will ever leave me. It ripped me apart."

"Thank God, he didn't say anything," Liesbeth said.

"Yes, that was a noble deed. I owe him for that. But it's so awful to think we were too late. If only Vader had made the decision last night ..."

"Don't say that. He knew he couldn't convince Moeder in front of us. At least this way, you had a chance. It was the blockade that set us back."

Liesbeth put her arm around her sister. Emmy sagged against her, deflated. "I failed them," she said, tears falling down her cheeks. "They're on their way to a concentration camp, and I know they are totally unfit for that."

They sat there for a while without speaking, because there was too much to say and none of it made sense yet. Emmy's mind flooded with questions that might take years to answer. Why had she assumed her parents would not have enough compassion, when she herself had also immediately resisted Mr. Hirsch's suggestion? How much had she let herself be influenced by a dislike of Mr. Hirsch? Didn't nobler souls take care of people regardless of like or dislike? The piercing questions didn't stop swirling through her mind.

"You know, Liesbeth, I heard a rooster crow. Did you hear it? Right after I said three times that I didn't know those people?"

She didn't wait for the answer, because she knew it had been the echo of her own conscience.

"Now I know how the Apostle Peter felt when he answered that he didn't know Jesus. But what could he say? It was sure death if he said yes. And it would have been the same for me. Or at least a concentration camp."

"I'm sure many people have been in that position and chose the same answer," Liesbeth said. "Don't be so hard on yourself. You've done a lot for that couple."

Emmy listened, but her mind told her she had failed.

"At least," she said, "Simon Peter had an advantage. Jesus gave him the name Peter, because he saw in him the rock he could build his church on. So Simon Peter had a way to get back on his feet and do what was expected of him. But I am no rock. And I really don't know what to do with my future. Translate French books? I hope I can do better than that to make up for this failure."

Liesbeth got up and untangled their bicycles.

"Let's go home and tell Vader and Moeder that they will not have company today."

"Yes, they will be relieved," Emmy said. "And actually, so am I."

But feeling relieved made her think of herself as even more of a failure.

CHAPTER THIRTY-NINE

Walter – September 1944

Walter found a kind middle-aged woman willing to take care of Ruth's children while Ruth visited her husband in the sanatorium. Her name was Mrs. Schellink, the wife of an army officer who'd been sent to a concentration camp, like all Dutch officers. Her daughters were married and lived elsewhere. She would be delighted to be with the children for two days and two nights, she said.

The children were not quite so delighted. Walter could hear the girls crying downstairs, and there were many knocks on his study's door. Usually, it was Bram.

"Dominee Vlaskamp, can I come in and read my book here?"

"Of course. But only if you're quiet, because I'm writing the sermon for Sunday."

"I'll be quiet. I promise."

Bram made himself comfortable in the chair reserved for visitors and spread out a book for second graders on his lap. He had grown in the two years since Walter had taken over the congregation from his father.

"Dominee Vlaskamp, can I ask you a question?"

"All right, one question."

"Is my mother going to bring my father back from that place?"

Walter screwed the top back on his fountain pen. The sermon could wait.

"Not yet, Bram."

"But when? Mama always says he will come back. And you said so too!"

Bram got up and wanted to sit on his lap. Walter lifted him and cradled him in his arms.

"Your father is very sick, Bram. He's not ready to come home yet. The doctors think it is better for him to be in the sanatorium."

"Why is that better than to be at home?"

"For many reasons. The sanatorium is like a hospital, with doctors and nurses who can help your father all day. And his lungs need pure air for him to breathe. In a sanatorium, they always leave the windows open, even all night long. Even in wintertime."

Walter resisted the temptation to reassure Bram. There was no known cure for tuberculosis. The best the medical profession had to offer was to bring the patient to a place with pure, dry air, such as existed on de Veluwe, a vast sandy area not too far from Ede. Even then, there was only a 50 percent chance of recovery. And it seemed clear from latest developments that Bram's father didn't belong in the 50-percent-survival category.

"I can't remember what Papa looks like," Bram whispered.

"That's why it's so nice to have a picture of him. Click! And the camera snapped a moment that nobody can take away from you. It will always be in your heart. Your father has a picture of you too. So, you will be in his heart. Forever."

"How long is forever?" Bram asked as he nestled his head in the crook of Walter's arm.

"Forever is a very, very long time, miles and miles long. To the end of the earth."

"To the end of the earth? I like that."

He climbed down from Walter's lap and settled back into his

chair with his book again spread on his lap. He seemed satisfied with the answers. Why give him more information than he asked for?

For the next hour, it was quiet in the study, except for Walter's fountain pen scratching over his pad of paper and Bram turning over the pages of his book.

He looked at the clock. It was time to get to the castle for supper.

Downstairs, Mrs. Schellink looked exhausted, just short of frantic. Her hair fell in peaks around her face from perspiration. The girls sat in their highchairs at the dining room table. They'd made a mess of their food. Lideke, not a baby anymore, had smeared applesauce all over the chair's tray. Emily didn't seem to behave any better. She loudly proclaimed she didn't like green beans and flipped them off her plate. When Walter stood in the doorway, they stopped their noises. He made a quick decision. He would stay and relieve poor, exhausted Mrs. Schellink.

"Could I share the meal with you all? Is there enough?" he asked.

Mrs. Schellink gave him a grateful look and went to the kitchen while he pulled up a chair. He looked sternly at the girls.

"I expect you both to behave. Finish your plates. You know that's what your mother asked you to do."

My God, I'm acting like a father!

The children turned very quiet. Afterward, Walter made a call to the castle to say he wasn't coming home that night, and neither would he be coming home the next night. He thanked Mrs. Schellink for her services and sent her home. She didn't object.

He didn't have any experience with taking care of children, but he remembered his father taking him and Carla for a long walk after supper. It would tire them out, and afterward they fell into bed. That's what he would do. He got everybody outside. They walked to the town's central square and back. Lideke could barely keep up. He had to carry her part of the way. Bram challenged Emily to hopscotch over the square tiles in the sidewalk. It all worked as planned. Walter had no trouble goading the girls upstairs and putting them to bed.

"Where will you sleep, Dominee?" Bram asked. "You didn't bring your pajamas, did you? I think you should sleep in my parents' room, and I can find you my father's pajamas. But only if you let me sleep with you."

Bram rushed upstairs. Walter hesitated. Sleeping in the bed of his hostess violated her privacy. And putting on another man's pajamas, the one who should be in bed with her, felt even more like trespassing. But he didn't have a better idea. Sleeping on the couch in the living room with the big window without curtains that looked out on the street? No!

Just as the sun went under, they both were in bed, and Walter read from *Gulliver's Travels* till Bram fell asleep. As for himself, sleep wouldn't come right away. He listened to the regular breathing of the little boy next to him. When sleep finally came, he drifted off into a field with daisies where little lambs and children darted around. At the end of the field stood a woman, looking at them and smiling. He couldn't tell who she was. The children ran to him. The daisies were as tall as the littlest girl. Only the top of her head with its mop of blond curls was visible as it bobbed among the flowers. He turned to look at the woman, but she had disappeared.

He woke up with a start and looked around. Bram was still there, breathing easily, his cheeks flushed from deep sleep. He tried to make sense of his dream. Who was that woman? Could it be Ruth? Or was it Bertha? Why did she leave? The dream stayed with him all through the next day. It didn't bring him closer to an answer, but his thinking was infused with a vague uncertainty.

Ruth returned after two days from the visit to her husband. She looked broken, but the children put a smile back on her face as they all wanted to talk at the same time, eager to tell her that Dominee Vlaskamp had sent Mrs. Schellink home and that he'd slept in Papa's pajamas in Papa's bed. Walter was uncomfortable with that revelation, but Ruth didn't react one way or the other. She had a very sick husband on her mind. She was grateful, she said, that things had worked out so well.

A few days later, it was Walter's turn to go on a trip. He needed to attend a meeting of area clergy about malnutrition. In every church, regardless of denomination, concerns grew about the chronic lack of food, which became especially evident in children. Poverty wasn't the cause. Many or most of the crops from Holland's rich soil could not reach the local markets, because the Nazis ordered them shipped to their own country. Something needed to be done, but it wasn't clear what or how. Intercepting the shipments would be one way, but the Bible was clear on that subject. "Thou shall not steal."

The meeting was to be held in a hotel. A church would have been a more logical place, but the choices were too numerous. A Catholic church, or a Remonstrant or a Netherlands Reformed church? Those were just a few of the possibilities. To avoid the appearance of dominance, neutral ground was decided upon. Being in a hotel also meant that deliberations could carry over into the next day.

Arnhem was just a short train trip from Ede. Bram wanted to bring him to the station. His mother wouldn't let him. She didn't like the idea of him walking home by himself. He pleaded vigorously. Walter solved the little crisis by telling Bram he could carry his overnight bag to the end of their street.

"This bag isn't very heavy, Dominee," Bram said. "Did you bring your pajamas?"

Walter laughed. "Yes, and my toothbrush. I'm only going for one night, Bram. I'll be back on Sunday morning before church."

That Sunday was the seventeenth of September 1944, but British Field Marshal Montgomery had another plan for that day. He'd named it Operation Market Garden. As the meeting broke up early on Sunday morning and the clergy prepared to return to their churches, the air filled with a buzzing sound. Walter's first thought was that it came from a swarm of bees outside the window, but it got very loud and turned into a steady drone that overwhelmed all other sound. Alarmed, the men rushed into the street. The sky looked as if a huge flock of starlings was about to descend on the city. Wherever they looked, they saw airplanes. The collective sound of their turning propellers was deafening. Then they saw men jump out of the planes—little specks that looked like candies shaken from a bag. Red-, green-, and cream-colored parachutes unfolded in the shape of magnum mushroom caps. Hundreds of soldiers—it could even be thousands—clung to the ropes. Walter could not see them hit ground. From the looks of it, they landed somewhere to the west and north of Arnhem.

The men of the cloth stood nailed to the pavement, staring at the sky as if the prophet Elijah had appeared to them. There was more awe than talk. This was the moment they had been waiting for these last four years, but they'd never thought their rescue would fall from the heavens. It was a miracle.

Anti-aircraft booms woke them up to the fact that war was dangerous. Instead of heading home—it was too late to get there in time—they headed for shelter.

"The bridges," a young minister sitting next to Walter said. "I bet that's what they're after."

"What makes you say that?" Walter asked.

"Just think of it. To make it to Berlin, they have to cross the Rijn River. But the Siegfried Defense Line is in the way. It runs from Basel in Switzerland along France, then all along Luxembourg, and then along our own country. It ends at the city of Kleve, and that's not far from here. If they can get over the Rijn in Arnhem, they're practically beyond the end of the Siegfried Line. They can walk into Germany."

"You're quite the strategist," Walter said. "I hope you're right. By the way, I forgot your name. There were so many to remember. Forgive me."

"My name is Theo Brouwer. And yours is Walter, right? But I

forgot your last name."

"I am Walter Vlaskamp."

"What do you think, Walter? Shall we go outside and see what's going on? My church isn't far from here. This shelter is small, and it will get smaller and smaller as time goes by."

Walter looked around. They sat crowded in the hotel's damp cellar, scrunched up against a rough brick wall, elbow to elbow. Getting out was tempting. The older clergy made them out for fools, but Theo was resolute and Walter followed. Once outside, they heard the sounds of war. *Boom!* And *rat-tat-tat*. It was not close by.

Walter was new to the city of Arnhem. All he knew about it was what he'd learned in school. Its most striking feature was its location on the Rijn. Second was the beauty of its parks and lovely homes that gave it a spa-like aura. The river was only a conduit for the traffic between the harbors on the North Sea and the industrial areas of Germany. Arnhem itself did not have significance as a harbor, but in times of peace, large barges traveled under its two bridges, each spanning 150 yards over the width of the Rijn River.

Theo Brouwer was tall and long-limbed, and his stride covered ground rapidly. Walter strained to keep up. The sky was clear. The parachutists had been dropped, and the planes had turned around to where they'd come from—England, no doubt. He felt a rush of excitement. There could be no battle without casualties, he knew, but the prospect of peace was stronger than the grip on his fears. He had no idea in which direction he was walking, but what did it matter? He would feel closer to God taking shelter in a church.

The city was holding its breath. Traffic was nonexistent, except for an occasional biker in a hurry. He saw not one German soldier. They'd been taken off guard, apparently. He took notice of the street names: Broerenstraat, Turfstraat.

Theo stopped in front of a small church on de Markt.

"Are we close to the river?" Walter asked.

"Somewhat," Theo said. "It is several streets over."

They heard cannon booms, but it still sounded far off. Theo opened the door to the house next to the church. A little girl came running down the narrow hall.

"Papa," she cried. "You came home!"

She flew into his arms, and Theo lifted her up.

"Here to stay," he said. He introduced Walter to his wife, who'd emerged from behind their daughter. She was pretty, with long blond hair done up in a roll, and her first name was Els.

"Did you know the Allies dropped parachutists around the city?" Theo asked her.

"Yes, I know. Our neighbor came over. Mijnheer Kant was so agitated that I took Stien outside to see what the excitement was all about. We saw airplanes that pulled gliders. Unbelievable! The most amazing thing I've ever seen. But I decided to go back inside and get the shelter ready, because I'm sure it won't stay this quiet for very long."

Smart woman, Walter thought.

They sat down for a meal of bread and strawberry jam and to get to know each other. Els asked which church Walter served, and showed genuine compassion about the sad prognosis for the minister he was replacing in Ede.

They also listened to the distribution radio to see if the Germans would say anything about paratroops being dropped around Arnhem. There was no news about Arnhem, but plenty about two other cities: Eindhoven and Nijmegen, both situated in a more or less straight line to the south of Arnhem. The Germans admitted that paratroops had landed around both. This was big news. Theo, the amateur strategist, predicted that the Allies were trying to squeeze the Germans away from the big rivers. If their strategy was to march northward from Belgium, they needed to cross three wide rivers: the Maas, Waal, and Rijn. The Maas was not far from Eindhoven. Nijmegen was on the Waal, and Arnhem was on the Rijn.

"Do you have a way to get news from the other side?" Walter

asked, without mentioning Radio Oranje in front of his daughter.

"We'll see what we can do." Theo gave Walter a wink.

But Els said, "We'd better get moving, Theo. Never mind trying to outguess the Allies. We have to think about how we'll get through the next days. We need more food. Other people may show up looking for shelter."

She reminded Walter of Bertha—always thinking ahead and not afraid of hard work. She had already brought a first aid kit to the church's cellar and all the blankets she could carry. Stien had brought towels and soap.

Walter asked if he could call the parsonage in Ede, and Els handed him the telephone. No dial tone.

"They must have cut the lines," Theo said.

They got busy putting canned food, matches, and candles in baskets. Theo and Walter carried them over to the church. Els and Stien followed with extra clothes. The sound of artillery fire had drawn closer, but was still far enough away to give them time to get their stuff inside the old Protestant church.

"We can save the sermons we made for today for next Sunday," Theo said.

"I doubt it," Walter said. "Whatever happens today will force us to strike a different chord next Sunday."

Theo nodded. He opened the door to a stairway with an iron-rod railing and uneven stone steps. It ended in the cellar.

Els had already lit a petroleum lamp. Its hissing sound echoed against the walls. Stien helped her mother turn the shelter into a homey place by placing blankets on the cots. Some old crates got shoved together to serve as a table. Theo strung an extra blanket in front of a corner with a washbasin and a chamber pot to create the illusion of privacy.

"Els," Walter said, "you didn't bring all this stuff down here after you saw the planes this morning, did you?"

"That's true, I didn't," she said. "Every night the bombers flew over our house on their way to Germany, I thought to myself, 'someday we could be their target.' So I prepared."

Stien overheard the conversation. "Are we going to be bombed, Mama?"

"*Nee liefje,*" Els said. "Those planes we saw today didn't hold bombs. They held soldiers to chase the Germans away."

Five minutes before eight o'clock, Theo got up and motioned Walter to follow him. When he opened the door to the sanctuary, the sound of artillery fire sounded much louder.

"They fought their way into the city," Theo said. He looked pleased. It verified his theory about the bridges.

He climbed up the curved stairs of the chancel, knelt down, and carefully removed a panel underneath the lectern that was part of the overall design. A radio came into view. He fiddled with the dial and winked at Walter.

"Let's see what Radio Oranje has to say about all of this."

The familiar voice opened with, "Here is an important message from the Dutch government. On account of a request received from Holland, and after consultation with the Supreme Command … the government is of the opinion that the moment has come to give instructions for a railroad strike in order to hinder enemy transport and troop concentrations."

They barely listened to the rest of the news. This announcement was obviously the go-ahead signal to the management of the railroad to tell its workforce to go on strike. Would the workers follow suit? The prospect was mind-boggling. Workers would put their lives on the line if they did. The Germans depended heavily on the Dutch railroad. Besides transporting stolen goods like brass for bullets, they'd used it to transport tens of thousands of Jews to concentration camps. The Nazis would put the workers under the gun to force them to go back to work, if they went into hiding and didn't show up. How patriotic would those workers turn out to be?

"This is drastic," Theo said. "It tells me that London thinks this fight will soon be over. Isn't it ironic," he added, "that the resolution at our clergy meeting amounted to sabotaging the trains to get food for the children?"

Theo couldn't resist opening the door to the street. The heavy sound of cannon booms in the distance had stopped. The world was in twilight. The *rat-tat-tat* of machine gun fire came from nearby. How far away was the river? Walter wondered.

A furtive movement caught their eye. Two soldiers, their machine guns held at the ready, were hugging the buildings on the Markt on the opposite side from the church. Their uniforms had a strange brown color, and their helmets were of a different design than what they were used to. These were definitely not German soldiers. Inch by inch, the soldiers made their way to the corner of the Markt. One of them waved his arm at two other soldiers, who materialized from a side street. They joined the first two and ran around the corner, out of sight. Walter looked at Theo and saw the expression of childish delight in his eyes.

"I can show them the way," he said, and got ready to sprint across the Markt. His body was taut with coiled energy. Walter grabbed his arm and held onto it. Theo resisted.

"Let go," he said.

"Let the Underground show them the way, Theo. You have other things to tend to."

The muscle in Theo's arm relaxed slowly, and Walter finally let go.

"I guess you're right," he said, and they walked back into the church.

They'd hardly made it back to the cellar door when one explosion after another made the church shiver in its foundations. With their bodies pressed flat against the oak cellar door, they watched as the tall window frames couldn't hold onto their glass under pressure from the sound waves that rushed randomly through the streets like an invisible monster. The blasts kept coming for at least ten minutes. When they suddenly stopped, the flagstone floor was littered with shards of glass.

"Good God," Theo said. "They must have hit the ammunition

depot down at the river."

There was no sense in trying to clean up the mess. Who knew what was yet to come?

That night and all of the next two days were spent in the cellar. Combat went on all around them. Machine-gun fire and an occasional *boom* or a grenade whistling through the air were loud enough to be heard through the brick walls.

Stien had sat curled up on her bed, shivering with her blanket wrapped around her, when the ammunition depot blew up, but after that she got used to the noise, more or less. They all did. They even managed to get some sleep. The fluorescent dial of an alarm clock told them whether it was night or day. Els periodically warmed up canned food on a small kerosene stove. She tried to maintain some form of decorum by insisting that they sit around the improvised table instead of lying on their beds, even if they ate from tin plates and other camping equipment she'd brought down. Walter caught on to her powerful effort to prevent slumping into fear or resignation or restlessness. He asked to say a prayer before each meal they shared.

It was hard to keep Theo down. His mind had been taken over by supposing what the strategic goals of the Allies might be. He paced the cellar floor, he watched the clock constantly, and he never sat down for more than five minutes.

"Were you the kind of boy that played with tin soldiers, Theo?" Walter asked at one point.

"How did you guess?" Els said with a hint of sarcasm in her voice.

"Yes, I was. My grandfather had a great collection. I dug a wide hole in his backyard and created armies and wars. They had to drag me inside to eat my dinners."

"I'm amazed you didn't apply to the Military Academy," Walter said.

"Actually, I had a harder time deciding between theology and history. I read every book about Alexander the Great, Julius Caesar, and Napoleon that I could get my hands on. I liked the idea of becoming a history teacher."

"How did theology win out?"

"Parental influence. My father was a minister. And compassion, I would like to think."

"How do you reconcile Jesus's message of peace with war games in your own personal faith?" Walter asked. He'd never met a man of the cloth so taken, if not obsessed, with the details of war.

"I don't believe in wars of aggression, like the one Hitler is waging," Theo said. "But I do believe it's justified to take up arms in defense."

"We could debate that for days," Walter said. "When is it right to take a life? What I have difficulty with is what these days is benignly called 'collateral damage.' Battles used to be fought in a field somewhere, between professional officers on horses with sabers, and hired footmen with bayonets. That was not even all that long ago. Now, whole villages and cities are demolished without regard for the civilians that live in them."

Theo sighed and ran a hand through his short blond curls. There was something childishly appealing about him, Walter thought. A man forever young and forever in conflict with himself, caught between the hobbies and interests of his youth and the seriousness of his adult life, during a time that had unleashed colossal threats against humanity that could not be fought with tin soldiers.

In the darkness of the cellar with the light from only one candle, they compared their own days with the times in which Jesus lived. The Roman imperial theology had clashed with the Jewish social world, as much as Hitler's National Socialism now clashed with Holland's culture of democracy. For ages, the prophets had railed against dominance, against elitism, against power in the hands of a few. But, as was demonstrated during the German Occupation, people reacted to domination in several ways. It could be with resignation—and even active collaboration—or it could be with violent rejection. In Jesus's day, the temple in Jerusalem had become a place for the powerful instead of a center of devotion and hope. Today, Den Haag's bureaucracy was saturated with turncoats. There were many parallels between those biblical times and the present.

"Of course," Walter said, "the Jewish people hoped for a divine intervention to get rid of Roman occupation. When I watched those paratroopers fall from the sky a few days ago, I wondered if we were watching just that: divine intervention!"

Theo chuckled. "And then we saw shards of glass fall in the sanctuary … and hoped that it meant the beginning of our own liberation."

"It is challenging, isn't it?" Walter said. "As ministers we preach nonviolence, like Jesus taught us. But I always hold on to the fact that Jesus scolded the high priests who collaborated with the Romans, and that he threw over the table of the tax collectors in the temple. He didn't mind calling a spade a spade. If only we could fight this war with spades instead of guns!"

"Spades would need a lot of sweat," Theo said. "And it would be ineffective. Knowing how to use guns—when and where to use them—takes skill and intelligence. A victorious general uses firepower wisely. It's more about outwitting than outgunning. The object is not to kill, but to conquer. Conquering sets people free."

Walter had no difficulty conjuring up a picture of Theo as a little boy in his grandfather's backyard, lining up his tin soldiers. Smart generals could do great things! It was charmingly innocent, and it seemed a foolproof way to fend off his innate aggressions and fears.

Radio Oranje could not be turned on because there was no electricity. It was anyone's guess what advances the Allies had managed to make. But on the morning of their third day of sitting in the cellar, with only an occasional trip upstairs by Theo to empty their smelly chamber pot, they were sure of only one thing: the battle for the bridges was still going on. The *rat-tat-tat* of the machine guns had never really stopped, and occasionally there were some fierce bursts of explosions that had to come from something bigger than a rifle.

Then, suddenly, they heard a terrific explosion that made them put their hands over their ears. Stien crawled back under her blanket. Another one, and another one followed. It sounded more like a bombardment than a gun battle between two sides. The terrifying sounds of crashing buildings seemed to come from overhead.

Theo got more than a little restless. He had been reading Stien a story, but since she'd pulled her blanket over her ears, he put the book down.

"Did you say collateral damage?" he said to Walter. "Homes around the Markt have been struck. I can hear it. They're my parishioners! I've got to go and help them."

"No, Theo!" Els cried. "Wait! You can tend to them later. It's too dangerous to go out now."

Theo had started up the stairs to the sanctuary, but he reluctantly turned back.

The explosions didn't stop for hours. The sounds of crumbling buildings above the ground were unnerving. Walter took out his pocket Bible and tried to read some of the Psalms, but his hands trembled, and his eyes wouldn't focus on the small print. Theo couldn't stand it any longer. His neighborhood was crumbling over his head, and he sat in the cellar. Ignoring his wife's entreaties and Walter's warnings, he went outside.

Later, eyewitnesses said that while Theo was attempting to help a man carry his injured wife out of a collapsing home, a German tank came around the bend, firing bullets aimlessly and continuously into the street, hoping to flush out Allied soldiers. Theo hadn't been the only victim.

Walter surveyed the smoldering ruins around the church. Curtains idly swung from broken windows. Crumbling ceilings hung inside collapsing walls. He heard cats howling.

Theo had said, "They're my parishioners! I've got to go and help them."

He took on the task Theo had set for himself and started the agonizing process of finding the wounded, burying the dead, and consoling the stunned human beings who'd been left behind in an unreal world of devastation.

Els, dazed and distraught, started to sweep up the shattered glass, but Walter urged her to take Stien and go to stay with a nearby relative.

For himself, he knew he wouldn't be returning to Ede for a while.

The memory of Theo explaining how he'd come to be a minister kept running through his mind. "… compassion, I would like to think." It kept him going.

CHAPTER FORTY

Anna – September–October 1944

"I've never seen Janus get excited in all the years he's been with us," the baroness said. "He maintains the same calm demeanor throughout. It's a wonderful quality to have for someone in his job. But today something happened that melted his professional coating."

Anna had just returned from a short walk with Frits. It was Sunday afternoon. The sun was bright, the air windless, perfect weather for a visit with the ponies. Their walks were kept to a bare minimum—maybe once a month—and very close to home, for fear of being seen by curious eyes.

"So what threw our unflappable Janus today?"

"He had good reason to be excited," Oma said. "Hendrik came by to say that paratroopers landed around Arnhem by the thousands."

"Seriously? Around Arnhem? By the thousands?"

"I never doubt the news Hendrik brings me."

"An end to the war? Dear God, do we dare hope?"

Anna danced around in a circle. Oma laughed.

"They landed to the west of Arnhem, in Heelsum and Oosterbeek. That is not that far from here."

That evening, the atmosphere around the dinner table was giddy with the prospect of an end to the war.

"There's only one drawback," the baroness said. "When peace comes, all of you will leave, and this place will be very quiet."

"I will stay, Oma," Frits said. "Maybe my parents can come and live with us."

He sat next to the baroness on his throne of pillows. She reached over and stroked his hair. "Of course, they can," she said.

Walter's chair remained disturbingly empty.

"I wonder if Walter made it to church this morning," Bertha said.

Anna decided to call the parsonage, but the telephone was dead, and Walter didn't come home that night.

Two days went by. No news from Walter.

On the third morning after the Allies were dropped, Anna was in the hallway when the doorbell rang. She opened the door and saw a young boy on the stoop. A woman, holding onto her bicycle, waited in the driveway.

"Is Dominee Vlaskamp home?" the boy asked.

"You must be Bram," Anna said.

"Is he home?" Bram asked again. His tone was urgent. He was on a mission.

"No, but come on in, and ask your mother to come in as well."

Janus appeared. Anna whispered to get Frits out of sight and warn the baroness she had company. She invited Mrs. Boskamp in. Her grandmother would want to see her, she said.

Bertha had taken Frits's place at the chessboard while he was dispatched to the kitchen. Mien and Janus never questioned why Frits had stayed long after he had recovered from whatever ailment had put him in the hospital. They didn't need to be told. They were discreet and loyal and followed their own common sense.

Bram was intimidated by the formality of the salon with its tall windows and heavy curtains, but he didn't let up on his inquiry about Walter. Nobody at the castle had heard from Dominee

Vlaskamp since he left. His lower lip trembled at the news, and he reached for his mother's hand.

Ruth told them about a parishioner, who was Ede's station chief. He'd come by to say that all railroad workers had gone on strike. Radio Oranje had asked for the strike, he'd told her, and 30,000 workers, minus a small number of cowards, were now going underground. He'd come to say good-bye before he became an onderduiker himself, and to ask Ruth and Dominee Vlaskamp to keep an eye on his wife and two children.

"Well, if that's the case," the baroness said, "we shouldn't be surprised that we haven't heard from Dominee Vlaskamp. He can't call us on the phone, and he can't take the train. So, Bram, I know you're worried, but you know what Dominee Vlaskamp would say, don't you? Have faith!"

"Ja, Mevrouw," Bram said. But the apprehensive look in his eyes betrayed the turmoil in his head. He had bonded with Walter just as Frits had bonded with Dirk.

Anna distracted Bram by taking him to the ballroom. He remembered seeing the ballet performance there and forgot about Walter for a moment, as he watched himself in the mirrors making silly faces.

It was time for Ruth and Bram to get back to Ede before the rain started.

"Mevrouw Bosma," the baroness said. "Please stop by again. I hope your husband will recover and return to his family soon."

Tears formed in her eyes. "Not likely," she said.

The baroness took Ruth's hand in both of hers. "If there's anything I can do, then please let me know. We will pray for your husband's recovery and for Walter's return."

"I add my prayers on both counts," Bertha said.

Ruth looked at the gathering clouds and told Bram to hurry up and get on the back of the bike. With his legs straddled over the luggage carrier, he waved at Anna with a shy smile on his face.

Anna didn't think that no news could be good news. Uncertainty about the fate of her parents — they lived in Arnhem, after all — and Walter snuck around her mind like a stealth robber, chipping away bits of her innate optimism; and it didn't help that the weather took a turn. After the bright weeks of September, constant rain soaked the earth and everything on it. She stood at the window of her office that looked out on the circular driveway and watched the rain flow down the glass in a sheet. It distorted everything that was outside, but something besides rain was moving out there. She focused. Two people on bicycles were approaching, soaking wet and slow going. Who would want to visit them in this pouring rain? As they came closer, she saw that they weren't strangers at all. They were her parents! She hurried to the hallway, opened the door, and pressed the doorbell so Janus would appear.

"Vader, Moeder," she cried out to them.

Moeder was barely able to get off her bike. Anna had to reach for it. Vader leaned his against the brick wall and stepped inside. A puddle of water formed around his shoes. He tossed off his raincoat and dropped it on the floor.

"This was a ride from hell," he said.

Moeder said nothing. She slowly set one foot in front of the other. Anna helped her out of the soaking wet raincoat and handed it to Janus.

"Francina," Oma exclaimed, joining them in the hall. "What happened to you?"

Her daughter didn't reply. Instead, she let herself be embraced and led to the sofa.

"The Moffen gave all the residents of Arnhem thirty-six hours to get out of the city," Vader said.

"Why, in God's name?" Oma said.

"We were not given a reason, just an order."

It was mind-bending. The place she'd grown up in, a proud city of 100,000 inhabitants, was being emptied out.

"What about your home? Is it still standing?" Oma asked.

"Yes, we're lucky in that regard," Vader said, "but many of the windows are blown out. Everywhere we set our feet, there was broken glass, and there wasn't plywood available to board them up. I taped the cracked windows. Then we just grabbed a few valuables and left."

"Maybe you can go back later," Anna said.

"Anyone who tries to reenter the city will be shot. That was the other part of their message."

Moeder sat like a bronze statue, staring into space, her hands folded in her lap. Her cotton blouse clung to her skin, front and back.

"You need a warm bath, my dears," Oma said.

Janus was summoned to draw a bath in one of the guest rooms on the first floor, and Oma went to find suitable clothing for both of them.

Bertha and Frits were in the library. They had made themselves scarce. Bertha, determined to homeschool Frits, was teaching him math.

"We have guests tonight," Anna said. "They came from Arnhem."

"Is it Dominee Vlaskamp?" Frits jumped up, all excited.

"Dominee Vlaskamp is not a guest here. He lives with us. These guests are my parents."

Calling her parents *guests* sounded weird. Her mother was born and raised in this place, for heaven's sake. Yet, calling them guests also reflected how she felt. Her parents had suddenly inserted themselves into the easy coexistence that had grown between herself, Oma, Walter, Frits, Bertha, and the loyal servants. The sweet side of the war was living with her grandmother—the bright side of the foreign coin.

They ambled over to the dining room. Oma and her parents had just entered, and she heard her mother ask, "Who sits on the chair with that pile of pillows?"

"You will find out in a moment, Francina," Oma answered.

Anna took Frits's hand and led him inside. She had all she could do not to laugh at the sight of her father in a tweed suit that was out of style by at least fifteen years and a size too large, and Moeder looked like a caricature of herself in Oma's dress, which hung around her frail body like a tent. But neither was in the mood to be made fun of, especially not by their daughter.

"Vader, Moeder, this is Frits," she said, pushing him forward.

With eyes cast downward, Frits just stood there. Their inquisitive looks as he'd entered the room had not escaped him.

"And this is Sylvia van Tongeren," Oma said, pointing at Bertha. "Like Frits, she is staying with us for a while. Now let's all sit down." Her tone cut off all probing.

Janus carried in a large soup tureen and placed it on the sideboard. He proudly told them that today's soup was made from mushrooms he'd found in the woods on his way to work early in the morning.

"I hope you know your mushrooms, Janus," Moeder said. She wasn't joking.

"Ja, Mevrouw, I've picked mushrooms since I was a boy. My father taught me. These are called cantharellen. They are sweet and very tasty."

"Thank you, Janus," Vader said. "That sounds delicious, and we haven't eaten anything warm in days."

The stories about the battle came out bit by bit. The picture that emerged was not complete—history would have to fill in the missing pieces. But the stories Vader told about initial surprise, hope, and then senseless destruction. The objective of the Allies had clearly been to capture the bridge. When the Allies couldn't hold onto it but refused to surrender, the German commander gave the order to lay the city to ruins.

"What good did that do?" Anna said.

"It clearly was their revenge for having been taken off guard," Vader said. "So, now the Allies lost their best chance to get into Germany. Holland lost one of its most beautiful cities, leave alone rendering thousands of people homeless, and the Nazis will have to live with that unsavory legacy."

It was awful news. The rest of the meal was taken in silence while each of them digested the defeat and the senseless destruction.

The next morning, Anna woke up with a heavy feeling. The day loomed large. Her parents' arrival threatened to throw off the established rhythm of daily life at the castle. Oma had allowed her a very loose rein in administering the affairs of the estate. She'd done a pretty good job, she thought. Now her father was here, a banker by profession. Did it make sense for her to continue?

Frits stirred in the bed next to hers. He felt safe in her room, because a secret door in the large walk-in closet led to a hiding place, big enough for his slender body to stand up in or sit down. He could close it from within, making it look like a wall instead of a door. There were several designated places on the ground floor he could rush to as well.

"Anna, are you awake?"

"Yes, I am. What's on your mind?"

"When are we going to see Dirk again?"

"Oh, how I wish I knew!"

His out-of-the-blue remark caught her off guard, and tears welled up in her eyes. It was all she could not to start crying. She had desperately tried to hide how she pined for Dirk, pushing memories of being with him in Utrecht to the outer reaches of her mind. Frits was quick to pick up on her reaction, though. He couldn't be fooled.

"You miss him too," he said. "Almost as much as I do."

This made her laugh. "Shall we have a contest of who loves Dirk the most?"

"You didn't answer my question, Anna," Frits reminded her.

"True. The trouble is," she said, "we cannot call Dirk because the telephone doesn't work. We cannot write him a letter because the mailbags move on trains, and the trains don't run anymore. So, we have to wait till the war is over."

"But he could take a bike, couldn't he?"

"Maybe yes, maybe no. I'm sure if he could, he would."

"I hate the war," Frits said.

"It will soon be over," Anna said. But in her heart, she wondered what it foretold that the Allies hadn't been able to hang on to that crucial bridge over the Rijn.

She found Oma at the breakfast table with her father.

"How was your night after that wet bike ride?" She planted a kiss on his unshaven cheek.

"Well enough to enjoy sharing a cup of *real* tea with your grandmother."

The dark circles under his eyes proved he hadn't slept well at all. Always a gentleman, he got up to help seat her. Oma lifted the tea cozy and poured her a cup of the real tea. Taking the first sip, she swore she never again would take tea for granted.

The different configuration of people at the breakfast table threw her off-kilter. She couldn't remember a time she'd been alone with just Oma and Vader. Moeder had always been the fourth person, and that meant the conversation got steered in ways that kept Moeder in mind. The unsaid rule was: don't upset her. Vader knew about the hiding of Jews and what roles Oma and Anna played in that, but they'd agreed it was best not to tell Moeder. Sitting here at the breakfast table with Oma and Vader felt conspiratorial.

"Oma tells me she is keeping Frits and Sylvia out of the hands of the Gestapo," her father said, "and that you do a good job of keeping the estate on an even keel. I am proud of you, Anna."

"Thank you, Vader. I never dreamed I would follow in your footsteps, but I still prefer medicine over finance."

Janus brought in a tray with food. The slices of bread in the silver basket were of an unappetizing gray, but the boiled eggs in their small porcelain cups were still as white as the linen tablecloth. Mien had made jelly from apples in the orchard. It lacked sweetness for a lack of sugar, which was scarce. Her challenge to provide tasty meals was getting harder by the day. The necessary ingredients just weren't there. Even living among farms, butter had to be replaced with bland margarine. Meat had become an unheard-of luxury. The farmers who raised cattle and pigs were under intense scrutiny from inspectors, who were all Nazi loyalists. They checked if the farmers cheated on their quotas, and if they found one pig more than the farmers were allowed, they took it for themselves.

"Did you bring your food stamps with you, Karel?" Oma asked.

"Yes, and we brought our IDs, but little else. Maybe I can chop wood to earn our room and board." It was meant as a joke, but it held a bitter truth. He now was a refugee, and his bank building lay in ruins by the side of the river. It was not a cheerful thought on this rainy morning, but Oma was undaunted by mere facts.

"Think of it this way, Karel," she said. "You still have a house, even with its windows blown out. You know your bank will be rebuilt, and you're not on a Gestapo's hit list. Plus, the war will end sooner or later. Have faith."

"You're right," her father said. "I wish Francina shared your outlook on life. Ever since we heard that Maarten was in a Japanese concentration camp, she has been in a morose mood. These latest developments don't help."

Rain pounded against the dining room windows. It hadn't stopped raining in more than two days. The trunks of the oak trees had turned a somber black. It was gray and dark outside, and the light inside wasn't much brighter. Several bulbs in the crystal chandelier over the table had been removed to save on electricity. It cast a gloomy pall over the table. Anna felt enveloped by it. She hadn't thought much about Maarten lately. Her memory of him was static, frozen in time. He would forever be the handsome, single-minded young man she'd seen off in Rotterdam, as he waved back from the big ocean liner that took him to the Dutch East Indies. Events here had overtaken worries about him. Her mind had been on people that were near her and in danger, and that she felt responsible for. For her mother, though, not directly engaged in the horrors of the war until now, Maarten's fate had become her focal point. Anna could understand her mother's funk, yet she didn't feel empathy. If Oma could be positive, cheerful even, while she put her life on the line for the good of others—for people she hadn't even known before the war—then why couldn't Moeder rise above her own anxiety?

Vader got up to check on his wife. When he opened the door, he stopped and turned around.

"Could it be that I hear someone playing the piano?"

"Yes," Oma said. "We have a concert pianist under our roof."

It was a welcome sound on a rainy day to hear Frits practice. Anna pictured his delicate fingers running over the ivory and ebony keys like a white mouse over a polished floor. He could be counted on to practice every morning before breakfast.

"Can this pianist do more than running scales?"

"Yes, he can," Oma said. "He'll give a concert this afternoon."

Vader looked mystified, but he had other things on his mind, and started up the wide staircase.

There would not be a concert. In the middle of the afternoon, Anna was on her way out the door to do some errands, when a sound that was hard to pinpoint stopped her. It was still raining some, but what she heard was not rainfall. There was nothing to see, but the sound came from the lane that led to the circular driveway. It was soft and nonthreatening, yet persistent and coming closer. Her curiosity was aroused. There was a stirring at the gate. It moved forward like a coiled ribbon that slowly unwound itself. The sound she'd heard was from shuffling feet; feet that belonged to a motley group of people, it turned out. They seemed to move as if in a trance. Some pushed baby carriages filled with things. Most carried backpacks and suitcases and small children. Without exception, they were soaking wet.

Hot tears ran down Anna's cheeks. She understood. She knew. These people had walked from Arnhem, and at the head of the slow-moving procession was Dominee Vlaskamp.

Anna ran over to him. "Walter," was all she could get out.

He stopped. His blue eyes were as alive as ever, standing out like lit candles in a dark, tired face that looked ten years older than on the day he'd left for Arnhem. His shoulders were hunched under his wet raincoat, weighted by misery.

"I didn't know where else to take these people, Anna."

The procession stopped in eerie silence. The people were too tired, too wet, too beaten-up to talk. Walter spoke for them.

"We need shelter."

"The stables," Anna said, seeing how many there were of them, at least fifty or sixty, she thought.

"I also thought of the stables, but please go inside and ask your grandmother first. We've sprung too many surprises on her."

She ran inside. Oma was at her usual place by the salon window. Bertha and Frits were absorbed in their game of chess.

"Quick," she said, "Oma, put on your raincoat. It's urgent. Frits, you stay here with Sylvia."

Oma looked surprised, but she put her book down and got up. In the hall, she fetched her raincoat and a walking stick. Through the open front door, she noticed Walter standing in the yard. A smile started over her face.

"Walter! You came back safely."

She stepped out the door, and to Anna's immense surprise, embraced him. When she let go of him, she took in the row of desolate people in her yard. She didn't need to be told where they'd come from.

"Oh, God, these people are in poor shape. They need help."

"The stables," Anna said. "Let's bring them to the stables."

"Yes, that's a good idea. There are too many of them to take them into my home."

She walked over to the row of refugees. Their eyes, set in sallow faces, followed her from under their wet caps and kerchiefs. She took the hands of the woman at the head of the line.

"We will take care of you," she said.

The woman nodded. She had no words left after walking for hours in the rain.

"No time to waste," the baroness said. "Anna, go to Hendrik and ask him to come over. And Walter, do you know how to get into the stables? We cannot let these people stand in the rain any longer."

"I know how to get in through the back door."

The baroness walked back into the castle. Anna grabbed her bike and sprinted off. Walter gave a sign to the people behind him to follow. The column started to move forward like a caterpillar, many feet, step by step.

Anna turned into Hendrik's yard out of breath. It being late September, the cows were still in the meadow, and she saw him walking toward the farmhouse with a pail. He had just milked them.

"Hendrik," she called out. "Oma wants you to come to the stables right away."

"Hello, Miss Anna. What's going on? Not a fire, I hope?"

"A whole lot of people walked over here from Arnhem. They are refugees with nowhere to go."

Hendrik brought the pail with milk inside. One of the things Anna liked about Hendrik was that he never got overly excited. He came back out and stood still, thinking.

"So, if I get this right, all those people are going to be put up in the stables?"

"That's the idea."

"Let me hitch up my horse. I'll bring over a load of straw. They'll need something to sleep on. At least straw is something I've enough of."

Anna jumped back on her bike. When she got back to the castle, only a few people were still standing outside the stables waiting to get in. It had stopped raining hard, thank God. She debated whether to go into the stables or into the castle. She decided on the latter. Bertha, Frits, and her parents were with Oma in the salon.

They didn't hear her come in.

"This is ridiculous," she heard her mother say.

Oma pointedly ignored the remark. "We will make this work," she said. "Sylvia, you are a nurse. Would you mind going over to see if any of these people are in need of medical care? Let me know if there are things they need."

Bertha, who'd gotten used to her new name, got up and made for the door.

"Karel," Oma said, "you're uniquely qualified to help these people find their way out of their predicament. See if they have IDs so we can register them for food stamps locally."

"I'll be happy to," Vader said.

"Hendrik is coming over with a load of straw, Oma."

"Splendid. I put you in charge of getting these poor people something to eat, Anna. That's no small task, I know, but you are now a capable young woman."

"I'll do my best."

"What can *I* do?" Frits said. "I want to go over there too, Oma. I want to help."

"He calls you Oma?" Moeder said.

"Of course. Why not?" Anna said. "We all do."

"Frits," Oma said, "I know you want to go over there, but you know the rules, don't you?"

"Yes, I do." Frits sighed.

"You come with me, Frits," Anna said. "I know of a way you can help."

She took him to the kitchen. The large woodstove threw off enveloping warmth, and a steady plume of steam rose from a copper kettle. The table was loaded with fresh vegetables from Mien's garden patch, which she tended with skills nobody had known she had. She wouldn't let anyone come close to it, except for Hendrik, who'd dropped off a load of cow manure in the spring.

With her apron on, a knife in her right hand, and freshly chopped onions on the chopping board, Mien was watching the yard from the kitchen window.

"Miss Anna, can you tell me what's going on out there?"

"Yes, Mien. Dominee Vlaskamp brought these people from Arnhem. They were told by the Germans to get out of town. They had no place to go, so he took some over here."

"But what are we going to do with that many people?"

"For the time being, we'll put them up in the stables. Hendrik is bringing a load of straw for them to bed down on. And we will have to find a way to feed them."

"Feed them?" Mien looked incredulous.

Feeding people was her territory, and the prospect of providing food for the crowd she'd watched coming into the yard terrified her. She put the chopping knife down and put her hands on her hips, as if to say, "Are you crazy?" But being the devout Christian she was, she thought of something, and a mischievous smile spread over her round face.

"Miss Anna, all I need is a few small fishes and seven loaves."

Anna laughed. "You'll have them, Mien. Except, we have more potatoes than bread. If the disciples had given Jesus potatoes instead of bread, I bet he would have fed the multitudes with those just as well, don't you think? Frits and I can start peeling them. Do we have some salt pork to throw in with them? Do we have a pot big enough to boil them in?"

They got to work. Janus went to the root cellar and came back with a sack of potatoes. Anna taught Frits how to peel a potato, and Mien went scouring for pans that would fit on her stove. She came up with very large copper pots she said she hadn't used since before the baron died, when they'd had big parties at the castle.

Anna warned Frits that he should be careful not to cut himself, but Frits didn't hear her. He sat on a kitchen stool with a basket in his lap, creating very fine curls of potato skin. Mien watched him and said if he was going to be that fussy, the people wouldn't get to eat till tomorrow night, and the peelings were going to be fed to Hendrik's pigs anyway, and those animals weren't fussy. But Frits did what he did best with his fingers. He treated the potatoes like the ivory keyboard: with a delicate touch. Anna told Janus that if Frits could learn how to peel potatoes, so could he.

By six o'clock, they had a meal of mashed potatoes mixed with kale and pieces of salt pork. Anna got permission from Oma to bring over plates and forks — whatever they needed — to the stables, so the food could be eaten.

The rain had let up. Logs and sticks had been stacked on a bed of straw on the bricks of the courtyard in front of the stables. Hendrik directed some of the refugees on how to set up racks that were normally used for horse blankets at a safe distance from the pile. As Anna came out with Mien and Janus, all three carrying stacks of plates, he took out a match and lit the straw. A tall flame flared to the top of the woodpile and then died back down to the bottom, but its brief life caught the attention of the people inside. Some, especially the younger ones, came out and made a circle around what soon would become a controlled bonfire. The older ones came out with the wet coats and hung them over the racks.

Inside, instead of the somber silence she remembered from the days she'd brought food to the American pilot, Anna was greeted by a buzz of voices. Vader sat behind a table taking down names, asking people for their IDs and other particulars. Bertha had improvised a clipboard on which she wrote down the supplies she would need to treat people who had suffered injuries or had a chronic disease, like diabetes. Walter was in the role of social worker, trying to find out if these refugees had relatives somewhere nearby who might temporarily house them. Hendrik, having delegated tending the fire to a competent-looking young man, created a makeshift privy.

Anna walked down the aisle with box stalls. They had sliding doors. Most were left open. Vader had told her there were fifty-four people in total, not counting young children. She watched them getting organized with the few belongings they still owned. It would be cruel to ask questions about the battle they'd witnessed.

They were too depleted to elaborate on any of it. They ate, they helped clean the dishes, they made sure the fire went out, and they went to sleep on the straw.

But at the castle, everyone was wide awake. The realization that they had started a refugee camp began to sink in. They needed food and blankets and medicine and money.

"This is ridiculous," Moeder said again, and it grated on Anna's nerves.

"Would you have left these people standing in the rain?" she asked.

"I wouldn't have brought them here in the first place," Moeder said. "Who is this Dominee Vlaskamp?"

Mercifully, Walter was talking with Bertha and not listening. Oma didn't waste a minute to put her daughter in her place, and it saved Anna from making a snide remark.

"Walter Vlaskamp is my guest, and I hold him in high regard. You may not like it, Francina, but he is the one who steered young people like your daughter toward standing up against the Nazis and defending our democracy. I praise him for that."

Moeder sighed. Either she didn't have the stamina to object, or she knew she would never win an argument with her mother.

Vader tactfully opened a conversation about what needed to be done. Walter and Bertha fell in with his ideas. The next day, they would go to the local churches and ask for help, maybe even the mayor, though he was a known Nazi sympathizer. Then they sent Walter to bed. He promised to be up early in the morning to help get things done.

The one who showed up early in the morning, though, was the commandant. When Janus answered the doorbell, Herr von Schloss stood before him in full uniform and demanded to see the baroness. Janus brought him to the dining room, where she was having breakfast with Anna.

"Herr von Schloss, I was afraid you might be engaged in battle."

He had come to warn her. Many refugees had made their way

to the castle, he knew, and he had to check if there were any Allied soldiers among them.

"My goodness," the baroness said, "I don't think so. It's my understanding that these are homeless Dutch citizens, who did not exactly fight their way out of the city."

The commandant ignored the innuendo in her remark. "It is my duty to search for Allied soldiers in retreat who may be trying to hide among the refugees. I give you the courtesy of advance notice."

"I thank you for that," she said, and looked him directly in the eye. "I will make sure I heed your warning."

The commandant took her hand and placed a kiss on it.

"It didn't surprise me, gnädige Frau, when I was told you were hosting refugees. You are a noble woman. Please be advised that my soldiers are surrounding your home as we speak."

"Thank you," the baroness said. "I will be quick to act on it."

Janus had already warned Frits, who had been on his way from the bedroom to the piano in the ballroom for his early morning exercises. Anna rushed upstairs and put him in the closet with the double door. When she returned, Oma had retaken her seat at the breakfast table.

Vader and Sylvia joined them for breakfast, but Oma wanted them to go to the stables and warn the people there would be a search, because the Germans thought retreating Allied soldiers might have mingled with them.

"Does it ever stop?" Vader said, but he got up after he'd just sat down and held the door open for Sylvia.

Oma and Anna were left alone in the dining room. It offered a golden opportunity to ask a question that had been on Anna's mind for a long time, but especially after her parents had unexpectedly shown up. She seized the moment.

"Oma, I have a question for you. How is it possible that you, who are so positive in your outlook on life, have a daughter who is so negative? I have a hard time understanding her, and it's always been that way."

The baroness didn't seem surprised at this outburst. Comfortably seated in her chair at the head of the table, she took her time to organize her thoughts while twisting her diamond ring, which came alive with the reflected lights of the overhead lamp. Anna thought that women with a diamond ring on their hand liked to twist it while they thought out something difficult.

"Your mother," she said, "was the survivor of a set of twins. Even though she and her sister looked alike, they were very different in character. Theresa came into the world first and weighed almost a pound more than Francina. It foreshadowed how they would grow up. Theresa was the bold one. She dominated your mother. Everything she touched turned to gold. They were very close throughout their early years. But, of course, there was also a lot of sibling rivalry going on. "

Anna was stunned. She'd never heard about a sibling of her mother, let alone a twin.

"When Theresa drowned in an unfortunate accident, your mother was devastated, as we all were. She was eleven years old. It shaped her life. She became hard to live with in her teen years. Rebellious. She turned against her father, her title, against the life she'd led as a child. Looking back, it explains why she looked for a husband with the most common name she could find: Smits. Your father crossed her path at an early age, and that was a very lucky thing. He helped her reconcile, to some extent, her past and present."

Anna's mind was doing somersaults. If Moeder had been rebellious against her status, then why did she dissect people's backgrounds at first meetings, as if the most important thing about a person was the color of their blood or their social status? It made no sense.

"You, Anna, can pursue an academic education. God willing, and after this war comes to an end, you will be a doctor with a status in life that's not connected to inherited title or gender.

Although no human being is ever totally free, it will open ways for you to feel independent. Your mother grew up in a time when a woman had to be extremely forward thinking and persistent against prejudice to go to university or to pursue any other unconventional course in life."

This was earthshaking news. It dawned on Anna that in spite of rebellion as a teenager, Moeder had hung onto her blue blood as a platform from which to tackle her lack of self-confidence. Some things fell into place. Was it possible that her often tense relations with Moeder had been set up, in part, by the domination of a twin sister who could do everything better?

"I always hoped," Oma said, "that your mother would turn her loss into something positive, like a career of some sort."

"Is that why you encouraged me to become a doctor, even against Moeder's wishes?"

Oma twisted the diamond ring back and forth on her finger and kept quiet for a moment.

"Yes," she finally said. "I was afraid the same thing might happen to you that happened to Francina, but in a different way, of course. You had a much older brother, and he could have easily dominated you. That did not happen. Sometimes, we worry about things that might happen but never do. You were the wiser one. Maarten, I'm afraid, has to learn the hard way. Hunting tigers on Java is not a profession."

Oma's insights were like a candle in a blacked-out room. Its light lifted the darkness of misunderstanding. Anna had never felt closer to her.

Janus came in to announce that an officer was at the front door demanding to search the inside of the castle. This was a surprise. Oma had hoped they would just search the barn. They got up in a hurry. Oma went to talk to the officer, and Anna raced up the stairs to talk to Frits through the secret door of his hiding place.

"Can I come out now?" he asked.

"Not yet. Don't move. I will tell you as soon as it's over. Try not to worry. Everything will turn out all right. I'll stay here in the room."

It didn't take long for the soldiers to find the way upstairs. They didn't knock on doors. They opened them. Anna could hear the commotion down the hall where Walter's bedroom was. Later, he said he thought he was in a nightmare, when a soldier shook him awake and asked for his ID. The next upset came when the soldiers rammed the door of her parents' bedroom. Moeder screamed. She was probably still in her nightgown. The scream took Anna back to the time Klaas had been taken away. The memory was unsettling, but she tried to steel herself for the search in her own room. Thank God she'd never needed a fake ID. She steadied her fears with the rational thought that if they were looking for Allied soldiers, they wouldn't be interested in women.

Instead of waiting for her door to be opened, she opened it herself and looked down the hallway. Two soldiers walked toward her.

"Kennkarte," the older looking of the two shouted.

She was prepared and handed him the ever-important ID. The other soldier poked his gun under the bed.

"There are two beds here. Who sleeps in the other bed?"

"A friend of mine," she lied. "She's helping me out with the refugees."

The older one opened the closet, poked the butt of his gun among her dresses. Having turned up nothing, he signaled to his mate to move on.

Of course, they didn't find an Allied soldier. Their steel-heeled boots clicked down the staircase. Down below her window, five soldiers poked the forsythia bushes that lined the terrace. Finally, they were hailed by an officer, and moved toward an army vehicle parked in the yard. They left empty-handed.

Janus appeared to say the decks were clear.

When Frits came out of the closet, his face had taken on the color of skim milk and his eyelids fluttered against the room's bright light. He threw himself in her arms, shivering. His nerves were taut, and so were hers. Where was Dirk? She needed him more than ever. He had a way of putting matters in perspective in his calm, deliberate tone.

"It's over," she said. "They're gone and they won't come back."

Frits didn't react, and she waited till she could feel the muscles in his arms around her relax a bit. It gave her a moment to reflect on how, when he'd first arrived, caring for him had felt like an awesome responsibility. Now, she couldn't imagine her life without Frits. He'd stolen her heart with his gentle nature and his ability to connect to people, once he trusted them. Whatever had happened to him in the past, he somehow knew how to separate it from the present. Who had taught him? Had he taught himself? At what cost? She could only guess. Often, she wondered what his parents were like, what had happened to them, and how they would fit back together as a family after such a long separation.

Walter told her once that the hardest time might still be ahead for Frits, adjusting to life after the war, whatever that would translate into. He'd compared it to a small robin that falls out of the nest and is picked up by human hands, and then is not accepted back. Anna couldn't imagine how Frits's mother would not take him back or love him again as she had before. She'd loved him so much, she'd given him away to a stranger in the face of deportation. But four years was a long time to be separated, and God only knew what horrors might have happened to her in those years. Anna fended off thoughts of having to let go of him. It was unthinkable, so better not think about it.

After breakfast, Vader took his bicycle and went to town to get help. He returned triumphantly after meeting with the *burgemeester*, the one who was a Nazi sympathizer. He had appealed to the man's humanity by reminding him that these poor people had done nothing to deserve their refugee status. They were victims and, above all, they were his compatriots. His reasoning had swayed the nonpatriot. Vader said that maybe the man worried about what might happen to him after the liberation, when Ede's citizens might hold him accountable. He promised that prepared food from the town's soup kitchen would be made available for as long as it was necessary, with the understanding that every effort would be made to find a more permanent solution for the refugess.

After days of steady rain, the sky turned the color of cornflowers, and a refreshing breeze shook off a myriad of raindrops from the dripping trees all around. Anna walked over to the stables, avoiding puddles that were gradually draining away. Vader sat behind a crude table in the courtyard, taking notes as people stood in line to be interviewed. He seemed completely comfortable in his role as clerk. Maybe the process wasn't all that different from interviewing clients who wanted to get a loan from his bank in Arnhem.

She looked for Walter and Bertha. The people in and around the stables appeared exhausted. Sleeping on straw, even with a generous layer of it on the brick floors, had not provided much relief after days in crowded shelters and walking many miles in the rain.

A woman with a red bandana covering her graying hair looked over at her and said, "Good morning, or maybe it is already afternoon. I'm losing track of the time of day. Are these stables yours?"

"They belong to my grandmother."

"Thank the lady for helping us out. Do you know the man who brought us here?"

"Dominee Vlaskamp? Yes, I know him well."

"Oh, I didn't know he was a man of the cloth, but he sure knocked himself out for us. He was right there in the rubble with us, pulling us out and getting us organized. He's someone special!"

"Yes, he is." Anna said. "I will tell him you said so."

She moved on. People were more talkative than the evening before. They asked if she had news about how the war was going, but she had none to give them, except that the railroad workers had gone on strike.

When she couldn't find Walter and Bertha in the stables, she tried the tack room, but as soon as she opened the door, she knew she was intruding. What should she do? Back out quietly? Bertha stood with her arms around Walter, as if he needed consolation. It wouldn't be surprising if he did. The last ten days must have been like a hell. Yet, there was more to the picture in front of her than that. It hadn't escaped her that when Walter had found Bertha in the salon of the castle, back when Dirk had brought her, he'd been absolutely stunned. Was there something between them that was more than a childhood friendship? And what would be wrong with that?

She quietly retreated, but she paused for a moment after she closed the door softly. Seeing them in a tender embrace heightened her yearning for Dirk, and she cringed at the prospect of a delayed liberation. How long was this damn war going to last? It had been so long since she had felt his embrace, smelled his sweat, felt the rub of his beard on her cheeks. Being separated was one thing, but to not hear from him — not over the phone and not through the mail — was quite another. Was he still working in the lab in Utrecht? Was that still enough of an excuse not to be forced to work in Germany? It was this nagging uncertainty that drove her to despondency sometimes. Maybe it was a blessing in disguise to suddenly be in charge of a refugee camp. There was enough to occupy her mind with, to keep her from dwelling on not seeing or hearing from Dirk. Or was it? Seeing Bertha and Walter in an embrace planted the seed in her mind to take her bike and get over to Utrecht. Someday …

Walter left for Ede to get back to his church duties and see if he could rouse his congregants to donate or lend blankets. He planned to beseech other ministers to help the refugees in any way they could.

By midafternoon, he was back. Dominee Boskamp was terminal, he told them. He wanted to accompany Ruth for a last visit, but he needed somebody to take care of the children in a hurry, and he hadn't found anyone yet.

Bertha volunteered, even though it was risky for her to leave the protection of the castle. She brushed off any concerns, packed a bag, and got her bike.

As Anna saw Walter and Bertha disappear around the bend of the circular driveway, she wondered if this was the start of a new phase for them. Time would tell. Time would have to solve many riddles and uncertainties for many people.

CHAPTER FORTY-ONE

Carla – October 1944

It was early October 1944. The leaves had fallen from the trees. The trains had stopped running. There was hardly any gas left to run trucks, and coal was hard to come by. Carla couldn't help thinking that the last four years had merely been a tame run-up to what was beginning to look like an unmitigated disaster. The pain of war increased day by day. What had brought it on was the railroad strike. It had infuriated Reichskommissar Arthur Seyss-Inquart. To get the trains moving again, he told the newspaper editors to immediately publish his dire warning that "the strikers will bring terrible disaster to their families and compatriots." But the editors didn't oblige. They knew the Dutch people were solidly behind the strikers.

In a rage, Seyss-Inquart ordered the presses of one of the papers, *de Haagsche Courant,* to be blown up. That was only the beginning of his revenge. Bicycles, cars, and the entire stocks of wholesalers were confiscated. The worst consequence of his revenge was a new ordnung, an embargo on all inland shipping. Barges were no longer allowed on the extensive network of rivers, canals, and the inland sea, het IJsselmeer.

Transportation came to a standstill.

It would mean famine.

Carla had taken over the task of standing in line for food coupons and provisions after she came home from Utrecht. It was a full-time job. Standing in the rain by the hour—it was the wettest autumn since 1864, so the paper said—she saw mold appear on her shoes, and she expected mushrooms to sprout any time now on her soaked raincoat that never dried out completely.

But, like much in life, there was a bright side to it. A professor in psychology couldn't have taught her what she learned from watching and talking with the people she shared the ordeal with. It helped her pass the time to guess how long it would take before someone "lost it." Men were more impatient than women, she observed. Women, after all, knew how to endure childbirth and to be subservient to their husbands. They knew a thing or two about resignation. There were exceptions, of course. Some women used their sharp elbows and tart tongues to their advantage. On one of those dreary days, an older woman standing behind Anna got vehemently angry with a younger one, who had wiggled ahead a few places in a long line at the bakery. She tried to put the girl back in her place, with words. A man tried to intervene, with his hands. A shuffle resulted.

The girl gave the man a piece of her mind. "I am pregnant," she shouted.

"Prove it," the man retorted. "How long have you been pregnant? An hour or so?"

A gasp went up among the waiting customers.

"None of your business," the girl screamed, and he screamed back that she was a liar.

A patrolling policeman separated the troublemakers and sent them to the back of the line, where they were told to make peace. If not bread, people took home the lesson that it paid to wait your turn.

Getting food was a hassle, but bringing it up to Jacob and Esther was a ritual Carla looked forward to every day. The snippets of news she could bring along were as important as the food. Jacob had asked if she had a spare atlas. With the precision of a cartographer, he marked the Allies' advances and red-penciled the dates of their major victories since the Normandy landing. Esther wasn't interested in those details. She waited for the end to the war in a resigned kind of way. The fiasco of *Dolle Dinsdag* — that day when the whole country thought Breda had been liberated, because Radio Oranje said so — had cut the ropes to her balloon of hope, and it had soared away, right through the closed window in the roof.

"I am bringing you one potato, two apples, a piece of cheese, and two slices of bread," Carla said one day as Jacob opened the door to their hiding place under the eaves. It was damp inside, and the window had fogged up. The small kerosene stove didn't have the capacity to dry out the place. Esther was lounging on the bed with an unopened book in her hands.

"I heard rumblings again, Carla," Jacob said. "It sounds like artillery fire. Did you hear it?"

She put down her basket. "You're right. It's artillery fire, and they say it comes from Baarle-Nassau. Can you believe it? They're close to our border."

They looked at the map together. The small border town was about twenty kilometers south of Breda. So close! If only …

"The Belgians are lucky," Jacob said. He made a gesture toward the open map. "It looks like the Allies are sweeping south of us on their way to Germany, bypassing us."

"Vader says they first have to set up a supply route for the front."

They looked at the map again. Jacob traced the long Schelde River that connected Antwerpen to the North Sea. His fingers were slender but also strong and decisive, and she remembered his handshake the first time she came up to bring food, and how she'd felt a carpenter or an engineer in it.

"That makes sense," he said. "The Allies will get their ships pounded before they make it to Antwerpen. And it will be from the Dutch side and the Belgian side."

Jacob looked at war the same way her father did, as it were played out on a chessboard. But Carla could not distance herself from the devastation she had no trouble conjuring up in her mind. Every place Jacob had marked as an Allied victory, she wondered what it looked like after the fighting was over and the conquering troops moved on. She ran her hand through her thick, wavy hair, which had taken on a dull look because of the lack of soap. War took away so much.

"What else is going on in the outside world?" Jacob asked.

"The Ortskommandant is forcing middle-aged men to work for them."

"To do what?"

"To build a defense belt around Breda. The farmers are upset and angry. Trenches are randomly dug in their fields. The Germans don't bother to ask them for permission. But the workers are sabotaging with a slow-does-it action."

It was time to get in line at the grocery store. Outside, the sky was the color of smoke and it was cold. Her raincoat felt as damp as the air. She tightened her wool scarf around her neck and braced for the oncoming ordeal. The line had already formed when she turned the corner into the Brugstraat. It would be a long wait. Surprisingly, there was animated banter among the people ahead of her. Her curiosity was aroused. People seemed less cautious about sharing information. What did they know that she didn't know? She tuned her ear to the voices.

Baarle-Nassau, the small town on the Belgian border, had fallen into Allied hands. It was believable, because for days they'd heard persistent artillery fire in the distance. And the news had only twenty kilometers to travel to reach their eager ears. No wonder the conversation was animated. But there was more.

By the time Carla reached the front of the line, she'd learned that a convoy of Dutch trucks had left Breda with the blessing of the Ortskommandant to pick up a large supply of food in Zuid Holland, north of the rivers. It seemed too good to be true. Why would the Ortskommandant give his consent, and not only that, provide gasoline to power the trucks? Answer: the German Army was as short of food as the Dutch citizens were since the railroad strike started. There were other questions. How could the Allied bombers overhead know this convoy wasn't a German troop transport? Answer: Large Dutch flags had been laid on the flat roofs of the trucks, to be seen by eyes in the sky.

Every person in the line wanted to believe those answers, and history would prove them correct.

Standing in line was suddenly bearable. Her raincoat stopped feeling like a wet blanket, and she hurried home with her canvas bag filled with the limits of what she was allowed of sugar, flour, and dried beans. Moeder was in the kitchen making applesauce from a bagful of apples that one of Vader's patients had bartered for dental care.

"Baarle-Nassau has fallen," she exclaimed, and danced while swinging her grocery bag around.

"Slow down, Carla," Moeder said. "We've gone through this excitement once before, remember? So, don't run up to Jacob and Esther with the news. We haven't seen any foreign soldiers in the street yet."

Vader said he had a patient who would come the next day to turn the cellar into a shelter they could stay in for up to a week.

"This will be like planning for one of our sailing trips, Carla," he said. "Think of every angle, every possibility, and prepare for it."

"Are you putting me in charge?"

"Yes. Get the place ready for five people."

"That includes Esther and Jacob, right?"

"Of course."

Immediately after dinner, Carla ventured to the cellar to see what needed to be done. The place was shockingly dirty. Close to the steel bulkhead on the street side was the storage bin for coal. A film of black dust layered every nook and cranny. She went upstairs, fashioned a cotton kerchief around her head, and then went back down with a broom, a pile of rags, and a pail of water. It took her till midnight to make the place livable.

Vader's patient brought a helper to place three fresh-cut trees to buttress the ceiling. Carla directed the men to build five narrow berths from planks and pieces of plywood. Shelves for storing food were also built into the curved brick walls. It took three days to get the shelter outfitted with canned beans, bottled water, a camping stove, matches, two lanterns, fuel for the lanterns, propane gas for the stove, a chamber pot, and a slop jar. Mattresses and blankets they would take from their beds when the time came.

They were prepared for the final siege. Every evening at eight o'clock, the hidden radio was tuned to the BBC, but there were no reports that hinted at an active front moving their way. The news was all about fighting around the River Schelde and how bombs had breached a dike in Zeeland, which flushed out the Germans but also inundated large parts of the farmland. What was happening in the neighboring province of Zeeland sounded absolutely awful, and they probably wouldn't hear the worst of it till after the war was over.

Prepared and eager, they waited for a sign. Surely, something had to happen soon.

Carla had kept Jacob and Esther in the dark about the fall of Baarle-Nassau. Having seen how the disappointment of *Dolle Dinsdag* had sent Esther into a tailspin, she'd heeded Moeder's remark. Jacob noticed the artillery fire rumbling in the distance had stopped, and he kept fishing for news, but she warded him off with reports of the fight for Antwerpen's harbor. That, after all, was the only news she really had.

To keep Jacob's mind and hands occupied, she begged her father for the kit to build a ship's model he'd received for his birthday but hadn't started yet. Jacob's face lit up when she came in with her present. It had been a good guess that he was capable with his hands. He opened the package as if its contents were made of glass. The parts were laid out on a plank he could move from the table to a place on the floor, because there was only one table that had to serve as kitchen counter, sink, and dinner table. He immediately went to work.

"You look like you have ship building in your blood," Carla said.

"Building, yes. Ship building, no. My father is an engineer, and that's what I started out to study for."

"'Did you go to the Technical Institute in Delft?"

"Yes, but only for three years until all Jews were banned from universities, professors and students alike. So, I went to work for my uncle in his photography shop here in Breda."

Carla watched as he organized the parts of what was to become a schooner with three square-rigged masts. The plank was hardly large enough to hold them all, as well as provide space for the slow birth of the schooner. She went down to the cellar and rummaged among scraps left over from building shelves. On her way back up, she grabbed a wool sweater from her closet and brought it to the attic as well.

"Here's a sturdy plank for you, Jacob, and a knitting project for you, Esther."

Esther sat on the edge of the bed, filing her fingernails. She had shown minimal interest in Jacob's new project. She needed to be jolted out of her depression. Looking at Jacob building a boat wasn't going to do it.

"My father complains of cold feet. I wonder if you could knit socks for him from this sweater? Do you know how to knit?"

Esther looked surprised, as if someone had just shaken her out of a deep sleep. She took the dark blue sweater from Carla's hand and studied it.

"Knit? I suppose I could. Do you have a pattern for it and his size?"

"Not yet, but I brought a pair of scissors, so we can start carding the wool."

She snipped a thread and started to unravel the fabric. Esther took the thread's end, winding it gradually into a ball, while Carla held the sweater up. It was a gratifying feeling to pass time with Esther in this silent cooperation of movements, giving and taking until the resulting ball was too big to hold in her hand and she had to start a second one.

"What are your dreams for after the liberation?" Carla asked, holding the sweater at shoulder height and weaving it back and forth as Esther pulled the thread.

Esther looked up, her expression betraying how unprepared she was for the question. Her eyes widened. Her forehead wrinkled into a frown, as if Carla had asked an improbable question, like how many cows grazed in the street. There were no cows in the street, there was no liberation, and didn't Carla know this?

"Come on, Esther, you must have some wishes, some dreams for when all of this is over?"

Esther stopped winding the ball and let her hands sink into her lap. If her face was pale when they first met, it was beyond pale now. She was petite to begin with, and she'd lost weight in the two months since Carla had come home. A strong wind would blow her over.

"I haven't allowed myself to dream, Carla. Dreams are like sand castles. They get washed away by the tides."

"Jesus told his followers to build their house on a rock. You have a rock right here in this room."

"I don't see a rock."

"Sure you do. Look at this man who's building a boat. Maybe it will be Noah's Ark that will float you out of these walls that have fenced you in for two years. You will float away to a new future with your lives and your dreams intact."

Jacob looked up from reading the sheet with assembly instructions. In their small attic space, there was no hiding from what another said.

"We may not be free to move around," he said, "but we are free to imagine a future. I for one hope to go back to Delft and finish my studies."

Esther looked back at him. There was envy, love, and fear all mixed together in her face. Her brown eyes held his. He responded by getting up and kneeling in front of her and holding her hands.

"Give it a try, Esther. What would you really like to have happen in your life? There's no penalty for dreaming."

Carla sat on the rug holding the sweater, wishing with all her might that Esther would give in and let her imagination soar. Nothing came out. She waited. But then suddenly, Esther blurted out that she would love to have a child, a home in the country, and a garden to tend. Tears formed in her eyes as she revealed her deepest wishes. Jacob got up and embraced her. Carla felt like she shouldn't be there, but she *was* there, so she said what she'd often heard in church: "May it be so."

Time crept toward the end of October. The waiting for Breda's liberation was excruciating. Then, on the twenty-second of October, the BBC reported that the war machine had woken up from its period of quiet preparation. Artillery booms in the distance confirmed that Operation Pheasant had started, and the behavior of the German occupiers went from arrogant to rogue. They saw the writing on the wall and started to plunder before they were turned out of the city in defeat.

Vader's best friend, Mr. Wetselaar, who lived around the corner on the market, came to their house out of breath to ask for help. A sympathetic German officer had come to warn him that his pharmacy would be raided within two hours. He needed help to get some precious medicines out of their reach. Vader dropped everything and called to Carla. Together, they went over with Mr. Wetselaar. On the way, he confided that he housed a depot of scarce medicines for the Underground for the entire western portion of the province. The Germans had systematically sidelined lifesaving drugs like insulin and digitalis for their own use, and the Underground foresaw a dangerous shortage. He had also stockpiled practical items like bandaging materials. Most of it was in a guest room in his home above the pharmacy.

Carla helped pack up as much as possible into rucksacks and schoolbags that Mr. Wetselaar's children took away on their bicycles to trusted friends' homes. But time ran out. An officer barged in and searched the entire place. He inspected everything in every room with unbridled greed leaking from his roaming eyes. She resented his dress uniform, which he trusted would give him license to steal.

As the officer searched downstairs, Mr. Wetselaar was upstairs putting his elderly mother-in-law in a double bed and stuffing the most precious medicines around her body, under the covers. He asked Carla to sit next to her bed, as if she were a nurse. When the officer entered the bedroom and asked who she was, Carla answered that it was Mrs. Westelaar's mother, who suffered from tuberculosis. The officer quickly turned on the heels of his shiny boots and left the room. The old woman winked at Carla, and they both had a good laugh after the danger passed.

The greedy officer never did find out about the Underground's depot. He was more interested in an antique brass scale that could weigh infinitesimal amounts of medicinal compounds inside its magnificent mahogany and glass housing. It had been in the pharmacy for generations. It was sad to see it taken, but things could have been worse. Much worse.

A day later, Carla was standing in line at the butcher shop when it sounded like the world was coming apart. The air raid had not sounded, and she didn't see bombers flying overhead, but for what seemed like an eternity, the air was filled with deafening sounds. Were the Allies that close already? Glass was jerked out of the window frame of the liquor store next door in one loud *bam*, and seconds later she stared at a pile of shards on the sidewalk. Sound waves bounced from side to side in the street, leaving a queer pattern of shops with their windows blown out and others miraculously spared. Nobody understood what was happening. People ran like scared chickens in the street, not knowing how to escape this strange threat. The butcher opened the store to let people in. Many were covered with blood from the flying pieces of glass. Carla asked the butcher if he had a first aid kit. After all, she'd been well on her way to becoming a doctor. Luckily, no one had any deep cuts. She carefully cleaned wounds and rid them of shattered pieces of glass. The Band-Aids she applied calmed the frayed nerves. After the explosions stopped, the customers decided they'd had enough excitement for the day and went home. The butcher thanked Carla for her help and sent her off with a pound of ham. That evening, the newscaster reported that the Germans had blown up their entire ammunition depot at the airport of Gilze-Rijen, near Breda.

The following day, Carla noticed unusual activity at the police station across the street. There was a constant coming and going of officers. She walked over to the market. Same thing. German officers carried out what looked like files and logs from the city hall. Cars with military license plates streamed by, packed to the roof with luggage. It was a different kind of retreat from the one she'd witnessed on *Dolle Dinsdag*, when a dilapidated stream of soldiers, who didn't care if their uniforms were unbuttoned, dirty, and torn, had passed through the city in an unending stream. What was happening before her eyes now was hasty but organized. The military in the cars were not combat soldiers. They were the officers of the Ortskommandantur, who'd been charged with ruling the city for four years and six months. Carla felt no hardship seeing them go. They'd made life miserable long enough with their stifling ordnungs.

It was time to move to the cellar. Artillery fire was not so distant anymore. Vader told Carla to go upstairs and alert Jacob and

Esther.

"Pack a bag with only important things," she told them. "And bring your blankets."

"The only thing that's important for me is to bring my wife," Jacob said.

"And our IDs?" Esther said.

"Good idea," he said. "But do the Allies really care about our false IDs? I'll bring our passports, so we can prove who we really are!"

Hearing him say that got Esther excited. She took a bag and quickly put some toiletries in it. Jacob folded their blankets while Carla waited at the door.

"We haven't been down this staircase for two years, Carla," he said. "I wonder if I can still negotiate treads."

"I'll go first, then you can fall on me. That might be a softer landing."

They all giggled, and it was such a happy moment. Now, if only Operation Pheasant would succeed better than Operation Market Garden, the fear and isolation of the war years could be behind them in a matter of a week, or maybe even days.

Carla opened the door to the hallway and separated the heavy winter coats. Vader stood there with an armful of pillows. He dropped them to the ground and stretched out his arms toward Esther.

"Welcome back to the world," he said.

Her father hadn't seen either one for months, and Carla noticed that the pallor of their faces took him aback, but he hid it well. He was in a jovial mood. He had convinced himself that the end of the war was at hand, and he relished the activity required to meet the last battle. Carla compared his excitement to a time when he had sailed their boat through a wicked storm and the coast had finally come into view.

Moeder was in the kitchen packing up bread, jam, and a chunk of cheese, as well as some of the ham that was left over from the butcher's gift. They went down the cellar stairs in a mood of happy anticipation, even though the electricity had been cut off and they descended into a pitch-dark basement. Vader lit a match and got the gas lamp going. The pillows they'd carried down were arranged on the berths, and they decided it would be nice to have mattresses as well. Jacob, Vader, and Carla went back upstairs. As they were undoing the beds, the front doorbell rang. Jacob stiffened. Carla pulled him by his sleeve, parted the coats in front of the attic door, and practically shoved him onto the staircase.

She could hear Vader talking to a patient downstairs. He was sorry, but without electricity he couldn't use his dental tools, and he gave the man a prescription for pain medicine. Back in the cellar, Jacob vowed he would stay down till the liberation. Recovering from the scare, Vader challenged him to a game of chess. The women busied themselves setting up some sort of housekeeping order.

"Esther," Moeder said, "we never talked about your family. Where did you grow up?"

"I was born and raised in Amsterdam. My father taught French at the university. I loved Amsterdam. Jacob and I were married there."

"How did you meet?"

"At the home of a mutual friend. It was love at first sight. Jacob was a student in Delft, and I was working at the university's library."

Carla had not seen Esther this animated since they met. Her eyes shone in the darkness of the cellar with only the flickering light of the gas lamp, and her voice lacked the lethargy Carla had gotten used to. She welcomed the change. Two years of staring at walls was enough to take away anyone's desire to talk, and it was the more surprising that Jacob had maintained such an upbeat outlook on life. He seemed to engage every aspect of it, good or bad. Right now, the world around him had fallen away while he concentrated on trying to beat her father at chess.

She had more questions for Esther, like where are your parents now and do you have siblings, but she suppressed the urge. The answers might be too painful.

Through the heavy steel bulkhead, they heard explosions that seemed closer than any they'd heard before. There was a war going on above their heads.

"What time is it?" Moeder asked. "I don't even know what day of the week it is."

"It's Friday, October 27," Vader said. He moved closer to the lamp and looked at his watch. "It's eight o'clock in the evening. Time to eat, I would say."

The women got into action and produced a meal of reheated beans, slices of the precious ham, and some applesauce. With nothing more to do and no light to do it by—if they wanted to save fuel—each tried to get comfortable on their individual berths. Carla could hear the others toss and turn. Every time there was an explosion, they talked about where that bomb might have landed.

She couldn't sleep. Random images of things that had happened over the past four years kept floating into her mind, coalescing around the Group of Eight. Her rented room in Utrecht that became its center; the sermon that Walter gave in the church that had set her friends off on an uncharted path and put him in prison; the indelible memories of being at the castle and of Anna's formidable grandmother rose up. She couldn't remember how the castle was situated in relation to Arnhem. How had they fared during the assault of the failed Market Garden Operation? Pray, if you don't know the answer, Walter would say. She prayed.

There was another loud bang, and another one. They seemed to get closer. What would Breda look like once they got out of the cellar? The feeling of elation at the prospect of liberation ebbed. There was a price to be paid, and it might be steep, if bridges were blown up and homes destroyed and people homeless and, worse, killed.

Carla's mind sank back into ruminations about the events that had led to this moment. What would have happened if she hadn't invited her friends to hear Walter preach? Piet might still be alive. Anna and Dirk might not be living in constant danger. Neither would the baroness and all those farmers around the castle that were hiding Jews. How about Betty and Jan? They had given cover to Anna, Dirk, Emmy, Bertha, and herself. All these people had put their lives on the line because of Walter's challenge. Herman and Otto had made choices for different reasons, and they were not related to Walter's call for solidarity with the Jewish people. They acted because the university closed. Herman had taken the option of working for the Germans, and Otto had preferred the adventure of getting to England. She hadn't forgiven Herman for the choice he made. And she hadn't thought much about Otto, even if he had tweaked her curiosity with that little note in the cookie jar.

They had spent two nights and two days in their shelter when they noticed the loud bangs of direct hits close by had stopped. Were they liberated? Once in a while, they heard a lone gunshot. Most sounded far-off, a few were nearby. Vader was torn between curiosity and caution, but curiosity won out. He told everyone to stay in the cellar. He would scout out the situation above the ground. When he came back, his face was flushed with excitement. He had seen soldiers with the word *Poland* on the sleeves of their uniforms.

"Poland?" Jacob said. "Are you sure they're not Germans?"

"No, no, I'm sure they're not German. They have a funny-color brown uniform and their helmets have a very different shape. I'm sure they're part of the Allies. Their guns, their boots, their helmets, everything about them looks different."

They were sitting on their cots around the improvised table with the gas lamp in the middle. Its flickering light created weird shadows on the walls behind them, turning their bodies into grotesque shapes.

Suddenly, Esther sprang up and raced over to the staircase.

"I want to see them!" she cried. "We're free!"

"Esther, wait," Vader shouted. "It's still dangerous. The soldiers motioned me to go back inside. It's not over yet."

But Esther was caught up in the excitement of the moment. She was determined to go out and embrace freedom. She ran up the stairs. Carla heard her open the door from the kitchen to the hall, followed by footsteps overhead toward the front door.

Jacob leapt to his feet. In his haste, he almost threw over the gas lamp. It teetered on the rickety table, and he bent over to straighten it.

"Stop her, Jacob!" Vader said.

Jacob raced after his wife. It was eerily quiet until one shot rang out. Carla froze with a terrifying feeling of premonition. Seconds later, she heard two other shots, all of them nearby. She ran up the stairs, ignoring her father's shouts. When she came through the kitchen, she heard the most heartrending cry she'd ever heard in her life. The front door was wide open, and she saw a foreign soldier trying to hold on to Jacob and push him back into the doorway, but Jacob resisted with all his might and ran into the middle of the street. And there lay Esther, slumped on her back, her legs askew, her eyes open—sightless. Her blouse darkened, and the cobblestones around her body glistened in the late afternoon sun with her fresh blood.

Carla's impulse was to go over to Jacob, but the soldier who'd tried to hold Jacob back was firm with her. He pointed at the house across the street beside the police station. There was an open window upstairs. The window next to it had a hole the size of a bullet and a spider-like crack around it.

"Sniper," he said. "I got him, but there could be another one."

"I'm a doctor," she said to the soldier. An impulse to save Esther coursed through her, and she tried to move by him, but he looked at her with eyes that had seen many deaths before, many more than she had, and those eyes told her it was too late. He waved to his mate across the street. Together they walked over to Jacob, who'd fallen to his knees beside Esther, and they said something to him. Jacob got up, dazed and stumbling. The soldiers brought Esther inside and laid her on a bench in the hall, the one meant for waiting patients. They turned back into the street, their guns at the ready. Then they evaporated.

Carla had the weird sensation of being disembodied, floating above the place where she actually stood and looking down at herself and Esther and Jacob. She was a spectator at a scene in which Esther looked beautiful and peaceful, like Snow White; Jacob beside her, holding Esther's lifeless hands and sobbing; and she watching herself holding back at first, and then kneeling next to Jacob and crying with him.

When she telescoped back to reality, Jacob lifted his head toward her and in stifled tones said how he'd always hoped they would be able to survive the war together. It broke her heart to hear him say the very things Esther had voiced, only a few days before: a home, a garden, a child.

"Oh, Carla, why, why, why did this have to happen? This so unfair!"

His light brown eyes, usually so full of life, were wet with tears, and it pained her to look into them. There was immeasurable sadness in them. She put her arm around his shaking body and said nothing, because as far as she knew there was no answer to that question. All she had to offer him was compassion.

That was how Vader found them.

The next days formed a weird combination of mourning and rejoicing. Inside the Vlaskamp home, Esther's passing had to be dealt with, and getting her buried while the city was still partly under siege was a challenge. Outside, the people of Breda danced and sang in the streets, and church bells rang. The carillon in the spire of the Grote Kerk played patriotic songs, in spite of the many direct hits it had suffered. It was this juxtaposition of feelings that was hard to deal with, and Carla realized that many more families were in the same painful and awkward position. Esther wasn't the only casualty. The undertaker Vader contacted said he was overwhelmed with demands for caskets. Carla's parents took care of the practical details that come with a death, but under the circumstances, a formal funeral was out of the question.

They moved out of the cellar for good, although artillery fire still sounded in the distance. It was clearly moving away from the center of the city where they lived.

Jacob said he didn't want to go back to the attic. Carla helped him move into Walter's room, and then went upstairs to get some of his belongings, of which there weren't many. But two items struck her as important: the schooner and the wedding picture. Jacob pressed the frame against his heart. Tears ran down his cheeks. It was hard to watch this tall, handsome man so broken up. She had no words. It seemed best just to be and not to say meaningless things. He seemed to appreciate just having her there, and she had to admit that she needed him too. She had never lost anyone close to her. Esther was the first direct hit in her life, and she was unprepared for the feelings of loss and anger it loosened. Death was a thief. War was a robber.

She was equally unprepared for another unexpected happening.

Four days after Breda was declared free, the bell rang. She opened the front door. A man in battle dress, with a big smile under his officer's cap, stood in front of her.

"Carla!"

He called her name with the force of someone who had imagined saying that name over and over in his mind.

She reeled.

"Aren't you going to invite me in?" he said.

"Otto!"

He stepped inside and embraced her and kissed her. She was not ready for this. Her emotions were bound up with death. It was somber inside her heart. There was nothing left of the lightheartedness of that day in Utrecht, when she and Anna had laughed about their discovery of Otto's cryptic note in the cookie jar.

"Come in," she said. She was aware how detached and distant her words sounded.

He took off his cap and tucked it under his arm. She noticed he had the insignia of the Prinses Irene Brigade on the sleeve of his uniform.

"Did you liberate us, Otto?"

"Yes, we had a hand in it. All of us Dutchmen had trained hard for this, so it was very rewarding. We liberated the city of Tilburg, your neighbor."

She led him into the living room and introduced him to her mother, who was busy mending sheets.

"This is my reentry into a Dutch home," Otto said.

He treated them to stories of how he'd made it to England, and how hard fought the advance from Normandy to Breda had been. Vader came in and was introduced. He had many questions to ask Otto about the war and the battle for Breda. Carla felt like she was watching a play, like this wasn't about her at all. She looked over at Otto, smart in his uniform, his sleek black hair shorter than she remembered it. She felt disconnected from the Otto she remembered from Utrecht. He represented something very different now. He was part of the conquering army. All of which was admirable, of course. It couldn't have been easy to get himself to England; to become a lieutenant; to do battle that could end in death. But she couldn't rid herself of the feeling that, all the same, he'd taken an easier path than Dirk and Klaas and Piet, who had made the moral decision to keep helping Jews survive, risking concentration camp and the death penalty.

Carla was only half present throughout the visit. The other half of her was with Jacob. While listening to the heroic advances the Allies had made—and praise the Lord that they had—she thought of the contrast between a uniformed man full of brave stories and another man who was thin and pale from spending two years in hiding, and who had just lost what was most dear to him. Her heart, she realized, was not with Otto. It had never been. A note in a cookie jar hadn't been enough of a declaration of eternal love.

What was love?

With a sudden deep insight, she knew that love had to be earned. It had to be lived. It had to be shared. Love had to sacrifice. It had to suffer, like steel needs to be tempered before it can be useful.

This was not the kind of love she shared with Otto.

Life would show her with whom she would share that kind of love.

CHAPTER FORTY-TWO

Dirk -- November 1944

Dirk hung his white coat on a hook in the lab's closet. It was a raw early-November day, and he wasn't looking forward to the bike ride home against a strong wind.

Dr. Hamel had asked him to stop by his office. He said he had an important message from Dirk's father. It had to be something serious. His father wasn't given to idle talk or unnecessary action.

The important message was about a worrisome shortage of insulin in the western part of Holland. Many diabetics were at their wit's end. The Germans grabbed what they could, and that included vital drugs like insulin.

"I take it my father has a plan to remedy that?" Dirk asked.

"Yes, he does. He wants you to cross the rivers. There is a depot of crucial medicines in Breda."

"*Allemachtig!*"

"I know. He asks a lot of you. His reasoning is that, in the first place, you are strong and in reasonably good shape, which can't be said for many men these days. Secondly, as a medical student, nobody can sell you apples for oranges."

Dirk took a deep breath. Many questions rushed at him. How

was he to get across the rivers undetected? How could he carry enough insulin for an entire population? How would anyone in Breda believe him? Dirk van Enthoven, a medical student, taking all that precious insulin? Did he have enough guts?

Dr. Hamel gave him time to digest the news. Like his father, he was not a man of many words, but he could be counted on. Only last week, the Gestapo had shown up looking for one of Dirk's coworkers, but Dr. Hamel had literally blocked their way to give the man time to escape. The incident made clear that, as was the case with Bertha, others at the hospital were as engaged in some form of illegal work as he was, and were protected by Dr. Hamel.

The fact that his father had sent a message through Dr. Hamel pointed to the fact that both men were deeply into resistance work at a high level. Dirk trusted that neither man would send him on a dangerous mission without a good reason, or without the necessary strategy for getting it accomplished.

Dr. Hamel told him not go home to get instructions. It was too dangerous. The Germans had carried out a razzia in Rotterdam the day before. All roads connecting the city to the outside world had been hermetically closed off, including the tunnel under the Maas River. The local police had been disarmed, and every household had received a notice that men between the ages of seventeen and fifty needed to pack a few things and be ready to go to work camps. It was expected that the same thing would happen in Den Haag.

"Don't they have enough of us working for them already?" Dirk asked.

"At the rate their soldiers are killed on both fronts, Hitler is running out of able-bodied men to replace them. You even see sixteen-year-olds in uniform."

"How soon must I take this trip?"

"As soon as possible. It's November, and the water is cold. It will only get colder. Let me know tomorrow."

He biked home with the wind in his face, a reminder of the shift in seasons. Much to his surprise, Emmy was there. She'd come on her bike from Haarlem, saying she couldn't stand being at home any longer, and begging if she could stay with Jan and Betty if she helped distribute the illegal newspaper. They'd taken her in. Over their meager dinner of potatoes and applesauce, Betty asked how her Jewish couple was doing.

"They were found," Emmy said.

Before she looked away, Dirk saw a huge hurt in her eyes.

Betty's question had the sound of a book being slammed shut. There was more to Emmy's escape from home than she was willing to share, Dirk thought, but he didn't press her. Neither did Betty, who'd sewn Mr. Hirsch's money into Anna's and Emmy's raincoats, now more than a year ago.

"You can sleep in Anna's room, Emmy," Dirk said. "I know she would like that. I may be gone for a while."

At that moment, he realized he'd decided to take on the task his father had trusted him with, even though he hadn't admitted it to himself yet.

"Gone?" Betty asked.

"Yes, for a while."

No more questions were asked.

The next morning, he told Dr. Hamel that he was willing to go, on the condition that a messenger was sent to Anna with a personal letter. There was no other way to let her know, and he was acutely aware that he'd left her hanging with a lot of responsibilities, not the least of which was the care of Frits.

There was a lot to be done in a hurry. Dr. Hamel described the hurdles he would have to overcome. The first one was to get to the Merwede River without being stopped. The Germans were not only on the lookout for line crossers, but for males they could put to work. So, there would be roadblocks to clear on his way to the boat that would take him across. The second hurdle was the actual crossing. The longest part of the trip was through the Biesbosch, that mysterious delta between the Waal and Maas Rivers. It had been done already a few times, Dr. Hamel said, so far without casualties.

It was a sobering statement.

"How will I prove that I'm the contact coming for the insulin once I get to Breda?"

"The appropriate authorities will know you're coming and what for. You will have to memorize my instructions. Carrying any kind of papers is too dangerous."

The plans were made carefully, and Dirk memorized them down to the tiniest minutiae.

Saying good-bye to Jan was the first hurdle. After the railroad strike had drastically diminished food supplies, Jan had visibly lost weight. Being the skinny type to begin with, and having to do without his customary meat and potato dinners, his face had developed a hollow look. It worried Dirk, and he took Emmy aside and encouraged her to try to get extra food by biking to farms around Utrecht. He left her some money to pay for it. She refused to take it, but Dirk insisted.

With a small bag with long underwear, a toothbrush, and an extra sweater, he left for the hospital, checked into the lab as he normally would, and put on his white lab coat. Dr. Hamel was waiting for him. Together they walked over to the morgue, the one he'd brought Bertha to when the Gestapo raided her office. He took off his lab coat and got himself comfortable on an empty gurney.

"You'll have tall tales to tell, Dirk," Dr. Hamel said. "Tell the Allies to hurry up and liberate us."

"I'll do my best."

"I will put your bag here as a footrest. Any more questions before I put this sheet over you?"

"Be sure to get my letter to Anna Smits. And pray for me."

"You are an instrument in God's hands. He will guide you," Dr. Hamel said, and then he unfolded the sheet and draped it over Dirk's lanky body.

From under the cover, he could hear the door of the morgue close. What if Dr. Hamel forgot to notify the undertaker? This was not a place to be left for any length of time.

His mind took him through the paces of the trip ahead. Many links in the chain of events would have to be foolproof to make it a success. For relief, he turned his thoughts to Anna. He'd written her a long letter, explaining—short of giving her details—that he carried her with him in his heart on an adventurous trip that would benefit many hard-put people. He'd ended it with the hope that the next time they met, the war would be over and they could plan their wedding. It was his way of proposing to her. He wouldn't know her answer until after he'd battled many odds. He folded his hands under the sheet and prayed, more fervently than at any time in his life. There were so many odds to overcome, and there was so much to lose.

He heard the creaking of the door being opened and Dr. Hamel's voice telling somebody that this was the one to take out. The next thing he knew, his whole body was shaking as the gurney was carried through the hall to the cool outdoors. A car door opened. He felt himself being shoved inside, head first, feet last. The car started moving. He was on his way to the same place Bertha had been brought. After a short journey, his gurney was taken out of the vehicle and carried inside. The sheet was pulled back, and he looked up at the undertaker in his somber black suit.

"Good morning," the man said in a solemn voice. "We have instructions to prepare you for burial in a cemetery close to the Merwede River. You will be taken care of from there. Have you had breakfast?"

Dirk briefly thought the undertaker had a keen sense of humor, but looking into his melancholy face, he realized it was a practical question.

"I had some oatmeal."

"You will need more than oatmeal to get across. Dr. Hamel provided an extra bread coupon, so before we prepare you, I'll get you a slice with butter and ham."

The man left him in a large room with a variety of caskets.

Looking at them robbed him of his appetite for the ham sandwich. What did it mean to be "prepared for burial"? Which of these caskets would be his?

The undertaker, whose name he didn't know—just as well—came back with the promised ham sandwich and a tall glass of milk, both scarce items.

"This is the plan," the man said, his voice still solemn. "We will bring you to a trusted undertaker in Avelingen, a small town on the Boven Merwede River. We have made up a death certificate for a fifty-year-old man. We named him Karel Bongers. Died of tuberculosis on November 2 at his home in Utrecht. The Moffen are scared stiff of TB, but that's not your concern. I will need the death certificate in case we get stopped. It's unlikely the casket would be opened, but always a possibility. When we get to Avelingen, you can get out of the casket, and there will be people to help you get across."

It was a dry summing up of what loomed as a creepy adventure. It was one thing to be lying briefly on a gurney in a morgue, but lying inside a casket in a moving hearse was—now that he was close up to it—quite another.

"I will dress you in a black raincoat," the unperturbed undertaker went on. "You will be less visible that way once you're outside." He looked at his watch. "We should leave in about an hour. My hearse doesn't go fast with that cumbersome gas balloon on top. It would have been a lot faster with the motor working on regular gasoline. But those days are behind us, at least for the time being."

"How long will it take? Can I get air in that thing?" Dirk said, pointing at a casket.

"About two hours, if we don't get stopped. We have a special casket for transporting live bodies. It has vents close to where your head will be."

Dirk almost choked on his ham sandwich at the thought.

"There's a soft mattress for you to lie on," the dry undertaker added.

An hour later he was "prepared for burial." Dressed in a black raincoat—courtesy of the Resistance, the man said—he climbed inside the plain pine coffin. It was lined with satin, and the mattress underneath him was indeed soft, but there wasn't much room for movement. But then, that's not what coffin builders had to take into consideration. The undertaker took Dirk's hands and folded them over each other. Before closing the lid, the man, as solemn as ever, said he would let him out as soon as they got to Avelingen.

"I commend my soul into your hands," Dirk said. Then everything went dark around him.

He could breathe. That was a relief. All the same, this was a macabre experience. To be alive while pretending to be dead was not the same as actually being dead. When he opened his eyes, he could see the lined cover of the coffin. With dead eyes, he would never again see the sun rise or set. Being lifeless wasn't a condition he was ready to contemplate any further, so he let his mind roam while his body was held rigid. Why was he doing this weird and dangerous thing? He examined his motivation, and almost immediately his parents came to mind. They had seen early on the dangers of National Socialism and what it would lead to. He thought of how they had made room for a Jewish family on the escape vessel to England; how Walter Vlaskamp had shown the Group of Eight that only an open, charitable mind could overcome prejudice; and men like Dr. Boot and Dr. Hamel were examples of the defiance it took to counter a soulless enemy. With examples set by people like that, he would never be able to respect himself if he didn't stick out his neck to prevent innocent people from dying for lack of insulin. And anyway, it wasn't that different from being a doctor. Just a little riskier way of saving lives.

They were stopped only once. He heard German-speaking voices outside, but they weren't argumentative. The wheels got moving again underneath him. Finally, the hearse again came to a stop. This time, Dutch-speaking voices were outside. He had arrived. It wasn't long before the lid opened, and he could climb out of his confining coffin. To limber up, he took a deep breath and did some push-ups. He felt alive again, and hoped to feel that way for a long time to come.

The undertaker introduced him to a tall blond man. His name was Rolf. No last name was given, as was customary in Resistance circles. After some brief small talk with the undertaker in Avelingen, Dirk thanked the undertaker from Utrecht, and was given a bicycle to follow Rolf through a flat landscape of dikes and polders. The sky was gray, the air humid and heavy. Rain was likely to follow. They didn't talk as they biked. Finally, they stopped at a ship's wharf with a small brick house beside it. Inside, he found two men, a woman, and two young children, all seated around a crude wooden kitchen table, while a woodstove kept the place toasty warm. The two men were Allied pilots who'd crashed, survived, and were now on their way back to England. They didn't say so, but Dirk didn't need to be told. In their ill-fitting civilian clothes, they looked thoroughly foreign. He wondered if these two men would join him on the trip across the rivers.

Rolf asked the woman, obviously his wife, if she could have dinner ready in two hours. The children were sent out to play. Rolf spread out a wrinkled map on the table. His calloused hand traced the area they would have to traverse. The trip would be divided in stages. First, they had to cross the Merwede River. The next phase would be getting to and through the Biesbosch. The last phase was getting across the Maas River to Noord-Brabant.

"The first part is the hardest," Rolf said, "because we have to row upstream." He pointed at a spot on the map. "When we make it to here, we don't have to row at all. The river will take us."

Dirk asked if there were many Germans patrolling the area. Rolf sighed and said there were. "When they hear something, they send up flares, and they shoot at anything that moves."

The airmen were lucky they didn't understand enough Dutch to know what dangers were facing them. Dirk was in awe of this man with a wife and children, who was willing to risk his life for the cause of the Resistance.

He went outside to get some fresh air. The shipyard was located on a sheltered tributary of the Merwede River. It was twilight, and it had started to rain, though just a sprinkle. The damp air brought out the smell of tar, and he was reminded of the days he was on the barge on his way to Maastricht. Back inside, the wife had set the table. Steam rose from a cast-iron pan filled with a thick pea soup with chunks of carrots, celery root, potatoes, and ham.

"That will get me across the river in good shape," Dirk said to the wife.

"You'll need it. Do you have your long undies on? It gets cold on the river."

The men rested after the meal until it was midnight and pitch dark outside. It had rained a bit, but the river wasn't high, and that was important, Rolf said. Another big, strong man was waiting for them in a large rowboat, large enough to hold the five of them. It was tricky getting into it in total darkness over a narrow gangplank.

Rolf and the other man took the oars. When everyone was settled, they struck out, forcefully and gently. As soon as they left the protection of their sheltered spot, the water got rough. Rowing against the current was hard work, and it was almost impossible to know whether they made any headway. The landscape was the same all around, flat and dark in the rainy night. After what seemed like ages, they made it across without being detected. For a long while, they rowed along the shore, going slowly to not arouse any living thing, like waterfowl.

The boat stopped at another wharf. It was still raining, and that was their good luck, Rolf said. German guards liked to stay inside their patrol huts during rainfall. He led them to a brick house that was similar to Rolf's own, only bigger, and they spent the rest of the night there on straw in the barn.

The next day, they walked over to a farm at the edge of the Biesbosch. Its peculiar lowlands lay beyond. Dirk wondered how anyone could even contemplate getting through that maze of grasslands, ditches, and creeks. Only people whose cradle had stood on its shore would be able to come out at the other end.

The farm belonged to a couple in their forties. Their son, Ari, would be helping them get across to Brabant. Ari was as solidly built as Rolf. Each had biceps the size of tennis balls, and their hulking bodies emanated power. Ari spread out a more detailed map on the kitchen table and explained the route. They would have to sneak through the Biesbosch from island to island until they reached the Maas River. All in all, they would cover an area of about twenty-five miles.

Night fell. It was time to leave, fortified by another hearty meal. Rolf issued Dirk and the two pilots high rubber boots, which were a true blessing, as they had to walk through knee-deep mud for quite a while before they reached a narrow canal. There they halted. It was hard to make out any kind of shape in the thick mist. Everyone was silent as they waited, well aware of how voices carry over the water. Finally, they heard a soft bird call. Rolf answered it. The vague outline of a boat appeared. To Dirk's surprise, Ari was in it.

It was still raining. Rolf and Ari took the oars and eased them into the water to avoid splashing. They rowed with short, powerful strokes. The oars were covered with cloth, and rope had been wound around the oarlocks to make them smoother, as a precaution against any noise they might make. Dirk noticed they stayed close to the shore, where the man-high reeds provided cover. Once in a while, a heron flew over.

They floated along like this, slowly but carefully, and Dirk almost forgot the danger he was in until the boat came to an abrupt stop. He looked up and saw a guardhouse on a dike above him. Lights were on inside. The five men all crouched as low as possible as they floated underneath the dike in the narrow passage between the shores of two islands. Rolf had told him how the guards might turn on the searchlights if they heard noise—any noise—and there would be no place to hide. The guards would use their guns and shoot randomly. Dirk's hands tightened into fists, and a cold sweat broke out over his entire body. He could be killed like a duck in water. But it didn't happen. He fervently praised the Lord.

They reached het Stemgat, the halfway point, through the maze of small islands. The next leg of the trip took them to de Reugt, where even higher reeds kept them out of sight. Rolf and Ari maneuvered the boat into the reeds and took a deserved rest for half an hour. A bottle of gin got passed around. One good swig chased away the bitter cold and the overall feeling of numbness.

The rain had stopped, but it was overcast. As Dirk tried to remember the map, he realized they still had to pass by two guard posts. He prayed the cloud cover would hang on, so they wouldn't have to go by the posts in the light of the moon. There again would be no place to hide while sliding between the dikes on both sides of the narrow creeks. Still, they arrived at de Kerksloot, the last leg of the long trip, without incident.

Just as they thought they were free and could relax, they heard a motorboat approach at high speed. Water birds flew up out of the reeds, flapping their wings and making quite a racket. Rolf abruptly turned the boat into the reeds. The motorboat passed by only a few feet away, and the rowboat danced in its turbulent wake. They could hear the Germans talk and laugh. Would the bent reeds give them away? They collectively held their breath. The danger passed.

"You're bringing us luck, Dirk," Rolf said.

"I'm glad. It scared the hell out of me."

Rolf and Ari rowed for another hour, staying close to the bank. Eventually, they aimed for a hidden spot in the reeds on the bank of the Maas River, which at this point was called the Amer. Their spot was far away from the last German post. Ari said the Germans wouldn't venture out this far to go after them. Dirk was inclined to believe him. These guys had earned his total trust. They stretched out, relaxed, and ate crackers. All that was left to do was wait for daylight and the incoming tide.

The biting wind from the North Sea had calmed down. At daybreak, they could see the other side of the river through a veil of mist. In the current of the incoming tide, the boat floated along with only a little steering needed till a small town loomed up. It was the town of Drimmelen. It was the province of Noord-Brabant. It was the promised land of freedom.

Rolf steered their humble rowboat into the small harbor, and Ari, Rolf, and Dirk sang the Dutch national anthem, "Het Wilhelmus," as loudly as they could to let the soldiers standing on the shore know that they were Dutch. As he belted out the song he hadn't sung for over four years, tears of emotion rolled over Dirk's cheeks. They'd made it! The two Englishmen sang "God Save the King," which proved they were Brits. They were free, and the feeling overwhelmed all of them.

With solid ground under his feet, Dirk threw his arms around Rolf.

"I don't know how to thank you. The people up north will be eternally grateful to you for taking on this risk."

"Voor Koningin en Vaderland," Rolf said. For Queen and country.

Men in khaki uniforms with distinct orange armbands around their sleeves greeted them. They were Resistance people who'd been given a uniform and the task to keep order—*de Ordedienst*, or OD for short.

Now came the hard part. He had to convince them that he was not an adventurer, or a spy for the Nazis. Dr. Hamel had warned him that he would be met with caution and even suspicion, but he passed the immediate test by identifying himself as Dirk van Amstel. The surname seemed to ring a bell in the ears of the OD sergeant.

They were given bread with Spam, English cigarettes, and bars of chocolate. Dirk was not a smoker, but he could appreciate that the smoke coming from a Pall Mall was heavenly compared to the smoke that had come from the strange concoctions Jan had struck up.

It was time to say good-bye to Rolf and Ari, who said they would row back the next day. Rolf expected to see Dirk again for his return trip, and he said this with total confidence. The skipper, with his work-hardened body and calloused hands, was a God-given blessing. Men like Rolf and Ari followed their moral compass, which pointed them in the direction of freedom and away from the Nazis' racially motivated ideology. They were willing to give their lives for it.

Dirk lost track of the Brits after the hearty breakfast, when an OD soldier told Dirk he would bring him to Breda. The vehicle he used was unlike any car Dirk had ever seen. Called a jeep, it was as rugged as a tank, but unlike a tank it was open. It could turn on a dime and jump over ditches. The resistance fighter turned soldier visibly reveled in his macho toy, and put it to the test every chance he got.

The half-hour trip was an eye-opener. The area had been a war zone only a week ago, and it bore every sign of it. Bomb craters pockmarked the fields; buildings lay crumbled in their own rubble; there were burned-out tanks with the hated swastika sign by the side of the road; homes looked violated with their windows blown out. Dirk was heartbroken to see the devastation, and it would have been totally depressing were it not for the overwhelming might the Allies displayed. Already, blown-up bridges were being replaced by prefabricated steel Bailey bridges. Huge tanks with white stars painted on their sides dwarfed the small village farms as they screeched over cobblestone roads that dated back to Napoleonic times. War was devastating. Dirk saw it all around, but it was also exciting to see how soldiers from countries around the world had come together to free the Continent from the Nazi yoke.

The Polish First Armored Division, which was part of the Second Canadian Army, had liberated Breda, and thus Breda had received a temporary Canadian mayor. Dirk was taken to his office to be interrogated by two officers.

The interrogation was conducted in English, which sounded a lot kinder than the snarls of the Gestapo. Even the khaki uniforms were a relief from the steel-gray ones the Germans had sported. The officers' demeanor was relaxed, and they even handed him a bar of chocolate, offered a cigarette and a cup of coffee before they got down to business.

"Who are you? Did anyone send you?" the highest-ranking officer asked him.

"I am Dirk van Amstel, and I was sent by the Resistance."

"Do you have identification?"

Dirk unbuttoned his raincoat, which was still damp from the rain and fog. He reached for the gold chain around his neck and showed the small rubber tube hanging from it.

"Quite ingenuous!" the younger officer said.

"You learn to be ingenuous with Nazis around."

He unclipped the tube and handed it over. What came out had survived the trip. It was his ID. The officers looked at the picture and his name: Dirk van Enthoven.

"So Dirk van Amstel is Dirk van Enthoven?"

"Yes, officer. I was told that the surname van Amstel would indicate that I am headed for the headquarters of His Royal Highness, Prince Bernhard."

"Well, well. What's your mission?"

"I am to bring insulin back up north. There's an acute shortage *of this essential drug, and diabetics are in severe danger."

The officer looked at his ID and back at him. "You are twenty-four. Isn't that a little young to be trusted with such an important mission and with that much precious insulin?"

"It depends on what you call young, sir. Many of your soldiers are my age or younger. I'm a medical student, and I was chosen because I am still strong enough to survive a trip like this."

They considered his answer, but seemed more interested in what was going on north of the rivers. He informed them that a few days earlier, tens of thousands of men had been rounded up in

Rotterdam and forced to walk to work camps, mostly in Germany. More razzias in other cities were expected. People were hungry and cold. To make things worse, he said, the Germans demanded that each household hand over either a blanket or a winter coat for the "poor people in Germany" who'd been bombed by the Allies. Most people had tried to sabotage that order, but few successfully.

"I still don't understand why you were chosen for this delicate job. Can you explain?" the older officer asked.

Dirk wondered how he could ever convince them that he was a legitimate line crosser with a detailed task, and not an adventurer or a spy for the Germans.

"There simply aren't enough men left who are free to move around," he said. "Men between the ages of seventeen and fifty are picked up by the Gestapo and sent to work in German factories. Most students like me have gone into hiding. So have 30,000 railroad workers. I am considered essential because I work in a hospital laboratory, so I can still move around. My superior, Dr. Hamel, is the one who sent me on this mission."

The younger officer studied his ID. "I see you work at a hospital in Utrecht."

"Yes, sir. That's where I studied medicine before the university closed because its students refused to sign a Declaration of Loyalty."

"Loyalty? To whom?"

"To the rules the Nazis imposed on us."

The officers got interested in his stories. He was probably one of the first line crossers they'd had the chance to interview. After all, Breda had scarcely been liberated. What had been going on in Holland during the war, and what was still going on in the as-yet-unconquered provinces, was unknown to them. Dirk used their ignorance to fortify his position, but he decided not to tell them about his trip in the coffin. It might sound a bit too fantastic.

"So, how do you think you're going to get to your prince?" the older officer asked.

He welcomed the question. This was where the information Dr. Hamel had pumped into his head would be invaluable.

"Once I get out on the street, I will look for the tower of the cathedral as a guide to get me to the city's center. From de Grote Markt, I will walk over het Kerkplein, through de Torenstraat and de Vismarktstraat to de Haven. There I'll take a right and announce myself at the Old Post Office, which is now Prins Bernhard's headquarters."

"And then?"

"I will ask for Majoor Buma. He is expecting me, sir."

"Let's see what Majoor Buma has to say about this," the older officer said, and picked up the phone.

"I can give you the number," Dirk said. He prayed he'd remembered it right.

The officer dialed the number, and after working through several layers of secretaries and adjutants, he got through to Majoor Buma. They talked briefly, and then the officer hung up the phone.

"Okay, young man. Major Buma is expecting you. He will send up a jeep. You can wait in the hall. Don't forget to take your bar of chocolate," he added with a smile, and handed it to him. "Good luck, Dirk van Enthoven. You have guts."

The same driver who'd brought him over from the river arrived moments later.

"Were they tough on you?" he asked

"As tough as they should be," Dirk said.

The cathedral — de Grote Kerk to locals — showed signs of many direct hits. Shorn pieces lay strewn around its base, but it was still standing, as majestic and inspiring as ever. The jeep hopped over the chunks and got them to the harbor. At the end of the quay stood a building of unusual architecture. It had the pretense of a medieval castle with its round tower. A guard held watch in front.

Dirk was led to the office of Majoor Buma, who rose from behind his desk. An unusually tall man with a head that was small in proportion to his body, he looked somewhat like an asparagus.

"Dirk van Enthoven, how was your trip?" he asked.

"Cold, but successful, sir."

Dirk spent the next ten minutes answering pointed questions. Once it was established that he was indeed Dirk van Enthoven, the major lit a pipe and allowed that he knew Dirk's father well. When Dirk looked surprised, because he'd never heard of a Majoor Buma among his father's friends or acquaintances, he smiled and said that his real name wasn't Buma. Few people around there used their own names, he said, for fear that the Gestapo back home might take it out on their families.

Dirk began to relax, and deep tiredness set in. His coat was still damp, and he shivered. Majoor Buma noticed and said he'd made arrangements with the pharmacist for Dirk to sleep at his home above his pharmacy. But Dirk told him of a good friend on the Veemarktstraat who he was sure would take him in.

Carla answered his ringing of the bell. She burst into tears at the sight of him and didn't stop. He took her in his arms and waited for her to tell him what was wrong.

"You're alive, Dirk. Thank God. I'm so worried about all of you up north."

He couldn't help wondering if that was all there was to her tears. They leaned into each other, giving in to the comfort of familiarity.

With a sudden impulse, Carla held him at arm's length and said, "Dirk, your coat is wet, and it isn't raining."

"Yes, I know. May I come in?"

"Oh, my God, of course."

As spontaneous as Carla, her mother welcomed him in. A man who tried to stay discreetly in the background was introduced to him as Jacob.

"What's the story, Dirk?" Carla asked as she took his damp raincoat.

"It's hard to get through de Biesbosch without getting wet."

"When did you get across?"

"I arrived this morning."

His statement sent Mrs. Vlaskamp into action. She told Carla to raid her father's closet and get Dirk some dry clothes.

After a good nap, he sat down to dinner with the entire family, which now included Jacob, a handsome man with sad light-brown eyes. Carla's father wanted to know the details of his trip through the Biesbosch. Carla wanted to know how the others of the Group of Eight were doing. He told them about conditions in the north, but all the way through the conversation, he felt as if a somber cloud hung over this family. That surprised him, because they had been liberated. They were free.

After dinner, he fell into a deep sleep, the kind that offers no dreams. When he woke up the next morning, he felt disoriented. Bit by bit, the reality set in that he was in Carla's home, in a liberated province, and that his head was filled with cotton balls. The day loomed large. He had to make contact with the pharmacist and get to work.

Carla determined over breakfast that the pharmacist in question was none other than her father's best friend. She painted an agreeable picture of the man. On the way to the pharmacy, she told the story of how she had helped keep the most essential medicines in the secret depot out of the hands of a marauding German officer.

Directly across from the stately city hall and in the shadow of the cathedral, the pharmacy sat prominently on the marketplace. Its interior looked wonderfully authentic. Delft ceramic pots, indicating various substances, sat decoratively on mahogany shelves behind the eight assistants, who reached for them as they prepared prescriptions, each at their place on a long counter, and each with a precision scale. It was a busy place.

Carla introduced him to Mr. Wetselaar, who was short in stature but long in geniality. His witty eyes gave credence to Carla's opinion that this man was the best joketeller in Breda. People came to his pharmacy to fill prescriptions, to be sure, but to hear him tell jokes was another draw. The pharmacy had also become a place where Resistance people could safely leave a message and get one back.

Mr. Wetselaar had expected him, but he was pleasantly surprised that Dirk turned out to be Carla's friend. Like the Canadian officers, he was eager to hear how things were up north, and he invited them to come upstairs so Dirk could share the stories with his wife as well. Dirk was led into a sunny, comfortable living room.

When Mrs. Wetselaar entered the room, Dirk was taken aback by the physical contrast between man and wife. She was at least a head taller than her husband with eyes as pure blue as Anna's, and her calm, gracious demeanor was reminiscent of Anna's grandmother. A quiver of recognition ran through him.

He tried to give them an accurate picture of what conditions were like in Utrecht. That the Germans were out for themselves was not news to them. All the same, they were shocked to hear that entire factories and telephone networks had been dismantled and the equipment brought to the Heimat. That the proud harbors of Amsterdam and Rotterdam had been systematically demolished with callous, vengeful brutality made them shake their heads in heartbreak and disbelief. He hated to tell them that electricity was scarce, water supplies marginal, fuel almost unobtainable, and food in short supply. He didn't spare them, though. They wanted the unvarnished truth. They had relatives up north to worry about.

"We will have to rebuild our country from scratch," Mr. Wetselaar said. He let out a deep sigh. "And it will have to be done by people who are sick and exhausted."

"Don't despair, Gerard," his wife said. "We are a resilient people. We'll be back on our feet in no time. You'll see!" She didn't just look like the baroness. She sounded like her.

Carla said good-bye. Mr. Wetselaar took Dirk to a large storage room behind the pharmacy. Part of it was called *de watten zolder*, an attic where bandages and cotton balls were stored. It also held the most essential medicines that the pharmacist had accumulated over the last months of the war, when it became clear the Germans were prioritizing production for their own use. He foresaw a calamitous shortage, and had convinced pharmaceutical manufacturers to allow him to set up a depot for his region with a secret portion of their production.

The insulin was typically packaged in 10 cc vials. They wouldn't take up much space, but they were fragile and there were many. Mr. Wetselaar suggested they could bind them together with tape into clumps of ten vials. But what could they put these clumps into? They considered the inner tube of a bicycle or a car tire that could float, but even if they could get hold of one, it was not a foolproof solution. They rejected the idea. In the end, a wooden crate seemed the best idea. The clumps could rest inside *houtswol*, a kind of curled wood shavings. They planned to tie a rope with a handle around the crate and put a brick inside. In case of detection, Dirk could throw it overboard. Or, if he was lucky, he could hide it in tall reeds and come back for it later.

The better part of the day was spent on the project, until Dirk started to cough. It didn't escape Mr. Wetselaar's keen eye.

"If you don't mind me saying so, Dirk," he said, "you look like you could use some rest."

Dirk didn't want to give in, but the next bout of dry coughing seemed to come up from the underworld. He was sent back to Carla's home with a bottle of aspirins.

The next days passed in a daze. Dirk ran a high fever, he was coughing up some ugly green mucus, and his throat and chest were sore from the incessant coughing spells. Between Carla and her mother, he was fussed over night and day. And he had to admit, he needed all the care he could get. The endless coughing, the wheezing, the sore throat, and the shortness of breath—he felt like he was on his way out. A doctor was called in, who declared he had pneumonia. Rest, he said, and drink a lot of water. That and nourishing food will get you back on your feet.

Mrs. Wetselaar talked the English officer who billeted in their home into scaring up some good old-fashioned oatmeal. Carla biked to a farmer to get eggs and bacon. Gradually, with all this care and good food, he emerged from his stupor. His voice came back, and his mind cleared from the fog he'd lived in for several days. With it came the realization that he had to get up and bring the insulin back over the rivers. The very thought gave him shivers.

Later that day, Carla came into his room with chicken soup. She'd lost weight, yet she'd retained her easy elegance and spontaneity. But the look in her eyes gave away that something had profoundly touched her. Was it related to the cloud he'd felt hanging over this family from the moment he'd stepped into their lives?

"You won't believe this, Dirk," she said. "A few days after *de Bevrijding,* Otto rang the bell."

"Otto? Did he come to cash in on 'Geef Carla een zoen'?"

She didn't smile at what he'd meant as a joke.

"He's an officer in the Prinses Irene brigade. I forget his rank. He was in uniform. Rather dashing, and enjoying every minute of it. He'd been part of liberating Tilburg."

It was exciting news, but she delivered it in a flat tone of voice.

"I'm glad to hear he survived his escape to England," Dirk said. "You don't know this, but I brought him to Maastricht on a barge over de Maas to put him in contact with English Intelligence people. I said good-bye to him in the caves of St. Pietersberg."

"So, that's why you were gone so long right after the university closed! Anna and I were worried sick about you."

"Yes, I know. Sorry about that. But it must have been a happy surprise to see Otto on your doorstep?"

She was silent, looking at her hands, rubbing them together in a nervous gesture. This was not the Carla he remembered from their happy days in Utrecht.

"Something wrong?" he asked carefully.

She looked up at him with moistened eyes. "Oh, Dirk, it was the wrong moment. It couldn't have been worse."

The story she told was very, very sad. After spending a few days in the cellar during Breda's liberation, Jacob's wife had run out and been shot by a sniper across the street. For two years, the Jewish couple had lived in their attic.

"My God. The poor man must be heartbroken."

"We all are. I had brought up their food every day after I came home in August, so I got to know them both quite well. And that makes it so much harder."

Dirk was sitting in a comfortable chair, wrapped in a bathrobe. Carla got up, knelt in front of him, and rested her head in his lap. It surprised him, but he knew what to do. He stroked her hair and waited.

"I am so confused, Dirk."

"About what?"

"About everything. We've been liberated, and I should feel happy. Yet there's darkness all around. It was so weird to see Otto standing there in uniform. He looked triumphant, and he had a right to be, of course, coming fresh from helping to liberate Tilburg. But I saw something very different."

"Like what?"

She had difficulty expressing at first what had bothered her, although it was understandable that she hadn't been in the mood for triumph right after witnessing a friend being murdered. It went deeper than that, though. It went back to something that happened while he was on the barge with Otto. Herman had come to Betty's house to say he was going to do what the Germans wanted him to do: work in German factories. Dirk had always wondered what in the world had motivated Herman. Carla framed it as greed. His parents were wealthy and in danger of losing it all if he didn't show up at the Arbeitseinsatz bureau. Herman and his parents had taken the threat by Seyss-Inquart seriously and literally. Carla and Anna had tried to talk him out of it, and he'd left piqued and angry. She couldn't forgive him. In her mind, Herman was a coward. Shortly after that incident, Piet was executed because he refused to go to Germany. The contrast couldn't be greater. He had stood by his principles and given his life for them. And then she learned that Otto had gone to England, leaving Dirk as the only male student of the Group of Eight to carry out their commitment to help Jews survive, and most of that task had fallen to Anna. Emmy and she had lived up to at least some of their commitment, she said.

Dirk heard remorse and condemnation in her voice. Most of all, he sensed she was at loose ends. One boyfriend had fallen far short of her expectations. The one who had hoped to become her boyfriend hadn't fared much better. What had been so excruciatingly difficult, she told him, was that Otto had represented the victorious student who could boast of a heroic escape to England and managing to get military training, while in the same room was Jacob, also a student without a chance to finish his studies, but who'd spent two years in an attic with his wife, who then got killed. She said it had been insufferable to compare the two.

Dirk sensed her sympathies lay with Jacob.

"I have a hard time making sense of life," she said, getting up. She shoved a chair closer to his. "What's the point of it all? We've already wasted four years of precious youth. Where will we go from here?"

"That's an existential question, Carla. If we're in a good mood, it's not so hard to find an answer, but when things are down we seem to only think of life as a tough assignment. All right, that's not an answer to your question. I'll have to do better."

"Go on, Dirk, I'm all ears."

"If we survive this wretched war, we have an enormous task to replace the societal fabric that Hitler wove from threads that couldn't hold together. Although they may have glittered at first, they were really brittle with hate. And now it's torn and ripped to pieces."

"You're poetic, Dirk. Maybe, if Hitler had used poetry instead of brutality, he wouldn't find himself at a dead end."

Dirk searched for words that could get Carla out of her funk.

Mankind's history was littered with moments like this. One country swallowed another under the pretense of a false ideology, driven by greed, vanity, and an outsized ego that craved power. Time and again, this scenario had played out, from even before Roman times till now. It could turn your heart into a cynical stone. Maybe it was better to look at the miracle of victims dusting themselves off and working to create a better world, or at least trying to. Were there eternal values that survived the wicked minds that concocted those self-serving scenarios? Love for mankind came to mind. That really had to be the foundation for everything. The rest followed from that.

"Carla, think of the rest of your life as an opportunity to weave a fabric of moral threads that will hold up. It's our generation that has to translate the disaster we've witnessed into something positive and beautiful."

"Would you say that to Jacob, who just lost his wife?"

"Yes, I would. Absolutely."

"Are you an incorrigible optimist, Dirk? Can you reconcile the hate, the racism, the brutality, and the beastly treatment of innocent people? Shall I go on with this list?"

"You don't have to. I can recite it by heart. An immoral leader misled his people. We have to restore the tenets we live by or, to speak from my faith, what God clearly wants us to do, and that is to love one another."

"It sound so simple. Love one another."

"It isn't simple. Hitler didn't love the Jews, so he made other people hate them, even if they'd never thought of hating them before. We have to turn that around. Germans cannot just love Germans. Christians cannot just love Christians. We have to love people who are other than us. It is uncomfortable at times, and inconvenient, but it's the only way humanity can move forward. I am deeply convinced of it. Hate is no replacement for love."

His throat felt scratchy, and he started to cough. What a way to chitchat over a bowl of chicken soup! He let his head fall back and closed his eyes. When he opened them, Carla was gone.

A week had passed since he'd set foot in Drimmelen. The temperatures were dropping, the water in the rivers getting colder. His return trip was overdue. Majoor Buma called to ask if Dirk felt up to it. Dirk answered that, yes, he was. All right, Majoor Buma said, that's fine. We will arrange for you to leave in a few days. Depending on the weather, of course.

Dirk shared this news at the dinner table. Carla was on the verge of tears, wondering if he was suicidal. How could he go on a trip like that when he was still weak as a kitten?

"I don't have to do the rowing, Carla. Don't worry."

Her mother was worried too, he could tell from the frown on her face, but she didn't give her opinion. Neither did her father.

Jacob spoke up. "I can go in your stead, Dirk. I have nothing more to lose."

This was too much for Carla. She exploded. She squished her napkin into a ball and threw it on the table. "You have nothing to lose? Your life is worth nothing? What if you get caught and the Nazis put you in a concentration camp, like they've always wanted to do?"

There was stone silence around the table until Carla started sobbing. Dirk realized he was probably the only one who truly understood her outburst. She thought of Herman as a coward. She blamed Otto for skipping out on their oath of solidarity with the Jews. But she respected Jacob, and she didn't want to lose him too.

Jacob didn't know what to make of Carla's explosion. He was too deep into his grief to have noticed her feelings for him, that she was genuinely concerned. He looked baffled and at a loss for words.

"Jacob, thank you for the generous offer," Dirk said, but before he could finish the sentence, Carla cried out, "No, Dirk!"

"Let me finish, Carla." She nodded, obviously understanding from his severe tone that he meant business.

"I will not take you up on it, Jacob," he said. "It is a matter of honor for me to bring the medicine back. What I would appreciate, though, is if you could help me with getting the loot packaged and together."

"I'll be glad to," Jacob said.

A few days later, Dirk met Rolf and Ari in the darkness of a cold November night. He'd been dropped off in Drimmelen with the crate, which wasn't heavy but bulky. They walked over to the Amer River and transferred the crate to the same rowboat he'd arrived in ten days earlier.

The coast was clear, the air cold and moist. Rolf and Ari picked up the oars.

"Here we go again, Dirk," Rolf said.

Indeed. The soft sound of the oars dipping into the water, the soft lapping of the waves against the hull, it was déjà vu. But this time, he had a precious load to bring home.

He placed his trust in the two strong men in front of him and thanked God for his restored health. Mr. Wetselaar had given him medicine to suppress his cough. Carla had put homemade cookies in his bag, and her father had donated a flask with jenever. God was good. He stretched and settled in for the trip, his mind filled with memories he wouldn't soon forget.

CHAPTER FORTY-THREE

Anna – February 1945

A crust of ice had formed on her blanket and rubbed against her cheek. Anna didn't want to move. She watched her exhaled breath turn into a plume. Nothing enticed her to get out of bed. It was still dark outside. The nights were long and the days short in this coldest of winters. Did God have any compassion for a suffering nation? Couldn't he, in his omnipotence, turn up the heat a few degrees?

She sighed. How dare she complain? There would be a breakfast of sorts awaiting her. There were still some logs to put on the fire. Nobody in the castle had as yet succumbed to hunger or disease. The same couldn't be said for the people who lived in the big cities. Every day, people roamed the farms around the castle to find food and bring it back to their hungry families out west. They brought valuables to barter with. If Grandmother's golden necklace could get them a sack of potatoes or a side of bacon, they were willing to part with the heirloom. Hendrik told her the things he was offered for food embarrassed him.

Finally, she willed herself to get up and face the layer of ice in the washbowl. She cracked the surface with a cloth. Maybe cold water on her face could wake her to the day. She quickly threw on some warm clothes and slipped out. There was no use in waking Frits. He was better off staying under wool blankets. Without enough wood to stoke a fire in the ballroom, practice on the piano with fingers that felt like icicles was unproductive and frustrating. These cold winter days, Frits spent much of his time in the warm kitchen. Mien had taken him under her wing, and he felt safe with her.

"Good morning, Miss Anna," Janus said as she walked into the dining room. "It's a little warmer today than yesterday. Maybe we've had the worst of this freezing weather."

"Good morning, Janus. You're the eternal optimist."

"Got to be, Miss Anna. Things are bad enough without us getting down in the dumps. I talked to a woman yesterday on my way home. She said she came from Utrecht, and —"

Anna interrupted him. "From Utrecht?"

"Yes. She said they were now eating sugar beets over there. They don't have much else they can get with their coupons, she said."

"That's awful, Janus."

He poured her a cup of surrogate tea. Oma's secret cache of real tea was long gone. The news Janus brought put a lump in her throat. She stirred the tea, but didn't feel like drinking it. Her mind was in Utrecht. Where was Dirk these days? Living in a news vacuum was nerve-racking. No mail. No telephone. No trains. No buses. Life had come to a standstill. Maybe it hadn't been such a good idea to ask the railroad workers to strike. Life had taken a dark turn ever since. The strike had stopped all transport, and it had made the Germans so furious that they wanted to take revenge in any way they saw fit.

"Shall I ask Mien to boil you an egg to go with your bread, Miss Anna?"

"Yes, Janus, that would be nice, but you know? I almost feel I should refuse it after what you told me about the people in Utrecht."

"It wouldn't help the people over there, Miss Anna, if you didn't eat that egg. You need to take care of yourself. You have a lot to do."

He was right, and she was touched that he thought of her that way.

"Ask Mien to boil one for you too, Janus. We depend on you!"

He allowed a little smile and left the room. Anna picked up her silver napkin ring and twirled it round and round her finger. A sugar beet! The next thing might be a tulip bulb, for heaven's sake. Could people survive on pig fodder? She shivered at the thought, and her heart grew angry at the gross lack of compassion her countrymen were treated to. Stone-cold hearts in Den Haag and Berlin turned a blind eye to famine. Could it be that they hated the Dutch people the way they hated the Jews, so much that they wanted them to starve to death? It was incomprehensible, yet all signs pointed at a calculated strategy.

While these depressing thoughts roamed Anna's mind, Oma walked into the dining room. She wore a wool shawl over a heavy tweed jacket, and she still looked cold.

"Good morning, Oma. Did you sleep well?"

"As long as I stayed under the covers, I slept well. I was very grateful for the Austrian eiderdown quilt your grandfather insisted on importing so many years ago."

Anna didn't waste a minute to share her agony. "Oma, Janus just told me that he met a woman from Utrecht. She said they now have to eat sugar beets there."

Oma seated herself at the head of the table and carefully unfolded her napkin.

"I see. I thought you looked rather down, Anna. Your heart is in Utrecht with somebody you love."

There was no denying Oma's astute observation. The minute Janus uttered the word *Utrecht*, her mind shot directly to Dirk, whom she hadn't heard from for over a month. He had let her know by courier via a trusted intermediary of his safe return from what he called an "adventurous journey." She regularly received the necessary coupons for the Jews they were hiding around the castle. Dirk had never let her down on his promise to provide them. But the break in any form of communication was killing her.

"You're right, Oma," she said. "I love Dirk. If we survive this cussed war, we will get married. That's the one thing I am absolutely sure of. But, my God, we have to stay alive to see that day."

The thought put the lump back in her throat. She couldn't go on.

"My dear Anna," Oma said. "I can see that you are wrought up about this. What can I do to lighten your mood?"

Anna wiped the tears that had crept into her eyes. "I want to go there," she said. "But I don't see how I can walk away from my responsibilities. The Jews, Frits, the farmers. You!"

"Follow your heart, Anna. Dirk is a good man. I wholeheartedly approve of your choice. Your father can run the affairs of the estate in your absence. He hasn't wanted to interfere with your work, because he's impressed with your abilities. But you know that he is a capable administrator. Mien can mother Frits. And I can bring the coupons around."

"You can't be serious, Oma."

"Of course I am. I have lived in this place for forty years. The people around here are no strangers to me, Anna. It will give me pleasure to get reacquainted."

"But couldn't we ask Sylvia or my mother?"

"Think again. Sylvia is needed at the parsonage to help poor Mrs. Bosma with her young children, now that her husband has died. She is safer there than out on the road. And you know very well, Anna, that your mother would not be an ideal choice to bring clandestine material around to people she never bothered much with."

As usual, her grandmother made a lot of sense.

The next morning, Anna told Frits to be good while she was gone. Janus pumped up her bicycle tires, which were still in good enough shape. Hendrik filled her rucksack with a ham, carrots, and

Brussels sprouts; and baskets with potatoes hung from both sides of the luggage carrier. Frits talked Mien into parting with a jar of homemade strawberry jam. For Dirk, he insisted. Since money couldn't buy much of anything these days, Oma sent her off with twelve gold coins. Anna tucked them in a velvet sack and put the sack in a pocket of her tweed jacket.

In spite of the early hour—it was still dark outside—Vader, Oma, Frits, Walter, Mien, and Janus stood in the front yard as she climbed on her bike. Moeder was still upstairs, her way of signaling disapproval of her daughter's folly to go to the city while city people were trying to get to the country. As Anna rounded the curve of the circular driveway, they all waved, and she felt their support. She would need it. Keeping her heavily laden bike going forward took extra push. Besides, she felt like a stuffed sausage. With her grandmother's hiking boots on her feet, extra underwear, and a wide raincoat that hid linen bags filled with dried beans, sugar, and two bars of soap, she didn't feel very athletic. But in case German patrols confiscated the obvious cargo hanging from her bike, she would at least have a few things to offer Betty's household.

A biting wind blew through the trees that lined the path between the castle and the town of Ede, but mercifully, the sun came out as she passed the barracks where Herr von Schloss kept his troops on alert. Over the winter months, every now and then, a parcel had been left on the castle's kitchen doorstep. Mien said she didn't have a clue how it had landed there; never saw anybody put it there. Invariably, it contained supplies that were unavailable in stores, like soap or canned meat. At first, she didn't want to use it. Maybe it had been left by mistake. But Oma told her to use it since obviously, someone meant well. Privately, Oma was convinced it was Herr von Schloss's doing. She had refused his offer to help, saying she could not accept food from the enemy, but he had found a way of getting it to her.

The back roads Anna took to get to Utrecht led through small farm communities. The fallow fields were snowed under. Winter had silenced the landscape. Cows were tied in their stanchions; farmers sat inside sharpening their tools for when spring came. As the morning wore on and a feeble sun threw shadows over the narrow paths, Anna began to meet people traveling in the opposite direction on bikes that no longer had rubber tires. Wood or thick ropes had replaced them, and some just rode on the wheels' rims. These people were what the farmers called the "hunger trippers," and they were mostly women and teenagers. The closer she got to the city, the more haggard they looked. It wasn't just their worn clothes. Their faces were sunken and gray.

She took a break in Maarsbergen, the halfway point. There she ran into a group of people that seemed to have gathered for the purpose of commiserating. She listened closely as they talked about a roadblock German soldiers had set up with the help of traitors. A woman who said she had biked from Amsterdam held her audience captive with stories of how she'd watched hunger trippers being relieved of the goods they had dearly paid for. The stories of conditions in the capital were beyond sad. They were frightening.

"We haven't laughed in ages," the woman said. "Nothing works anymore, not even the sewerage. Kids can't go to school, and the trams don't run, because people have taken up the blocks between the rails for firewood. It's awful."

Anna was more determined than ever to get the food to Dirk, Betty, and Jan. Now that she knew where the roadblock was, she changed course. It made the trip longer but safer. She pushed hard to get to Utrecht before curfew, and prayed no German soldier would ask her what was in the baskets hanging from her bike.

As soon as she got to the outskirts of Utrecht, she noticed differences, and they weren't subtle. She was riding into a ghost town. Life, if there was any, was invisible. Garbage in the streets—once unthinkable in proper Holland—was a sure sign of breakdown in municipal services. As she pedaled by a city park, she saw a teenage boy hack off tree branches and bundle them onto his sleigh. There was nobody around to forbid him. Once in a while a car with German officers drove by, or a biker, or a wagon pulled by a horse that was too run-down to trot.

Anna was tired and hungry, but she kept pushing through the snowy sludge on the streets. It was getting close to curfew time. Finally, she could step off her bike and take it to the back gate of Jan and Betty's house. With trembling legs, she leaned it against the fence and took a few minutes to catch her breath. A look through the window in the kitchen door gave her a feeling of foreboding. For a woman who was a meticulous housekeeper, Betty's kitchen was in disarray. Once inside, she missed the usual enticing smell of something cooking on the stove, and dirty dishes were piled in the sink. She opened the door to the hallway and called out, "Oo-hoo." No answer. She opened the door to the living room. Deserted. A cold fear gripped her heart. What had happened?

Back in the hallway, she repeated her call. A door opened upstairs. A woman leaned over the stair railing and looked down. Anna couldn't believe her eyes. It was Emmy. What was she doing here? In spite of her tired legs, she raced upstairs.

"Emmy! Where is everybody?"

Emmy's answer was to drop into her arms without saying a word. Even through her heavy sweater, Anna could count Emmy's ribs. Holding her at arm's length, she saw the face of hunger. To be sure, Anna had thinned herself, but nothing like what she saw in front of her. She had prepared herself for the worst, but this was worse than the worst she had imagined. An official diet of 350 calories per day had put people on a downward spiral.

Anna let go of Emmy and looked through the open door into Jan and Betty's bedroom. Dirk sat at the side of the bed where Jan lay under a pile of blankets. She repressed the impulse to rush to him. Something about the way he was leaning over Jan held her back. She motioned Emmy to come downstairs. She needed explanations.

"I am glad to see you, Emmy," she said, "but I'm very worried that it's not for good reasons."

"I came here in November because I couldn't stand staying at home. I told Betty and Jan I would distribute the newspaper and do whatever they wanted me to do, if I could just stay with them."

"Jan doesn't look in good shape. What's going on with him?"

"He steadily lost weight. We all did, but he lost it faster. When he caught pneumonia, he had no reserve to fight it off."

Anna swallowed hard. Low reserve, no resistance, no wonder drugs. This spelled disaster. Then she remembered she had left her supplies outside. They might get stolen.

"Quick, Emmy, help me get my things inside."

"Things?"

"Yes, you know, potatoes, ham, things like that."

Emmy's eyes widened, and she grabbed her jacket from a hook on the wall. By faint twilight, they unhitched the baskets with potatoes and the rucksack from the baggage carrier and lugged them inside.

"Why aren't the dishes done?" Anna asked, even as she hated to sound like a scolding mother.

"No water most of the time. Same for electricity. We can only do them some of the time. And we don't have soap."

Anna fought off tears and concentrated on lining her gifts up on the kitchen table. She opened her raincoat and undid the sacks of beans and sugar. Emmy clapped her hands in amazement.

"I haven't seen food like this since last summer," she said. "Where did you get it?"

"I live in a rural area, and I was very, very lucky not to get stopped. Is Betty upstairs? I haven't seen her in over a year. How is she?"

"Very sad and very strong."

It was time to face what she hated to see and admit to. On the way up the stairs, she heard Jan's hacking, labored coughing. Anna hesitated on the doorstep. She felt like an intruder. It had been so long since she had been a daily member of the family, so to speak.

Dirk and Emmy had taken that place. But the feeling that Jan and Betty were her surrogate parents had never left her. To the extent a person can be changed, Jan and Betty had changed her in fundamental ways. In spite of their differences in background, conventional and superficial barriers had been wiped away. Jan and Betty's emphasis had been on hospitality and on vigorous defense of freedom.

Anna felt shy as she put one foot into the bedroom. Dirk looked up and was noticeably shocked to see her standing there, as if she were an apparition—someone he carried deeply in his heart, but was startled to see in reality. He got up slowly. Anna didn't want to move. Something very private and tender was going on in this room. She could read his mood, but didn't know how to react to it. Should she turn around and leave?

But he came up to her and took both her hands in his. "Anna," he whispered. "You came!"

He had lost weight, as she'd expected he would, but the hollow look in his eyes took her aback. Dark rings circled them. His hands felt bony inside hers.

"I came to bring food." It was all she could think of to say.

"Too late," he said, and turned his head toward Jan.

A jab of pain stabbed her soul, the pain of regret that she hadn't acted sooner. She leaned into Dirk, seeking reassurance. He responded by putting his arm around her shoulders.

"I'm glad you came," he said. "Say hello to Betty."

And there was Betty, sitting on a chair near her side of the bed. She looked like she had retreated into herself, and Anna wasn't sure if Betty was aware of what was going on around her, except that she was losing her man.

"Betty," she whispered.

The woman looked up, and as with Dirk, Anna had the sensation that her unexpected presence was more like an apparition than a reality to Betty. The people under the roof of this house had lived in a state of hunger and exhaustion from trying to stay alive, while the means to do so had gradually been taken away, sapping their vitality.

Anna knelt next to Betty's chair. She looked like a shadow of the plump woman Anna remembered.

"I'm glad you came, Anna. I've missed you."

"I should have come earlier, Betty, but I brought some food."

"Thank you," she said softly.

Then Betty retreated back into herself.

Anna thought the best thing to do now was put some order into this household. Dishes needed to be washed, a dinner prepared. There must be things she could do to buck these people up. Downstairs, the first thing she did was to take a spoonful of the sugar she'd brought. After a day of bicycling, she was badly in need of instant energy. Emmy was put to work peeling potatoes while Anna reorganized the dishes and washed them in cold water with the bar of soap she'd brought. There was just enough petroleum left to fire up the small countertop stove and boil the potatoes. She found a sharp knife to slice into Hendrik's smoked ham. Well aware that hungry people couldn't stomach a lot of food all at once, or it would make them sick, she cubed the ham and the potatoes into small portions and carried them upstairs.

The thought of food seemed to bring them back to life a bit, except for Jan, who was very quiet in between bouts of coughing. It was a situation unlike any she'd been in before, sitting silently around the bed of a dying man with people who hadn't eaten a decent meal in for God knows how long.

Night had fallen. Electricity was shut off from the outside. It got pitch dark in the house, except for a lit candle in Betty and Jan's bedroom. There was nothing more she could do. Emmy, who had taken over her room, offered it back. But Anna had only one desire, and that was to be close to Dirk. He had camped out in Jan's hobby room on a mattress on the floor since he'd returned from his adventure. Anna threw all pretentions and conventions to the wind and let her exhausted body fall on the mattress, not even bothering to take off her clothes. She dropped into a deep sleep.

It was still dark when she woke up with a start, wondering where she was until she felt a warm body next to her. A blanket covered them both. Dirk! How often had she imagined sharing a bed with the man she loved? She raised herself up on her elbows to take a better look at him, even though it was dark in the room. Like her, he'd fallen asleep with his clothes on, ready to get up if Betty needed him. His chest rose and fell with his breathing. She didn't have the heart to wake him, as he had probably not wanted to wake her. After her eyes adjusted to the dark, she saw how exhausted and gaunt he looked. As with everything else about their future, what they might desire most had to be postponed. They were both too exhausted to make love, and this was not the place or the time.

Sleep wouldn't return. The many impressions of the day crowded her mind. The excursion to bring food had been bleak — the landscape frozen, the roads messy with sludge. But that was the least of it. The people she'd met on the way had foretold what she'd found here in Utrecht. Besides hunger and deprivation, a thick blanket of melancholy had fallen over everyone and everything. She would have to fight hard not to be buried by it as well.

Dirk stirred in his sleep and briefly opened his eyes. "Anna," he whispered. She waited for him to say more, but he fell asleep again. And so did she, with her arm draped over his body. It was eerily quiet, except for Jan's frequent coughing spells.

The next morning, as she stood in the kitchen, Anna noticed the apple tree in the backyard was gone. Dirk had cut it down for firewood, Emmy told her, because they'd run out of coal. Anna had come downstairs with the thought of making tea and bringing breakfast upstairs to Betty and Dirk. Jan, she'd seen through the open bedroom door, was lying very still except for when he coughed. Dirk sat next to his bed, exactly the way she'd found them the day before.

Only a trickle of water came out of the faucet. There was no bread in the breadbox, and no gas burner would light up on the kitchen stove. The last bit of petroleum had been used up to boil the potatoes last night. What good did it do to bring potatoes, beans, and carrots if they couldn't be cooked? There had to be a way to make things better.

She slipped into her coat and out of the house and knocked on the neighbors' door. It was as much a shock to see the woman who opened the door as it had been to see Betty. Anna remembered her to be in her forties, but today she looked over sixty, with folds in her neck and creases in her face that hadn't been there before. With her body whittled down by lack of food, her tailored dress hung around her like a grainsack.

"Hi. I am Anna. I don't know if you remember me, but I used to live with Jan and Betty next door."

A light of recognition came into the woman's eyes. She invited her in.

"How is Jan?" she asked immediately. "He looked sick to me last I saw him."

"He has pneumonia, and we're very worried about him."

"Oh, dear. That's not good news. There isn't any good news these days, unless you're bringing some?"

"I wish I could tell you the end is in sight, but that would be a lie. I came to ask if you know of a way I could buy petroleum. We ran out last night."

The neighbor told her that it was only available on the black market, and it would cost her a mint. Anna said she didn't care what it cost. They needed it. She got the name of an *olie boer* at the edge of the city. She didn't waste any time, and took her bike with its two empty baskets out of the backyard. She divided the twelve gold coins Oma had given her into equal portions over her various pockets.

The address brought her to a machine shop. Or was it a dump? All manner of machine parts, in dilapidated condition, lay strewn about the yard. By the standards of the day, the man who opened the door was fat. His smug smile told her he thought he had the world by the tail, and there wasn't much he couldn't afford to do, and that probably included fleecing people like her.

"Good morning," she said. "I wonder if I could buy some petroleum from you."

"That stuff is pretty scarce, *juffrouw*. Money can't buy it anymore," the fat man said.

"I know that. Would gold do?"

"What do you have to offer?"

"I have rare gold coins."

"I don't care if they're rare as long as they're gold."

She produced three coins from her raincoat pocket and showed them. They were quite large and heavy.

"That won't get you much. Petroleum is like liquid gold these days."

"Well," Anna said, "then I will have to look elsewhere."

She turned back from the door, but before she got to her bike, the fat man called to her. "Wait a minute, *juffrouw*. Not so fast. We can come to an agreement."

"All right," Anna said. "I showed you what I have to offer. How much petroleum can you give me for that?"

"I can give you a one-liter bottle."

"I need three, at least." Anna was surprised at herself. She'd never bargained before in her life. But this was a matter of life and death.

The fat man grumbled, turned his back on her, and went back into his shop. She paused. Should she walk away from this? What was the alternative? The door opened again, and he came out with two bottles.

"Two liters for three coins. That's final," the fat man said.

She handed him the coins, placed the bottles carefully in the bike baskets, and left without saying good-bye. She'd met society's underbelly.

On her way back to Betty's house, she saw things she later wished she'd never seen. As she reentered the city, she passed by a park. Maybe it was the same one she'd passed the day before, where a boy hacked off tree branches. At the entrance to the park, four men in handcuffs stood lined up in front of German soldiers, who raised their rifles to their shoulders. Before she could stop her bike, they aimed and pulled the triggers. The men fell forward onto the ground and lay there, slumped. Anna stopped and asked a woman what was going on.

The woman shrugged. "Who knows? Maybe they'd cut down trees," she said, and walked on.

The soldiers got into their truck and peeled off, leaving the men bleeding on the ground. Anna went over, as she had done in Ede, what now seemed ages ago. One by one she turned them over carefully, felt their pulses, raised their eyelids and touched their corneas. They were all dead. Did anyone care? The park was deserted. She looked around, wondering what she should do and what her responsibility was. Finally, an old man on a bike came by. She stopped him. He told her to move on. This happened every day. The police would eventually come to identify them.

"And then what?" she asked.

"They bring them to an old empty church. That's where all dead bodies go these days. The undertakers have run out of coffins, and anyway, the ground is frozen."

"But that's awful," Anna said, close to tears.

"That's the war for you," he said, and climbed back on his bike. "Go home! Take care of yourself."

Go home and take care of myself? How about these poor men, lying here in their blood, shot and deserted? She bent over the youngest of them, who could be Dirk's age. If the Nazis simply bypassed the law and didn't bother to bring people to a police station, but instead shot them on the spot as they pleased, then Dirk was in ever greater danger. She shivered all over.

There was no sense in staying, yet she hated to leave. Kneeling down at the feet of the four men who had not been shown justice, she said the Lord's Prayer out loud. "*Uw will geschiede*. Thy will be done, on earth as it is in heaven." As she spoke these words, she wondered if it made any sense to say them now, at the feet of these poor men. Whose will was done? The world had gone absolutely crazy. She hadn't been brought up to understand a society without a hint of dignity, where people could walk by dead bodies and just shrug. A world in which people starved.

She got back on her bike and pushed hard on the pedals, trying to escape the disintegration of a way of life she had taken for granted, even after five years of war that had drastically lowered life's standards. She impelled her bike forward in a rage. It was this rage that made her stop abruptly as she passed a man pushing a bakery cart. On impulse, she asked him if she could buy bread.

"You must be kidding," the baker said. "I have to deliver these at the barracks down there."

Anna looked down the street and saw the barracks with a sentry in front. She reached into her coat pocket and produced three shiny gold coins. The man blinked at the sight.

"Three breads, at least," she said. She was surprised at her commanding tone of voice.

The man looked furtively up and down the street. He took the coins from her hand, opened the lid of his cart, and gave her three breads.

"Get lost," he said.

She grabbed the breads and tucked them next to the bottles of petroleum, then rode away as fast as she could.

It was very quiet in the house when she entered with her gifts. She plunked the bottles and breads on the kitchen counter and went upstairs. Emmy and Dirk stood around Jan's bed. She stepped closer. It was the first good look she'd had of Jan, and she reeled at the sight. His face was sallow, thin, and exhausted. Not at all the kind man she remembered. Betty lay on the bed next to him, holding his hand. She felt Dirk's helplessness as he stood next to Jan, staring down at him. She took his hand. He squeezed hers, but said nothing.

Jan's breathing was very shallow, and became even more so until there was no more breath to exhale. It was over. Jan was gone, a victim of the Hunger Winter. Betty reached over and kissed him. Dirk took Jan's hands and folded them on his chest. Emmy cried softly. Anna wondered what her role was in this terribly sad moment. She didn't want to say another Our Father. The people in this room who had cared for Jan over the last months needed her practical help more than words, or they would go under as well. She was still strong enough to prevent that. In fact, she considered herself the only one strong enough to tackle what they might not know was ahead of them. There could be no funeral in the ordinary sense. But first, she had to give them sustenance to withstand their bleak emotions.

Back in the kitchen, she sliced one of the breads and spread the slices with the strawberry jam Frits had handed her. It was prosaic to think first of food after the man of the house had passed away, but these were not ordinary times.

"Here!" she said as she reentered the bedroom. "You all have to eat something. Jan would want you to."

They looked up at her in a daze.

"Let's make this an Irish wake," she went on.

"An Irish wake? What's that?" Emmy asked.

"It's a social gathering around a loved one who's passed away. It's an old Celtic custom. People gather, reminisce, and celebrate his life. And they also share food. The Irish don't hesitate to add a pint of beer. We'll have to do without that. But I think it's proper for us to give thanks for the life of Jan and to eat something while we do it."

Betty was sitting on the bed, still holding onto Jan's hand. She looked up at Anna, her eyes moist with tears. "Yes, Anna. That's what we should do."

"Here's a sandwich for you, Betty. You haven't eaten much lately. And that goes for all of you."

Dirk seemed to come out of his stupor when she held a sandwich out to him.

"Anna, you're an angel. Where did you get this?" he asked.

"The strawberry jam is a gift from Frits. And I was lucky to find bread."

"Who is Frits?" Emmy asked.

"He's a nine-year-old who lives at my grandmother's place and who's very fond of Dirk."

But she was anxious to steer the conversation away from the castle. This gathering was about Jan.

"Betty, where did you meet Jan?" she asked.

It worked. Betty looked down at Jan and told them they'd met at the beach of Scheveningen. She became more animated as she dug into her memories. It had been a good life, she said. Their one regret had been that they didn't have children.

"*You* became our children," she said. "You have done what our own blood children would have done for us." She wiped away her tears.

After a while of sitting around Jan's bed, Anna thought it was time for Betty to get out of this room. She encouraged her to go downstairs. Betty greeted the kitchen like an old friend she hadn't seen in a long time. The primary reality she had lived in had been death. When she surveyed what was on the kitchen table, her survival instincts kicked in, and she clapped her hands at the sight of bread, ham, potatoes, vegetables, and, most of all, petroleum. There was fuel to cook with, and it fueled her will to survive.

It was equally important to get Dirk downstairs after he'd properly laid out his friend. Anna could see that Jan's passing had taken over his mind—the man with whom he had set up the secret business of providing truthful news to people without access to Radio Oranje.

Anna returned to Jan's room and called Dirk's name. "Come with me. You need fresh air."

He obeyed. They put on coats and stepped out onto the street, which was virtually deserted. Anna hooked her arm through his, and they walked a while without saying a word. A bench in a nearby park looked inviting, and she steered them that way.

"You've been a true friend to Jan and Betty," she said.

"I couldn't save him, Anna. He was too run-down. It was too hard to play doctor without tools and medicine."

"Don't blame yourself, Dirk. The blame squarely falls on the Nazis for withholding food and medicine."

He was quiet, and sat studying his hands. This was a Dirk she didn't know. He had always been the one with positive answers to perplexing questions; one who solved dilemmas with unblinking courage.

"I brought as much food and fuel as I could carry," she said, because she didn't know what else to say. "Be sure to build yourself up slowly, Dirk."

He nodded in response. She had a hundred questions to ask and a hundred stories to tell, but he wasn't ready for any of it. Malnutrition had dropped a veil of apathy over him.

Back at the house, Betty had taken command of the kitchen. Something was cooking on the small petroleum stove, and the distinct aroma of boiling Brussels sprouts filled their nostrils.

"We'll eat in the dining room," she said. "I can hardly remember the last time we sat down at the table."

It was a smart move to have everyone sit down and share a meal after their haphazard style of eating whatever and whenever some food was available. Without the regular gathering at meals, each had lived with agonizing thoughts and fears. Anna knew one good meal would not wipe that away, but she hoped to find ways to make things better for them until the liberation, which was bound to come.

But when? It became the main topic at the dinner table. Because electricity got shut down early every evening, listening to Radio Oranje had become impossible. People who could charge a dynamo by hitching a bicycle up to it had some news some of the time, and they'd learned that the front was stalled at the Rhine River. Things hadn't gone well for the Allies in northwest Europe after their initial success. Trying to take the bridge at Arnhem had been a terrible failure, and the Germans had shown unexpected strength at the Ardennen in Luxemburg in December. It would go down in history as the Battle of the Bulge. Hitler was digging in his heels and turning Holland into a fortress. *Festung Holland*, he called it. A quarter of the arable land had already been flooded at his command, and his minions were busy preparing to dynamite the dikes if the Allies started an offensive in Holland. Flooding its land had been Holland's defense since time immemorial, and now Hitler wanted to use Dutch ingenuity to postpone the final collapse of the Third Reich.

"Of course," Dirk said, "Eisenhower and Montgomery know only too well the Germans would flood the polders and everything behind it. It's probably what's holding them back. Their tanks would get mired in mud."

It was a devastating outlook. Even so, Anna was glad to hear Dirk say it. She saw light returning to his hazel eyes. And where there was light, there was life, she thought.

"Betty," he said as they got up from the table, "would you allow me to make arrangements for Jan's funeral? Through the hospital, I got to know an undertaker very well."

Betty nodded. "That would be a load off my mind, Dirk."

He got his coat and was ready to go when Anna blocked his way, saying she wanted to go with him.

"Are you sure?"

"I am absolutely sure."

They got on their bikes, and Dirk led the way. Near the city's center, they passed a soup kitchen where people stood in line with a pail in their hands, waiting for the only food they would get that day. Anna had to look away from the faces that had hunger written on them—deep lines, sunken cheeks, dull eyes, resignation. Two boys, dressed in rags and wearing wooden shoes without socks, were raiding the trash barrels beside the kitchen door.

Not far from the hospital, Dirk stopped in front of the funeral home, a brick building with a driveway next to it, which set it apart from the other houses in the row.

"I know this undertaker from work," he said to Anna. "I can't tell you more right now."

She got the message.

A man in a somber black suit and with a somber, emaciated face answered the door. He recognized Dirk and invited them inside. After introducing Anna, Dirk came right to the point. He was there to arrange the funeral of a very dear friend.

"Impossible," the man said.

"Impossible? What do you mean?" Dirk asked.

"I have no caskets left, and there isn't wood anywhere to make one."

Anna had been prepared, but Dirk was aghast. He hadn't been able to save his good friend, and now he couldn't give him a decent burial? He wasn't going to take no for an answer.

"There must be a way," he said.

"Not with wood," the undertaker said.

"If not with wood, with what?"

"Cardboard, at best. I hate to tell you this, Mijnheer van Enthoven, but bodies these days are brought to the old Vincent Church, wrapped in a sheet. We can't bury bodies. The ground is frozen. And the morgues are full. I am sorry I can't help you."

"But you could bring my friend to that church, right?" Dirk said.

The look on his face told Anna he didn't want to give up on a decent funeral for Jan. He understood that with the ground frozen, the burial had to be postponed, and bringing the body temporarily to a church didn't sound as awful as a morgue, but he should be brought there in something better than a sheet.

"I have no means of getting him there," the undertaker said. "The Nazis took my horses a year ago, and I don't have gas for the hearse."

"Well, that's a hell of a way to make a living!" Dirk said. "No caskets to sell, no transportation, no burial grounds."

"You mentioned a cardboard casket," Anna said. "How much would that cost?"

"Oh, I don't know." He was evasive.

She reached into her pocket and produced three more gold coins. The undertaker's eyes came to life at the sight of them. She knew she wouldn't have to push hard to get him to provide some sort of transport as well.

"Maybe I can get one for that," the man said.

"That would be great." She reached into another pocket and showed him the last of the twelve gold coins Oma had given her. "I bet that for these you can also come and get our friend and bring him to the church. That would be very much appreciated."

Dirk looked at her in amazement.

"I will do my best," the undertaker said.

She nodded. "We will be looking for you before the day is out."

"I will do my best," the undertaker said again.

She turned around and made for the door, but before she got there, she stopped with her hand on the door handle. "I will have the coins ready when I see you this afternoon."

The undertaker nodded. Dirk followed her out.

Back on their bikes, Dirk asked where she got those gold coins.

"Oma gave them to me to use on this trip. She knew people weren't interested in paper money. That's how I got the bread and the petroleum."

"You're amazing."

"No, Dirk. These are amazing times. Please don't mention it to Betty."

They pedaled back through streets that were practically deserted. Few men were out and about. Even teenage boys were nowhere to be seen. They all knew they were targets for labor in Germany. University students weren't the only onderduikers. Anna was anxious to get Dirk back safely inside Betty's house. But they got stopped on the way. Not by the Gestapo, but by an older gentleman who collapsed on the sidewalk right in front of them. Dirk got off his bike and helped the man up. He was disoriented and dangerously underfed. Luckily, someone opened the door and took him in. The man had collapsed in front of his home.

"Doesn't that make you feel helpless?" Dirk said. "You know what he needs is *food*."

Before curfew went into effect, a strange vehicle parked in front of Betty's home. Anna had been on the lookout for the undertaker from the living room window, but what she saw in the street was not what she had expected. It was a sort of tricycle with a wide front axis with a wheel on either side ahead of the handlebars. A steel pole connected the single rear wheel to the front ones. Between the two front wheels was a wide loading platform made of wood. A large cardboard box rested on it, shaped like a coffin. No, it *was* a coffin. The operator of this odd vehicle was dressed in a long black coat that might have once been tightfitting, but was no longer. He wore black gloves and a black top hat.

Window curtains in several homes were pushed aside as curious neighbors wondered what was going on. Dirk had told Betty what to expect, but all of them were amazed at the sight of the tall undertaker in his traditional outfit sitting on a tricycle. It was a sign of the times.

Dirk helped the man carry the coffin inside and up the staircase. Before the undertaker had arrived, they had stood around Jan's bed, holding hands, and said their good-byes. Dirk promised Betty there would be an official burial as soon as possible and then said a prayer. His voice rough with emotion, he told everyone to go downstairs and wait in the living room. He would take care of the removal.

Neighbors, all women, who'd known Jan for many years came out to say farewell. Through the gauze curtains, Anna watched the intensely sad, and at the same time totally bizarre, sight that was unfolding in the street. The undertaker, as he climbed onto the tricycle's seat, looked like death himself. The people around him didn't look much healthier. If a picture were taken of the scene, it could become the poster for Holland's Hunger Winter. Anna wished she could create that poster and show it to the powers that could influence the end of this wretched war. The country known for its cheese, flowers, and vegetables, as well as for its proud inhabitants' rosy cheeks, was sliding into poverty and misery. Not through its own fault, but because its resources had been plundered by a zany leader with a merciless ideology. Seeing Jan being carted away, followed by Dirk on his bike, was the truest illustration of how low her country had sunk.

Dirk came back a few minutes after curfew went into effect. He looked beat. Nobody dared ask him what it had been like to bring Jan's body to a church building where reportedly hundreds of other bodies were being warehoused. Anna didn't need to ask. She could tell the experience had taken the last ounce of his reserves.

When the electricity was shut off and the house returned to darkness, there was nothing better to do than wish each other a good night's sleep. The evening's cold crept into the unheated house, dropping the temperature several degrees. Anna reflected, as she lay down on the mattress next to Dirk, that few things in life could make a person feel more miserable than a combination of cold and hunger.

"Dirk," she whispered in the dark. "Shall we make our wedding plans? This is as good a time as any I can think of."

He rolled over to face her. "You didn't forget?"

"How could I forget? It was the last thing you communicated to me before you went on your adventure. And I didn't have to think about the answer for a second. Does your invitation still hold?"

"Oh, Anna. I have nothing to offer you. I am a nonstudent with a meager job and a decrepit body that isn't even capable of making love to you, even if societal rules allowed it. You should have second thoughts, Anna."

"Dirk, listen to me." She shifted closer to him. "I love you. Do you hear me? I love you. There will be an end to this war. We will be strong again. We will study again. We will make the strongest couple that ever was. I have faith, and I know you do too."

She felt his hand touch her hair, then her face, and finally her breasts. The warmth of his fingers seeped through the sweater she'd kept on, and a quick shiver vibrated through her whole body. Dirk moved his face close to hers and kissed her passionately. Then he fell back, exhausted.

"Thank you, Anna. You've saved me."

He slipped into a deep sleep next to her, and Anna did the same, nestled in the curve of his lanky body.

CHAPTER FORTY-FOUR

Anna – April 1945

It had been exactly a year since Anna stood in this same place with Klaas and Walter, watching the Allied Air Armada fly over. That had been in April of 1944. The American airman they'd saved, after one bomber was shot down, had told her that General Eisenhower was the best general any army had ever had, and that the Continent would soon be freed. That prediction had come true for France, Belgium, Italy, and a small portion of Holland, but Holland's three most populous provinces—North Holland, South Holland, and Utrecht—were still suffering under the German boot. And so was most of her province of Gelderland.

Anna had run up the stairs to the balcony to see if Janus was right when he declared he could hear artillery fire in the distance. She had to agree with him. The staccato firings of bullets sounded muffled and far off, but they were proof of an advancing army, and it filled her with excitement. It was rumored the Allies had taken Arnhem. Could Ede be next? Would Herr von Schloss's soldiers put up a tough fight?

The grass around the circular driveway below had turned a vibrant green. Every living thing had come back to life. The forsythia bushes were in full bloom, and looked as bright as the sun itself. Seeing the swollen buds on the beech trees filled her with hope, and she wanted to believe in their message of renewal. She hadn't felt this optimistic in a very long time, although at the edge of her mind was the nagging fear that victory might come too late for many, and that included Dirk, Betty, and Emmy.

When she'd said good-bye to them two months ago, she'd told Emmy to use the clothes that still hung in her closet at Betty's as barter for food. A wool skirt, a pair of shoes, a cotton blouse, or a sweater could buy a sack of potatoes, bread, milk, and butter. Hopefully, Emmy had been up to the task. It filled Anna with dread every time she saw hunger trippers in the vicinity. They looked increasingly desperate and thin. Not that she lived in the land of plenty herself, but living among farms was a true blessing. Even with the sharp control traitorous inspectors exercised on the number of pigs, cows, and chickens the farmers kept, some milk or bacon could still be found. What was harder to find was soap to do the laundry. Clothes were wearing out, and shops had nothing new to offer.

"Do you hear anything, Anna?"

Frits had gotten behind her. He knew he shouldn't show himself on the balcony. Seeing his pale face made her pray extra hard for a quick liberation. This boy needed to return to a normal way of life.

"Yes. Janus is right. We'd better get prepared."

Excited, Frits ran down the staircase and burst into the salon. "Oma, they're coming! Anna heard them."

"That's wonderful, Frits," the baroness said. "I'll have to start thinking about unfurling our flag. It must be in a cedar chest somewhere."

That evening at dinner, Walter unexpectedly said he was worried.

"What are you worried about?" Anna asked.

He said he had it on the best authority that the way Germans defended cities was by placing snipers inside people's homes. It came down to hand-to-hand combat. They ordered people out of their houses so they could take up positions behind their windows.

"I have heard enough, Walter," the baroness said. "I want you to bring Ruth, Sylvia, and the children here as soon as possible. No sense in waiting till it's too late."

Nobody argued with her common sense. The next day, as the rumbling sounds of the artillery got nearer, Walter showed up with Bertha and the Bosma family in tow. Each adult brought a child on the baggage carrier of his or her bike, and each child held a bag with pajamas. There was excitement in the air, and the children sensed that this was no ordinary outing.

The baroness welcomed them on the stoop of the front door. Bram was the least intimidated, because he'd been to the castle twice before, but the little girls hid behind their mother's skirt. Frits was ecstatic to see other children. He took Bram by the hand and showed him around. When Anna went to look for them, they were in the ballroom where Frits was demonstrating how to play the piano. After that, they were inseparable.

The baroness left the room assignments to Ruth and Bertha, but she had the children come to the living room. They sat on the floor around her chair, looking up in rapt attention at the gracious lady in her ankle-length dress, decorated with a single string of pearls. Anna smiled at the serious little faces and at her grandmother, who had a way of getting her message across that something big and exciting was going to happen, and that everything would go well if they did what they were told.

"What's going to happen, Mevrouw?" Bram asked.

"We call it *de Bevrijding*. Once again we will be free. We've had soldiers here from another country telling us what to do for a long while. But now we're wishing them to go back home. It's been hard to convince them to go, so we've called for help from friends. We call those friends Allies. We've been waiting for the Allies to come, and now they're coming. Of course, the soldiers we don't like want to stay, so it will take a little doing to get them out of our country. Sometimes that doing may make a lot of noise, and when that happens, I will tell you to go to the cellar with the grown-ups. No ifs or buts."

"What are the soldiers called that you don't like?" Bram asked.

"Nazis," the baroness answered.

"That's a funny word. I thought they were called Germans."

"It may sound funny to you," Frits said, "but what they do is not funny."

"All right, children," the baroness said, cutting Frits off. "Mien will have a meal ready for you, and Frits will bring you to the kitchen."

Everybody was assigned a place to sleep. Walter took Bram in his bedroom. Bertha and Ruth shared a bedroom with the two little girls. All the children went to bed warned that they might be awakened during the night and taken to the cellar for protection. It made for a restless night's sleep for the adults with one ear open to the booms in the distance, but they didn't seem to get closer, Anna thought.

At breakfast, Janus said he'd run into a scouting mission of the Allies on his way over. Janus hardly ever fell out of his butler role, but he couldn't contain himself. He was almost gleeful as he told them that he had shown the Allies the way to the German military base.

"What do they look like?" Bram asked.

"Their uniforms are brown and their helmets are very different from the Germans. The most amazing thing was the rig they drove. It could drive right through the thicket of the woods, like a little tank on rubber wheels. Amazing!"

It wasn't long before they heard noises outside. Nobody wanted to go down to the cellar, and they gathered at the windows to watch a troop of Allied soldiers tread slowly down the road from Hendrik's farm. They carried their rifles as if they were ready to shoot, the barrels pointing downward, and each soldier looked carefully right and left. Three huge tanks, screeching over the pebbles in the road, followed them. It was an exhilarating sight.

More soldiers followed the tanks. They looked ready to take on the enemy.

Half an hour after they passed, they heard shots farther down in the woods that led to Ede, then some loud booms, and the baroness ordered everyone to the cellar. Nobody minded. What they'd seen held a promise that the end of the war was near.

They didn't have to stay there for very long; three hours in all. That was how long it took for Herr von Schloss to surrender. When Hendrik came over to tell them Ede had fallen into Allied hands, the baroness said she wasn't surprised that the Germans hadn't put up a fierce fight. Although he was a career officer, Herr von Schloss was too sensible to put more lives at risk when the Third Reich was collapsing fast. Walter and Anna agreed. His heart had never been in defending Hitler's agenda.

"What will happen to him?" Anna asked.

"If the past is any guide," the baroness said, "he will be made a prisoner of war. But probably not for long since he cannot be accused of acts against humanity, unlike Reichskommissar Seyss-Inquart, who couldn't care less that thousands of people died of hunger and cold. The Allies will undoubtedly have him pay for his callousness."

They couldn't be sure if the German forces in the area were definitely defeated. Walter warned not to go out before the area had been officially declared liberated. Occasionally, they heard shots being fired. But the next morning when the area was declared cleared of enemies, Anna went up to the attic to find the Dutch flag. With Walter's help, she hoisted it on the flagpole that had been silently waiting for five years in the middle of the rosebushes that graced the center of the circular driveway. Her parents, Sylvia, Ruth, the children, and all the servants came out of the castle and formed a circle around the flag. The baroness started to sing "Het Wilhelmus." Her voice was hoarse with emotion, but it gathered strength as everyone joined in. She then thanked the servants for their loyalty and fortitude during these very trying times.

"*Leve de Koningin,*" she called out.

"*Hiep, Hiep, Hoera,*" everyone shouted.

"I give everyone the rest of the day off, but let's first celebrate inside with a glass of wine I saved for just this happy occasion."

Janus got the wine. Mien found the glasses, and the baroness insisted on filling the glasses herself. Tongues were loosened. The wine had an equalizing effect.

"I advise everyone to go home—as long as it's safe—and celebrate with your families. Just be sure to be back tomorrow."

The war was over, Anna thought with amazement, but only locally. Seyss-Inquart was still in Den Haag, following Hitler's orders. He could still do awful things, like blowing up dikes and flooding valuable land to keep the Allied armies out. Her throat constricted at the thought.

The baroness noticed the worry that shadowed Anna's otherwise upbeat mood.

"Come on, Anna, let's hitch the ponies up and go to Ede. This will be a once-in-a-lifetime experience. Let's take Frits and Bram with us."

When Anna opened the barn, the boys, all excited, raced up and down the aisle. Frits, who'd only seen the building from the castle's windows, was wide-eyed at the vastness of the place. Outside, the ponies were in for a surprise. The baroness coaxed them toward the gate and hitched their halters to leashes. With a pony on either side of her, she entered the barn.

"We have work to do, boys," she said. "The ponies need to be cleaned. I'll show you how."

She reached for a box with curry combs and went to work, showing how brushing with a circular motion would work out the dirt embedded in their fur. Each boy got a comb. Bram had no fear, but Frits was tentative.

"What if the pony doesn't like to be brushed?" he asked.

"To the pony it feels the way a warm bath feels to you," the baroness said.

Anna brought in the pony wagon and started to untangle the harnesses. It had been ages since she'd hitched up a pony, leave alone two of them. There was a lot of leather involved, and she struggled to get the various parts lined up.

"We can't be too fussy," the baroness said. "We don't want to miss out on the celebration in town."

Soon they were on their way. The baroness sat on the coachbox; Anna shared the back part with Frits and Bram. The ponies, sensing the excitement, set a lively pace.

"Anna," Frits said, "am I really free now?"

"Yes, Frits, you are really free. They won't be looking for you anymore."

"Who was looking for you?" Bram asked.

"The Nazis."

"The people your oma said she didn't like?"

"Yes, those people. They don't like Jewish people, and I am a Jew," Frits said.

"What's a Jew?"

Bram wasn't going to let go of the subject, being thoroughly intrigued by his new friend, and Anna thought it was time to interfere.

"The Nazis," she said, "think differently about people than we do. They divide people into groups, called races. They call their own race Aryan, and they believe it is superior to any other race, which is total nonsense. Frits belongs to the Jewish race. You and I belong to the Caucasian race. But to God, we look all the same."

"You don't look different to me," Bram said to Frits.

"Let's not talk about it anymore," Frits said. "Oma says we're going to a big party."

The baroness turned around. "That's right," she said. She'd obviously overheard the conversation. "This is a day to celebrate that all of us are free again. Even the ponies are excited. They're stepping out smartly to get us there."

As they came closer to town, more people were leaving their

homes. Every street that emptied out to the main road to Ede brought even more people. The crowd looked like a river being fed to overflowing by its rivulets.

Despite the many boisterous people, the ponies behaved admirably. The baroness had them firmly in hand with minimal use of the carriage whip. Even as they entered the town's square, the ponies didn't shy from the rowdy scene of people dancing and singing "*Oranje boven, Oranje boven, Leve de Koningin.*" Over and over, they sang the song that had been forbidden for five years. There were orange decorations everywhere, on houses and on people's clothes. At the castle, Anna had even found orange plumes to put on top of the ponies' bridles, and they bobbed up and down with their movements.

"I have never seen anything like this," the baroness said over her shoulder. "This is a true, spontaneous expression of patriotism. People are drunk with happiness and relief. And that's without any beer flowing!"

She parked the ponies in a safe place off the market, telling Anna to let the boys join the dancing crowd and to get back in half an hour. Anna took the two boys by the hand, and they plunged into the crowd, hooking arms with complete strangers. It was over! With the collective release of tension, people danced with abandon. The heavy yoke of the Occupation had been thrown off. The coming of the Allies returned to Ede's population its voice after it had been stifled for so long. Anna joyfully gave herself over to the exuberance around her.

The ponies had their deserved rest, and by the time Anna and the boys returned, they were ready to trot back to the castle. Bram and Frits fell over their own words as they tried to tell the baroness what they'd witnessed. Their eyes shone like stars. They wouldn't forget this day.

The other sight they would likely never forget occurred when the baroness halted the ponies to let a bedraggled troop of German soldiers walk by, their heads downcast. They were on their way to become POWs. An Allied sergeant walked alongside them. Anna couldn't help remembering the image of Jews being marched to the railroad station in Utrecht three years ago, with German sergeants in front, to the side, and in back of them.

"Are they Nazis?" Bram asked.

"No, Bram," the baroness said. "These are German soldiers. They were told by the Nazis to do things they really didn't want to do. Most of them didn't, anyway."

Anna looked at the soldiers' faces. They were just teenagers who hadn't even grown a beard yet. Even so, they'd been ordered by a madman to carry a rifle to defend a lost cause and a bankrupted philosophy. She didn't rejoice in seeing them taken prisoner. What a waste of their youth. So many broken lives.

The baroness let the ponies set a more leisurely pace on the way back to the castle. Over the course of the war, their portion of oats had been rationed to nearly zero, but now the grass in their pasture was turning green. Their flanks had begun to fill out again.

They saw Walter, Sylvia, and Ruth riding toward them with the two little girls on the backs of the women's bikes, holding on to their waists.

"Poppa!" Bram called to Walter with great excitement.

"Is Dominee Vlaskamp your father?" Frits asked.

"Sort of," Bram said. "My own father was very sick and he died."

"Oh," Frits said.

As usual, Bram didn't let go. "Do you have a father?" he asked.

"Yes," Frits said. "Everybody has a father to begin with. But the Nazis took my father and my mother, and I don't know where they are."

"Maybe Dominee Vlaskamp will want to be your father as well," Bram suggested happily. "Then we would be brothers."

The baroness looked around and winked at Anna. "If that is so, then I could be your oma, Bram. One big, happy family."

She stopped the ponies to say hello to the bikers, who were on their way back home, now that danger had passed. But Bram didn't want to go home with them.

"I want to stay with Frits," he said. "Can I stay, Oma?"

"You certainly can, Bram."

The baroness steered the ponies back to the barn, and Anna unharnessed them with Bram's help. As she hung the harnesses back on their hooks in the tack room, she mulled over the revealing conversation between the boys and what it would mean for Walter's future—and Ruth's and Bertha's. The time for making choices was near for all three of them. It would require a lot of soul searching, and it wouldn't be without pain.

The next weeks were like a movie on fast forward. One town after another fell into Allied hands. Events roller-coasted at a dizzying speed. Anna listened religiously to Radio Oranje every evening. President Roosevelt sadly died on April 12 of a heart attack. Five days later, she heard that the Nazis—as though they hadn't caused enough suffering—had flooded the Wieringermeer Polder in Noord-Holland. Fifty thousand acres, all fertile agricultural land, were inundated after the surrounding dikes were breached. It destroyed the granary of Holland. Seven thousand citizens had been forced to evacuate; more than five hundred farms were underwater.

It was also reported that the Allies had stopped advancing after they freed Amersfoort, a city close to Utrecht, and held the line there. General Eisenhower thought that operations west of Utrecht would involve too many casualties, and it was better to wait till the whole operation was accomplished. But when would "the whole operation" be over? Anna wondered. It was unbearable to think that she was liberated and Dirk was still suffering. After Jan's death, she had tried to convince Dirk to come back with her to the castle, but he brushed her suggestion off, saying that he might be picked up on the way and deported to a work camp in Germany. Besides, he didn't want to abandon Betty and Dr. Hamel. So,

Anna's first rush of joy at being liberated abated with her worries about Dirk. She had nightmares thinking about how much worse things might have gotten since she'd been in Utrecht, back at the end of February.

Finally, good news came on April 29, when 253 Lancaster bombers flew at very low altitude over areas near Amsterdam, Den Haag, Rotterdam, and Utrecht. It was called Operation Manna. Instead of bombs, the planes dropped food packages weighing twenty-three pounds each. After agonizing back-and-forth negotiations, the Germans had finally agreed to allow this long-awaited aid. Radio Oranje reported that the pilots flew at such low altitude, they could see the people waving at them, some standing on the roofs of their homes. Over the course of a few days, the Allies dropped more than six million pounds of food on Holland. Anna's joy surged again. Food! Justice! Finally! What had taken them so long?

And then came the most amazing news, on the first of May. Hitler had died! Radio Hamburg announced, "Our Führer, Adolf Hitler, has fallen this afternoon at his command post in the Reich Chancellery, fighting to the last breath against Bolshevism and for Germany."

Good riddance. That's what Anna thought unabashedly. And the world agreed with her. It wasn't known until much later that Hitler had committed suicide in his bunker. The Russians stood at Berlin's gates, and several British, Canadian, and French armies were zeroing in on Berlin as well. The ship of state was sinking fast. Hitler didn't have the courage to face a whopping defeat.

But the war still wasn't over. In Ede, they were free, but it didn't mean they had more food, or electricity, or that the trains were running and mail was delivered. Anna had brought the radio, which they had hidden in the attic rather than giving it to the Germans, down to the living room. It was turned on every evening as she, Oma, Walter, and her father listened breathlessly to Radio Oranje, waiting for the promised end of the war. It was clear to everyone except the Nazis that the writing was on the wall. Germany was like a worm without its head, still crawling, but barely.

Then, on the fourth of May, Walter came home all excited. He had heard rumors that negotiations were going on between Canadian and German generals close by in Wageningen, a city just down the road.

That evening, Oma, Walter, Anna, Frits, and Bram, as well as Anna's parents, sat around the radio, anxious and nervous. Was it possible the Germans would give in? Radio Oranje came on and announced that British Field Marshal Montgomery had read his conditions for capitulation to Admiral Friedeburg and General Kinzel in his tent on the Luneburg Heath in Germany. The ceremony took all of five minutes. One million German soldiers surrendered unconditionally. Simultaneously, the capitulation document was signed in Wageningen between the Canadian General Foulkes and the German General Blaskowitz. The announcer said with a trembling voice that as of 8 a.m., Saturday, May 5, 1945, the capitulation would be in force.

"Now we are *really* free," the baroness said. "It's over. Let's celebrate."

Anna embraced her, hugged Walter, and swept up Frits in her arms. Bram ran into Walter's arms. Tears were flowing freely. Even her mother was moved.

The baroness went down to the wine cellar and produced a Margaux from before the war. Anna found the fine crystal wineglasses, which had been neglected since the Normandy Invasion, when they had thought the end was near. It had taken another eleven months, and those months had been the worst of the five war years.

After the wine was poured, the baroness lifted her glass. "I want to make a toast to Her Majesty the Queen, for her perseverance, and to General Eisenhower and all the other generals and soldiers who fought to free us. I deeply honor the victims of this horrible war.

Lastly, I want to thank Walter and Anna for having lived up to your principles and your faith. You have set an example for these young boys."

To which Anna added, "May Dirk van Enthoven come back to us soon."

The crystal glasses tinkled.

THE VERY LAST CHAPTER

September 23, 1950

It was the kind of weather Oma would have loved, Anna thought, as the sun rose over the fields behind the castle. It promised to turn into the kind of day that had clarity, crispness, unlimited visibility, and enough warmth to make it pleasant to be out and about, the kind of day that personified her grandmother.

It was hard, if not impossible, to think of Oma in the past tense. Four days ago, Anna had received a telephone call from the castle. Janus had found the baroness slumped in her favorite chair by the window in the salon. He had waited in vain for her to show up at the breakfast table and gone on a search. A doctor was called, but he could do no more than pronounce her dead. Eventually, it was determined she had died from a ruptured cerebral aneurysm.

Anna couldn't remember any time in her life when she had been this perplexed and devastated; and the war had not lacked in moments for comparison.

She had stood numb with anguish with the telephone gone dead, dangling from her hand. That's how Betty found her.

"Oma died."

Betty was the right person to be with in such an agonizing

moment. To lean into her warm body and let her tears flow was the best release for her all-encompassing sadness.

Dirk and Anna had moved in with Betty shortly after they got married. It was an ideal solution for several reasons. To begin with, Betty now lived alone and she needed the income. Also, it was impossible to find housing so soon after the war. The country couldn't rebuild itself fast enough to provide housing for young married couples. It worked out as well for Dirk and Anna as for Betty, as they took up their studies again. And when their son Hendrik Jan was born, Betty was the ideal person to take care of him while they crammed for exams.

Dirk stirred as Anna walked back from the window to their bed. It was still a miracle to her that he was there for her to see, to feel, to touch, after her fears of losing him to either the Nazis' zeal or to the horrible Hunger Winter. Dirk had come close to losing his life in the last two months of the war. An SS roadblock outside Utrecht had almost snagged him while he was carrying illegal food coupons for hidden Jews. Acting on a tip from a total stranger, he'd changed his route at the very last minute. And the signing of the capitulation had come just in time to save him from starvation. By the time Anna could make it to Utrecht, he was skin over bones. She convinced a member of Prince Bernhard's Interior Forces, who had access to a vehicle, to transport Dirk to the castle. There, with Mien's help, she fattened him up, enough so they could get married without much pomp and circumstance.

Anna pulled the blanket aside and slipped back into bed, snuggling up to Dirk. He responded by pulling her close.

"This will be a tough day for you," he murmured.

"Yes, it will be, and I'm not ready for it."

"What will carry you through, Anna, is remembering what Oma would do on a day like this."

"That's a tall order, Dirk."

But she knew he was right. As soon as she heard that Oma had died, she knew it would be up to her to organize the funeral. Her

mother had fallen into a deep depression after Anna's brother
Maarten repatriated from Indonesia in 1946 with a native wife,
Matti, and infant son. Nobody had known he was married. It was
a tough reentry into Dutch domestic life for Maarten, who was
without a job. It was even harder for his wife, who shivered in the
cold climate of a country that was adjusting to life after the war,
and to the fact that what used to be the Dutch East Indies was now
the sovereign country of Indonesia. The colonial days were over.
Maarten's story was the story of many people like him who knew
the way back to their beloved East Indies was closed. After barely
surviving three horrendous years in Japanese prison camps, tens of
thousands returned to their Dutch families, who were licking their
own wounds after the years of the German Occupation. There
wasn't much room, literally and figuratively, to accommodate these
homeless repatriates. Anna's parents themselves were in upheaval.
Their home in Arnhem had been ransacked and plundered. Her
father's bank lay in ruins and needed to be rebuilt with scant
available materials.

Oma had looked at this dismal situation and offered to put
everyone under her roof. At least the castle was big enough for
people to be able to stay out of one another's way, but it had taken
all of Oma's tact to guide these unsettled lives. Mien had a hard
time accommodating the Indonesian wife in her kitchen. The Dutch
way of preparing food couldn't be more different from what
Maarten's wife, who desperately wanted to help, brought in
culinary ways to Mien's undisputed domain. Eventually, they
worked it out, but not until the baroness intervened.

What was harder to resolve was the standoff between Maarten
and his mother. In fact, it didn't get resolved. Although she had
pined for Maarten during the war years, his mother could not
accept his native Indonesian wife, who stepped off the boat in a
sarong. Anna was embarrassed and ashamed at how her mother
ignored Matti and her first grandchild.

"Moeder," she said one day. "Do you realize that we fought the

Nazis because we didn't share their ideology?"

"Yes. Of course, I do."

"That they thought the Aryan race was supreme?"

"Yes, Anna, of course. Why do you ask?"

"Because the Nazis also believed in white supremacy."

"Anna! That's different."

"How is it different, Moeder? You seem to think that Matti, being of another race, is not worthy of being Maarten's wife. And that's what white supremacy is all about."

"I never said that, Anna. How dare you?"

"Then why do you act that way? Matti is a beautiful woman, devoted to Maarten and devoted to little Ben. Yet you treat them as if they don't exist."

It may not have been the most diplomatic approach to solving the problem that was growing like a poisonous plant in their midst. In fact, instead of solving it, the noxious plant exploded into a full-blown tree. Not able to take the criticism from her daughter, Anna's mother retreated into an even more severe depression. Anna felt some remorse at the way she'd confronted her mother, but she couldn't swallow the neglect shown her sister-in-law.

Oma reprimanded Anna for being too direct with her mother, but she agreed with her in principle. How much she agreed with her was evident when the estate lawyer read Oma's will to the assembled family. Anna and Maarten would inherit the castle. Anna's father was the executor of the will. A sum of money and jewelry were left to Moeder. There were generous legacies for Frits, Mien, Janus, and Hendrik. Oma had, for the last time, spoken with a loud and clear voice.

There was a timid knock on the bedroom door. Anna quickly jumped out of bed and opened it. As she expected, it was her son Hendrik Jan, now all of three years old. He had escaped from the bedroom he shared with Betty, who'd offered to come and take charge of him on this demanding day of the funeral. She was his grandmother-in-fact.

"Mamma," he said, clutching his teddy bear with a big smile on his round face. He was obviously proud of himself that he'd found her in this place that was many times the size of the small city house they lived in.

Anna picked him up and swung him onto the bed next to his father. Hendrik Jan had light blue eyes like hers, but he resembled his father in build and disposition—even-tempered and determined. Looking at him now, climbing over Dirk and giggling, she felt a pang of regret that Oma wouldn't play as big a role in his life as she had in Anna's growing-up years. There had not been a greater influence on her life than her grandmother. That had been clear to her all along, but in these last few days, confronted with the fact that Oma was gone forever, she realized to the depths of her soul the gift Oma had been for her. In a curious way, that recognition somewhat balanced the deep feeling of loss.

"Oma Betty says there will be girls for me to play with," Hendrik Jan said.

"Yes, that's right," Anna said. "Their names are Emily and Lideke."

They were the Bosma girls. There had not been a moment's doubt in Anna's mind over whom to ask to lead Oma's funeral. Walter Vlaskamp, of course. She was convinced that would have been Oma's wish. After Dominee Bosma died, the deacons of the Remonstrantse Kerk in Ede had asked Walter to stay on, and, after the liberation, gave him the permanent position as their pastor.

There was only one problem with asking Walter to do the service. Oma had been a member of the nearby Nederlands Hervormde Kerk, like every member of the van Haersolte family had been before her; and her husband was buried in its graveyard. It was a delicate issue. In spite of the hope of many, the war had not resolved the sharp delineations between the various Protestant churches. Even the queen had fervently hoped her country could let go of the divisions that ran through the churches directly into governance. Practically every political party, except for the

Communists and the Socialists, was rooted in a particular church, including the Catholic Church. It was one of the great disappointments of life after the war that the old patterns simply returned and continued. It would take roughly another twenty years before the divisions crumbled, and that slow process would go hand in hand with the crumbling of the churches themselves.

But Walter wouldn't be Walter if he didn't know how to smooth the ruffled feathers of the minister of the small Hervormde Kerk down the country lane. It was agreed that Dominee van Houten would lead the service and Walter would give the sermon.

It was time to go downstairs for breakfast. Anna brought Hendrik Jan back to Oma Betty and then returned to her room to change into a black tailored suit. She decorated it with a gold pin Oma had given her when she turned eighteen. Dirk was already showered and getting into his formal morning coat. He looked dashing and handsome, and she was proud to have him at her side on this day, and any day.

Every chair around the breakfast table was taken. Besides her parents, Maarten, and his wife, there was Klaas, who was Daan again. Three months after the liberation, he had walked into the castle's front yard. At first, Janus hadn't recognized him. He'd watched a man in torn, dirty clothes stumble along the circular driveway on shoes that could hardly be called that for the holes in them. He leaned on a walking stick; a grain sack was draped over his shoulder. Before the war, Janus would have labeled him a *landloper*, a no-good tramp. But this was after the war, and people weren't measured in the same manner. Not until Daan stood before him and said, "Hello, Janus," did he realize it was Klaas.

They had celebrated his return, alive and well enough to have walked hundreds of miles from the last work camp he'd been in, since there had not been any available form of transportation. Trains and buses weren't running. Germany was flat on its back. Along the way, he'd had to beg for food or steal it. But the amazing thing was: Daan wasn't the worse for the experience. He considered it a miracle that the Nazis never discovered that he was a Jew. In spite of the hardship, he thought himself extremely lucky.

Her grandmother had been so impressed with Daan's attitude that she offered him the job of administrator of her estate. He took over from Anna and her father, and the timing couldn't have been better. Vader needed to go back to Arnhem to rebuild his bank, and Anna needed to restart her studies.

Of course, Daan's return made Anna wonder what might have happened to Herman, who'd gone to work in Germany voluntarily. Nobody had heard from him since he left. Then Emmy ran into a friend of Herman's family. He told her that Herman's mother had died during the Hunger Winter. His father had remarried before Herman returned. Like Daan, Herman had walked back from a part of Germany that had been brutally conquered by the Russian Army. He had lasted one month at home and then vanished. It was assumed he'd joined the French Foreign Legion, which was the most effective way of disappearing from the face of the earth, short of actually dying. He might be fighting in Algeria for all they knew.

Anna wondered if Emmy had told Carla about how things had turned out for Herman. She could never forget that day at Betty's house when Herman walked in and said he would work in Germany instead of hiding, because he was afraid the Nazis would take his parents' wealth away if he didn't. Carla and Herman had been very close, but Carla could never forgive Herman for what she considered an unpatriotic deed. Carla had not returned to finish her studies in Utrecht. Instead, she'd fallen in love with Jacob, the man who had been hidden by her parents in Breda. They had seemed happy when they visited Dirk and Anna in Utrecht, right after Carla and Jacob got married three years ago.

As was the custom, Anna had sent out announcements the day after the baroness's death. She had consulted Oma's address book and come upon many names of people she didn't know, and others she was surprised were still in there. In that last category, two names stood out: Jack Foster from Barksdale, Texas, USA, the pilot they'd saved and hidden. The other one was Herr von Schloss from Oldenburg, Germany. She looked at the two names for a while, hesitated, but decided to send the announcement to both men, even though Oma would be buried before they could receive them. Still, they deserved to know. They'd played a role in Oma's life, although in opposite ways.

The hallways were filling with delicious aromas that emanated from the kitchen. A reception would be held in the ballroom after the service and burial, and Mien was cooking up a storm. After coping with shortages during the war years, she finally could get her hands on the kind of ingredients she needed to create finger food like *bitterballen* and *saucijzenbroodjes*. She had summoned relatives to help her out in the kitchen and for the serving. This would be her last big event for the baroness, whom she had served for practically her entire life, and she was going to make it memorable. Embroidered linens were laid out on the tables. The silver was polished. It was Mien's way of dealing with grief. As long as she stayed busy, she would be all right, she said to Anna.

Oma had left only two wishes for her funeral. She wanted her coffin to be carried in a horse-drawn hearse, and she wanted to be buried next to her husband. It had not been easy to fulfill the first wish, but with Hendrik's help, Anna located an old-fashioned hearse, open on three sides with a fringed roof. It appeared in front of the castle, pulled by two black Friesian horses, and followed by three carriages for members of the family.

When the cortege arrived at the church, six pallbearers stood waiting outside the church's oak door to carry the coffin inside. They were Dirk, Maarten, Hendrik, Janus, Daan, and Daan's brother, all dressed in black suits. They shouldered the weight of the coffin that held the woman who'd played an outsized role in their lives. The family followed the coffin inside.

Walking down the aisle, Anna noticed a few people had already taken their seats. A warm feeling washed over her as she saw the familiar faces of Daan's parents, who sat with Bertien, and next to them Bertha and Ruth, each face representing a page in Oma's life story. Memories of the war came back in a flash. The fact that Ruth and Bertha were happily sitting next to each other was in itself remarkable. Anna remembered the day shortly after the liberation, when Bertha had arrived at the castle in an emotional state to ask for advice. Ever since Dominee Bosma had passed away, she had stayed with Ruth to help take care of the children. She had attached herself to both the children and Ruth. There was just one problem, and it was huge. She was in love with Walter and always had been.

"Is that a problem?" Oma had asked.

"It is when one is Roman Catholic and the other is a Protestant minister."

"Is that insurmountable?"

"It is in the eyes of many, I'm afraid. There would be complications, like having to bring up our children in the Catholic faith. That's apart from the wrath of my family. And what does it do to a minister's career to be married to a Catholic?"

"My dear Sylvia," the baroness said. She wasn't used yet to Bertha's real name. "You have stated your dilemma well. There's no denying it would be difficult. Love is a complicated thing, or it can turn out to be. To fall in love is not hard, but to have love last beyond the obstacles society puts in its path, rightly or wrongly, is much harder."

"There is another aspect to this," Bertha said. She hesitated, wringing her hands in obvious agony. Anna, who was coping with fears about Dirk's well-being at the time, felt a deep compassion for Bertha. The love between Walter and Bertha was no secret to her.

"Walter should marry Ruth instead of me," Bertha went on. "Ruth is the perfect minister's wife. What's more, the children already consider Walter their father. They adore him, and so does Ruth, even if she tries to hide it. It would be best for everyone concerned."

"Except for you," Oma said.

At this, Bertha covered her face with her hands and cried. Oma, sitting next to Bertha on the couch, put her arm around her shoulders.

"Have you ever considered, Sylvia, that the deepest form of love is the sacrificial one?"

"Yes." Bertha's voice was hoarse, yet definite.

The next day, Bertha took her bike and headed for Utrecht. She reported for duty at the hospital. Walter found a letter on his desk. It took him a few months to digest the message that Bertha had left him. In the fall of 1945, he and Ruth were married.

The undertaker had handed Anna a large spray of fern greens and red roses. As the pallbearers placed the casket on the bier in the sanctuary, she laid the flowers on top and curtsied. She joined her relatives, who had gathered in a room off the sanctuary, then reentered the church on the arm of Dirk, following her parents, Maarten, and his wife while deep organ tones swelled the interior of the old church. The sight of rows upon rows of people overwhelmed her. The church was chock-full. She spotted members of the Group of Eight in a pew close to the front. It held Daan, Emmy, Otto, and Carla, who sat next to her husband Jacob.

After Dominee van Houten spoke a word of welcome to the mourners and some psalms were recited, Walter climbed up the curved stairs to the pulpit. He opened the Bible and read the parable of the Good Samaritan.

"Most of us are familiar with this parable," he began. "It is one in which Jesus touched on some difficult issues. Those issues have not gone away over the past nineteen hundred and fifty years. We have seen how much they were still a part of everyday life during the years just behind us. Blatant racism, lack of empathy, callousness, hypocrisy. These undesirable traits were all on display.

"I understand that you may wonder why I chose this parable on the day we celebrate the life of Baroness van Haersolte. But there is good reason, and it has a history. In the second year of the war, I was asked to preach in a church in a small town outside of Utrecht.

At that time, it had become apparent what the Nazis had in mind for the Jews who lived among us, although the full extent of their scheme was not known. We were simply incapable of imagining what later would become known as the Holocaust. I asked the congregation in that small church whom they identified with. The poor man by the side of the road? The priest? The Levite? The Samaritan? The innkeeper? I admit that it was a veiled admonition that we had a moral obligation to show mercy for defenseless citizens, and especially the Jews among us."

Anna was transported back to that Sunday, when she had joined Dirk on a lark to attend a church service. It had changed the course of her life, and not hers alone.

"My sister," Walter continued, "who studied in Utrecht at the time, was in the congregation with her friends. Among her friends was the baroness's granddaughter, Anna. And she is the reason I chose the Good Samaritan parable for today's sermon, because Anna and her friends took the sermon's lesson to heart. They put faces on the characters Jesus used to symbolize his message. Looking back on those war years, it is easy to see how they personified the Good Samaritan, who took mercy on the victim by the side of the road and brought him to the inn. Anna and her friends went to work to hide Jews, and took care of them for as long as the war lasted. The castle became the inn, and Baroness van Haersolte personifies for me the innkeeper as well as the Good Samaritan. She allowed Anna to bring to her home many people who needed a place to hide."

Anna had a hard time keeping back her tears. Oma absolutely deserved this analogy.

"The baroness," Walter said, "was very much helped in these good deeds by the people of this community. She set an example that many followed. So many of you present here today were involved in the attempt to hide people who were persecuted, among them the pilot who was downed over the woods next to Kasteel Koppelburg. He was hidden in the castle's stable."

Anna, who sat in a direct line of vision with Hendrik, looked over at him. He acknowledged her glance with a little smile. She also noticed that the local people in the pews gave each other a look of, "So that's where that pilot was hidden!"

Walter wrapped up his short sermon by saying that the baroness did these remarkable things with grace, intelligence, and great courage. "She was gifted," he said, "with a noble title that lent her a natural authority. But what was truly remarkable about her was her faith in humanity. She understood humanity. And she never forgot she was a servant in God's employ. She truly lived out her faith. All of us here are privileged to have known a woman who was a true Christian."

Before he climbed down from the pulpit, Walter announced that someone very special to the baroness had asked to be allowed to play one of her favorite music pieces on the piano.

Frits got up from his seat and walked over to the piano, which had been brought in earlier for this special occasion. He had grown into a handsome young man, now sixteen years old, and he carried himself with dignity. Seeing him standing there next to his favorite instrument made Anna's emotions overflow. If anyone could personify how Oma had protected people, it was Frits. After the war was over, it gradually became known what awful things the Nazis had done, and names like Dachau and Buchenwald became more than geographical locations. Oma initiated a search for Frits's relatives. They had all perished. Frits was devastated. He stayed at the castle with Oma until Walter married Ruth. Frits, who had become good friends with Bram, moved in with the newly formed family, and Oma saw to it that Frits got the best piano instruction available. It soon became evident that he was truly gifted, and it wasn't hard to convince a famous concert pianist to tutor him.

"My name is Arthur Goldberg," Frits said, looking at the congregation. "Over the course of the war, I was given four different names. I didn't like any of them, because they weren't my own. By the time I came to the castle, I was called Frits. There I felt safe for the first time. The baroness was Oma to me. She accepted me as one of her own. And when my own turned out to exist no longer, she took me into her protection. I have a deep, abiding love for her, and I would like to play this piece by Johan Sebastian Bach in her honor. Its title says it all: 'Sheep May Safely Graze.'"

He sat down behind the piano and played the piece from memory with a sensitive touch, his long fingers dancing over the keyboard with ease and purpose. His composure was astonishing, and as he played, Anna let her tears flow. So did many others. When the congregation sang the last hymn—"Het Wilhelmus," the national anthem—many voices struggled to get the patriotic and God-fearing words out.

The pallbearers moved into position to lift the casket and carry it to its last resting place in the graveyard by the side of the church. Anna and her parents followed. As she stepped outside into the bright sunlight, she saw a man striding quickly up the lane to the church. He held a bouquet of flowers. She wondered who it could be. When the pallbearers stopped at the graveside, the man placed his spray of white roses on the casket. Through her tears, Anna recognized Herr von Schloss.

Walter said some consoling words, ending with the Lord's Prayer as the pallbearers carefully lowered the ropes that held the casket into the grave.

"From dust to dust," Walter said.

Anna snapped off one of the red roses in the spray that had covered the casket and threw it down.

"I will love you forever, Oma."

She sensed that somebody was moving to stand next to her. It was Herr von Schloss. He had taken one of the white roses from the bouquet he had brought.

"The white rose of peace, gnädige Frau," he said softly as he threw it down on her casket.

Anna took his hand and squeezed it.

Statistics of World War II in the Netherlands.

18,000 Dutch men, women, and children starved to death during the Hunger Winter.

104,000 of the 120,000 Jews who were dragged away to extermination camps did not survive.

23,000 Dutchmen died in air raids.

More than 5000 succumbed in prisons and concentration camps.

Of the 550,000 Dutch men who were forced to work in the Third Reich or for the Nazis in Holland, 16 percent of the male population—30,000 men—never returned.

Executions, most of them summary, claimed 2800 victims.

The liberation of the country cost the lives of more than 50,000 Allied soldiers—American, Canadian, Polish, British, Belgian, French.

4500 Dutch soldiers died for their own country.

More than 1500 sailors found a grave at sea.

Statistics suggest 50,000 Netherlanders died during the war simply because medical help was inadequate.

Out of a population of 8.8 million people, 237,300 Netherlanders lost their lives.

Taken from: *The Hunger Winter* by Henri A. van der Zee
(University of Nebraska Press, 1998)

TITIA BOZUWA emigrated from the Netherlands to the United States in 1957 with her husband, a physician. They settled in Wakefield, New Hampshire, where her husband practiced family medicine. A Montessori teacher in Amsterdam before she emigrated, Titia took up photography in the States. In 1991, she began studying creative writing at UNH with Martha Barrett and Sue Wheeler; and for seventeen years, she operated the Twin Farms Writers Workshop at her home during the summer months. She has published four memoirs.

CPSIA information can be obtained
at www.ICGtesting.com
Printed in the USA
FFOW02n1803251117
43672639-42486FF